DAVID EBSWORTH is the pen name of writer Dave McCall, a former negotiator for Britain's Transport & General Workers' Union. He was born in Liverpool but has lived in Wrexham, North Wales, with his wife Ann since 1981.

Following his retirement, Dave began to write historical fiction in 2009 and has subsequently published six novels: political thrillers dealing with the 1745 Jacobite rebellion, the 1879 Anglo-Zulu War, the Battle of Waterloo, warlord rivalry in sixth century Britain, and the Spanish Civil War. His sixth book, *Until the Curtain Falls* returns to that same Spanish conflict, following the story of journalist Jack Telford, and is published in Spanish under the title *Hasta Que Caiga el Telón*. Jack Telford, as it happens, is also the main protagonist in a separate novella, *The Lisbon Labyrinth*.

Each of Dave's novels has been critically acclaimed by the Historical Novel Society and been awarded the coveted B.R.A.G. Medallion for independent authors.

This eighth novel, *Mistress Yale, The Glorious Return*, is the second in a trilogy about the life of nabob, philanthropist (and slave-trader) Elihu Yale, who gave his name to Yale University, but told through the eyes of his much-maligned and largely forgotten wife, Catherine.

For more information on the author and his work, visit his website at www.davidebsworth.com.

CH00763308

Also by David Ebsworth

The Jacobites' Apprentice
A story of the 1745 Rebellion. Finalist in the
Historical Novel Society's 2014 Indie Award

The Jack Telford Series
Political thrillers set towards the end of the Spanish Civil War.
The first of these is *The Assassin's Mark*. "This is not
a novel you will be able to put down."
– Rachel Malone, Historical Novel Society

The sequel is the much-acclaimed *Until the Curtain Falls*, published in
Spanish as *Hasta Que Caiga el Telón*. Telford also features in the e-book
novella, *The Lisbon Labyrinth*, which follows Jack's later misadventures
during the Portuguese Revolution of April 1974.

The Kraals of Ulundi: A Novel of the Zulu War
Picks up the story of the Zulu War where Michael Caine left off. "An
accomplished, rich, beautifully produced and very rewarding read that
brings a lesser-known era of history to life."
– Cristoph Fischer, Historical Novel Society

The Last Campaign of Marianne Tambour: A Novel of Waterloo
Action and intrigue based on the real-life exploits of two women
who fought, in their own right, within Napoleon's army. "Superb!
David Ebsworth has really brought these dramatic events to life. His
description of the fighting is particularly vivid and compelling."
– Andrew W. Field, author of *Waterloo: The French Perspective*

The Song-Sayer's Lament
"A rich, glorious, intricate tapestry of the time we know of as the Dark
Ages, With echoes of Rosemary Sutcliff's magnificent *Sword at Sunset*
and Mary Stewart's, *Crystal Cave* series. It's steeped
in authenticity and heart. I loved it!"
– Manda Scott, author of the bestselling *Boudica* series and *Into the Fire*

The Doubtful Diaries of Wicked Mistress Yale
Part One of the Yale Trilogy

To Gwy & Chao

Mistress Yale's
DIARIES
The
Glorious Return

DAVID EBSWORTH

Happy Reading &
¡Hasta Ponto!

Dave

SilverWood

Published in 2019 by SilverWood Books

SilverWood Books Ltd
14 Small Street, Bristol, BS1 1DE, United Kingdom
www.silverwoodbooks.co.uk

ISBN 978-1-78132-936-8 (paperback)
ISBN 978-1-78132-937-5 (ebook)

British Library Cataloguing in Publication Data
A CIP catalogue record for this book is
available from the British Library

Page design and typesetting by SilverWood Books
Printed on responsibly sourced paper

Dedicated to Joe C. Dwek CBE and his Family Trust for their considerable support in the publishing process for this novel.

Author's Note

As I said in the introduction to *The Doubtful Diaries of Wicked Mistress Yale* – the preceding part of this trilogy – this is, of course, a work of fiction, though very firmly rooted in history and, for the period in question, this throws up a couple of issues. The first of these is the dating of Catherine Yale's diary entries. These are written as they would have been at the time and as seen in the personal correspondence of Elihu Yale and other real-life characters from the story, as well as the records of the English East India Company. Under the old Julian Calendar, then in use, the new year officially began in April of one year and ended in March of the next (although the 'calendar year' still began on 1st January, of course), so that February would, for example be dated as 1674/5, while May three months later would simply be dated as 1675.

Second, there are a lot of real-life characters to be recalled from Part One, so here is a quick summary of some significant family and related members…

Catherine Hynmers Yale (née Elford), born 1651
Joseph Hynmers, Catherine's first husband, born 1641, died 1680
Joseph Hynmers Junior, born 1670
Richard Hynmers, born 1672
Walter Hynmers (probably fictional), born and died 1674
Elford Hynmers, born 1676
Benjamin Hynmers, born 1678
Elihu Yale, Catherine's second husband (married 1680), born 1649
David Yale, born 1684, died 1687

Katherine (Katie) Yale, born 1685
Anne (Nan) Yale, born 1687
Ursula (Ursi) Yale, born 1689
Katherine Nicks (née Barker), Yale's alleged mistress at Fort St. George, Madras
John Nicks, her husband
Jeronima de Paiva, Yale's "other" mistress at Fort St. George
Carlos Almanza Yale (Don Carlos), her illegitimate son
Streynsham Master, a former governor of Fort St. George
Sir William Langhorn, another former governor

Volume Three

London

Six weeks ago, and the other ship was sinking, that much was plain. Thus the sight of our own sails, coming up over the horizon, should have been as wondrous to them as the descent of God's angels from Heaven on the Day of Judgement. No trumpet fanfare, however, simply a single shot from one of the *Rochester's* guns to alert them of our proximity, should their lookouts somehow now be more focused on survival than their duties.

They were fortunate to be in such peril in that precise spot, though a piece of fortune, it later transpired, entirely due to the skills and tenacity of her navigators in bringing her there. One of the few places where outbound vessels from the European ports and destined for the Cape of Good Hope and beyond – after following the trade winds across the Atlantic from the coast of Brazil, and then swinging north with the favourable current – could cross paths with those inbound and driving up the west coast of Africa. Yet, when the *Rochester* sighted them they were far from land and in heavy seas.

By the time we were hove-to and within hailing distance – and Captain Sutton able to satisfy himself they posed no piratical danger – the Dutch seamen had taken to their boats and their vessel, the *Johane*, was down by the bow, listing to starboard, her decks almost entirely awash, bails of cargo rising and falling on the swell.

They wanted to be taken into Cape Town, of course, though Captain Sutton would have none of it. We had already been delayed in that port longer than he would have liked, taking on water, fruit and other fresh supplies. But mainly the foul weather blowing in from the northwest. And the news. Oh, astonishing news. News now making it even more imperative for us to reach England with all possible speed.

Yet his decision causes great unrest among our crew. Some of them are veterans of our own recent wars with the Hollanders, and suffered horribly in one or other of the defeats inflicted upon our navy. Besides, we are a John Company ship and they our bitter rivals from the Dutch East India Company – Jan Company, as we disparagingly name them. Anyway, so many additional bodies make the *Rochester* badly overcrowded, seriously increases the number of mouths to be fed. Our nearest landfall now will be the Azores, still more than a month distant, despite the favourable wind that keeps us heeled at this strange angle. I have become accustomed to it, and to the scents of timber, hemp, bilge water and tar now infused into my soul. Yet the wind sings in our rigging and we make good headway.

'I could put you and your men ashore there, sirrah,' our captain told the Dutch skipper as, this evening, we shared a precarious supper together in the lurching quarters Sutton had taken for himself after surrendering his own, and a neighbouring cabin, for the use of myself, my three baby girls, and our Gentue *ayah*, Tanani, when we left Madras Patnam.

'*Nee*, my friend,' said Captain De Groet. 'If more supplies you take at Ponta Delgada, we can sail to London. Our new big city, *ja*? Our capital too now.' He slapped his meaty hand down on the sloping table with unbounded joy, considering how close he had come to disaster.

'England conquered,' said Captain Sutton. 'I can scarce believe it.'

England liberated, more like, though Sutton's weather-beaten officers obediently shook their heads in shared dismay. De Groet's sailing master, however, a fellow with a strangely nobbled pate, and normally taciturn from the little time I had known him, could barely contain his excitement.

'Conquer?' he said, with an irony in his voice that echoed my own thoughts. 'We are one now. *Goede vrienden*. Good friend.'

The news we had picked up in Cape Town, though Captain Sutton had almost refused to believe it. Yet here it was again, confirmed by the *Johane*. There had been a revolution in England. To my ears, a glorious one. In June, Mary of Modena, the Catholic queen of Catholic King James, had borne him a Catholic babe, also named James. Or had she? The news told how rumours quickly spread, soon became accepted as fact, that the infant was not truly the king's son, and had been substituted for a child still-born.

In any case, much of England had hoped having a Catholic monarchy again after one hundred and fifty years – with the exception of Bloody Mary's brief interlude, of course – would be a temporary aberration, would disappear with James's death, the succession of his Protestant daughter, another Mary. And suddenly that hope was dashed.

'I can scarce believe it,' I said, unable to restrain my enthusiasm any further. 'There we were, all Christmas at Fort St. George, continuing with our normal round while, in England, the world was being turned upside down.'

It was something of an exaggeration, the comment about our normal social round. It was over Christmas, after all, that I had finally determined to seek some revenge: to leave my husband Elihu to his avarice and licentiousness at Fort St. George; to poison the woman who had betrayed my secrets to that popish agent, Vincent Seaton – though sadly I seem only to have succeeded in poisoning the creature's husband; and to cheat Elihu's two harlot concubines, as well as John Company itself, from a small fortune, and thus enhance my own. But at what price? It all seemed so simple, so equitable at the time, but now I am plagued by visions of how the Almighty shall punish me.

'Good friends we may be.' Sutton paused with a piece of salted cod halfway to his mouth. 'And I am no adherent to the Church of Rome. Far from it. But the king? He is anointed by God. And none but God should set him aside.'

Oh, how bored I am with that foolish opinion.

Within a week of the baby's supposed birth, a group of noble gentlemen had written to Mary's husband, James's son-in-law, the staunchly Protestant Hollander William of Orange, and invited him to force James, through military intervention if necessary, to confirm Mary as his heir. Word of the letter had spread rapidly and James, it was said, had been horrified by the level of popular support surrounding it.

'And was this true – about William landing at Torbay?' I asked De Groet. 'It seemed such an unlikely story when we heard it. The details so confused.'

'True, *ja*.'

Torbay, with an army of twenty thousand Dutchmen at his back. It seems he had quickly marched on London, but halted his advance outside the city, making a declaration that the sovereign English Parliament should decide what might happen next. Oh, joy! Parliament. The word alone makes my heart sing. But this much was all the news we had at Cape Town, and the uncertainty, the way England's future hung in the balance, had gnawed at me ever since. So I thank God for this encounter with the *Johane*, and word of what has been happening, at least until just after Christmas.

'It seems, sir,' I said to Captain Sutton, 'the king has rather set himself aside, has he not?'

'That is what we hear, *mevrouw* Yale,' said De Groet. 'Your King James, he run away. He throws away your *Grote Zegel* – how you say?'

'The Great Seal,' I replied, thankful that all my years of close proximity to the merchant communities of Portugal, Holland, Spain and India have gifted me at least a working knowledge of several other tongues. 'You heard he threw it in the Thames?'

'*Ja*, in the *Theems*. Then run to France. He come back. Then go again. *Stadhouder Willem* – William – now is in London. December, that was. He is there. Our soldiers in London too. Your Westminster.'

'But the people,' said Sutton. 'They shall not accept it, surely. A Dutchman on the throne of England. A Dutch army of occupation in London.'

'Perhaps a *republiek* you shall be. Like us.'

'Could such a thing be possible?' I wondered.

'We tried that, sirrah,' Captain Sutton smiled. 'Cromwell, you know? It turned out very badly.'

'The English,' I said, 'fear uncertainty more than the devil himself. If the throne is empty, I can see no reason why they should not accept Stadholder William as King, if Mary rules as Queen. After all, it is little more than eighty years since we brought James's grandfather from Scotland to reign over us after the death of Queen Bess – and shared a common monarch for the two separate kingdoms ever since.'

'Different kettle of fish entirely, mistress,' Sutton laughed. 'Between a Scotsman, and a Dutchie – begging your pardon, De Groet.'

Captain De Groet shrugged.

'*Ja*, different. You English at war with Scotland five hundred years. With *Nederland* just fifty. And your husband, *mevrouw* Yale. Big man, him. *Nederlandse* king, he will like?'

Elihu will almost certainly be too occupied with his infidelities, his concubines – *Senhor* de Paiva's Jewish widow, Jeronima, and that drab, Katherine Nicks, with her brood of children and several of them, it seems, his by-blows. But that would not suffice for answer here.

'My husband is the Governor of the Honourable English East India Company's post at Madras. At Fort St. George, Captain De Groet, as you must know. As such, Elihu has a responsibility to whoever sits upon that throne. He was required to serve King James loyally and he can do no other than to serve whoever might now succeed him.'

Of course he would. How could he not? These were the things driving Elihu. Primarily, the imperative for a male heir – an imperative destroyed with the death of our dear son, Davy, now entombed with my first husband, sweet Joseph, and alongside the shattered headstone of the third among five sons into whom Joseph and myself breathed life. Tragic deaths still causing me to drown often in the darkest humours, the worst of nightmares.

'And others at Fort St. George, *mevrouw* – they will see same way?'

'England has been divided, Captain, for the past fifty years. Fort St. George is no different. When I arrived there, we were divided too. Now, my husband governs a Presidency where the Cavalier faction, those we presently call Tories, entirely holds sway. A faction that has worked studiously to rid itself of the most vociferous among its opponents. Dismissals. And perhaps worse. Men who will remain loyal to Catholic King James for as long as their purses allow them.'

Elihu's second imperative. The accumulation of wealth. He sees it as a gift from God, a sin if he fails to ignore that flair.

'Dismissals – and perhaps worse?' said Sutton, and I saw his officers were all poised over their plates, hanging upon my words. But this was neither the time nor the place to discuss the possible murders in which Vincent Seaton is implicated – Major Puckle, that poor cove Sawcer, *Senhor* de Paiva and my dear friend, Sathiri.

'I fear my tongue ran away with me, Captain. Dismissals, certainly. Each of the Governors before Elihu, in fact. Streynsham Master, for example. An exemplary fellow but driven out through those same political machinations. But my husband will do his duty, as I say.'

Of course he will. His third imperative, blind loyalty to John Company – after he has fulfilled imperatives numbers one and two.

Yet I shall do my duty too. I thought about Matthew Parrish, wounded in a fight with that scrub Seaton – mouthpiece for the Cavalier faction and an agent for the papal nuncio in London. Matthew was shipped home last year but not before his discovery that Seaton had forced me to betray our associate, Jewish diamond trader Jacques de Paiva – a betrayal that led to de Paiva's murder. The revelation has ruptured the trust between Matthew and myself, but I know that, if he has survived the journey back to England, he will now be in the thick of things.

Given the chance, I will play my part too. Salve my conscience. Compensate for any wickedness I may have done in the eyes of God. Gather my family about me – Mama and Pa, the boys already in London, the three girls asleep here on the *Rochester*, safe in their cots. And perhaps even find some modicum of happiness. Strike a blow against my own enemies and those of England.

That is, if my enemies do not strike me first.

The nightmare visits me afresh. The impossibility of the choice I must make – to rescue either little Kate or baby Ursula, knowing I cannot do both without killing us all. Green waters foaming and crashing through the cabin door. The *Rochester* at such an angle I can barely keep myself upright. The surging brine already around my thighs, trapping my skirts ice-cold against my flesh, making it almost impossible to move at all. The creak and crack of timbers besieged by the flood, and the frantic yelling above, the ship's bell tolling its own sad demise.

A nightmare. Yet one that I lived almost in truth.

The Azores were behind us and even more news from England. In January, Parliament agreed that James had, indeed, vacated the throne. In February, William and Mary were proclaimed co-rulers. In March, James landed in Ireland with an army of six thousand French soldiers, seemingly having decided he does not wish to vacate the throne after all. In April, William and Mary crowned in St. Peter's, at Westminster's ancient abbey while, in Ireland, James had laid siege to Derry. And, in May, new legislation, the Toleration Act, guaranteeing freedom of worship for all Nonconformist and Dissenter Protestants – though not to Papists.

The Azores behind us and, somewhere ahead, Ushant and the entrance to the English Channel. And then, from nowhere, a storm as brutal as that which had taken the *Johane*. The sky blackened in moments and the seamen on the overcrowded deck, Englishman and Dutchman alike, gazed in horror at the black maw promising to swallow us.

Captain Sutton gave orders for our sails to be shortened and, as the sailors fell to their duties, a terrible stillness fell over the scene, an instant when the ocean became like rancid grease and into the silence the labouring seamen could easily be heard, profane oaths and a simple conclusion reached.

A Jonah, they said. It began almost as a jest. They should have known, should they not? It had almost been spelled out for them. Literally. The *Johane*. What good could come of picking up a vessel called the *Johane*? And had those same Dutchies not already attracted misfortune? Hard lines. Yet that did not last long and, quickly, others were shouting that no, it was not the Dutchies at all. It was the inevitable result of having a Mahometan heathen on board. Tanani, of course.

'Best to get below, mistress,' Sutton shouted, 'and I'll send Mister Hackett to make everything secure with his tarpawlings. Make you as snug as we're able. Perhaps best though if you and your party keeps to your cabins, if you take my drift.'

Mister Hackett is the appropriately named and bark-gnarled carpenter aboard the *Rochester* and, as promised, he had soon followed me down to the master's cabin, where he sealed up the windows with his nailed canvas. Yet he had no sooner finished than that unnatural silence was broken. There was a roar of some beast, which sounded like it might devour the whole world, and the *Rochester* was picked up, shaken in the monster's jaws and then spat forward, lurching, rolling, so that I fell, cracked my head on the swinging gimbals of the baby's crib and she, poor mite, let out a screech of pure terror, while little Kate tried to catch at my skirts, missed her grip and, with a pitiful face, was sent tumbling across the cabin floor. Through the adjoining bulkhead I could hear Tanani's shriek.

The space she shared with Annie was much smaller than my own and, immediately, I knew we would all be safer there. Safer, or quicker the drowning. So, in a brief lull, I lifted the girls in my arms and, though buffeted and badly pounded in the process, I managed to stumble and bounce my way to Tanani's door. I hammered upon it until she opened, wiping vomit from the seaman's jacket that, since we left Ponta Delgada, it had been her wont to wear over her *saree* to keep herself warm.

'*Memsahib*,' she cried, 'the Death God Kala has us.'

'Yes,' I said. 'But we must all stay together. Fight Kala together. Here…'

I passed her the two girls, saw her fall back as the next surge hurled us sideways so I was certain we must broach. Yet somehow the *Rochester* righted herself and I was able to regain the master's cabin, thrown this way and that, to gather up our palliasses, our blankets. I paused a moment, thought about trying to push the travel chest ahead of me, or at least the treasure within, but knew it would be impossible. I made my way back to Tanani and the children so that, in their more limited space, we used everything available to wedge and cushion ourselves together. And we prayed. Gentue and Christian together, for there was naught else that might save us.

Thus we endured. Endless hours, singing to the girls in one or other of our languages, trying our best to avoid being hurled about, or to drown out the howls of the storm, or to ignore the rending of timber and canvas we knew must be bringing the *Rochester* close to her end, or to relish the defiant clamour of our seamen, the rhythmic pounding of the pumps, the occasional roar of their chanties, letting us know this fight was far from over.

At one point, Captain Sutton managed to thrust open the door, hung there a moment between one mountainous swell and the next. He flinched, for the ebb and flow stench of *mal de mer* and other odours in that confined space must have been overpowering, though we were all long past caring.

'Just raised Ushant,' he yelled. 'Almost certain, sure. Cannot be other. Taking on a lot of water though, mistress. But thank the Lord we picked up those Dutchies. Without them to work the pumps so hard we'd have been sunk hours ago.'

'No Jonah among them, then, Captain Sutton?' I croaked, for the ship may have been awash with water yet I had never been so thirsty in my life.

'Well, ma'am…' he replied, and glanced at Tanani, somehow mercifully asleep by then and curled tightly in the corner with Annie in her arms.

'Never mind. Can we make it?'

'Storm's driving us straight into the Chops of the Channel. All we can do is ride it as long as we may. Pray, madam. And then pray again.'

So I prayed some more. Little Katie was old enough to pray also, never once doubting the Lord would deliver us, for I had schooled her well in the ways of the Almighty. And Tanani prayed to Shiva, destroyer of evil and great transformer. We prayed until, an eternity later, even above that horrendous Armageddon, we heard the lookout sing the sighting of Deadman's Point and, six hours later, we clawed our leaky but now somewhat gentler passage into Plymouth's Sound.

Captain Sutton is convinced the *Rochester* has made her final voyage and, indeed, as we were rowed ashore I gazed back at her in amazement that she had brought us here at all. She looks as though she has fought a great battle – as indeed she has. Each of her yards sprung and lashed all a-jumble upon deck, her main yard gone by the board along with the snapped mizzen mast, her canvas shredded, her rigging in tatters, mats and frapping in parts along her hull where, I imagine, her planks must be sprung also. She is anchored, though leaning at such an angle she must surely topple completely if the wind does not abate soon. Though, wind? Did I write wind? Sirrah, this is no more than the merest breeze compared to that screeching banshee we encountered four days ago.

Our deliverance, of course, has not diminished the sailors' superstitions and they were almost silent, mutinous – exhausted too, of course – kept their eyes averted from Tanani as they worked their oars to deliver us onto the wharf.

All things are relative, however. So while this may be dry land, and my eyes tell me I am sitting here, at my writing slope, in busy Plymouth's *Minerva Inn*, the chair upon which I sit refuses to be still. It pitches and heaves beneath me as though I am still upon the ocean. I recall the sensation from my passage out to India over twenty years ago, but this is surely more enduring, for we have been here since yesterday noon.

And my second observation relates to Tanani as well as myself. Black faces are far from unknown in this town, yet the innkeeper required considerable persuasion when I explained that, yes, I required room and board for my maidservant too. That one, indeed. And no, she was not a Mahometan. Rather, a Gentue and been in my service a score of years. But then he looked askance at me, also. I suppose it must be difficult to live at a place like Madras Patnam for two decades and not accumulate some of the manner, the colour – literally, the colour – of the place. There are plenty of women at Fort St. George who managed that difficulty with aplomb, naturally. Those who never ventured into the sun, beyond their own social circle, nor beyond the gates and into the labyrinth of Black Town. Yet I was never comfortable with those ladies and now I feel like a stranger in my own strange land. This unbroken sea of white faces.

Why does it affect me so? Perhaps I have underestimated the power of dear Sathiri's words to me, when poor Joseph died. I had been there ten years and that, she said, was enough for the land to be in my blood. Besides, she reminded me, my blood was in the land, too. Baby Walter's blood. I had been so anxious to leave and yet now I would give almost anything to be back there. So how will we fare, Tanani and myself, upon the streets of London?

Well, we shall see. I add a final flourish to Mama's letter, her address at the house in George Yard. Just off Lombard Street. They will be astonished at my return, I collect. I had posted short notes aboard those vessels, both at Cape Town and at Ponta Delgada, bound for London, for family and friends, with a likelihood of arrival there before the *Rochester*, though I had no idea whether they might have reached England ahead of us. And while I am certain Mama and Pa would wish to accommodate us all there while I search for a suitable house of our own, I have made it very plain we shall not impose, that Papa must reserve rooms for us at the *George*, which – in those brief notes he always appends to Mama's lengthy missives – he has always lauded as a fine establishment indeed.

It is probably a wasted effort though, the letter. Even if the post-boys are diligent and the roads in decent condition, it is unlikely to reach them in less than five days. And, by then, the vessel upon which we have booked our onward sailing, tomorrow, will almost certainly have deposited us at the Pool of London.

As I say, we shall see. But meanwhile I must try to adjust. My own world turned upside down, as England itself has been. For, here in England, events seem to be galloping with a speed that seems impossible, unreal.

And such events!

I should have known better than to sail from Plymouth on a vessel with such an ominous name. The *Revanche*, captured long since from the French, it seems, and sold into service as a merchantman, running tin ingots, sheep's wool and mail from Plymouth to the Pool of London, returning with cargoes of beer, soap, iron, hops or any other commodity so much in short supply within Devon.

An old tub of a ship, far from comfortable accommodation – barely adequate for myself, Tanani and the three girls, as well as two other gentleman passengers – yet she made good progress all the way along the south coast at a steady four knots, the skipper would frequently boast, around into the Thames Estuary and, finally, dropping anchor opposite the Custom House Stairs after a tedious haul up the river. A full week for the journey and all that while I troubled about the cursed name. *Revanche*. Revenge. Retribution.

'London Bridge, Mama,' Katie squealed as we waited for the jolly boat to be lowered. I had sung the rhyme to them so many times. 'It still stands.'

Such a long time. But there she lay, in all her jumbled glory, as she had done since ancient days. When I left for Madras only the buildings along the Southwark half had survived the Great Fire but now all was new and modern housing towering above the northern archways, though crowded all together as they had always been.

'So much change though, my dears,' I said. My mother had kept me abreast of everything, naturally, from the year I sailed until the Fire Courts were deemed no longer necessary. But even so I could scarce believe the difference in the city's outline now that I saw it for myself. So many steeples. And the glorious white temple of St. Paul's, the tracery of its scaffolds climbing skywards, though still without whatever tower may finally crown its magnificence. Praise be! For we had all wept so, the lucky survivors of the conflagration, mourned with our entire collective soul, when the old cathedral had been so cruelly destroyed, London's very heart ripped from its breast.

The oarsmen obligingly carried us from the anchorage, past Sabb's Quay, to the Billingsgate Stair. I had no real expectation that my family would be there to meet us, but it was just possible, for my letters from Plymouth had set this as my most likely point of disembarkation – and the good natur'd fellows of the *Revanche* were happy to help me make it so. Thus we cut our way through the hoys, fishing luggers and coal boats plying the river, and the bigger square-riggers that must moor here, since plainly none of these masted vessels could progress further westward for the obstacle presented by the bridge.

Yet as we drew near I searched in vain for any familiar face. And one face in particular. Oh, how I had hoped Matthew Parrish might somehow have heard about my arrival. But he was not there. The wharf was crowded, however, though with none that I knew. Customers mainly from the nearby stalls and arcades, the fish vendors mostly. I was therefore surprised when, as the sailors hauled our travel chests, my precious treasure, up the evil-smelling slime-smeared steps, or lifted the girls to safety – while still keeping their distance from poor Tanani – I heard my name shouted from above. In an imperious tone, too, that promised nothing by way of warm welcome.

'Mistress Yale?'

The man's clothes seemed somewhat outlandish. More costly perhaps, than he could afford. As though he had recently purchased them to suit a position in which he was not yet entirely comfortable. A brace of minions jostled at his elbows among the bystanders, and the jostling set a cloud of powder blossoming upon the wind from his ill-fitting periwig.

'A fine greeting,' I told him, coughing as the white dust caught at my throat. 'And you, sirrah?'

'Fleet, madam. Sir John.' His surreptitious attempt to shift the peruke back into position served only to highlight how much it was plainly made for a considerably larger head. 'Fleet by name and nature. Sheriff for this fair city of London. And a warrant.' He drew from his pocket a parchment, unrolled the document. 'Yes, a warrant. In the name of the Honourable English East India Company.' So, here it was. The retribution I had feared. 'To be precise, in the name of Sir Josiah Child. Charged with...'

One of the sailors, the boatswain Amos Damerell had just set both Anne and Ursula down upon *terra firma*.

'Trouble, ma'am?' he said.

'Only for yourself,' said the Sheriff, 'should you interfere with my judicial duties.'

One of Fleet's Constables stepped forward and set a foolish hand upon the boatswain's arm, and Demerell shook himself free as the crowd parted, made way for a figure who tore at my heart. Papa, the rebellious Dissenter of my memory, now become old and frail.

'Catherine, dear girl,' he cried. 'What is this?'

'Stand back, sir,' said the Sheriff. 'I have a warrant to serve. An arrest to make.'

'My daughter? Why, you pompous ass. I voted for you, sir.'

'All the same, charges. Complicit in defrauding accredited officers of the Company.'

He did not need to name them. Those members of the Fort St. George Council. Higginson, Briggs, Littleton and the rest. But by then Amos Demerell had stepped in front of me.'

'Back to the ship, ma'am?' he said. 'Safe there, I think.'

And that absurd Constable, again trying to push him aside, Amos turning swiftly on his heel and bringing a fist down upon the cove's skull, felling him like a pole-axed pig. The second Constable drew a rapier from the hanger at his hip and I was sure there must be blood.

'Arrest them all!' Fleet was shouting.

'No need for that, Sir John.'

A voice I recognised. Streynsham Master, his own pair of retainers forcing a passage through the crowd and Streynsham himself waving papers of his own. It is eight years since I saw him, and he has not changed a great deal. Turned fifty now, of course, but still seems young. Not a wrinkle to be seen, except for those crows' feet at the corner of his eyes, which more accentuate the laughter within him than his age. He always reminds me of a Roman statue I once saw, the features proud and aquiline. Even now one of the few men who can easily excite my fantasies with the seductive drawl of his voice – though perhaps only on better days than this.

'There is a warrant,' Fleet whined, a mere child by comparison with Streynsham's authority – and a child about to have its favourite toy stolen from him.

'And here,' said Streynsham, 'an order rescinding that warrant. Signed by the Lord Advocate himself.'

'That could have been difficult,' said Streynsham, taking my arm and guiding me into the shade afforded by the carriage, while Papa sweated with the supervision of loading Tanani, the girls and our possessions into that conveyance on Thames Street he had arranged for our transportation. 'I am just glad I had business at Leadenhall Street. The place all a-buzz with this nonsense. Great heavens, Catherine. They say you sold shares to Council members. To John Company itself. In a worthless mine.'

Sir John Fleet had been far from happy that his duties were so frustrated but he had left the wharf with as much good grace as he was able.

'My mark was elsewhere,' I explained. 'But those fools, Higginson and the others, insisted on purchasing their own portions as well as investing the Company's own finances. In truth I could not stop them.'

'Gracious,' he laughed. 'Then you are fortunate indeed that Josiah Child is now so far out of favour. Gone to war with the Mughal Emperor indeed! The old jackanapes. Fortunate that I was able to appeal on your behalf over his head, to those with whom he is in such debt.'

'In debt to…?'

'Among others, William Cavendish, my dear. Now, there is a man with the Midas touch, so far as charmed lives are concerned. And the very fellow who enabled Matthew Parrish to maintain his position at Fort St. George for so long when the entire Cavalier faction would gladly have seen him hanged.'

The Earl of Devonshire, one of those who signed the letter to Stadholder William – our King William now. My father had mentioned him frequently when he wrote, praised him, though with reservation. All those years in the Commons as member for Derbyshire and led our faction through one Parliament after another – and despite his family's natural loyalties to the Court and Catholic factions.

'And Josiah Child himself?' I asked. 'What now for him? And for John Company?'

'Both outlived their usefulness, as you must have guessed. There will be a pension, naturally. But the Company has been living on borrowed time for quite a while, enormous payments to the Crown for the privilege of maintaining their licence, those payments even greater when James came to the throne. And King William seems to have no love for the English East India Company. Perhaps,' he laughed, 'to do with being a Hollander and the Dutch somewhat in competition so far as the East Indies trade is concerned.'

'Elihu?' I said, as he handed me up into the carriage.

'Stands or falls with the Company.'

'Me?'

'You have made enemies, Catherine,' he whispered, looking to make certain that Papa was busy with the girls. 'The lesser of them may have been rebuffed this once, yet you cannot expect them to forgive and forget. I fear they will seek...'

The very thing I have feared.

'Retribution,' I said.

'I thought we must surely all drown,' I told Papa, but almost choked upon the words, tears coming yet again unbidden to my eyes. Dinner at Mama's very fine food-laden table. 'Then to survive simply to be threatened with imprisonment.'

'Such an ordeal,' Mama said, fussing to make sure our plates were filled. 'But look at us. Give you joy of this moment, my dear. All of us together.'

'I think I must be a little overwhelmed.' I tried to smile, gazed around those seated about me. Papa at the table's head, immediately to my left; opposite me, Joseph Junior, at nineteen his features almost identical to those of his father – almost hawk-like; next to Joseph, my sister Roberta, twenty-six, her husband Richard Banner away in Porto, with the wine trade; then my fractious younger brothers – Richard, twenty-four, and already almost running the coffee house on Papa's behalf, and Benjamin, twenty, employed alongside Joseph Junior at Mister Bentley's counting house; at the opposite extremity of the table, my ageless mother, with little Kate on a stool alongside; and, finally, on my own side of the table, my other three sons. Closest to Mama and Katie, the obdurate Richie, seventeen, and Elford, thirteen – the latter now at the rebuilt Merchant Taylors' Company day school in Suffolk Street – and, nestling just to my right, dear Benjamin, at eleven, just finished at petty school.

Those missing from the feast? Tanani and the two little ones, of course, both still exhausted from the journey, resting upstairs. And my two older brothers – John, thirty-four, a merchant in Smyrna, as Papa had been, and Walter Junior, thirty, also a wine factor, in Alicante, where I was born.

'It would have been easier for you to adjust, my dear,' said Mama, 'if you had not so stubbornly insisted upon the *George*.'

'There is barely room for us at table,' I protested. 'Where in Heaven's name would we all sleep? And the *George* is most amenable, just as Papa knew it would be.'

'In any case,' said Joseph Junior, pausing between mouthfuls of his beef, 'it would be difficult for Mama to share with so many of us who are strangers to her. Is that not so, Mama?'

'It is the nomadic existence we have chosen,' I told him, irritated that he still failed to understand this. 'We pursue our trade, as overseas merchants, in the hope we may – well, look around you. This elegant house that provides so much for you, Joseph, is a product of your grandfather's sacrifices. In Smyrna. And in Spain. And yourself – am I wrong in thinking you, too, have ambition to follow in your father's footsteps?'

'As soon as I'm able, Mother, I shall go back to India.'

I suppose I should have been proud of him, but I could not help feeling rebuffed.

'But first,' my father patted his arm, 'we need to get you employed by John Company. That is,' he said, with a quick glance in my direction, 'if such a thing may still be possible.'

'Elihu will help, will he not?' said Mama. 'Such a pity he did not sail with you, Catherine. A short visit, perhaps. So we could have known him. And surely he could have resolved this foolishness. Warrant, indeed!'

It was a thinly disguised attempt to seek an explanation from me, but I still fear the reproach I might have to endure if I reveal the separation from my husband, or those events that have transpired in Madras.

'There are rogues upon the Council,' I said, my knife chiming against the porcelain as I abruptly set it down, 'who would unseat Governor Yale if they were able. They must have sent word to Leadenhall Street with their preposterous allegations, hoping they would damage both of us. Though a pity? Yes.' Time to change the conversation. 'But Richie,' I said, 'you never finished telling us about Probation Day. How was the examination? And what does it feel like now, to be finished with school?'

He rolled his eyes. And they are not attractive eyes. Piggish, I should say.

'I began to tell you last night,' he complained, 'but you were too busy with those girls. In any case, it was two years ago.'

'Richard!' Mama scolded him, and threw down her napkin. 'That is no way to speak to your mother. And those girls are your sisters.'

'It was the English into Latin I collect from my own,' said Joseph Junior. '"*The Atheist went to Amsterdam to choose his religion.*" A phrase for which I could imagine me having not the slightest use in either tongue.'

Perhaps there is, after all, hope of being fully reconciled with my boys, for his face lit up, exactly as his father's would have done and I wept openly at the sight.

'It is all so new, so very contemporary,' I told Papa as we stood outside the house after dinner. A fine afternoon, with the scent of roasted meats and woodsmoke thick upon the air. I admired the place once more, three storeys, all brick-faced as required of new dwellings, the upper floor extending out above the adjoining coffee house, and the whole thing just a stone's throw across the alley from the *George*. It could not have been better. A veritable crossroads for their collective passing trade, standing at a junction of various passageways – down one of which we began to wander, my arm in his.

'And that?' he asked, turning his head and pointing to the bruising, which had spread from my forehead to my cheek. 'You're certain there's no serious damage?'

'I told you. We were thrown about during the storm. But a chirurgeon in Plymouth was certain there will be no lasting effects. Of course, I may never play the harpsichord again.'

He laughed. It was an old jest, but still he laughed.

'I believe that is the first time I've caught a glimpse of my own dear girl once more. You seem so...'

'Entirely confused, Pa. At this moment I have no idea where

I am, nor even *who* I am. But come, show me this fine church again. I still cannot believe it. The last time I was here, all was charred rubble.' We strolled among the other passers-by into the open square next to the churchyard, almost at the corner where the narrow lane spills out onto Lombard Street itself, and I looked up at the tower of St. Edmund's. 'But yes,' I said, 'so very contemporary. I barely took note of it this morning.'

'Italian style, they tell me.'

'Sirrah, it looks more like one of our Black Town temples.'

'Still, all new. Even the dear old *George*.' He turned back towards the re-built inn. Its sign marks it as the *George and Dragon*, of course, but nobody bothers with anything but its shorter title.

'And a printer's shop,' I said. There it was, tucked into the corner of George Yard, its leaded diamond-pane window filled with books and, inside, line upon line of drying pages. The sign above the door displayed a printing press. 'Is this,' I asked, 'where Mama purchased the copies of Bunyan? They were a great comfort to me.'

More than just a comfort. I believe that they sometimes served to keep me sane.

'Of course.' Pa smiled. 'Northcott. Fine fellow. He supplies the Meetings of Friends. Gracechurch Street. And a new place they've now been permitted to use from time to time. Devonshire House. A room there. They flourish, of course, since the Toleration Act.'

I released his arm, moved closer to the window, shielded my eyes that I might peer within.

'The Earl of Devonshire – a Quaker?'

'Hardly that, Catherine. But the present leaseholder a sympathiser, I understand.'

I turned back to him, wagged my finger at him.

'And you, Papa – have you succumbed to the lure of the Society yet?'

'I seem many times to have walked a parallel path. And I was certainly taken for one in Smyrna. Dissenters, Quakers, we were all one to Sir Sackville Crow.' The Royalist Ambassador to Constantinople, who had left my father to rot in gaol for thirty months. 'Why do you ask?' he said.

'Oh, you were the subject of some interest at Fort St. George. I was interrogated about your beliefs more than once.'

He was suddenly alert. More than alert. His eyelids flickered and he chewed upon his lower lip, pulling me closer to him.

'By?' he said.

'A wretch called Vincent Seaton. At first simply a mouth for the Cavalier faction along the Bay of Bengal. But later it became clear he may be an agent of the papal nuncio, here in London.'

'He threatened you?' He looked all about, checking that we were not overheard.

'To be precise,' I said, 'he threatened Mama and yourself, gave me to understand his arm was long. A word in the right ear, about your associations with certain folk...'

I could not bring myself to confess that the threats had been sufficient for me to present Seaton with an affidavit against *Senhor* de Paiva, who was then engaged in employing the diamond trade to raise funds for our faction in England – for those, I now realise, who have also been instrumental in that same invitation to Stadholder William. The same affidavit, of course, which immediately preceded de Paiva's murder.

'You're certain – about this Seaton being an agent of the pope? These are strange times. The allegations and the plots. First one side, then the other, until it's almost impossible to believe anything we hear or read.'

It pained me to see him so uncertain, and the colour had drained from his normally weatherworn cheeks.

'Are you well, Papa?'

He took my arm again, turned us back towards the *George*.

'I survived the pestilences of Smyrna and Alicante,' he said. 'Then thirty months in a dungeon. Thirty more years fighting for compensation from the Crown. The damn'd fire. The Great Plague too, of course. Poor little Barbara.' She had been just one of the eighty thousand taken by the sickness, and a miracle more of us had not succumbed. 'We have each lost so much,' he went on. 'And now here you are, in danger too.'

'Governor Master shall, I think, keep me from harm's way so

far as John Company is concerned.'

Yes, I am certain of that. But in that case, why has this feeling of dread not left me?

'Come,' said Papa, 'let me show you my pride and joy.'

Yet he stopped outside the coffee house door.

'What?' I said. 'You will tell me, I suppose, that after all this time, this new age in which we find ourselves, women are still not allowed across a coffee house threshold.'

'Just one of the many health benefits from such establishments,' he laughed, and took an unsteady step to one side, trying to dodge the punch I aimed at his arm. 'Yet I suppose we can make an exception today, at least.' He opened the door and we both stepped into the tobacco fug hanging from the ceiling beams to the height of the tabletops. Yet the smell was agreeable, reminded me of the Dutch blend my sweet Joseph had been accustomed to smoking. 'Gentlemen,' Papa shouted. 'Please forgive this breach of our regulation, but allow me to name my long-lost daughter, Catherine, just returned from the Coromandel Coast. Needless to say, she is one of my major investors.'

My watery eyes were slowly adjusting to the miasma, and I could see the well-dressed customers raising their penny dishes of coffee, tea or chocolate in salute, or murmuring greetings while, at the hearth, with its row of pots, my brother Richard, regarding me, I thought, with some disdain.

I gave him a jaunty wave, all the same.

'Coffee, sister?' he asked, offering one of the pewter jugs.

'I never developed a taste for it, Rich. But a saucer of chocolate would serve nicely.'

He shrugged, chose the appropriate pot and poured. For a moment I thought he might charge me the penny. But instead he held the dish to my nose, allowed me to savour the rich, bittersweet aroma.

'Come,' said Papa, as I accepted Richard's offering. 'Upstairs, I think. We can talk more easily there.'

It took some time, several of my father's customers blocking our progress up the staircase, either to offer me greetings, or with questions about the East Indies trade, or more dangerously threatening to spill the chocolate down my satins.

'You open on Sundays now?' I said, when we were finally seated near a window.

'Trade must flow,' he replied, and it could have been Elihu speaking.

'You miss the old place?' I sipped at the saucer, pleased to see that he now seemed more fully himself again, less agitated, his complexion restored.

'Exchange Alley? It was very grand, was it not? But the lease-holders were never going to let me back on the site. They'd had an offer from old Garway I could never have matched. So he has a new coffee house there now. Even more grand. Mostly merchants trading with the American colonies. Hudson's Bay Company. Auctions of their furs and other goods. Yes, other goods.' He seemed distressed. 'Well – slaves, my dear. African slaves.'

'The trade existed at Fort St. George too. Though mainly Indian slaves. Abominable.'

'Your husband?'

I nodded, but I was spared elaboration by one of Papa's friends coming to give me joy of my return.

'Simply one matter among many,' I said, when he had left us alone once more. 'But you shall say nothing to Mama? She has a particular image of Elihu, and I should not like to spoil it.'

'I collect that you expected your return to be different.'

'The boys mainly. I had envisioned a tearful and joyous reunion though, in truth, and apart from Benjamin, I seem to have received nothing from them but resentments. From Joseph Junior because, somehow, I was responsible for him not being there when his father died. From Richard because he hated being separated from Joseph Junior. From Elford because he felt abandoned, being sent back here so young. From all three of them, apparently, because I have the girls. I fear I have scarred them all. But at least they were delighted Tanani is with me. Still, it seemed like the right thing to do, coming home.'

'For the rest, you wish you were back in Madras Patnam.'

'I did not say so.' It was a waspish reply and I found myself turning from him, setting my elbow upon the table, raising the hand so that I might rest a petulant chin upon the palm, gazing around the walls filled with posters announcing the sale of one commodity or another, many of the auctions here in his own establishment.

'Catherine, you are your father's daughter,' he laughed. 'I remember what it was like. I still yearn for it, despite my age. Seventy-eight this year, and none of my friends left. Except your Mama, of course. But if I had my way, I should settle myself on some vessel bound for the Levant and make my final peace with the Almighty during the passage, simply go to sleep with the sound of the wind and waves in my ears.'

'Such sentimental stuff, Papa. You have many years in you still.' But I doubted this was true. So frail now, compared to when I left. 'And Fort St. George? You are correct, of course. I miss the colour, the sounds, the scents. Even with all this modernity, everything seems lifeless by comparison. And besides, all that time the Tories were gaining the upper hand out there. Seaton. My certainty that we should have to tolerate domination and repression by the Romish Church for heaven knows how long. And without my knowledge, all has been thrown to the winds. King William the Third! Oh, if I could be there to rub their noses in this victory.'

'A victory far from secured, I fear.'

Mixed messages. A rising in Scotland led by John Graham of Claverhouse, James's most fervent supporter, ambushed and slaughtered a Williamite force in a mountain pass called Killiecrankie – though Claverhouse himself at least slain in the process. Better news from Ireland, where the Siege of Derry has been lifted after one hundred and five days of heroic struggle by the defenders. But then the Archbishop of Canterbury and a whole host of clergymen suspended for refusing to swear allegiance to William and Mary.

'I imagine,' I said, 'this establishment to be a hotbed of revolutionary fervor.'

I intended the comment as an irony, for the walls displayed nothing but commercial purpose. But by then Richard was up the stairs to replenish our drinks.

'Indeed, the beverages are exhilarating, the ambience conducive to social discourse and fine business. Plans and intrigues of one sort or another. Is that not so, Rich?'

'Intrigues galore, Pa,' he replied. 'But only in your head, I think.'

But I was not so certain, and when Rich was back about his duties, after I had blown upon the saucer to cool it, I reached across and set my fingers upon his wrist.

'I have often wondered, Papa. In Smyrna, were you merely a merchant, or something more?'

He grimaced, his face set in a scowl as, without a word, he rose from the booth and took a pipe from the rack on the opposite wall, filled the bowl from one of the pots he supplied for his customers' comfort and exchanged hearty greetings with a fellow whose belly was impressively large. A boy came scurrying around the tables, trying to find anybody foolish enough to purchase the penny ballads he was peddling.

'Be gone, boy,' shouted Papa as he crossed the floor again. 'How many times?' He cuffed the lad for good measure, and this seemed to restore his normally more affable demeanour.

'Why ask me this now?' he said, as he resumed his seat.

'My father's daughter, as you say. There were things I did, Papa – at Fort St. George. Things I believed were in the interests of our faction. Other things too, of a more personal nature. Some I regret. But revenge against those I believe have wronged me.'

It overwhelmed me, I think. The dangers I have faced these past few years rising up to renew my prideful satisfaction on one hand, the threat of God's punishment on the other.

'Your husband?' he said, stroking my own hand now, in his turn.

'Not directly, no. Not then. But I fear I must act. It was eating at me all through our cruel voyage, and yes, it was often Mama's words that came back to me. Holding the moral high ground, having right on your side alone, it is rarely enough in itself to protect us from harm. Sometimes we are required to climb down into the depths ourselves, sup with the devil, if needs be, to make sure right prevails.'

Saturday 21st September 1689

They have a name, these rebels, these followers of Catholic James – no longer King of England – this confederacy that has risen on his behalf in Scotland and Ireland. According to the broadsides they now style themselves as a 'Jacobite' faction, using *Jacobus*, the Latin for James, presumably to lend themselves some modicum of legality, of superiority.

'I simply refuse to employ the word,' said Streynsham Master as we took tea this morning in the withdrawing room of his elegant house in newly built Red Lion Square. 'Jamesites, if we must. But rather just 'the rebels', don't you think?'

I could not quite agree with him, and reached down into the portmanteau I had brought with me on that cold and nauseous chair ride, two miles through the busy streets from the *George*. September, the weather already unseasonably chill, so the modest blaze in the broad fireplace was most welcome.

'I read,' I said, waving one of the sheets published by old Northcott the Quaker, 'that there are associations sprung up in several towns, in Wales too, which openly style themselves as Jacobite Clubs. It may be difficult to avoid the term, Governor.'

'Governor? Good gracious, Catherine, I walked you down the aisle at St. Mary's. I think we might allow ourselves a little less formality.'

We had already spent an hour reminiscing about our time in India: the tragedy of Joseph's death; the way I had sought his counsel about my plans to wed Elihu so soon afterwards; and the way Fort St. George flourished under his governorship. He gestured towards

27

a pipe rack and tobacco jar on the table alongside his chair, asked whether it would trouble me.

'Of course not,' I said. He had filled the pipe's bowl, took a spill and lit it from the fire. Puffs of sweet-scented tobacco smoke as he took his seat again. 'And Streynsham then,' I conceded. The smile he gave me brought to mind the day he had tried to persuade me Elihu might not be the right man for me. There was no love lost between them, this much was certain. And there had been one brief moment when I had thought he might – well, that had simply been foolish. 'Streynsham,' I repeated. 'Was it difficult, when you came back?'

'I can see by your face you already know the answer. Difficult for us all, is it not? To spend so many years in India and then – but how can I complain?' He gestured around the room, the elegant furnishings, the silken hangings, all the rich colours of the East, depictions of the Mughal Emperor's court. 'And there was much to occupy my mind.'

'A day of infamy. I remember it so well, Gyfford arriving with news of your dismissal. Unbelievable.'

'Elihu must have believed it.'

'Well, that is Elihu. And John Company, of course.'

The door opened and Streynsham's footman ushered the housemaid inside with another pot of tea to replenish our dishes. She was accompanied by the scents of fresh baking, a plate of Shrewsbury cake on a black lacquer tray, the design of which I recognised from Madras Patnam.

'Yet the false testimony against you by Seaton and others who sealed the thing?'

'Ah, Seaton. Now, there was a rogue if ever I saw one. And trapped in Bombay, you say, by the Mughal siege?'

'Certainly when I left. Let us hope he perishes there.'

'Indeed. And I have seen Parrish, by the way – before you ask.'

My hand wavered. I could not help it, and some of the tea slopped over the saucer's edge, onto the folds of my skirts.

'He is well?' I said, dabbing at the stain with my kerchief.

'Recovered. His injury, at least. Still writing poetry, though most of it too melancholy now, for my liking. Left the Company and engaged in some minor diplomatic role. He frequently reminded me of the superb intelligence you provided him.'

'You mean spying on my husband? Matthew once told me it was the only reason he countenanced my marriage to Elihu. And, as you have seen, it has put me somewhat in harm's way.'

'John Company has more serious issues with which to concern itself now. Besides, attack may be your best means of defence, Catherine. So might you do the same for us again, do you think?'

'Spy on Elihu? That might be difficult.'

'But his family. They are prominent, the Yales. Welsh. And it's always good to know where the loyalties of the Welsh may lie.'

My eyes were drawn back to a painting I had admired when I first entered the room. By Courtois, Streynsham had said during the tour he had given me. Horsemen in combat.

'Prominent, yes,' I said. 'Whenever anybody uses that word I am always minded of something my father learned from Winstanley. About men of property, those who inherit the earth, who measure their ability to act as they choose, regardless of the law, in direct proportion to the amount of land they possess – when, in truth, the land should be a common treasury for all of us to share.'

'Yet, at times, those same men see their inheritance as endowing them with a duty on behalf of the nation as a whole. For the common good. As William Cavendish has done.'

I set down the empty tea dish, dabbed with my kerchief at some bisket crumbs in the corner of my mouth.

'And it helps, I suppose, when those men of property are able to further expand their purses at the same time. The Earl of Devonshire is now also King William's Lord Steward, I collect.'

'Well, Catherine, whether you decide to assist us or not, I know we can rely on your own discretion. Though things seem to be moving in our favour. The Jamesites beaten at Dunkeld and our own ships taking Carrickfergus. Yet we need eyes and ears everywhere.'

I wondered whether Matthew Parrish would agree that point about my discretion. He had, after all, discovered the way in which I had betrayed Jacques de Paiva.

'Tell me,' I said. 'Matthew. Is this the diplomatic mission in which he is engaged too?'

'I have no brief to tell you, my dear. Perhaps you should ask him yourself.'

'We hardly parted company on the best of terms. Not even a farewell before he sailed. He blames me. For his wound. For allowing Seaton to escape. And – well, other things.'

'Secrets abound, it seems. Which reminds me, you asked me to find out about those two Gentue youngsters. The dwarfs?' I had, indeed. The note I had sent, suggesting we might meet, a couple of quick sentences to see whether he might discover their fate. That request from Josiah Child on behalf of the Court, two young Gentues to be dispatched for the entertainment of the king, the stipulation they must be dwarfs. 'Might I ask why you thought to enquire?'

'Seaton again, as it happens. He claimed that, after Charles died – you must know far more about the confusions surrounding his death than I – it was discovered they were in possession of Poison Nut seeds and thrown into gaol suspected of complicity.'

'I know nothing about the seeds,' he said. 'But to the dungeons they certainly went. And perished there, I'm afraid. Fever, or some such. Did you know them?'

'I did not. At least, not directly. Though Elihu selected them. It was simply – well, another connection to Fort St. George, I suppose. They have been on my mind. Such a tragedy. Those poor wretches. And the Company, I hope, might not fall too quickly, despite its attempts to see me in Newgate. My eldest, you see, Joseph Junior, has his heart set on following his father into their service.'

'I shall do all in my power to assist him. Fortunately I still have the ear of several Directors on whom we can rely. But no, these things take time. The Crown will wish to see its own interests in the East Indies protected. So this is perhaps not so much to do with the Company's fate but, rather, with how we choose to replace it.'

'Then these might be of interest.' I lifted sheaves of papers from the portmanteau. 'Documents demonstrating the way Elihu has been evading the payment of proper taxes on his private trade goods. Others that show how selective he has been in the collection of poll taxes. They are damning so far as Elihu is concerned but they may also shed some light on how deficient the Company's own processes remain. While these others relate to the Company's recent injudicious investment in their China venture. And then, this. An absurd purchase of interests in a diamond mine that was never going to yield them anything in return. Fiduciary impropriety, all of it.'

He laughed.

'The mine may just be pushing things just a little too far,' he said. 'But the rest are invaluable. And your return to England, you implied it was for the girls' sake. Reunion with your boys. Yet is there something more? Vengeance, Catherine? But for what, my dear?'

'Nothing that need concern you, sirrah. Private matters, all of them. Though I prefer to think of those documents as a measure of justice, not revenge. Or protection, perhaps. Revenge would be too base a thing. Yet I shall do what I can for the cause. I have already promised as much to my Papa. I wrote to Elihu's family last week, suggested I might bring the girls to meet them, though I am unsure of my reception there, at Plas Grono.'

'How could there be any doubt about it – your reception, I mean?'

'It seems there is a great deal I cannot share, I fear. And you must not press me. Not yet. In any case, I have explained to Elihu's Ma and Pa I cannot make the journey until we are settled here. My own investments to make. And a house to be found.'

'You have somewhere in mind?'

'A very adequate house in the fine parish of St. Peter-le-Poor. Broad Street. Just at the junction with Austin Friars.'

'If I can help in any way…'

'Of course. But I think I may have taken up too much of your time already.' I picked up the portmanteau, stood to leave.

'Catherine,' he said, standing too and taking my hand, 'you may always take as much of my time as you need.'

I was almost moved to tears. Dear man. And he had suffered his own misfortunes. Married before I first knew him. Diana, his wife's name. Yet he had been wed and widowed in the same twelve-month.

'You are kind, Streynsham. You have always been kind to me, even when perhaps I did not deserve your kindness. And I suppose that, in different circumstances, after Joseph died, perhaps…'

'My dear,' he said, and he touched his hand to my arm. I recalled the gesture perfectly, for it was precisely the same as I had employed with him, that day when he had tried to counsel me against marrying Elihu, the moment when I had known he was about to suggest an alternative, and I was desperate to prevent him saying something we might each later regret.

'Better to confine our words to the matter in hand?' I said now, as I had said then, nine years before.

'I have finally met somebody, Catherine.' He was almost apologetic. 'We plan to be married next year.'

'Then give you joy of it, Streynsham. And all I ask is to be allowed to dance at your wedding.'

Too late. I delayed over-long. A polite letter by return from Elihu's Mama, inviting me to bring the girls and stay as long as we should like at Plas Grono. No hint of the pity, shame or contempt I had feared if the family had been told of Elihu's infidelities. So yes, I had replied. We would make the journey before the winter's weather made the roads impossible. Or did I say impassible? I cannot now recall.

But then there were more weeks than I should have liked concluding negotiations for the house on Broad Street. The move too, of course. Furniture to be selected. In the midst of all this, a more urgent missive from Wrexham – Elihu's father fallen ill, a suggestion that perhaps I should bring the girls as speedily as might be feasible. My apologies sent back, but the trip would now have to wait until after Christmas – and, late in January, the inevitable news that Mister Yale senior had passed away.

I have fretted away the two months since then, the weather foul, snow for days on end, followed by melting slush, the slush freezing before thawing into cloying mud, then the snow and its cycle commencing afresh. Over and over again.

'Too late for both funerals, my dear,' said Elihu's mother. It seemed she had rather taken against me for this sin, for I only arrived at Plas Grono this morning after church, and our reception was less than warm. To begin, there had been the household's reaction to Tanani. It has been bad enough in London at times, and at each of the places we have stopped along our route here, but the sight of her black face as she climbed out of the carriage sent to collect us from town brought from the servants both gasps of astonishment and outbursts in the Welsh tongue I did not understand. Yet they were spoken with such invective that the meaning could not have been clearer. And the *ayah*'s presence produced a similar response when we were all ushered into the presence of that more elderly Madam Yale and her simple-minded sister-in-law, while the girls' own expressions of distress upon my attempt to introduce them to this pair of desiccated crones in their mourning weeds, their seemingly disembodied ancient faces floating in the darkened reception room, caused the children and Tanani to be quickly exiled into another part of the house.

'Both, yes,' I replied. 'Such ill fortune. I could scarce believe it.'

Her husband had passed away early in January.

'The ice,' croaked Mistress Hopkins, the sister-in-law. 'It were the ice.'

I could almost feel it. The reception we had received hardly a warm one. And the house itself frigid too, its many hearths unlit. I had not expected cheer in this twice-bereaved household but I was surprised by the paucity of its furnishings, their banality. Elihu had always been so flamboyant in his attire and I suppose I had expected this to be an inheritance from one or other of his parents.

'Yes,' I said, perhaps a little too loudly. 'Your nephew. My condolences. To you both.'

'Ill fortune,' said Madam Yale. 'Is that all you have to say about it?'

It was hard to know what else I might add. Mister Yale died of an apoplexy while, outside, a severe snowstorm had raged, the household trapped at home with the deceased for many days. It had finally become necessary to transfer his mortal remains to the small ice-house and, when it was thought safe, Elihu's elder brother David – Elihu had only rarely spoken of him, some jealousy I think – had set out for town to make the necessary arrangements. Yet he had gone no more than a mile when, it seemed, his horse had skittered on the ice and the poor man had been thrown, broke his neck. The horse had returned and Elihu's brother had been found soon afterwards.

'The tracks of our lives,' I said, 'are marked along the wayside by the shrines of those we have lost, do you not find?'

The old lady turned towards the fireplace, hid her face, hand resting on the mantelpiece into which was carved a coat-of-arms. It was similar to that with which Elihu had familiarised me, though not precisely the same. He has never been here, of course. So far as I know. Born in Massachusetts, raised in London. Yet she tapped a fingernail against the red paint within the design.

'Elihu's grandfather, Thomas,' she said. 'And his father, both grew up here. Do you believe, Catherine, we shall be reunited with them all again? In Heaven?'

'Heaven,' repeated Mistress Hopkins. 'Poor David. Dead, you know.'

I was not sure whether she meant her brother, or his eldest son, but yes, I said, I knew. Yet I succeeded in ignoring Madam Yale's question about whether Heaven would ever bring us all together again with those we have lost. I simply do not know any more.

'My poor husband,' said Elihu's mother. 'He sickened so quickly. I have sometimes wondered... Tell me, you met my Thomas?'

'Yes, several times. I counted him a friend.'

'A strange response. Was there some reason you should not have counted him as such? Or perhaps he did not return your friendship?'

I cannot recall ever having felt so intimidated by anybody in my life except, perhaps, for Vincent Seaton. In truth, any reticence in my reply had simply arisen from my continuing uncertainty about whether Thomas may or may not have written home about Elihu's dalliances.

'Far from it,' I said. 'I assume Thomas may have mentioned our meetings with some fondness.'

'Difficult to say, my dear. I have never seen the last letter he sent. My husband read it, I know he did. And then lost the thing. Is that not strange? Almost immediately after, he suffered the first of his apoplexies. It left him almost without speech, palsied. The leeches bled him, of course. But all their medicaments were useless. I asked him about the letter again but that same night another apoplexy and this time he did not survive.'

'Thomas returned from China just before I sailed for England. He was somewhat distressed that his trade mission there had been less than successful – to say the least, unsuccessful. Perhaps he conveyed the scale of his disappointment to your husband?'

'And if he did, what business of yours? Though you may be correct, I suppose. It was his life, after all.'

As it was for so many of us. And David Yale senior was something of a legend. Mercantile trade in Boston, then continued the same trade between London and New England when he returned from Massachusetts, opened up further opportunities with the Hanseatic League factories in Bristol and Ipswich, furs and timbers imported, cloth and manufactured goods sent out in exchange to the Baltic. He had even, at one point, been an ambassador to the Danish Court. Then Church Warden, here at St. Giles, where father and son are now both buried.

'Trade takes us along some strange roads,' I said.

'Strange roads,' said Mistress Hopkins.

'That creature.' Elihu's mother flicked her aged head towards the door. 'Do you think it appropriate for my granddaughters to spend so much time in company with a heathen?'

'She is their *ayah*, my maidservant. The journey would have been impossible without her.'

In fact, I felt guilty for having subjected poor Tanani to the various rigours of the trip. We had taken the coach on Tuesday at dawn from Aldgate and travelled until dusk, forty-seven miles to the *Woolsack* at Woburn. Four more similarly arduous days. But the real hardship had been the insulting behaviour of so many along the way. Fellow passengers who would not even look in Tanani's direction, or spent the endless hours with their noses wrinkled in distaste at thus having to share their space with her, or pointedly chose, despite the weather, to ride atop. Two borachios at Coleshill who refused entirely to board unless "that savage" was removed – and subsequently declared they would rather remain there than travel with us.

'Expensive?' said Madam Yale.

'Thirty-five shillings for each of our four seats. Little Ursula taking turns upon our knees. I could not have managed without Tanani. And it is true she is a Gentue, not a Christian, though at Fort St. George I believe I observed more Christian acts from those we might call heathens than from some who profess themselves devotees of our Lord Jesus. Tanani is such a one, ma'am.'

'Then I wonder the Company has not brought her kind to the Holy Bible, my dear. I have written to Elihu on the matter many times.' Her annual letters to her son had usually conveyed some greeting or word of advice for his "good wife" also. 'But I forget myself.' She seemed to soften a little. 'You mentioned little Ursula. It was dutiful of Elihu – and yourself, naturally – to name the girl for me.'

'Ursula,' said Mistress Hopkins. 'Married my brother. Did you know her?'

Madam Yale regarded her with something that might almost have been pity.

'My husband,' she whispered, 'insisted we should care for her, though the task now grows somewhat tedious. I am not gifted with sufficient patience, I fear. Ah, that reminds me. Our neighbour, Mister Edisbury, he has a gift for you. More precisely, for this new home you have acquired. Broad Street, I collect.'

'Edisbury? The name – ah, I have it. He wrote most kindly to Elihu when he was first promoted to Council. He sent a gift too. Sandpatch ale. Building a new house in the vicinity – the same gentleman?'

'It is a very grand hall, my dear. I invited him to have dinner with us. His wife too.'

'To whom Elihu dispatched a rather elegant lacquered screen, if my memory serves me well. Yet I fear we would be imposing too much, though the invitation is kind. Perhaps better if…'

'You would deprive me of the chance to know my granddaughters, sirrah?'

'Less than polite to descend upon a generous host with the whole of one's household, ma'am.'

'It seems you care more for your heathen than for my hospitality, Catherine. But you need not fear. I shall ensure she is treated with the respect due to my son's retinue. No more and no less. And beyond dinner we shall send to the inn for your baggage. You must stay. My husband would have wished it so. Besides, we are not, now, without room to spare.'

Indeed they are not. The exterior? A three-gabled façade, tall chimneys at each end of the building, neat gardens all about, and high hedging to separate the formal layout from the considerable park lands and woods of sycamore or horse-chestnut beyond. Inside, four reception and two withdrawing rooms, seven bedchambers, eight third floor garret rooms for servants – though not all of them occupied – extensive kitchen and storage cellars, and this dining hall, with two hearths, which would have graced the castles of their ancestors, the Princes of Iâl, Yale in its anglicised form.

'We were fortunate,' said Mister Edisbury, helping himself to another slice of lamb. 'To be able to make the purchase. Your husband thought seriously about taking the land back into the possession of your family, did he not?'

'He always thought it had been a mistake for his grandfather to sell those acres,' Madam Yale replied. 'He frequently regaled me with tales of the happy hours he had spent as a small boy, on his visits here, rampaging on the hillside where, they say, the old castle once stood.'

'I must admit I thought of building on that end of the escarpment. Yet it seemed like a sacrilege.'

'Castle?' I asked, and spooned some scrambled egg and spinach into Katie's mouth. Being almost five she was deemed old enough by my mother-in-law to sit at table with us, while the smaller ones and Tanani were taking food out in the kitchens. I only hoped they were being treated with more civility than displayed by the surly servants in here. Only the young wench charged with feeding Mistress Hopkins seemed to have any enthusiasm about her duties.

'Joshua,' Mistress Edisbury scolded him, 'once you are set on this topic you are quite incapable of desisting again. But you must visit, Catherine. The house is a joy to behold. And yet the cost of furnishings. La! You would not believe.'

'I took a quick look earlier,' I said. 'Through the trees. A short walk with my daughters just before you arrived.'

The place was hard to avoid, and I only wonder I had not noticed the hall earlier, when I arrived. For it makes this Plas Grono seem like a ploughman's cottage in comparison. I had found the right spot, it seemed. Turn in one direction and there was the tower of St. Giles. In the other, the splendour of Edisbury's palatial home. A fitting home, he plainly felt, for a man who had once served his year as High Sheriff of Denbighshire.

'And shall we expect your husband home soon, my dear?' he said.

'Quite soon, I imagine,' I said, picturing again the documents I had placed in Streynsham Master's hands. 'He will be overwhelmed by your generosity, Mister Edisbury, I am certain.'

I tried little Kate with the eel pie, but she wrinkled her nose, spat it back onto the spoon and I saw Mistress Hopkins copy the gesture. They had become firm friends, blathering inanities at each other almost without pausing for breath.

'The clock?' said Edisbury. 'It may help you count the hours until your blissful reunion, I hope.'

It stands now in the entrance hall below, waiting for a fly wagon to convey it, in its crate, back to London – a service he has also provided. A Maysmore, one of the finest that can be purchased here in Wrexham, this home of clock makers.

'And until our unhappy country is at peace again, Mister Edisbury.'

'Does your husband permit political discourse at table, my dear?' Madam Yale snapped at me.

'We rarely speak of anything else.'

Kate was craving the lemon syllabub and I indulged her – which I soon saw was a mistake. For Mistress Hopkins desired she should have some too, though the young maid insisted that, first, she must eat a little more of the rabbit stew and steamed artichoke. There were tears, a great deal of shouting.

'Then you share Joshua's second passion,' shouted Edisbury's wife, Grace. She was a lady of some breeding, I had gleaned, the daughter of Sir Henry Delves. And oh, how I hope my own girls might marry so well.

'Court party, Country party.' Elihu's mother was forced to shout also, above the clamour of her sister-in-law's distress. 'Is there any difference? A plague on all politicians, I say. And for heaven's sake girl,' she yelled at the young maid, 'if she wants syllabub, let her eat syllabub.'

Peace restored, and the affable Mister Edisbury had settled into a defence of his own local politicians.

'Not bad fellows. Any of them. By my troth, we are a drab bunch here in Wales, I fear.'

'Yet I suppose,' I said, 'that, as in London, there must always be those disaffected by one thing or the other, flocking to join the rabble-rousers. The ubiquitous aggrieved.'

'And rarely conscious of the true causes for their grievances,' said Madam Yale, grimacing to see the syllabub dribbling down her sister-in-law's chin.

'I have heard some foolish remarks among the young men in town.' Mister Edisbury was thoughtful for a moment. 'Yes, ill-advised comments, I suppose. Animosity towards King William from some quarters.'

'Gossip from the cock-pit,' sneered his wife. 'Or the gaming tables. My dear, you should keep better company.'

Well, it seems there is little enough for me to feed back to Streynsham about the Yales themselves, or about the local politicians, though he may be interested in this gossip about Wrexham town's wayward youth. A shame though, for I had hoped for something tasty to break the ice with Parrish.

'All a matter of education,' said Madam Yale. 'Do you not think? If there were more educational opportunities for our young men, they would understand more about how the world is run. My husband was a great believer in education, made considerable subscription to several of our colleges. Though he never managed to quite match the notoriety of Reverend Harvard. They were friends, you know? And I think David was always a little jealous of that one thing.'

'Prime!' said Edisbury. 'To have a college named after you.'

I seem to recall Elihu once told me the very same story, about his father's friendship in Massachusetts with John Harvard. The college on the Charles River. Told it with perhaps the same level of relish as Mister Edisbury has done.

Streynsham Master's wedding feast and Sir Christopher Wren – yes, the very same – holding forth, loudly, in his cups, about the injustice he supposed done to him in the recent elections, the questionable result in his favour set aside.

'Perhaps,' my father suggested to him, 'the honest men of New Windsor, paying their taxes as they are required, should surely be entitled, in return for that taxation, to a voice in how they are represented, rather than it simply being a privilege for men of property.'

'God blind me, sirrah. Are you a republican?'

'No, sirrah. Simply a Parliamentarian.'

'Come, Joseph,' I murmured to my son. 'Time to rescue Grandpapa.'

The boy is so tall. Though a boy no longer.

'Ah, Sir Christopher,' my father beamed, almost as inebriated as the great man himself. 'Allow me to name my daughter, Catherine. And her fine son, Joseph Hynmers.'

There were pleasantries and we quietly extracted Papa while Sir Christopher was otherwise engaged.

'Is this not prime?' I said. 'Are you both pleased I secured the invitations?'

'The biggest damn'd tent I've ever seen,' said Papa.

'I heard somebody describe it as a marquee,' I told him. 'A tent, I think, might not be graced with these fine carpets, the tapestries and the chandeliers.'

It entirely filled the substantial courtyard of the College of

Arms, almost in the shadow of the still incomplete St. Paul's – Sir Christopher refuses to be drawn on the final form the tower may take, though there is talk of a dome now – and a mere step from St. Bennet's, Paul's Wharf, where the marriage ceremony itself had been performed. Another of Sir Christopher's accomplishments, naturally, an exceptionally elegant church, almost square, built in dark red brick but with alternate courses of pale Portland stone at the corners. Exquisite.

But at that moment, in the marquee, a small orchestra was playing Sandley's *Suite*, the first movement – that gentle air, the melodious singing – already completed, and the second section, the *courante*, now encouraging many of the guests to the dance floor. Joyous occasion, a fine day outside and the ambience within scented by the grandiose arrangements of blossoms, in blues and lavenders and pinks, as well as the rich aromas of the feast. On the side boards, platters of roasted meats, puddings and pickles in infinite variety, and the largest bride pie I have ever seen.

And there was Streynsham himself, admiring the thing, with his new wife upon his arm and surrounded by several others, including my mama.

'Come,' I said. 'Time for introductions, though I see Mama is there before us. Mama!' I cried, as we drew near. 'We thought you lost.'

It drew Streynsham's attention, naturally.

'Ah, my dear,' he said to his bride, 'here is the very lady I have mentioned so many times. An old friend from my Fort St. George days – and wife of the present Governor there. Allow me to name Mistress Catherine Yale. And – great heavens, can this be young Joseph?'

There was a deal of bowing, the proffering of hands to be shaken or kissed, the usual polite comments, the scratching assessment of each other's attire, while I studied this latest addition to Streynsham's life. Elizabeth Legh – as she had been before the wedding – was, I judged, in her mid-thirties, twenty years younger than her husband, though you would hardly have guessed it, for he had retained a youthful manner that softened the passage of his birthing days. She was slender, her features long, equine, full-lipped, and something of mischief in her eyes. Streynsham had told me a little about her at our last encounter. Daughter of Richard Legh, Lyme Park in Cheshire – though her father sadly dead these past three summers. One of thirteen children, her mother also named Elizabeth and now chatting amiably to Mama about the cost of haberdashery.

'An old friend,' said Mistress Elizabeth Streynsham, the mischievous amusement changing swiftly to something entirely different. What was it? Commiseration? Gloating? 'I should have recognised your India association, naturally. Like having a real Gentue at the wedding.' She laughed, very lightly. Just too lightly. 'La, your complexion, madam. Is it not injurious, to spend so much time in the sun? My husband has such a way with words, does he not? Old friend, indeed.'

In other circumstances I might have pressed the matter. Several matters. Apart from all else, I have been back in England more than a year and still accused of swarthy flesh? For myself, I cannot see it. Though perhaps that is because, now being almost entirely and permanently surrounded by milk-white faces, I imagine myself the same. Indeed, even to me, Tanani has come to seem exotic, out of place. But, just then, there was another familiar voice in my ear.

'And perhaps you might have time for another old acquaintance?'

I turned to find myself confronted by the beaming smile of Sir William Langhorn.

'Good gracious, Governor,' I said, quite taken back in time.

'Old habits die hard, do they not?'

'Indeed they do, Sir William.' Indeed they did. I had always respect for many of his actions at Fort St. George, his advocacy on behalf of the Gentues – in fact, each of Black Town's communities. But I had, of course, been responsible, along with Matthew Parrish, in compiling some of that substance against him.

'And this fine young man?' he said, as I fumbled with some vague guilt. 'He has about him something of...'

'My father,' said Joseph Junior. 'Joseph Hynmers, sir.'

'God's Hooks, young fellow. I should have known you anywhere. And my condolences, sirrah. Your pa was an exceptional man. I regret so much not being there when he was taken from us.'

'As do I, myself, Sir William.' Joseph gave me that disapproving look he seemed to reserve for me alone. It hurt me, as always.

'And what are you doing with yourself these days?' Langhorn asked him.

'A good question, Sir William.' Streynsham had placed a companionable hand on the fellow's shoulder and it seemed a strange gesture. Langhorn had left Madras Patnam, barely a word exchanged with his successor, and Streynsham Master left to pick up the pieces. 'And did I mention, Catherine, that our old colleague is now become one of John Company's Directors?'

The surprise – the fear perhaps – must have registered on my face.

'It was somewhat easier to settle old differences,' said Sir William, 'with Josiah now retired.'

Not to mention the shares you must have been able to purchase too, I thought. And I have never been sure whether news of Josiah Child's "retirement" as the Board of Directors' president is related somehow to whatever schemes Streynsham has been hatching. But, one way or the other, Josiah Child is gone at last. And, I hoped, any renewed threat of that arrest warrant gone with him.

'Perhaps also some new opportunities?' Streynsham said. 'For young men who have chosen to follow in their fathers' footsteps?'

'In truth?' Sir William appraised Joseph Junior afresh. 'Sirrah, I should be delighted to assist. Least I can do. Such a strange turn to the paths of our lives at times. You must have been no more than an infant last time I saw you. And there was another if I am not mistook…' He stopped, his face stricken. 'Oh, my apologies, my dear – for a moment I had forgotten.'

'Walter,' I said. 'The babe's name was Walter.'

'Awful tragedy,' Sir William stammered. 'And you married Yale,' he said. 'More children?' Yes, I explained, many more. 'Prime!' he cried, though he sounded less than certain. 'You shall be glad to be reunited, perhaps – you and our Governor Yale.'

It was not a question. Not a query about Elihu's plans. Rather a statement that his future was already decided, of inevitable fact.

*

We were all singing. *King William's Progress*, naturally. To the tune of *Valiant Jockey's Marched Away*. It had hit the streets like a storm since July.

Now our mighty William goes / To Ireland to subdue his foes.

Such a victory. On the Boyne River, near Drogheda, and the superior forces of King William and his loyal Duke of Schomberg had crushed the army of King James, along with his French allies and the Irish troops of Tyrconnell.

James had abandoned his rebellious Irish allies and fled, like the coward he is, back to France.

So we all sang. Loudly. To drown out the news that would otherwise have overshadowed our victory. The news that, William having drawn us into the mostly Protestant Grand Alliance's war against Catholic France, our Anglo-Dutch fleet had been thrashed by the French off Beachy Head,

Thus, we wedding guests sang for the Boyne to drown out Beachy Head. Though not all were singing, I saw. There was a significant group of younger men close to where I stood with my family and, at their heart, none other than the brother of Streynsham Master's new bride, Peter Legh. And my father, now somewhat cupped, was at them like a shot.

'You scoundrels,' he shouted at them. 'No pride in your nation's victories?'

'Because we do not sing?' Peter Legh laughed at him. 'I believe you may be suffering from an excess of wine, old fellow.'

'Oh,' said Papa, 'I could see you all a-huffing and a-puffing. I know your type. That would see honest Englishman in bondage to French Louis.'

I stepped in front of him.

'Papa,' I whispered. 'Streynsham's wedding. Perhaps another day...'

'Your father, madam?' said Legh. 'Best to remove him against he should cause harm to himself.'

Great heavens, how this cove annoyed me.

'Remove, sirrah? I think you speak above your station.'

'Truly, mistress?' he sneered. 'And you are?'

Joseph Junior was at my side, naming me as wife to the Company's Governor at Madras Patnam.

'Yale, you say?' said Peter Legh. 'Never heard of the fellow. And Madras Patnam – well, I had a close acquaintance there. You might have met. Seaton. Vincent Seaton.'

Perhaps he knew our connection already, for he never troubled to await my response. But Seaton. God's hooks, shall I never be free of him?

'Streynsham,' I said later, when I had a chance to catch him alone. 'Elizabeth's brother…'

'Precisely,' he beamed. 'You have read Machiavelli?' I had not, though Matthew was fond of quoting from *The Prince*, usually in its original. It had inspired much of his poetry too, and I wondered that he was not here. 'There is a section I like, though I shall not do justice to the translation, I fear. About how a new Prince must strive to hold close his allies, though understanding how it is perhaps of even more importance to hold close his enemies. If he is careful, he can bring them to pay for his much-needed patronage through real deeds rather than the lip-labour loyalty of his friends. And thus he exacts a value from his enemies.' He laughed. 'That rogue Peter is a leading light in their so-called Cheshire Club. Breeding ground for Jamesites. You see, Catherine, they are all around us. So there is one more gentleman I should like you to meet.'

'But Seaton,' I protested. 'He mentioned Seaton.'

'Seaton cannot harm you here, my dear,' he said, and set my hand upon his arm, leading me to the portion of the marquee that, without needing any physical barrier, marked itself as the preserve of the most wealthy among Streynsham's guests. Oh, there were a few of the dignitaries, like Sir Christopher, who might not be averse to mingling with the *hoi polloi*, as Dryden describes us, the common masses. But the rest…

It was William Cavendish, of course, the Earl of Devonshire.

There were polite introductions to his wife, Lady Mary and their younger son James, of a similar age to my Benjamin.

'Mistress Yale,' said the Earl, 'give you joy of your safe return to England and I am only sorry we had not the chance to meet earlier.' He seemed somewhat younger than Streynsham and regarded me with a cynical admiration appearing to go entirely unnoticed by his wife, who was deeply engaged in conversation with an older lady. 'Indeed, a great shame. God blind me, Streynsham, you should have told me we were so graced by this lady's presence in London.'

What did I know about this fellow, apart from his ability as a survivor in his parliamentary activities and his present position in King William's household? Only so much as the broadsides and several bawdy ballad sheets might tell: his concubines and a brood of by-blow offsprings; his brawls; his dueling; and his society marriage to Lady Mary, daughter to the recently deceased First Duke of Ormonde.

'Oh, Yale,' she said, as though suddenly remembering the name. 'You are the wife of the merchant fellow. In India was you not?'

'India, Lady Devonshire, yes. My husband is Governor and President at Fort St. George.'

'And Mistress Yale has been providing fine service for us there. Is that not so, Streynsham?' His Lordship was trying hard to mask Lady Mary's distinct lack of good manners.

'Fort St. George?' said Lady Mary's companion and, as this lady moved closer to inspect me, I saw that Streynsham's new wife, Elizabeth, had been standing alongside her. I noted the similarity between them, the same equine features. 'Where in Heaven's name, Streynsham, is Fort St. George?'

'The Coromandel Coast, Ma. India.' Streynsham smiled. Ma? Had I heard correctly? 'And Catherine, permit me to name Mistress Legh, Elizabeth's mother. Presently residing at Devonshire House.'

'Truly?' I said. 'I heard it was now a meeting place for the Society of Friends.'

'Gracious, you are well-informed,' said the lady. 'I permit them to use a room occasionally, with His Lordship's agreement, naturally. When I am in town. Rather in remembrance of my late husband. He always had some sympathy for Dissenters of all persuasions.'

'But you, Mistress Yale,' Elizabeth took her mother's arm, 'I understand from Streynsham you have recently acquired property of your own. Somewhere near the river, I collect?'

She spoke those last few words as though the entire area must be rat-infested.

'Not too close. On Broad Street. Near to my family.'

'All of them merchants too, I suppose?'

'My dear,' said her husband, 'we – all of us here, I collect – owe our fortune to trade in one form or another. Besides, Catherine's father also owns one of the finest coffee houses in London.'

'The finest coffee house,' said Elizabeth. 'Is that not an oxymoron? I am never sure. Though the consumption of that substance is a heathen practice, is it not, husband?'

'I fear my father would agree with you,' I told her. 'But then he is another simple tradesman – which brings to mind a few lines from our mutual associate, Mister Parrish. Something of this sort: *Respect is just a dream we sometimes trade, 'Twixt those who buy and barter, unafraid. Their trade no more than deeply shared respect, A modest, greedless profit to collect.* Is that not apt?'

'I think, daughter,' said Madam Legh, 'this is more a case of us being practiced upon. You have a sharp tongue, Mistress Yale.'

Oh, how I longed to hone its edge now, to draw blood about her seditious son and his association with Seaton. But somebody was speaking at my back.

'And a talent, it seems, for playing fast and loose with my verses.' I spun about and found Matthew Parrish himself looking sternly at me, before bending his knee to the earl. 'Lordship,' he said, 'perhaps you would allow me a private word with Mistress Yale before I offer my proper respects to this most joyous of couples. Apologies for my tardy arrival, Streynsham. And to you, Mistress Master.'

It was difficult not to smile, but permission granted, apologies accepted, and I was swept back across that invisible border between landed gentry and those of lesser breeding.

'Matthew…' I began, but could not quite find the words. Apart from anything else I had almost failed to recognise him. Gone were the Gentue *kurtas* and turbans I had become accustomed to him sporting in India. "Gone native" was a phrase I had often heard applied to him by the other wives of Fort St. George and, of course, to some extent they were correct, for he had lived entirely unashamed with his *bibi*, his Gentue wife Sathiri, whose wisdom I missed so much. Though now he sported a most lavish centre-parted periwig and a brick-red justaucorps day-coat that could only have come from Shudall's or one of their sartorial competitors on Holywell Street.

'You've been busy,' he said. 'Making the social rounds with His Lordship.'

'I knew Streynsham and the earl were associates. But that connection. Devonshire House.'

'A chance encounter, I believe.' He was being stiff, formal. 'Old Madam Legh was seeking a property here in London and a mutual acquaintance mentioned it to the Governor. He, in turn, knew His Lordship was vacating the Devonshire Street premises, moving out to Bloomsbury. Streynsham arranged a meeting and, in the process, struck up a friendship with Elizabeth.'

'But her brother. Do you know him?'

'Friend of Seaton's, you mean? That should not surprise you.'

The orchestra was playing the final notes of a rigadoon, Mister Purcell's piece, I think, and I had been surprised to see Mama and Pa attempting the thing. My mother remains sprightly but those leaping steps had brought a livid colour to my father's neck and cheeks. Still, his fatigue and pause for breath gave me a chance to name Matthew, though I quickly regretted the knowing look Mama gave me from behind her fan and I made the excuse that I must introduce Mister Parrish to Joseph Junior, if he could be found.

'Perhaps we could take the air instead.' I said, when we had escaped, and I allowed him to guide me to one of the marquee's many entrances, facing onto St. Bennet's Hill. But there we found young Peter Legh and his friends, in their cups and singing

Ho, Cavaliers. It was a long while since I had heard that sung, and much longer still since I heard it sung so badly.

'The other side?' said Matthew and led me back through the marquee's interior, out to the College of Arms courtyard. The weather is still fine, of course. A blessing for Streynsham's wedding day, but there was a stiff breeze blowing. Warm but stiff.

'There, better.' I said, though in truth I should have preferred to remain inside. The wind instantly began to make nonsense of the hours I had spent dressing my hair. I drew a deep breath, tried to put some of the wayward strands back into place, began to stumble through an apology. For not being honest with him about the threats Seaton had made against my family. For my betrayal of Jacques de Paiva. For – well, I cannot now quite recall all of them. Yet I remember this. 'One last thing,' I said. 'You remember when Walt died? Yes, of course you must. Though there is one thing you do not know. After we buried the poor mite, that dreadful storm. Elihu came stumbling to our *veranda*, carrying a bundle. It was the babe, the grave quite washed away. Dead then, though he swore he had heard the little one crying, had dug up the coffin with his bare hands, thought my poor boy still lived – though by the time he arrived at the house that was certainly not the case.'

There was a look of abject horror on his face and he took a few steps away from me, forcing me to lift my skirts and run to catch him. It was hardly dignified but I could not afford to leave matters this way.

'You tell me this now?' he said, halting to confront me. 'What, Catherine? You think this grotesque tale will engender pity in me? Help me forgive?'

Then he continued walking, towards the courtyard gate. Perhaps marching might be a better description, for I struggled to keep up.

'How could you think that of me?' I said, though somewhere inside me I suspected he might have seen more truth in this than I, myself, could perceive.

'It seems I could think it very easily, and I am unsure which of us is the more damned by that simple truth. Did Sathiri know?'

'Not even Sathiri. I could not bear the story to become known. Only myself and Joseph, Elihu and Reverend Warner.'

He stopped once more, in the shade of an ancient elm, left the path and leaned against the trunk.

'And Elihu has guarded your secret all this time?'

'He has.'

I was grateful for the respite, the chance to make some further temporary correction to my dishevelled hair.

'And is that the reason you married him?'

He was still vexed, though now, I thought, perhaps for some different reason.

'Not at all. At least – perhaps it played a part.'

'You've heard from him, I suppose?'

'Of course. He wrote at Christmas. Several letters, as it happens. The first two full of rage at his discovery of the way I practised upon Mistress Nicks. Called my actions nothing less than wicked. The pecksniff. Can you believe it? But in the third his ire seems tempered by the financial wounds I inflicted on those other investors in that worthless mine, his Council members like Fraser, Littleton and Briggs, who have apparently been giving him a difficult time.'

'He has forgiven you so easily?'

'Oh, the tone is still bitter. He seems to have had a cruel year.'

'Somebody making mischief for him then.'

Beyond the courtyard's railings, a convoy of carts hauled their loads up from the wharf and I had to shout somewhat to make myself heard above the cobblestone clatter.

'Streynsham has told you? About the documents with which I supplied him?'

'He did. But this is something else, I collect. Far too early for Streynsham to have acted. So, Seaton again?'

'It could be none other, I suppose. Though maybe Fraser or Littleton. Some revenge against the husband, which they could not take against the wicked wife.'

'Or a conspiracy between them all. Hatching while Seaton's been besieged at Bombay. The siege goes on, did you know? Yes, a foolish question. In any case, he would have known nothing about events here. Presumably thought he could make a clean sweep and have somebody in control of Fort St. George who was wholly in his own camp, rather than Elihu's feeble neutrality.'

'Harsh, Matthew.'

'Perhaps,' he said. 'But we should return to the celebrations, should we not?' I thought he might offer me his arm, but he did not. Simply stepped back onto the gravel. From inside, I caught the strains of young Purcell again, his *March and Quick-Step* so that, within moments, all those loyal Williamites within were howling out the latest version of *Lillibullero*. 'You miss him?' Matthew awoke me from my reverie.

'I miss Madras Patnam. And yes, I miss Elihu too, in some fashion. So do the girls. Though not so much as I might have imagined. Their ages, I suppose. And meanwhile he has other troubles. With John Nicks, of all people.'

'He'd had news of the coronation, I suppose?'

'Even that was strange. He has the constitution of an ox, as you know. Never a day's illness. Yet he professed himself struck down by some mysterious ailment.'

'He did not discover those Poison Nut seeds you guarded so carefully, I hope.'

'No – no, such would not be possible.'

Obviously not. I had powdered them for my intended revenge against Mistress Bridger.

'It was a jest, Catherine. Or do you have some other confession to make?'

'Not at all,' I barked, knowing the pitch of my protest was far too high. 'Anyway, the ship arrived with the news while he was ill, but he had to rouse himself and arrange all the normal celebrations for the King and Queen to be proclaimed.'

'He says nothing about how the news was received?'

'Received well, I think. Though he noted a certain hardening of attitudes towards him among the Council members afterwards. A dispute about a slave boy who had been tried for theft, sentenced to hang. But Elihu had some evidence that the boy had been tortured into a confession, had a mind to commute the boy's sentence to banishment. Bad enough, though he was then subjected to a torrent of complaint, says he finally had to agree at least to the child being branded.'

'I see your husband has not lost his penchant for mercy.'

'I am finding it difficult again to know when you jest – a problem I do not recall experiencing at Fort St. George. Have we grown so far apart, then?'

He shrugged. We had reached the entrance to the marquee again, but he did not immediately enter, stood in the doorway.

'You cannot have expected it to be otherwise,' he said. 'And that is all, from your husband?'

'The rest of his year seems to have been taken up with intercessions on behalf of English prisoners taken by Aurangzeb's army, and others who had been cast on the island of Ceylon, poor devils. But you, Matthew? Streynsham was close-lipped about your own activities. Tells me you are recovered and undertaking some diplomatic mission.'

'I doubt I shall ever be fully recovered, though I suppose it depends on how you measure the word. Yet I am made secretary to our embassy at The Hague. The reason for my late arrival.'

'You are leaving London?'

It struck me like a hammer blow, all the gaiety inside now turned to bitter cacophony.

'Tomorrow. And your good self, Catherine, have you plans? Elihu's father dead, Streynsham tells me. And little to interest us in Wales, it seems. For the moment, at least. But it's clear not a week passes without us picking up rumour of yet another Jacobite plot in one part of the country or another. We need eyes and ears everywhere if we are to prevent ourselves drifting into civil war again. You can still provide useful service, if you choose.'

My good self? Here I am, damned by that faint and false praise. But eyes and ears? Is that all I am to him now? A simple cipher in the secret struggle against sedition? I had so longed for more from our reunion. Yet it must suffice, I suppose. For now, at least. And a laudable enough responsibility, is it not? That mothers like myself

54

should no more be haunted by thoughts of bloody conflict. Well, I pray it shall be so, though that doom I had felt aboard the *Revanche* still seems to settle so often upon my shoulders.

They died on the same day. At the same hour. George Fox, most famous of Quakers, and my poor papa, Walter Elford, who had once professed to walking a parallel path alongside those Friends of the Society. Buried on the same day, too, though plainly in different locations – Fox at the Quaker Burial Ground on Bunhill Fields, and Papa in the churchyard of St. Edmund's. Three days ago.

It is said there were four thousand at the Bunhill Fields, yet even more remarkable that we had four hundred crammed into and around the church on Lombard Street. A great testimony to my father's own life and to all those he has touched during his seventy-nine years. Mama and my sister Roberta remain distraught, naturally, but my brother Richard seems almost unmoved, taking over full responsibility for the coffee house as though it were the most obvious thing in the world.

There has been time to add the news – about Papa, but also about George Fox, since I believed this would interest him – in my letter to Elihu. There is much else to tell him, of course. Apart from anything else, my riposte to his anger about Mistress Nicks and the mine. All she deserved, I told him, though my sarcasm was tempered by the belated condolences on the deaths of his own father and brother. Madam Yale had made arrangements for a fast post to carry word aboard the very final outbound vessel of last year, so I must assume he already knows about this double sadness, though I wove my wordings in such a way that if, for any reason, he had not heard earlier, it would break the thing gently to him.

And, speaking of Plas Grono, as I wrote those paragraphs,

the Maysmore clock struck the hour below, in the hallway, and reminded me to mention Mister Edisbury's kindness.

That has been my only other concession, however. Most of the rest written in a formal manner so I might not offer him even a crumb of affection to signal I have either forgiven or forgotten his infidelities and, in my eyes, his general failings as a husband, as a protector of my children. So I have taken some delight in advising him that, through my own intercession, Joseph Junior is now firmly ensconced with the Honourable English East India Company. And I could not help adding the phrase "for as long as it might survive", knowing this would both vex, pain and trouble him, leaving him no way by which he can query my meaning.

Of the other boys, I have made only the merest mention, except in Benjamin's case, adding my expectation that this might press Elihu to remember he has still never made good his promise of the eight hundred pounds, plus interest, due to my youngest son from his true father's inheritance.

I can almost see his enraged face as he reads those lines. I imagine he will have become florid since my departure, his dissolute lifestyle, his pair of harlots, having collectively taken their toll of his health and features. Yet I could not finish without mention of his daughters. Kate now has a tutor come to the house to assist me in her learning to read and write. Already turned five! I can scarce believe it but she has insisted on making her own addition to my letter, a picture of our new house on Broad Street and a few carefully crafted words. From Annie – good gracious, the child seems to grow more plain with every day that passes – some simple patterns along the lower edge of Kate's handiwork, and from Ursula a pair of inky little handprints on the reverse.

My postscript? I will tell him, without displaying any sign of the additional grief I feel, that he must be sensible to the fact that the letter is being borne back to Fort St. George by my faithful Tanani. I shall require him to ensure she finds an appropriate position there once more. It is a measure of how miserable her existence has been here that she is willing so soon to undertake once again the voyage that caused her such suffering to reach London.

*

I had no sooner finished the letter when there was a hammering at the street door and a boy delivered a brief note, signed by somebody who styled himself Ferñao Pereira and inviting me to meet him at his Cheapside premises, at the sign of the Golden Pheasant, to discuss matters of mutual interest.

Anyway, it was already my intention to visit Leadenhall Street this afternoon – entering the lion's den as I nervously perceived it. A surprise visit to Joseph Junior to confirm passage for Tanani as well as the cases of supplies Mama had already put into storage for delivery to Elihu – yet I decided to hire a chair, wrap myself in my furs against the January ice and snow, and make the detour. Such a contrast to the stately palanquin journeys I was accustomed to making through Black Town, here the bearers slipping and cursing their way along Threadneedle Street and the Poultry, until we reached the remaining stones where, in my youth, the castle-like bulk of the Great Conduit had stood. But then we were weaving our way between cart and carriage, past higgler and hawker, the shop fronts of Cheapside itself, until we reached the place, almost at the junction of Honey Lane.

Inside it was all noise, a treadmill driving a turning wheel within a large wooden frame and, supervising the operation, a handsome fellow of about my own age whose features I recognised from another of our old Black Town associates.

'Master Pereira?' I shouted from the doorway, and he turned, inclined his head by way of greeting.

'*Senhora* Yale,' he replied, his accent heavy with those familiar Sefardi tones I knew so well from Jacques de Paiva and Antonio do Porto but here laced with an additional element. Dutch, of course.

'Amsterdam?' I said.

'You can tell, from those two words?'

'If I am honest, it was perhaps more my recollection that the syndicate – your father's, do Porto's, whoever else might be involved – was based there. They never made mention of any operation in London though. Conclusion: you must be newly arrived. And the machinery, it is only recently installed unless I am much mistook.'

'My father, he told me you have a sharp eye.'

'And suggested you contact me?'

'With everything so much better now between England and the Dutch Republic, the heart of our trade is slowly shifting. From Goa and Amsterdam to Fort St. George and London. Since the ships bringing raw stones land first at London, it seems sensible to supply the English markets by cutting here. Rather than all that *ir e voltar*, you understand? With you, *senhora*, my father believed we might be able to conclude some business together.'

Diamonds, found nowhere else in the entire world than India, have made such a remarkable contribution to all our fortunes, and here was a young woman with a pox-ravaged face relentlessly working the treadmill powering the cutting and polishing rig.

'That girl, is she also of your race?' I said, for she did not truly have the appearance of any Jew I had ever known.

'*Nem pensar.* She came to us when we were installing the rig. Looking for work to supplement her – well, her usual income.'

'You can trust her, with the brilliants?'

'By the end,' said Fernão, 'we know each stone as though it were a new-born babe, each counted and settled in its bed at every day's end.'

'I have never seen this,' I said. 'All those years, the rough stones passing through my hands. And this...'

'My father believes you may have brought a quantity back with you to England.'

He was correct, naturally. Their syndicate associate, Antonio do Porto, had helped me convince Elihu's harlots to invest in a worthless diamond mine, just part of my revenge against them, and I had converted some of the gold they paid me into uncut stones in the short time available before I sailed. Not so many as I should have liked, but enough.

'Your father should know,' I laughed. 'He struck a hard enough bargain in the bartering for them.'

Even so, their estimated value, along with the rest of the gold pagodas, almost doubled the personal fortune I had already invested over the years with Mama.

'The fact is,' said Fernão, 'we simply cannot presently meet the demand for cut stones. So if you would care to bring us some or all of those you possess, perhaps you might enjoy bartering as our dinner guest.'

It was indeed an imposing frontage, three storeys of glorious mansion built, I think, during the reign of Queen Bess: the street level on Leadenhall itself very modest except for an imposing gateway; the first floor all windows and a fine balustraded balcony; and the second storey more windows with, in the centre of the façade, John Company's coat-of-arms. Above, that wooden structure imitating the stern of a ship, painted depictions of East Indiamen in a panel, a brace of gigantic carved dolphins at the corners, and the whole surmounted by an even greater timber statue of a seaman.

I had never before been inside, however. More than twenty years a bride of this establishment and never stepped across its threshold. A little like my association with the diamond trade, I suppose. So now I was handed from the hired chair and stood beyond the gate, with its old portcullis, finding myself unable to pass through, regardless of Streynsham's assurances. This still now felt like enemy territory and I was only rescued by the arrival of Sir William Langhorn himself, breaking away from a group of his fellows, just arriving back at the premises and seemingly having enjoyed an especially genial dinner.

'Mistress Yale,' he beamed. 'Great Heavens, how it does my failing eyes good to see you again. Here to see me, I hope?'

'Simply a word with my son. Freight to be paid on cargo for Elihu and passage for my *ayah*. You remember Tanani? Sadly she goes back to Fort St. George.'

'Yes, of course I remember. But your son? Not here I'm afraid. It is only, ma'am, that young Joseph's normal place of work is around the corner. Lime Street. We have further premises there. But I will send for him at once. And meanwhile, Mistress, perhaps a moment of your time if you would do me such kindness. Something perhaps we should discuss.'

He led me through the small yard, proudly showed me the main hall. A council chamber on the ground floor serving, Sir William explained, as the Directors' Court. It was grand, in the way a faded tapestry may still be grand long after its colours have waned and there is only one's imagination to reconstruct an image of the original. Yet as we wound our way up the dim main staircase, along its narrow passages, past the gloomy rooms, I struggled to remind myself that here treaties were regularly signed with Oriental princes ruling over territories larger than all Europe. Policies made, trading prices determined, wars commenced and peace concluded.

'It is more austere than I should have imagined, Sir William.'

There were busts of Directors and Governors now deceased, plenty of paintings or mezzotint engravings, some miniatures – yet all these pictures either seascapes, or depictions of the Company's ships in fair weather and foul plus, among them, an occasional rendering of one or other of the East India Presidencies. One I remembered well, a depiction of Fort St. George executed by Joseph. The whole house on Middle Street had been full of his sketchings and Elihu eventually insisted we should put all but the most precious into storage. These valuable examples of my Joseph's craft, mostly portraits of the boys, adorn the house on Broad Street. The rest? Still in one of Mister Yale's godowns, I assume.

'You recall it? Joseph gifted me that dainty before I sailed. A reminder of those happy days at Madras Patnam. Yet this whole place should be more exotic, do you not think?'

I agreed. Considering the quantity of fine art and furniture so regularly transported home from India, Sumatra, Taiwan and a dozen other locations, there was almost nothing of that sort on display here.

The upper level was more a warren even than the rest, but we finally passed through a counting room with young clerks busy at their ledgers and, beyond that, six rickety steps leading into a small office where Sir William made himself comfortable at a writing bureau and bade me take a more adequately upholstered chair. He fussed for a moment, shuffling papers, clearing his throat and harrumphing quietly.

'Easiest to simply say what it is on your mind, sirrah?' I said.

He stood and closed the door.

'Devilish,' he murmured. 'I understand Streynsham may have given you some flavour of what may be afoot?'

'With the Company?'

'Of course with the Company. Please, ma'am, it will not help me if you are coy. I believe the phrase "outlived its usefulness" may have been spoken.'

'It was.'

'Something about "not so much the Company's fate but, rather, how we choose to replace it" – that sort of thing?'

'Indeed.'

'And you, Mistress, may have offered our old colleague certain papers? Certain improprieties on the part of your husband, as well as fiduciary irregularities in the Company's systems.'

'That is so. As well as injudicious investments in mining ventures and the China trade.'

'Quite. Quite. And all that without this disastrous war with the Mughal Emperor. What in Heaven's name was Child thinking? Still besieged at Bombay. Next it will be Fort St. George, unless our envoys succeed in reaching some accommodation with the fellow – though I dread to think what the cost may be. By my troth, these are Presidencies, part of the Crown. King William's Crown!'

I recall Governor Langhorn being similarly enthusiastic about King Charles and I was reminded of Streynsham's words about Machiavelli. Here, for all the world, was a man with no natural affinity for our Commonwealth faction nor, I suspect, for King William in particular, but now dependent upon the patronage of this new regime for his future fortune and, therefore, more than happy to deliver whatever King William might desire so far as John Company was concerned. Keeping your enemies at least as close as your friends.

'A parlous state of affairs, Sir William. And His Majesty must be grateful indeed to have faithful subjects like yourself to help protect his interests.'

He regarded me quizzically, uncertain whether or not I was

practising upon him, but then took from his pocket a snuffbox and helped himself to a pinch. Offered me some too, though I declined, naturally.

'Well,' he said, 'where to begin? Confidentially, of course. But certain parties, myself included, have persuaded a parliamentary committee to investigate the Company and its affairs.'

'Might I ask the purpose?'

'Principally to remove the old managerial group and replace it with those who may be more loyal to our Williamite cause.' He placed a certain emphasis on this being a shared purpose. 'Your own purpose too, I must assume, putting King and Country above your wedding vows. Naturally, there are many among the Directors who believe themselves untouchable.'

'The papers I brought will play a small part in disabusing them, I hope. And an end to the Cavalier faction in the Company? Not before time, sirrah. There is my purpose. As you say, even at the cost of loyalty to my husband.'

'Yet there is the rub, ma'am. The papers, you see?' He waved them in the air, more harrumphing. 'You copied these accounts yourself?'

'The accounts, and those sheets on which I have recorded conversations about the matters I mentioned. And the problem?'

'That the parliamentary committee will only accept them in the form of an affidavit.'

'Because of my status as the Governor's wife?'

'In part. Though it is perhaps more connected to the cloud under which I, myself, originally left the Company's employ. A cloud of injustice, as you will collect.' I did not have the heart to tell him that the vast scale of his personal profiteering while Governor at Fort St. George was known to our entire community down to the last gold pagoda. 'So what they need,' he went on, 'is evidence that cannot be refuted, evidence like this, coming as it does, rather, unsullied from Caesar's wife, in fact.'

The words chilled me. Precisely the same as Vincent Seaton had used when he demanded I sign another affidavit testifying how Jacques de Paiva was using the diamond trade to assist those plotting against King James. Oh, how I wished to high heaven that Matthew Parrish was here to guide me, but he is long gone, to Amsterdam.

'Testifying against my own husband is hardly likely to make me seem unsullied in the eyes of this committee. Will they not simply see it as a quest for vengeance by a woman scorned?'

'But, my dear,' he smiled, 'is that not exactly the point? Scorned in what way? Surely there is nothing would lead them to believe your actions arise from anything other than your loyalty to the Crown? Is there?' He must have known. Of course he must, yet he simply cantered on, at a pace, for he had a good point. Who is there, here, that surely knows of Elihu's infidelities, apart from Streynsham and Matthew Parrish? 'In any case, how did you expect to employ these documents? Did you assume Streynsham Master or myself could, by some act of magic, produce the results you desire without you being identified as their source?'

'It would expose me, Sir William. Some public declaration of my involvement. I have my children to consider.'

'Then the affidavit is your only safe haven, ma'am. Your common law privilege, my dear. Lake versus King, I collect. The year sixty-seven. If the committee accepts your sworn statement and the papers you provide as valid evidence, you shall be protected in law, confidentiality guaranteed.'

'And if not?'

'Oh, I am certain we do not need to trouble ourselves in that regard. And it will help in this way also. That when the committee is done with the thing, it leaves me free to raise the necessary matters here in the Court of Directors too – though, naturally, I shall then be able to say I am bringing them evidence already accepted by parliamentary investigation but with the sources subject to privilege. Anonymous, therefore, though entirely trustworthy. By the time Parliament and the Crown conclude their deliberations about the Company's future, I shall already have been able to act on the specific issue of Fort St. George and your – well, your husband. As gently as I am able, plainly. That is, I assume, what you want?'

'As you say, Sir William, yet there is only this one last point to clarify, I think. You recall Vincent Seaton, of course?'

'Seaton? Yes, and what a surprise it was when Streynsham passed on Parrish's intelligence about the scrub. I should never have believed it. Agent for the papal nuncio, he says.'

I searched in his eyes, deep into his soul, for any indication this might be mere performance. For any sign he might already have known Seaton's nature. When poor Major Puckle had been sent out to India, to investigate the management of Fort St. George in general, and Governor Langhorn's conduct in particular, it was, to say the least, a fortunate accident that had seen the Major dead before he could take any significant action. But had Seaton murdered him, as Matthew suspected? And, if so, had Sir William been involved in any way? Well, from the profound innocence of his expression, I was no nearer to grasping the answers.

'Then let me add a further section to this affidavit you crave, sirrah. A section in which I relate the discussion I was forced to endure, by Seaton, in which he both admitted his work on behalf of the pope, as well as his part in the murder of diamond trader Jacques de Paiva – among other things I do not need to specify.'

He nodded his head appreciatively, pursed his lips.

'Yes,' he said, 'I think that will do nicely.' As he spoke, there was a knock at the door. 'Come!' Sir William shouted, and a breathless Joseph Junior stepped into the room, halted in surprise when he saw me there. 'Ah, Hynmers. Such timing. I was just about to break the news to your mama.' He turned to me. 'About his posting, Mistress Yale. Fort St. George, exactly as he desired. And – well, I shall make sure we keep a careful eye upon him out there. Make sure our plans proceed precisely as we should all wish. You follow my drift?'

There was just the slightest scent of menace lingering around the edges of his smile.

Saturday 26th October 1691

I fear I may have put myself in harm's way.

The day began innocently enough, Mama and myself taking the three girls, as well as the nursemaid I have hired to replace the irreplaceable Tanani, by carriage across the river and the tedious journey to Lambeth and the Vauxhall gardens.

A relatively short visit – though long enough to allow the children some play and to be amused by the jugglers there this morning – and then the return in time for my dinner appointment with Sir William and Streynsham Master at *Pontac's* on Lombard Street. Their usual provender at five shillings for some excellent French mutton.

'François,' cried Sir William, when he finally spotted the proprietor. 'Well, *très bien, monsieur. Très bien*, indeed.'

Monsieur Pontac gave a curt acknowledgement to the compliment.

'I suppose,' said Streynsham, 'that, with fare this good, we must almost forgive them for Leuze.'

The recent defeat of our Anglo-Dutch cavalry by the French. An image of the Courtois painting I had seen in Streynsham's house.

'It seems to always be the same,' I said, moving some of the meat around my plate. 'For every gain, another reverse.'

Before Leuze, the news had all been good. The war against the forces of Popish James in Ireland finally over. A treaty signed at Limerick and those forces still loyal to him flown to France, like wild geese, somebody has said, flown to milder climes for the winter – a winter that, for them, I trust, will never again turn to spring.

'Yet our own enterprise brings nothing but glad tidings, sirrah,' said Sir William.

There had been a letter from Elihu, which arrived early in August. Yet more anger about Katherine Nicks and the mine. But then his joy that the siege of Bombay was ended. Oh, in his normal fashion he claims it for a great victory by the Company. The Mughal Emperor forced to accept the peace and even concede to a new factory – on the east bank of the Hoogli River, a place we have called Calcutta.

'Glad tidings?' Streynsham almost choked on his food. 'Certainly the siege is lifted. But the indignity. Our envoys left with no alternative but to grovel before Aurangzeb in person. To prostrate themselves, literally, and offer ever more exorbitant levels of indemnity. The cost, Sir William. The cost.'

The final figure had been so large that, even without any intercession by parliamentary committee, it would likely have brought the enterprise to the brink of bankruptcy. But yes, Bombay released from the Mughal Emperor's claws, its trading concession re-affirmed, and the Company permitted to extend into this Calcutta simply because Aurangzeb thought the territory worthless.

'The cost, of course.' Sir William smiled. 'But that may prove the final nail in the coffin.'

'It seems to me,' I said, 'the official account and Elihu's version coincide really in only two places – that the siege is lifted and that, at its end, Vincent Seaton is missing. Missing? What does that mean?'

I wish the fellow dead, naturally, but I fear my optimism might be misplaced.

'Let us hope,' said Sir William, 'the cove is out of our hair forever. There are a couple of things in your husband's favour, however. This victory against the French fleet and our new fort, perhaps?'

A sea battle in the roads off Fort St. George, which took place last August – a French fleet driven off by a combined force of Dutch and English ships. And, in a similar vein, Thomas Yale had travelled to Tegnapatam, the area visited by Elihu ten years ago.

Then he had the ambition to build a fort there and name it Fort St. David. For the patron saint. In honour of Wales and long before our own ill-fated little Davy was born. Yet now he has finally achieved his dream.

'He seems very dismissive,' I said, 'of the Council's objections to the involvement of his brother in this venture.'

Objections, and a few disagreements, he had written, with the Council members also about that poor-quality cloth from John Nicks at Conimere. The true picture? Streynsham has shown me the Consultation Books and Diaries sent back for audit.

'How does he describe them?' Streynsham laughed. 'Certain jealousies. Was that it? And here we are, sitting on an entire folio of charges against him. He may still be your husband, my dear. But really! Arbitrary decisions. Personal avarice and vast ill-gotten fortune. Exorbitant treatment of native merchants. Foul language. Favouritism. Betrayal of the Company. Fraudulent activities. Page after page of supportive evidence.'

Well, on the one hand, I had seen similar allegations – with greater or lesser degrees of veracity – levelled against each of Elihu's predecessors, including both of these gentlemen. But so much smoke and no fire?

'Yet,' I said, 'even bearing in mind my own documents against him, this does not sound quite like the Elihu Yale I have come to know.'

And there, was that not the point? That while I suppose I should have welcomed these charges against him, the truth is I rather resented them. Did I want him brought down? Of course. But by those scoundrels of the Cavalier faction, the Tories of the Fort St. George Council? Oh, most certainly not. And the hypocrites. They could have raised issues about his personal morality – in my mind, his greatest crime. But, as Herbert wrote, those whose house is of glass must not throw stones at another. Each of them, I am guessing, would be guilty of moral impropriety at least as bad as Elihu's and probably far worse!

'Young Joseph will be out there soon enough,' said Sir William. 'Sails next month?' Indeed, though I do not wish to dwell on the matter, passage arranged aboard the *Samson*. 'He'll be able to keep you abreast of whether your husband's character has changed. It happens, you know. Even to the best of us.'

It would be, I imagined – as I had imagined so many times already – due to Elihu's debaucheries, taking their toll.

'And this affidavit, Catherine,' said Streynsham, 'are you certain about these additions?'

Once I had begun the process, given Sir William's assurances, it was hard to stop. Some added spice in my allegations against Seaton, naturally. But then the muse took me and I decided to indulge myself in the knowledge that Katherine Nicks had become impoverished by her losses from the diamond mine investment. So, what if...? I began to wonder. And I had soon concocted a vivid tale about how she had taken to entering the Company's godowns, removing large quantities of calicoes and selling them privately for the personal enrichment of herself and Elihu. The harlot should have left well alone, but that had been beyond her wit. Instead, she had written to me as well, demanding reparation for those losses, accusing me of the most terrible infamies. Such gall!

'Streynsham,' I replied, 'how could I ignore this embezzlement when I have it from the very finest authority – my husband's own latest letter to me, here in London.'

He knew I was lying, of course.

'All grist to one's mill,' said Sir William. 'And the committee proceedings going well already.' Indeed they are. 'This business,' he went on, 'with the Papillion Syndicate, for a start.' There had been a petition from a gentlemen called Thomas Papillion, another of the Directors, who has resigned from the Board, his petition calling for the Company to be dissolved and the Charter granted instead to his own syndicate. Naturally, the political nature of his syndicate would not lend itself to the service of King William any more than the present management, so the petition has been rejected. 'Yet some of the fools on the Board,' Sir William laughed, 'have taken the damn'd petition's rejection as a vote of confidence in them from the Crown.'

I suppose I was more taken with the news that the Company's vessel, the *Dorothy*, sails next month with instructions for the arrest of Katherine Nicks and, as additional measure – unintended on my part – the dismissal of her husband who, the committee has apparently assumed, must be aware of her illicit activities.

'They will wake up before too long,' said Streynsham. 'And you, my dear, you are still in correspondence with Elihu?'

Sir William had seen *Monsieur* Pontac passing through the dining hall and taking wine to one of the long tables. He called him over.

'*Monsieur,*' he said, 'are those samples of your father's superb produce?' Naturally. Château Haut-Brion, from the Bordeaux estates of Lord Arnaud de Pontac and imported into England through this French ordinary.

'Joseph will carry my usual letter to him,' I told Streynsham while Sir William was still engaged in the wine debate. 'He deserves word of his daughters, at least. And I should convey your own news, perhaps? He would wish to know.'

His wife, Elizabeth, had delivered him a fine baby girl, another Anne.

'As you desire,' he said.

Desire? I thought. Oh, Streynsham, if only you knew my desires. And I almost smiled, for I had been thinking about him last evening while perusing our latest broadsheet. *The Athenian Mercury* with its plethora of questions from readers. It was this one: *Whether a tender friendship between two persons of a different sex can be innocent?* And I had noted the gap in the various forms of advice proffered by Mister Dunton by way of reply. That of course such a friendship may be innocent – so long as the parties are not given the privacy and inclination to make it otherwise.

It was also Elihu's letter that then brought myself and Mama, in company with Joseph Junior and Richard, to the Boar's Head on Fleet Street.

'Must we do this?' said Rich, when we saw the crowds pressing to enter. 'It has already been a tiresome day.'

'Of course,' I replied. 'It must be fate, do you not think? Mister Yale makes such mention of this curiosity and by the time his letter arrives, here is Dampier in London with the self-same marvel.'

Captain Dampier had seemingly spent a considerable time at Fort St. George and brought with him this illustrated warrior from the Philippine islands, from Miangas, Elihu says, and purchased with the sole intention of exhibiting him as a wonder here in England.

'Make way there,' shouted Joseph. 'Please, let these ladies pass.' It could almost have been his father.

'Anyway,' I called to Richard, 'how many more opportunities might we all have to be together like this, with your brother due to leave us so soon.'

'Of course, Mama,' he replied. 'So important, is it not? To keep the family intact?'

It was easier to ignore him when his humour was thus and, by then, Joseph had made passage for us through the coaching gate and into the courtyard, where we paid for seating near the raised platform they had erected there.

'Have you met him before?' said Mama.

'Dampier, Mama? Gracious, no. He has made his living as a buccaneer. A privateer. The sort of fellow who threatened my life during the pirate raid. And in that way he has gained notoriety for his circumnavigation of the globe. Yet I am unsure how praiseworthy this might be. To make one's way around the whole world by piracy, regardless of whether such piracy might on occasion be in the name of the Crown.'

Yet there he was, mounting the scaffold. Forty, I suppose, weather-beaten, naturally, and his nose, his lips, his eyelids swollen, bloated. He spent some time speaking of the perils he had endured both in capturing his exhibit and then bringing him here for our pleasure and edification.

'Now let you marvel,' he shouted at last, 'at Giolo, the Painted Prince of Miangas.'

When the show was over, as a remembrance, I purchased a pack of playing cards with a reproduction of Giolo's image on the backs, though we declined the handbills inviting us to view him again, along with many other curiosities – a tiny fairy child from Sumatra, a giant Irishman and a Khoe Khoe dwarf, a Siberian dancing bear, the leopard-spotted Brazilian boy, the twin-headed girl from Tunis, and the Merman of Madagascar.

'Oh, a merman,' I said, and caused Mama to smile, for we had amused ourselves considerably with another reader's question in Dunton's *Athenian Mercury*. Whether, since mermen and mermaids have more of the human shape than other fishes, they may be thought to have more reason.

The handbill proudly announced this special performance would take place in a tent set up outside the gates of the Bethlem Hospital, at Moor Fields, now opened to the public, the admission price for the curiosity show also giving entitlement to view some of the more grotesque inmates. Oh, the world in which we live!

'Mama,' said Joseph Junior as we were leaving the courtyard, 'is that not...?'

'Indeed it is,' I replied, following the direction of his gaze.

Peter Legh, brother-in-law to Streynsham Master. The braggart who had boasted of his close association with Vincent Seaton. A couple of the coves I had seen constantly in his company at the wedding, all clustering like moths about a flame, and this bright centre of their existence another I recognised vaguely from Streynsham's nuptials.

'And that kind gentleman,' said Mama suddenly. She was plainly considering the very same fellow. 'Lord Bruce, is he not? Earl of Ailesbury. Were you introduced, my dear?'

'I was not, Mama.'

'Perfectly charming. Do you know he has been a Lord of the Royal Bedchamber?'

'Truly?' I said. 'To Catholic James, I assume.'

'Oh, Catherine, you have been out of the country too long. No, for him he was Page of Honour at the coronation.'

'Yet still here in England? Another of those who have sworn false allegiance to King William, I collect.'

I have to admit, though, that he did, as Mama had suggested, seem the most affable of men. Younger than me by several years, I think, and so richly dressed, his periwig full-bodied and of the very finest quality.

'Come, Mother,' said Joseph Junior, 'our curiosity has been noted.'

He was right. I was so taken by Ailesbury I had failed to properly observe Peter Legh. He was looking in our direction, one of his associates whispering in his ear, having – it seemed – drawn his attention to us. Our eyes met and he smiled. A frigid smile, before he turned and called to somebody on the farther side of their gathering. Then he laughed, stretched out his arm in greeting as their group parted and he placed it about the shoulders of his friend. Vincent Seaton.

The rage in me erupted like a flame, and I took a step towards them.

'Stay here,' I said, 'all of you.'

But there must have been a madness in my eyes and Joseph grasped my arm.

'Mother!' he said. 'What is this?'

How could I tell him? Yet I was glad of his restraint. It simply would not answer, to confront Seaton here, in this way. So I simply lifted my chin, looked into Seaton's own eyes, saw the venom there. Venom – and something else, something much more difficult to fathom.

Seaton seems to have vanished from the face of the earth though there have been times when I could have sworn I almost felt his breath upon my face.

The first occasion only two days after I had seen him at the Boar's Head and I was shopping at the Honey Lane Market with Susannah – the new nursemaid – and the children. I had turned around and, suddenly, they were all gone. It took me some minutes to find them and, when I did, the foolish girl told me they had been detained by a very pleasant gentleman who had admired her charges.

'Describe him,' I had said, and she gave me a perfect description of a cove who could so easily have been Seaton.

The second time, Gunpowder Treason Day, upon which we now also celebrate King William's birthing day, of course. We were in low spirits, Joseph Junior having so recently sailed on the *Samson*. It had not been the sweetest of partings, made worse for me by my failure to warn him what he might find at Fort St. George. He had said he was looking forward to renewing his acquaintance with Elihu and I did not have the stomach to tell him about Katherine Nicks or Jeronima de Paiva. A year is a long time, I reasoned, and much may have happened in that time. But as we were returning home from the Moor Fields, from the bonfires, fireworks and, this year, the burning of some very elegant effigies of the pope, the great guns still firing at the Tower, there was a cloaked figure lurking suspiciously in the shadows just across from the house. Richard saw him too.

'That fellow,' he said, now considering himself the man of the house, 'is he spying on us?' He set off across Broad Street to accost him, only to have the knave vanish entirely, almost literally in a whisper of air, and in the darkness.

The third, when the whole family made the journey in January to Wapping Stairs to bid farewell to Richard who, at the tender age of twenty, was sailing for the factories of Clark and Thornton at Porto. A muffled fellow of Seaton's build and stance was there too, just along the quayside.

Then it seemed he must have disappeared, though this was during February and March, the time when my seemingly innocent report to Streynsham Master turned into something far more significant.

'But it was nothing,' I had said to him. 'I simply reported seeing your brother-in-law and his friends in company with Ailesbury and Seaton.'

We were meeting at Fernão Pereira's Cheapside establishment, and Streynsham smiled.

'But in your own inimitable fashion, that snippet caused the king's agents to investigate Ailesbury's other connections more closely, his frequent trips to Paris. And in Paris he was observed by our old friend Parrish. From that we discovered Ailesbury's link to the Earl of Melfort in James's exiled court. Melfort, it seems, is involved in some plan for a French invasion, probably in April. Usual foolishness. The French will land and Ailesbury, as well as others of his kind from here in the south, will raise a force to join them. Well, we'll be ready for them and, meanwhile, we've already begun to round up the conspirators, Ailesbury included. Went into hiding in Berkeley Street but the wretch was found.'

'And your brother-in-law?'

'No evidence to implicate him in this. But he's under observation and, given enough rope...'

'Seaton, of course, will also not be implicated, I suppose. Or perhaps just sequestered himself more efficiently.'

'Both, as it happens.'

So, no sign of him. Until two weeks ago.

*

It happened after another of my meetings with Streynsham at the sign of the Golden Pheasant. I introduced Streynsham to Ferñao Pereira earlier in the year for he, too, wished to make some investments in the trade. Ferñao was happy to assist and I had suggested that, since we were there engaged, as it were, on business, we could take the opportunity of also exchanging intelligence at the same time, should the need arise. I believe *Senhor* Pereira may have seen something deeper in my suggestion, but he allowed us the use of his office whenever it was needed. A simple alcove, really, at the rear of his cutting room, far from private but, with the noise of the treadmill and the grinding wheel, sufficient for us to talk without being overheard.

'So,' said Streynsham, 'why the summons?'

We had arranged a simple enough system. A note, one to the other, with the regular message, *Investment to discuss. Ferñao.*

'I have received two letters from Fort St. George,' I said. 'One from Elihu, though unusual in its tone. And it is dated February of last year, as though he had, for some reason, kept it a long while before dispatch.'

'Is it significant?'

'Unusual.' I delved in my purse, pulled out the two pieces of correspondence, unfolded them both. 'This one. The usual unpleasantries, and then this. *"Through twenty years diligent service in India and trading I have accumulated an estate of above five hundred thousand pagodas though I have used all honest endeavour to do even better. I owe it to God Almighty that I should do so."* Five hundred thousand,' I said. 'Two hundred thousand in pounds. Great Heavens.'

It put my own meager fortune to shame, and finally made me realise how little he would have been affected by the loss of his own one thousand pound investment in the Chinese trade fiasco.

'Read on, my dear.'

'Where was I? Ah, yes. *"My actions have been just and honourable and the laws of England shall give me satisfaction for defamations by these knaves among the Council. So I shall not receive nor answer any more of their abusive papers."* Have you seen them, these papers?'

'Charge and counter-charge. Letter after letter. We have an entire collection of the damn'd things. Perfectly tiresome.'

'The same charges?'

'Probably worse. The normal things about him receiving substantial *pishcash* from dealings with our merchants and the local *polygars*. But now a new element. Threats made against the Council members themselves, physical threats of imprisonment and flogging, simply for their acts of defiance. Extraordinary. Then they parry with fresh charges against his brother.'

'You see?' I said. 'It is there the credibility fails. Thomas, I think, is an honest fellow. And even this final section of Elihu's letter shows contrition. *"I know I have become bitter, full of recrimination. And I ask myself why that should be. Some alteration in my manner occasioned by your sailing for England, perhaps. I felt myself a more modest fellow, more trusted when you were at my side."* You see?'

He looked at me as though I must be mad.

'Truly, Catherine? After all his philandering?'

'He has suffered too, Streynsham, as I have done. Listen. *"And the loss of our little Davy, I think, affected me more than I should care to admit. Baby Walter as well, of course. I felt that tragedy as though he were my own. And the nightmares, Catherine, which I know we share. The nightmares that fill the insanity of these tropical nights. This relentless heat, my dear. Perhaps if I had chosen to ignore the Almighty's gift and not sought to climb so high, I may have been a different man."* Contrition, Streynsham.'

'I hate to disappoint you, but that sounds to me like the sort of rambling scrawled by a man in his cups in the early hours of the morning when he has become maudlin and full of self-pity. Your leaving. The deaths of your poor children. His work. The heat of the tropics. Everything and everybody to blame but himself. And does he once mention *Senhora* de Paiva? Or Katherine Nicks?'

That was a particularly sore point – this other letter I held in my hand, though I was not ready to impart the contents. Not yet.

'Of course not. And I think he recognises his own faults. *"Now I am accused of being domineering, opinionated, aggressive. If it were so, it was a grievous fault and grievously hath Caesar answered it. Yet, even though these accusations are all falsehoods, I shall make amends for them regardless. You will see, my dear."* What does he mean by it, Streynsham?'

He laughed.

'He doesn't change, does he? Making amends, for a man who is become like Elihu Yale, simply means spending a portion of his considerable wealth – usually a portion he would never miss in a thousand years – to salve his conscience, to purchase atonement. Philanthropy, my dear, is so often driven simply by a fear of the Hereafter.'

'Marriage has hardened you, sirrah.' I said.

'Perhaps. I never realised children could be such hard work.'

'But she's well, your little Anne?'

'Almost one already. But Elizabeth is pining for her family, so we have made a decision. I've the chance to purchase Codnor Castle and some neighbouring estates.'

'Codnor?' I said, unable to place the name.

'Derbyshire, my dear.'

'Derbyshire. Oh...'

He laughed once more, and I must have seemed foolish. I could feel the colour rise in my neck and cheeks, my disappointment at the thought of losing his company written so plainly on my face.

'Not the far side of the world. And our move is hardly imminent, Catherine. Considerable repairs to be made, some legal chicanery to be found by which my lands in Kent may be exchanged for these in Derbyshire. And we must discover a way to still keep each other informed. You've heard, I suppose? Middleton sent to the Tower for his part in this plot of Ailesbury's?'

'And Churchill too. You believe the allegations against him?'

An associate of Ailesbury – I think that is correct – Robert Young, had delivered letters to Queen Mary. Correspondence between the plotters and the exiled court of James Stuart. Correspondence confirming their complicity, their plans to overthrow King William and restore that Papist to the throne. One of the letters allegedly from John Churchill, our renowned Earl of Marlborough.

'The letters?' said Streynsham. 'I've no idea. And in Churchill's case, I doubt he would have been so foolish as to put pen to paper.

But guilty? Of that I have no doubt. There's sufficient evidence without Young's letters of the rogue's dalliance with our enemies. He's accepted William's trust and betrayed it. Oh, his apologists may attribute high motive to his actions but he is, in the end, a traitor. It's said he is sorely rankled by William's failure to bestow even greater honours upon him. And the supposed affront, of course, to his wife.'

Rumours of John Churchill's dalliance with the Stuart court had been rampant for some time.

'Yet all of this brings us no closer to a final defeat of the invasion. And are we not better with generals like John Churchill in our ranks?'

'Only when they can be trusted. And William's amassed enough regiments along the south coast now to keep us safe, I think. And thank Heaven for those storms.'

The French invasion fleet had been bottled up in their harbours long enough for the king to muster and mobilise our own forces. Then our ships had given them a thrashing at Barfleur before heading off in pursuit of their remaining squadrons.

'We must pray for more good news,' I said.

'Indeed. But now, do you have there a second letter?'

Of course I did. But I had lost all will to share its contents with him.

'I shall not read it. Indeed, Streynsham, I am loath to have you know this at all. I do not love Elihu. I never did. But he is father to my girls and I see quality in him that, perhaps, you do not understand. I wished my own revenge upon him, but all this with the Council – it sometimes feels as though he has simply become a pawn in the Crown's game for control of the Company.'

'Bear-baiting?' he said.

'Yes, that precisely. The bear may be a brute yet there is no glory in him being ripped apart by savage dogs.'

'Is that how you see me? Or Sir William?'

'I do not, sirrah. And this…' I waved the second letter. 'Last year,' I explained, 'I received that note from Katherine Nicks, demanding reparation for the losses she had suffered. I ignored her, naturally. But now she writes again. This time a more direct threat, and I curse myself for a fool that I had not, after all, forewarned Joseph Junior. Unless I give her satisfaction, she will expose Elihu, bring disgrace upon his daughters. For heaven's sake, Streynsham, she is living under his roof. What sort of creature is she?'

'Expose him, for what?'

I took a deep breath.

'He now has that which he has always desired. A male heir. *Senhora* de Paiva has given him a baby boy.'

Two weeks ago. I awoke long past midnight in the humid summer darkness, knowing something was very wrong.

First, the silence. I lay there and listened to it for several moments before I realised why that should seem so strange, so far from normal. And then I knew. The clock, my fine Maysmore timepiece below in the hall. I could not hear it. Naturally, we had all become accustomed to its sonorous *tick-tock* since it was installed here, thanks to the generosity of Mister Edisbury. All of us oblivious to it, as a rule. But sometimes when I could not sleep at night I would listen for it, allow it to keep me company and then, yes, I would be conscious of its comforting presence. Yet now, nothing. A simple explanation? That Fletchley our manservant had somehow forgotten to wind the mechanism according to his schedule? Any other night, I might have considered that possibility. But not this night. This night there was evil in the hushed stillness.

And then there was the darkness itself. Profound. My door stood open to allow some circulation of air, yet no glimmer from the shuttered lanthorn we kept lit on the first floor landing in case the girls might wake and be perturbed. Annie in particular, at five now, seems especially prone to bad dreams, to tales of grim creatures she has seen in the shadows of their room, and Susannah finds it difficult to settle her unless the lamp is aglow. Though now the light seemed extinguished.

There was a smell too. To begin, simply something that did not belong. In summer the house was scented only by the beeswax keeping the furniture nourished and by the lavender with which our housekeeper, Ellen, stored the linen, lively and fresh, driving away the camphor I associated more with our winter months. But now? A faint odour of decay and something else. Damp earth. Something that reminded me of a long ago night in Madras Patnam, the *veranda* of our house on Middle Street, and Mister Yale with that small wet bundle in his arms.

Yes, something very wrong.

But for a minute or perhaps two I dared not stir, taking stock of my household. On the floor above there should be Ellen the housekeeper, Fletchley the manservant and Nanny Green, our cook. On this floor, Elford, now sixteen, and Benjamin, two years younger. Below, on the first floor, baby Ursula and Susannah sharing one bedroom, Annie and Kate in the other. If there was danger here, how might it be confronted? Hard to say unless I knew its nature. But it had to be connected to Seaton, surely. What else? And if it were so, who was there who might save us? Elford? Old Fletchley?

There was the taste of bile on my lips, my gorge rising. For I finally came to the certain intuition I was not alone. Not alone in my own bedchamber.

There was no weapon in the room except the candlestick standing on my bedside table, but as I slipped from beneath the linen sheet I grasped it by the neck and hefted the thing like a club.

Should I cry out, call for help? But I calculated this would somehow endanger my children even more, so I crouched there, allowing my eyes to accustom themselves to the darkness and listening, listening, for even the smallest of sounds. Nothing discernible though, now I was out of the bed, that smell of earthy decay was distinctly stronger.

My bedchamber is generally heavy with shadow, the area around the window drapes over to my left, and around the large dresser beyond the bed's foot posts. Deep enough to hide an assailant though?

I inched forward, my night vision improving all the time. And suddenly there was a flurry at the curtains, one of the drapes flapping upwards.

I cried out, raised the candlestick to defend myself but succeeded only in falling on my rump, scuttled backwards towards the open door, heard the sounds of movement in the servants' quarters above and my hand hit something solid, wooden, the stink of corruption and cloying clay now overpowering.

The curtain settled, nothing but the breeze through my open window. And now a light at last, bobbing down the stairs, Elford calling from his room, asking if all was well.

Me on my hands and knees, peering into the wooden box that should not have been there, shaking myself to wake me from the nightmare I must be having. But I could not succeed for I was not asleep. And my nightmare here had come to life.

I screamed and I could not stop, my horror-filled gaze fixed upon the small, dead, soil-encrusted thing laying within the box.

The Parish Constable was called, along with the ward's night watchmen, and the dead infant removed from the house. They were naturally confounded by the enormity of the crime, yet I was in no state to respond to their questions even had I known the answers. All the same, the Constable appraised my dishevelled appearance and listened to my story with the condescension he might have applied to one of those within the Bethlem Hospital.

By the time he finished, our family's physician had arrived too, Fletchley having been dispatched to bring him, and he dosed me with Sydenham's Elixir of Laudanum so that I soon drifted into a haunted, dreadful sleep – my last waking memory being a conversation with Elihu, when he first began to send back dried poppy seeds.

'My dear,' his voice echoed back to me, 'I shall soon be a merchant prince. As rich as Virji Vora.'

And I wondered whether this very elixir contained my husband's trade goods. I wondered too, about this child he had spawned with Jeronima de Paiva. Does he still live? His name? I told myself I did not care. Yet that is a lie. Far more than mere curiosity, the news wounds me in ways I can hardly describe.

Then there were simply the terrifying visions, until I finally awoke, at noon, my head thick with evil cobwebs, and Mama sitting beside my bed.

'Oh, my dear,' she wept, 'I have no words.'

I struggled to keep myself afloat in this waking world.

'The child?' I croaked.

'Ellen,' Mama yelled. 'Water for your Mistress!' Then she turned to me. 'The child,' she said, 'interred afresh. Precisely where he had been buried only two days past. In our own churchyard too. St. Edmund's, almost next to your father's grave. Extraordinary.'

'A boy?'

'Six months old, poor mite. But why?'

'What did the Constable say?'

'That he has rarely heard of such a thing. Grave-robbers, yes. But this? And the note.'

'Note?'

'Left in the child's empty grave.'

'You have it?'

'Of course not. The Constable has it. Trying to find the meaning behind the verse.'

I felt a chill run down my spine.

'Verse? I do not understand.'

'The note, it was all writ in verse. The only thing giving them pause.'

'You speak in riddles, Mama.'

'Why...' said Mama, and then stopped. 'Can you not imagine?'

'I can imagine nothing beyond the horror of finding that poor soul. No, wait. Something to do with my own lost babes?'

We were interrupted by Ellen, with a jug of water, but I waved her away as soon as she had set down the pitcher and glass.

'The Constable has only experienced anything even remotely similar once – when a bereaved mother dug up her own recently buried child. He wanted to know – if you had lost a child recently. And they have been making enquiries among your neighbours here.'

'For heaven's sake, can we not get to the point? I assume the Constable has been asking whether they may have seen any evidence of witchcraft hereabouts.' Mama poured me some water and I sipped at it gratefully. 'They think,' I said, 'I may have dug up the child myself. And how was I supposed to have done this, in my shift, in the middle of the night, my household asleep all around me and none of them disturbed by my nocturnal meanderings?'

'Is that any less understandable than the alternative, my sweet girl? A total stranger breaking silently into your house in those same circumstances and left a dead child for you to find? Unless, of course...'

'Unless?'

'Unless it was no stranger, naturally.'

'Naturally. The sort of thing my acquaintances might be wont to do. Mama, are you being serious?'

'Oh yes, my dear. Because this does not have to be a friendly acquaintance, does it?'

Today the Constable returned, though not alone. He arrived in company with one of London's two Sheriffs for this year, Sir Richard Levett, and a sergeant-at-arms. It was early and I was dressing, still shaky and confused after that horror, wary after my earlier brush with the law. But I sent Fletchley to escort them into my best reception room. He was back moments later to pass on Sir Richard's request that, if Cook would be so kind as to provide refreshments for his companions, he would prefer to meet me in private.

'Mistress Yale,' said the Sheriff, lightly kissing my extended fingers, 'you will not consider it fro'ward – meeting me thus without appointment?'

For an older gentleman, his attire was all-a-mode, and suited to this heat, an elegant and lightweight topcoat I thought most handsome.

'I am glad cook was able to oblige, Sir Richard. And we shall have tea, too, I hope. In any case, it would be difficult to refuse the Sheriff, would it not? And especially one of whom my father spoke so highly.'

'Your father?'

'Please,' I said, and offered him my most commodious chair. 'My father was Walter Elford, Sir Richard. He admired you greatly.'

'Elford? God blind me, I had not made the association. Of course. Yet we did not meet at the funeral.'

'Four hundred mourners, though I should have named myself. My brother pointed you out in the crowd.'

'Richard? A decent young man. Not his father, of course, if you would not mind me saying, but able enough, the coffee house still the very best for our trade.'

And such a trade. One of our most successful London merchants. Unbelievable tonnage of tobacco imported each year from Turkey and Virginia, then exported again to Holland, Germany and the Baltic. A Tory but, in my father's opinion at least, a harmless one. Of the old-school, Papa would say – misguided, but heart in the right place. More or less.

'And trade still flows free, I hear,' I said, as Ellen the housekeeper arrived with our tea, set down the tray on the Spanish chestnut occasional table. 'That will do, Ellen,' I told her. 'I shall pour.'

'It does, ma'am,' said Sir Richard, after Ellen had gone, 'though that is not, of course, what brings me here.'

I offered him milk, which he thankfully declined, for I despise this peculiar affectation, but the sugar he accepted. Two lumps.

'Naturally,' I said, 'but I really cannot add anything to the details I gave the Constable, nor...'

'Mistress,' he stopped me, taking the proffered tea-bowl and spoon. 'Perhaps I should first explain that Sir William Langhorn and myself are old acquaintances. And it seems, soon, we may both become acquainted even more. You take my drift?'

He stirred the amber liquid and sipped at it with care.

'John Company?'

'Enough said, I think. But when the Constable reported this case to me, mentioned your name, your connection to the Company was hard to ignore. So I spoke with Sir William yesterday. He told me – well, I suppose it matters little, that which he told me in confidence about the debts you are owed. This business with Ailesbury and the rest.'

'I am owed no debt, sirrah. All credit should be reserved for our bold sailors from La Hogue.'

The news we had been waiting for, at last. The remainder of the French and Jacobite invasion fleet caught at La Hogue and eleven of their vessels burned to the waterline by our fireships.

'Too modest, ma'am. And whatever private pretense you may have maintained, I believe we both know the root of this other invasion – the invasion of your own household, Mistress Yale. It simply will not answer. Indeed not.'

Pretense. Indeed. Keeping my suspicions from Mama and the boys, feigning complete mystification, though I knew she did not believe me.

I took some moments before replying, filling the silver teapot afresh from the hot water jug and pouring the dregs of my own bowl into the slops dish.

'A little more, Sir Richard?' He gave me thanks and paid me some small compliment about the quality of my Chinese porcelain, then another about the elegance, the etiquette, with which I handled it. 'Oh,' I said, 'we managed to observe some modest standards, even at Fort St. George.' His face reddened and he apologised profusely, swore he had not intended... And so on, until I felt guilty for having practised so upon him. He gulped down the last of his tea, then clumsily turned it over on the tray, having drunk his fill. 'No offence taken, Sir Richard,' I went on. 'And this invasion of my home? I have still not come to terms with whether there may be any connection. Your concern is welcome, but I should not like to jump to conclusions.'

He smiled, pleased, I think, to be back on firmer ground, though there was a harsh edge to his lips now.

'Truly? God's hooks, Sir William told me of your mettle but perhaps you should read this.'

From the pocket of that luxurious coat he took a folded sheet of clean vellum, opened it to display the neat script.

'This, from the child's grave?'

'The original is somewhat the worse for wear, I fear. Legible, though only just. I ordered this fair copy made for you. Please...'

He handed it across and I set down my empty tea-bowl, upturned beside his own. I read the words, then did so a second time, while Sir Richard produced a silver snuffbox, along with an over-sized kerchief and began to imbibe.

Silence, a commodity like gold.
Darkness masks the actions of the bold.
Odours of the grave, remembered well,
Suffering and tolling of the bell.
Easy comes the loss, the touch of death,
Hearth or street, 'tis there with every breath,
Can reach our children, without a bar,
Home, abroad, it matters not how far.
It comes for those with meddlesome tongue,
Heart of the traitor, dark souls of dung.
Yet join me, salvation you shall find,
Recover those two you left behind.
A simple tryst, a lover's sweet kiss,
Exchange of tokens, fresh dreams of bliss.
Though trust not in master, poet or will,
Lest your dear ones' clocks may soon be still.

'A parody of Parrish's *End of Times*,' I said.

'Indeed. And from the details you gave the Constable, are these not the very things you remembered from that night? The silence. The darkness. And…'

'The smell. The stink of the grave.'

It was all there again. My Walter. The unavoidable conclusion that the writer knew all the details of that tragedy – details that could only have been divulged by Elihu, damn his soul.

'And then the threats. To your children and your family. Sir William told me about this wretch, this Seaton. It must be his work, surely?'

It could be none other. The thinly veiled reference to each of my associates as well. To Streynsham Master, to Matthew himself, to Sir William.

87

'A parody,' I said, 'yet a fractured thing, the lines lacking all Matthew's finesse.'

'Though to take this trouble, this macabre charade, but leave you unharmed when he could so easily – well, you take my point, I think.'

'I believe he has some delusion about me. Some fantasy perhaps. This part about a simple tryst. A meeting. He speaks of a lover's kiss though his intention is not so simple, I collect.'

No, I thought. Something more. He succeeded in controlling me once, after all, persuaded me to give him the affidavit that caused Jacques de Paiva's assassination, though I had never really considered the mechanism of this. Seaton already knew *Senhor* de Paiva was helping to raise the funds that would eventually be needed for the overthrow of James Stuart, so why need the affidavit? Unless for some other purpose. Proof for another end. For another player. The most obvious answer? That he was, indeed, an agent of the papal nuncio. Yet murder was a sin, and even a murder committed in the name of the Church would still require absolution, the remission of Seaton's guilt. The papal nuncio, I guessed, would require some proof before giving the act divine sanction.

'Still, the threat is plain. Chilling. And against your family. But he shall not succeed, ma'am. There is a warrant out for the fellow's arrest and I need not caution you, I trust, against this nonsense of a meeting, whatever that means. No, Mistress, I have already assigned two of our best thief-takers to watch over your house and your person. You will not see them, but they shall be there. We will catch this rogue, I assure you.'

I doubt he is right. After his incursion into my very bedchamber I have come to see Seaton as something less than natural, less than material, some demon sprite coming and going silently at will. Though there was little silence in the house just then, Elford and Benjamin charging down the stairs and on their way to Mama's.

'Forgive me,' I said. 'My two youngest boys.'

'Their futures secured, I hope?'

'Benjamin's portion of his father's estate is held in trust by Elihu. Elford, like his older brothers, had his inheritance invested by Mama – perhaps with some guidance from my father, though she would never admit it. The evidence is clear, I think, all the same.'

'How so?'

'Because, sirrah, almost all of Elford's stock is invested in Sir Richard Levett and Company. Most of his eggs in one basket, even though it be an ample one.'

'You jest, ma'am?'

'I do not.'

'Does he follow my company's fortunes then?'

I saw his glance turn to the tobacco pot I always keep upon the mantle shelf. Joseph's tobacco pot, replenished regularly in his memory with the Dutch blend he had favoured so.

'Avidly, almost haunting his Uncle Richard each day at the coffee house for news of your latest successes.'

'His prospects?'

'He is recently through his probation year.'

'And has he – proved himself?'

'With all his banners flying and instantly offered three lucrative positions.'

'You say so? Well, it will not answer. I must have young men of such talent at my own beck and call, Mistress Yale. If he is interested, you must send him to me.'

I agreed I would do so, barely able to contain my delight that this awful affair should have, in Master Milton's words, at least one silver lining. It pleases me more than I can say, this opening of opportunities for each of the boys in turn, though in this world we inhabit, this strange world of the mercantile adventurer, every such opportunity is likely to take one of them from my side, send them to Madras Patnam, or Porto, or Smyrna. Some such distant place. Perhaps Benjamin, at least, may follow a different path.

These thoughts all crowded around me as Sir Richard took his leave, though I fear I may have seemed somewhat distracted, for I was thinking most about Walt and Davy, wondering what would have become of them, had they survived. And I touched a hand to my throat, to the locket I often wear with their tiny portraits inside, though I had not fastened it about my neck this morning. Indeed, I have not worn it in a while. Normally in the evenings, or...

The gold chain always lies coiled, embracing the locket itself, upon my bedside table. Yet when had I seen it last?

I dropped the sheet of vellum Sir Richard had left with me, fled back up the stairs, and although I had abandoned the poem below, that couplet played itself again and again in my mind.

Yet join me, salvation you shall find,
Recover those two you left behind.

And though I knew the meaning now, I still prayed I might be wrong. But, of course, I was not. The locket had gone and I had no doubt about who had taken it.

Thursday 20th July 1693

A veritable library of letters arrived, and an entirely unforeseen threat.

Among the correspondence, my heart leapt at the sight of my name and direction in Joseph Junior's hand on the sealed, ribboned packet, and I only wish Richie could be so punctilious in his communications.

First, there is an apology. Somewhat difficult to write this letter, Joseph says. Some disturbing news – as though I cannot guess what that might be. And therefore he hopes I might forgive him if he writes chronologically, coming to the point in due course. Perfectly logical, exactly as I might have expected from his father. So, there is an account of the tedious voyage, of course, and then this:

Upon landing here, I expected to see Mister Yale himself. But no, not even a welcome. Instead, the Secretary to the Council, a Mister Proby. And I was not accommodated in the Fort House along with the other new arrivals and the existing writers but, rather, in a private lodging some way from Fort St. George itself. This struck me as strange, though Mister Proby put it down to privilege, to Papa's significance here and, for some time, I was kept busy, day after day, by Mister Proby in person. Still no sign of Mister Yale and ever more implausible stories about his absence. Visiting a local dignitary. Illness. Legal duties to be carried out. A stream of them. And even more suspicious were the excuses for keeping me out of White Town entirely.

I almost smiled, for I remember Elihu's propensity for making himself scarce whenever there was something he needed to avoid.

Naturally, I used my limited free time to visit the tomb of my father and your son, David, as well as the headstone of our little Walter, though I fear it is even more decayed and broken than you may have imagined. Almost entirely overgrown, though I have arranged for the grave to now be tidied. Sad, so terribly sad, and especially finding myself at Papa's final resting place for the first time. Lonely there. Lonely.

Davy and Walt. This brought them closer, I think, for I did not even have the locket now as a remembrance. A year gone and no further sign of Seaton or the treasure he stole from me. But at least my accounts, my precious journals remain safe. Seaton would have taken those too, I think, had he known where they are hidden. The two thief-catchers, however, have long since given up their fruitless duty.

And I am trying to familiarise myself with the local politicks, wishing I had taken the trouble to discourse with you about these matters before I sailed.

The endless wars between the Mughal Emperor's Mahometans and the Gentue Marathas rage on, it seems, and Joseph finds it necessary to include an especially graphic description of the way in which Aurangzeb had tortured to death the Maratha leader, Sambhaji. Now, he writes, Sambhaji's successor Rajaram has escaped to Gingee with the help of Sambhaji's warrior widow, the Maharani Yesubai, though they are now under siege there.

Yet I can scarce believe the tales I hear, the countless thousands of lives lost, the interminable occurrence of disease, the periods of starvation occasioned by these conflicts.

Well, that is my India, I thought, and moved on to the next section of his news.

Just before my own arrival, the Dorothy *came here bringing orders that John Nicks, who has been Second in Council, must be replaced. You will know him, Mama, I collect. He has been Chief at Conimere and Porto Novo, further down the coast.*

Oh yes, I knew Nicks, and that ugly drab who calls herself his wife.

Did you know, Mama, that Mister Yale is godfather to not one but four of Nicks's children? There are ten of them, all told, and he is not only god-father to them but several are named for members of his family. One for his mother, Ursula, for example. Or did he name the child for your own daughter? I have no idea. And one of them — well, this is difficult — is named Elihu too. I have sought for some physical resemblance but they are all, like their mother, Katherine Nicks, swarthy of complexion.

How delicate of my son, to break the news this way. He seems to leave no room for doubt about his own conclusions. Though he is wrong, of course. The older members of Katherine's brood rather favour John Nicks, yet the two she bore in the couple of years before I sailed from there, certainly those were shaped by the mother's Portuguese blood. But the latest? Since she has been all but sharing the Garden House? How would I know? And to have the girl named Ursula? What does this signify? Truly, I have no idea either.

Katherine Nicks seems in even deeper trouble than her husband. Charges against her of notorious frauds committed at Porto Novo and Conimere while her husband was Chief. Inveigling her way into the Company's godowns and stealing cloth, which she then sold on behalf of your husband for his personal profit. Extraordinary. There was great commotion, it seems, when she demanded to see copies of the evidence against her and was told these are subject to parliamentary privilege, confidential, though their authenticity verified by the king himself.

Oh, how I laughed at that part. To hell with you, Mistress Nicks.

At first she refused to recognise the jurisdiction of the Court and a file of musketeers was sent to her house to confine her there, and she only narrowly avoided, due to the number of her dependent children, being hauled off to the gaol.

Her own house, then, not the Garden House. Well, I suppose it must be difficult, sharing space not only with a second concubine, but also with the bastards you have each spawned.

Mistress Nicks was, in any event, fined the sum of six hundred gold pagodas, which she paid at once, but her husband was fined eight thousand. They were tried in the Choultry Court so I was able to attend and saw the poor wretch break down entirely. He collapsed upon the floor, looked to his wife for succour and, receiving none, declared he was unable to pay. On this basis he was hauled off to that dreadful prison.

Prison at Fort St. George? Punishment indeed and though I have no love for Nicks himself, that seems excessive, even for John Company.

Immediately afterwards, the wife sought leave to return to England. The Court agreed but declared she must pay twenty-six pagodas for each of their passages and, apparently being unable to pay that amount, she is sailing back alone. And the devil, apparently, take her brood. Father in prison, mother on the high seas, I have no idea what may become of them, though I suspect the Court will make some provision.

What? Katherine Nicks coming to England? Or perhaps already here?

But then, Mama, came my greatest shock, though I now suspect it might not create so much surprise for your good self. Mama, did you know? Was this the reason for your own return? Am I the only one who was not aware? I decided to take matters into my own hands, for my enquiries about Mister Yale had been perfectly fruitless.

If even a fraction of the complaints against Elihu have substance, then he is become a tyrant, ruling those around him through fear, so who among them would have dared break the discipline my husband must have imposed upon them and shared their knowledge about Jeronima's child with my son?

So I went alone to the Garden House, hoping to find Mister Yale there. But he was not present. Servants aplenty, of course. All Gentues. And then a most stately lady. Beautiful, I should say and, as I now know, merely suspected at the time, one of the Hebrew race. There was a child at her hip, a little boy. Two years of age, he seemed. Handsome. Somehow familiar. I introduced myself, and this lady – Madam Paiva, she told me – expressed herself delighted to make my acquaintance, had heard a great deal about me, told me how much she missed your company, how greatly she admired you. She apologised, Mama, for Mister Yale's regrettable absence but she bade me enter, then named the boy. Charles, she said. Carlos, in truth. Almost related, she said. Virtually brothers, she said. And then came her own brother to stand beside her. A scar-faced rogue. Joseph, his name. She laughed. Yes, she said, another Joseph. Joseph Almanza. Mama, did you know, about the child?

She came to my door. I had just finished reading Elihu's own astonishing letter for the third time, scarce able to believe my own eyes, when Fletchley announced there was a lady at the front door. Only he spoke the word 'lady' in that tone he had for the expression of something distasteful.

'Does this *lady* have a name?'

'Nicks, Mistress. Says how you is old acquaintances. Friends, like.'

'Nicks?' I was incredulous she should have such temerity. But I instructed that she should be told to wait. 'In the lower parlour, Fletchley, not the front withdrawing room.' Not my best room, not for Katherine Nicks.

'Serve tea, ma'am?'

'Indeed not.'

And then I dressed. My favourite striped mantua, dripping with silver embroidery and enough pearls about my person to have made Cleopatra swoon. Though I need not have bothered.

I found her drifting from piece to piece of my furniture. The voyage, I think, had done her no favours, for her usually dark features – no less homely than they have always been – are now become sallow, her black hair bearing the same characteristic as her attire, that result when one has done one's best to impress but has failed miserably.

'This?' she said, simply, running her fingers along the back of a settle.

'The frame and boulle-work by Jensen. The Turkey-weave by Edmonds of Carlisle. They go so well together.'

'And this?'

My very elegant veneered walnut cabinet and writing desk.

'A Guilbaud. I had it made especially.'

'Your dress?'

'Imported from Paris. *Madame* Rémond.'

I have, as I promised myself so many times during that cruel voyage back to England, begun to use my new fortune in the way I, alone, have chosen.

'All from the money you stole from me.'

'You came to admire my possessions, Katherine, or my propensity for exacting justice when I am wronged?'

'It was you – who provided the charges I had stolen the Company's calicoes and sold them to enrich your husband.'

'Sadly I was not there to see the trial in person, though I should have enjoyed the spectacle, I think. But my son was there. He tells me many of the documents were restricted, subject to parliamentary privilege. It would be a breach, of course, to comment further.'

'You have climbed so high, Mistress? The king himself must needs lend veracity to your lies?'

'Well, you managed to see London,' I said. 'You always had that ambition, I collect.'

She was still pacing the room, but I kept myself stationed behind the great chair, for there was a savagery about her I did not trust.

'I am taking John's case to the Privy Council,' she said. 'We shall have justice of our own. True justice.'

'It is to be hoped your children appreciate the sacrifice. Do you even know who cares for them?'

'Some of us have friends at Fort St. George and Porto Novo. They will want for nothing.'

'Affection, perhaps? Their mother half a world away. Their father imprisoned. Well, one of their fathers at least. The other likely to join him soon if Elihu's trial goes as I think it must.'

She turned, at bay.

'You accuse me, of...?'

But I stopped her.

'Please, my dear, I am so tired of denials today. Your youngest children all sired with your husband down at Porto Novo. Each of them named for Elihu's family and one even for Elihu himself?'

She seemed not the least perturbed. Indeed, she laughed.

'He is their god-father,' she said.

'Indeed,' I replied and took from my skirts pocket the letter from my husband. 'From Elihu himself,' I said. 'No, please listen. You shall be interested. *"My dearest girl"*, he begins. Is that not prime? *"I write to you in haste, fearing you may, by now, be suffering from some serious misinformation. It seems young Joseph..."* – my son, of course – *"...young Joseph visited the garden house, which you know is still occupied by* Senhora de Paiva, *and that Jeronima may have practised upon him. About her child and giving the implication – well, I am sure you know the implication. Sensitivity prevents me from revealing her true story but you must believe me, my sweet. The child is not my son."* Do you see, Mistress Nicks, the lies that abound in the Gomorrah you share with my husband and Jeronima?'

'I share them no more, not since you ruined me. You and your other Jewish friends.'

'For my own part I would plead guilty – if I felt any guilt at all. But this other, you must needs explain a little. My husband's letter, once he is done with his lies, is much consumed with some rambling account of silver sent to Jeronima's husband by *Senhor* de Paiva's syndicate in Amsterdam. For the purchase of diamonds. A sorry affair – that touched you too, I see. Oh, how sweet!'

'Your son may have seen Joseph Almanza at the garden house but this would have been immediately before the wretch disappeared with half the money. Five hundred Spanish silver dollars, *pesos de ocho.*'

'And you the other five hundred. Or am I mistook?'

'A loan from Elihu to pay off the debts I incurred from your clever little scheme, Catherine.'

She spat out my name and I now took special care to keep my distance. The silver, naturally, had been sent to de Paiva on Stadholder William's behalf, to help raise funds for our cause but, by the time of its arrival, *Senhor* de Paiva was long dead and, unknown to me, Elihu had impounded this additional small fortune. He makes excuses for doing so, of course, but now seems genuinely fearful. The syndicate making threats he does not specify – if, indeed, they are true – against the return of their investment. Being Elihu Yale, he cannot resist quoting Portia and that "pound of flesh" episode but, overall, he has had to find half the amount from his own purse, he says. And the other half...

'He called in the loan,' I laughed.

'Every penny and more besides. Five hundred pieces of eight. Five hundred pounds. The silver, which might have brought my children back to England with me.'

I should have known. Though why had Ferñao Pereira said nothing to me of this? That troubled me.

'Everybody's fault but your own?' I said. 'I think I should have found a way. Somehow. To bring them.'

'You, Mistress Yale? So good at caring for your own. Two sons lost?'

The locket. The rhyme. If I have despised Elihu for nothing else, then his sharing my tragedies with that creature, Seaton, caps all else. Did she know too? I wondered. Pillow talk? And I also began to think about those other words. About keeping your friends close but your enemies closer still. Here was a desperate woman, but could I set her in my debt now?

'You know,' I said, 'my own Mama keeps asking me. What is he really like? She wants to know. Elihu. Great heavens, Katherine Nicks, where would I begin?'

She had stopped pacing the room, flopped herself down upon the Turkey-weave upholstery of the settle.

'He is not as I thought,' she said.

'Men never are as we think. All that time you pursued him, yet now he treats you like a common creditor. And your own little Elihu, does he lie about the boy, just as he lies to me about Jeronima's son?'

'Lies? You think so? Jeronima's child truly bears his name, whether Elihu wills it or not. Charles Almanza Yale, Jeronima has declared him. But all this sweetness – you think it will prevent me going to the Directors? Tell them your part in this embezzlement? Their investment too, remember. The mine.'

'My dear,' I said, 'you must do as you wish. And I collect it would please you to know the Directors already issued a warrant for my arrest. Embezzlement, as you say.' It was impossible for her to mask the delight in her eyes. 'Yet you should also know,' I said, and saw the spark extinguished, 'that those friends to whom you alluded – well, they had it quashed. Besides, by the time you make the appointment, the Company as we know it will no longer exist. What – you think I lie? They have already been forced to offer a loan to the Crown in excess of a million pounds, simply to keep their Charter this long. But the king is shortly to announce a new Charter. As you say, climbing high.'

She was suddenly unsure of herself.

'Then you will recompense me, as I demanded, for my losses.'

'In Madras Patnam, Katherine, I was almost alone. Susceptible to threats. From the Cavalier faction. From that scrub, Seaton. From the evil tongues of women like you over their chatter-broth. Here, my dear, your threats hold little weight. Sathiri taught me well, how to deal with my devils. For though I have not the slightest guilt about the revenge I took, some of the things I have done most definitely fill me with remorse. Just not enough to make me feel the slightest obligation to you, or anybody else.'

'Truly? Yet you should feel guilt. And your mama? Tell her if she wishes to know the real nature of your husband, she must first understand how he has been cuckolded by you.'

She was back on the feet, fire aglow in her ebon eyes once more.

'Cuckolded by me, you drab?' I shouted. 'From whence do you receive this nonsense?'

'Deny it, if you will. But he has been in my arms sufficient times for me to know. Sometimes it is his resentment at your own immodest proposal of marriage that emasculates him, burns him. A request, through pity for you, he could hardly refuse, he says. At other times it is your dalliance with Parrish that drives him to seek comfort elsewhere.'

I was astonished. And angered. He had many times voiced his annoyance that the proposal was mine, though I believed he had long-since accepted how much I had needed to secure the boys' futures. If I had my time over again, would I have done the same? Well, hindsight, as they say, is a wonderful thing, and now my fantasies tend to stray, rather, to how my life might have been if I had taken my problem to Streynsham instead of Elihu. But, at the time, Governor Streynsham Master seemed to exist on another level of society entirely, and there is no point dwelling upon the might-have-beens in one's life. Yet this...

'You dare come to my house,' I spat, advancing now towards her, 'boast of the times my husband might have had you like some common whore, then spew forth the lies he told you – and himself too, I imagine – to justify his adultery, your perversions? Oh, poor Elihu. Forced into a marriage he did not want yet without which he could never have enriched himself. Forced to wed somebody he did not love, yet resentful of my innocent friendships.'

Her turn now to keep the furniture between us.

'We all know,' she said, 'about you and Parrish.'

I moved a little faster and I saw her glance towards the door, but I was determined to reach it first.

'Tittle-tattle. And what? You thought because he kept a *bibi*, he must be lacking in morals. You sanctimonious little pounce pot. Sathiri and Matthew had more morality in their little fingers than your whole brood of White Town witches.'

I think, had it not been for the exigencies of her journey to England, she might have defended herself better, but my passion was up and I was far past the point of considering the outcome in any rational way.

'You owe me, you jade,' she yelled. 'And I shall collect.'

There was a moment when her head turned and she reached for the door that was not entirely shut. In this moment, I closed with her, snatched at her hair and caught a goodly handful, twisted it around my fist and heaved her head downwards, while she screamed and flailed about with her own hands, raking a deep and bloody scratch along my forearm. So I spun her around, kicked the door fully open and dragged her out into reception hall. The servants were all out now upon the stairs. Even the three girls, each of them beginning to weep pitifully as the screaming and cursing echoed around the walls.

'Fletchley, the door!' I shouted, and the old fellow edged his way around the fracas, knocking my favourite Chinese vase from its lovely little side table. 'Have a care, sirrah. And hurry, I would have this viper out of my house.'

She struck out with her foot, though I dodged the blow, and she cried out as her ankle cracked against the solid body of the Maysmore timepiece. Then I heaved on her hair again, earning myself another armful of her claws. And God's hooks, how it hurt! But I would not let loose my grip until the street door was fully opened, Fletchley retreating in haste down the hall, the other servants all shouting and my daughters' howls ringing in my ears.

Yet somehow I managed to bundle her to the top of the steps, then pushed with all my might so she stumbled down into the road.

For a moment I thought she would charge back up at me, for there was such hatred in her. Though after a moment she subsided, sat upon the paving and rubbed at her bruised back.

'You have changed, Mistress Yale,' she sneered. 'Now you owe me twice-over.'

We were attracting a crowd, coachmen and wagoners, riders and passers-by turning their heads, or halting on their journeys. So I descended the steps towards her. Well, that made her stagger to her feet soon enough, wincing with the misery from the damaged ankle.

'I will say this only once, Katherine,' I told her. 'Climbing high, lady, you remember? My most personal friend is Sir Richard Levett, Sheriff of London. You may believe what you like of me, but at least believe what I tell you now. My personal friend. So if you ever come to my house again uninvited – indeed, if I ever so much as hear you have set foot in Broad Street – I shall see you installed in Newgate just so fast as the Constables can carry you away. Or perhaps have you declared quite mad and locked away with those sad grotesques in the Bethlem Hospital. Do you attend me?'

I fear she did not, for she simply took a pain-wracked step forward and spat in my direction. The gobbet of spittle fell very short, naturally.

'I will have my due,' she said.

'You shall have your due in one way only. For I have work for which I can pay handsomely. If you wish to take up my offer, you may message me and I will arrange a meeting. Neutral ground. And then...'

But she had already spat once more, this time upon the paving, and had turned on her heal, limping off towards Threadneedle Street.

Will she message me – or have I humiliated her, enraged her, just too much? And if she does make contact, crawl back to take the offer I have for her, can I trust her not to use my plans against me?

I finally managed to quieten my household, the girls too, and Ellen the housekeeper applied an unguent of adder's tongue leaf and suet to my cuts and scratches – but, oh, how I wish now I had worn something below the elbow – before I returned to Joseph's letter.

Elihu was in far more trouble than even Katherine Nicks seemed to know, and it was illuminating. I ran through the lines again, his visit to the Garden House, Jeronima's revelation. Great heavens, I thought, if only she knew about Elihu's denial of her son. Like Peter's denial of our Lord Jesus. Perhaps I should write to her. Then I found myself wondering whether the boy had even been baptised, Jeronima being of the Jewish faith. But I had found the place where I left off, Joseph's shock at Elihu's lack of integrity.

I therefore decided it was fitting when, last month, Sir John Goldsborough arrived with Judge Dolben and an entire team of officials to investigate multiple charges against Mister Yale though, sadly, the state of his morality does not appear on the list. You will know, I think, that Sir John is here as Commissary General for India and his initial brief from the Company, we are told, expressed the desire he should attempt to settle any differences and allow Mister Yale to sail home to a cordial welcome.

Yes, they would hope so, those of John Company's Directors unaware of the hammer about to fall upon them, still hoping to keep everything within doors and show to the outside world a façade of efficiency and business as usual.

But in the past few weeks your husband has been accused of misappropriating Company funds for the repair of the walls and fined three thousand and five hundred gold pagodas by way of recompense. Then Mister Proby was dismissed and I was left without any supervision of any kind.

Elihu, of course, tells a different story. What did they expect of him? he complains. That he should have raised the costs through yet more taxation of Black Town? Or left the walls without repair so the Frenchies could simply climb over the rubble? Poor fellow, I smiled to myself, always thinking of others. Those Gentues and Moors under his care. Good enough to be sold into slavery though. Still, damned if he does, damned if he does not. And is he offered any credit, he groans, for having driven away the French again that very summer? Well no, husband. The credit, I fear, goes to those Dutch and English sailors who saw them off.

So I took it upon myself to remove my person, without any authority, to the Fort House. I spent some time at our own old house, now seemingly abandoned. And, by then, Mister Yale himself was on trial, one of his ships, the Diamond, *seized as surety against any additional fines that may be levied against him.*

It is sad, to think of Joseph Junior there alone, at the house on Middle Street – even more sad to think of the place abandoned, ravaged by the termites perhaps. And Elihu? The ink splatter testified to the splitting of his quill as he screamed his opprobrium at their temerity in seizing the *Diamond* – though he quickly goes on to tell me he still has three vessels more with which to continue his private trade, the *David*, the *Jagenott* and the *George*.

The investigations into Mister Yale now seem set to continue all through the coming year. And against his brother Thomas too.

Good gracious, I thought, how are the mighty brought low. And yet I was mindful too of that huge fortune he had amassed. Two hundred thousand pounds. All this would seem as nothing but a gnat bite to my husband.

He adds almost an afterthought. Oh, my dear, he exhorts me, perhaps it might be best to advise young Joseph he should disregard *Senhora* de Paiva's little jest. Elihu would apparently hate very much for my Mama or others in the family to hear such foolishness. The girls, of course. He would want this kept from the girls, especially as they grow old enough to understand. A short message, therefore, for each of them from their loving Papa. Well, he need not fear. I have already penned my response to Joseph Junior, though Heaven alone knows when it might reach him. As if I could bear the shame, myself, of Mama knowing all this.

Even his dismissal features as a footnote, a trivial and temporary inconvenience, he is sure.

And such a way to treat a fellow, my dear, he writes. *A simple dispatch addressed, not to me, but to "President Higginson."* Nathaniel Higginson, I collect was then Second, as Joseph had been, and a distant cousin from Connecticut also. The first mayor of our little township when it became incorporated not long before I left. *I continued a while, of course,* Elihu goes on, *until we received confirmation.*

But there it is! Dismissed. Five years and two months as Governor and President. I shall stay here and fight this calumny, however.

I almost felt pity for him, particularly when I read Joseph Junior's account of his demeanour in the weeks that followed.

Yet the thing that seemed to sting him most, the accusations against Katherine Nicks – poor Katherine Nicks – the charge she could have broken into the Company's godowns and stolen cloth for his enrichment. Who could have invented such lies?

Who indeed, Elihu? Who indeed?

Oh, how they irked me through the rest of the day, those sad excuses for his own dalliances. But this evening was intended to dispel my dark humours, a time for gaiety. At the Theatre Royal.

Elford and I were to be guests of Sir Richard and Lady Levett, and that gentleman had arranged a carriage to convey us in relative comfort to Drury Lane.

'I am still not certain,' I said as we passed along Fleet Street, 'whether the theme of this play is entirely appropriate for one of your tender years, my dear.'

'Mama, I am seventeen years old. And a working man, now.'

'Still, I have heard very mixed reviews. A certain amount of bawdiness, I collect.'

The carriage dropped us at the Bridges Street Yard entrance and we showed our tickets. Box seats at five shillings each, the very best, and emblazoned with an image of the principal characters. In bold print, *The Old Bachelor* by William Congreve. Then down the entrance passage, around the rear of the amphitheatre pit with its green-covered benches already seething with all manner of rakes, a few fellows of quality and their ladies, and all those damsels of simple or easy virtue. Riotous noise that would likely lessen little even during the performance, and the air heavy with the scent of ale or the steaming grease of mutton pies.

'Mistress Yale! Mistress Yale!' Sir Richard, yelling at us from his box, his arms waving like wind-whipped willow branches. 'Gracious me, ma'am, it is prime to see you again. And allow me to name my good wife, Lady Mary. Mary, this is Mistress Yale, of whom I have spoke so often, and this – well, this is my most promising Writer, Master Elford Hynmers. Such ability, my dear.'

Elford blushed as deeply scarlet as my mantua, making polite obeisance to his employer and to Lady Levett. We settled in our seats and I glanced up into the first gallery, where my mercantile class would normally have placed me. But at least better there in the two-shilling rows than in the very highest and most distant balcony among the twelve-penny servants and ordinaries.

'Yet I can scarce believe, Sir Richard,' I said, 'that Elford's abilities alone could be sufficient to warrant the honour done by your invitation.'

'On the contrary,' he replied. 'But perhaps we should come to this later. Look, we begin.'

The story seemed somewhat slow. Some surly old fellow, Heartwell, falls in love with a younger woman – Silvia, her name – without realising she has an immoral background and predictable mayhem ensues.

Three boxes along to our right and there was Sir Christopher Wren once more. Away to our left, Sir William Langhorn and companions, including a lady who I knew could not be his wife. Below us, in the pit, a parcel of rogues: the Earl of Ailesbury, never punished, it seems, for whatever part he played in last year's failed plot; Peter Legh, Streynsham's Jacobite brother-in-law; and John Churchill, Earl of Marlborough – who had languished in the Tower for five weeks for signing one of the plotters' letters, now seemingly shown to have been forgeries, but released anyway through mercy when his younger son died. I had almost expected Seaton to be there as well.

'Yes, I see them too,' Sir Richard leaned across to whisper. 'If I were still Sheriff...'

But he was not, of course, his year in office ended just after our first encounter.

'Still scheming though,' I said.

'Fellows like those know nothing else,' he said. 'And this affair in the Highlands has given them more fuel for their fires.'

The previous year, winter, and a bunch of those brigands from the barbarous mountain fastness of Scotland had been massacred by a company of King's soldiers. Glencoe, I think, the place. And few here in London with any sympathy for the thieving tribesmen themselves – all the same, I think, those rogues, one tribe constantly at war with another, reiving their stock-in-trade – but there was general contempt too for those who had committed the slaughter, for they had, at that time, been enjoying the hospitality and shelter provided by those they later butchered. And there were rumours. Dark rumours. Rumours they might have been acting with the expressed authority of King William himself.

Yet the play's first half seemed to be reaching its climax, so I tried my best to focus on the actors' polished faces, white lead paint and powdered periwigs, beauty-spots and brightly scarlet lips, male or female roles alike, but all sharp enough to shine beyond the candle lighting.

'There is a fellow with jolly countenance,' I said to Elford. 'Fondlewife, is that not his part?' Plainly a very young actor, though his features so cleverly disguised to represent those of an uxurious old banker.

'Colley Cibber,' Elford shook his head in despair. 'Sure to become the greatest actor in all England. The whole world says so.' Then he became more thoughtful. 'Yet you could be forgiven, I suppose, for not knowing he is entirely smitten by Annie Bracegirdle.' I could imagine. The actress playing Silvia was not the greatest beauty but, goodness, what a presence. She exuded desirability with every word, every action, and I could see that almost every man in the theatre, rich and poor alike, had a taste for the strumpet. 'Yet you may be correct, Mama,' Elford told me. 'This play stretches credibility to the limit, does it not?'

From the little I had followed, this was a tale of simple debaucheries and deceits, which would have been easily eclipsed by the carryings-on at Fort St. George.

'Well,' I said, thinking again of Joseph Junior's letter, 'you might be surprised.'

The orchestra again, applause and shouting. An interval.

'Now, Mistress,' said Sir Richard immediately, 'to business, if we may?' He turned to his manservant, instructed him to fetch the refreshments hamper. 'Well – Smyrna, ma'am.'

'Smyrna? I do not understand.'

'Smyrna, the perfect collection point for tobacco from all over the Balkans and western Turkey itself.'

'Yes, my father was based there a while.'

'Indeed he was. Though not in my own godowns, naturally. And trade is booming. The Ottomans have a dilemma – they make great profit from growing the weed though do not wish their people to become addicted to its habit. Where two or more are gathered together to smoke tobacco, there insurrection is bred. A little like our coffee houses, what?' He laughed loudly. 'I am now shipping almost more than we can manage. Need to expand, ma'am. Expand.'

'You want Elford in Smyrna?'

'Truly, sir?' Elford jumped to his feet in excitement.

'He is seventeen,' I said.

'Mama...' he began, though he checked himself. He might resent me for sending him away from my side so young, and he might consider me, with my forty-two years, an old and foolish woman who knows little of his modern world and its ways, yet he would never cross nor contradict me in public. That was his father in him too.

'Yet imagine, Mistress Yale. The grandson of Walter Elford himself, making his fortune in the very place where his grandsire first began to build his own.'

'And spent three years festering in prison for his pains, sirrah. But I would not stand in his way, Sir Richard.' Elford grasped my arm, squeezed it, caused me to gasp in pain, a little blood appearing through the Flemish lace of my sleeve.

'God's hooks,' said Sir Richard as I pulled my arm free, 'you are wounded, ma'am.' And Elford, as well as Lady Mary, began to fuss around me.

'Please,' I said, 'it is nothing. And this of my son's future – well, it is difficult. One boy already in the East Indies. Another in

Portugal. Now my third to become a Turkey merchant like Papa. When shall I ever see them again?'

Tears came unbidden to my eyes, though I bit them back savagely.

'The life of the merchant adventurer, I fear,' said Sir Richard.

'I know,' I said, and begged leave for a moment by myself, shook away Elford's tender hand upon my shoulder, and turned away from them, stared up into the lower gallery so they might not see me weep. And there, moving towards an aisle, I saw Fernão Pereira, the diamond trader. With his family, I assumed. I took from my purse a cambric handkerchief, dabbed at my eyes and asked to be excused, then moved with as much speed and elegance as I was able to muster, making for the stairs, which would take me up to that higher level.

'*Senhor* Pereira,' I said when I finally caught up with him. He was buying chicken gizzards from a vendor at the place where the first gallery climbed up towards the second.

'Give you joy of the performance, Mistress Yale. I pointed you out to Miriam earlier. She admired your attire greatly.'

I scanned the double row of benches, saw a woman astonishingly similar in looks to Jeronima de Paiva, gazing stoically back at me.'

'I wanted to ask you…' I began.

'Please, Mistress, if this is anything related to trade, or perhaps to your husband, it might wait until we next meet at Cheapside?'

Where had all his normal courtesy gone? Indeed, I had almost thought us friends.

'Of course it concerns my husband,' I said. 'He owes your syndicate a considerable amount of silver. I simply wondered why you had never mentioned the fact.'

'Did you know,' he said, 'that my father was charged by the syndicate with pursuing the debt through the Madras Patnam courts? But before the claim could be fully filed, your husband had him arrested for a French spy. My father, Mistress Yale.'

I was astonished, entirely embarrassed.

'Yet surely he is released?'

'Only when Sir John Goldsborough arrived and your husband realised that, with all the charges against him, this was simply one issue too many.'

'Truly, I am sorry to hear this. But payment has now been made?'

'It has. Justice done, after a fashion. But it shows, does it not, the way a man like Governor Yale can be entirely above the law – especially if those seeking justice are nothing more than Jews.'

'He is Governor Yale no more. And I trust my own diamonds will not be needed as surety any further.'

He had the good grace, at least, to offer me an apologetic smile, a shrug of his shoulders.

'What can I tell you, Mistress?'

Oh, I had fathomed it as soon as I saw him, my conversation with Katherine Nicks about Elihu's debt to the syndicate so much to the forefront of my mind. I had wondered from the beginning why they should have taken such trouble to contact me. And now I knew.

'You can tell me, *Senhor* Pereira, I might expect some additional interest on my investment, given the circumstances.'

'I will speak with my associates, you can rest assured.'

'And might I rest assured also that Streynsham Master's brilliants have not similarly been held as ransom against my husband's debts?'

'*Padre bendicho.*' He threw up his hands. 'What sort of dishonest rogues do you take us for?'

Streynsham was, of course, by now far distant in Derby with his wife while, below, his brother-in-law was busy at some mischief – with others, furtively distributing handbills. And by the time I reached Sir Richard's box again, Sir William Langhorn had joined him for refreshments from the hamper. Cheeses, slices of ham, pickled eggs and copious quantities of wine. *Alicantino* wine, I saw.

'From your birthplace, Catherine,' Sir William raised his cup in salute. 'Am I not correct?'

'An excellent memory, sirrah. But that, below. What is it, do we know? The pamphlet Peter Legh and Ailesbury are so busy handing about.'

'I think,' said Sir Richard, 'it is hardly likely to be anything less than seditious.'

'Should I go down and fetch a copy, sir?' Elford asked him, and was rewarded with a beaming grin of approval.

'You see, Mistress Yale? Initiative and enthusiasm.'

Elford was duly dispatched upon his mission with appropriate words of caution.

'And is there news, Sir William?' I asked. 'About the Company?' It was the visit from Katherine Nicks again. I hoped I had not been premature in predicting the downfall of the Directors. But I saw from his grimace I may have committed precisely that mistake.

'His Majesty in his wisdom,' he replied in a whisper, 'has agreed to a partial renewal of the Charter, my dear. I wish it had been otherwise but I understand his reasoning. The expertise and facilities built up by its servants in the East Indies cannot be replaced overnight. But privately a number of us have been charged with the responsibility of working towards a new East India Company just so soon as that may be accomplished.'

'Next year?' I said.

'Longer, I fear. And I have obviously heard the news about Elihu's dismissal. Yet I confess I find it hard to know what to say, having been in the very circumstance myself.'

Heavens, was that a confession? And a look of feigned commiseration on the face of Sir Richard Levett, whispering at his wife to share the news, to earn me her pity too.

'Then my own work...'

'Has been of inestimable value, my dear. Without it we could not have made such progress. At least, not so far as your husband's displacement is concerned.' Well, that made me feel better, bathing in my own inner sarcasm. 'And Parrish, have you heard from him?'

Another of the day's letters. Formal. A careful description of The Hague's delights.

'Ah,' he replied. 'The Hague. It seems the place is much on everybody's lips today. Have you seen it, Levett, this paper Penn has written? Extraordinary idea, even for a Quaker. That we could resolve an end to all these wars if only we took a leaf from the Dutchies' book. United Provinces, indeed. And Penn going one further. Many steps further, in fact. A European parliament, sirrah.'

'The fellow's a dreamer,' Sir Richard laughed. 'And United Provinces? Well, it cost them enough in blood to get it.'

'Dreamer or no,' I said, 'Penn is right to want an end to all this fighting.'

'But he seems well, I trust?' said Sir William. 'Parrish, I mean.'

I was about to say yes, he seemed perfectly well and enjoying his duties, for this was just about all I had gleaned from him. But then, with the play about to commence afresh, there was a commotion down in the pit. Needless to say, Elford.

'God damn their eyes,' Sir Richard swore, as we looked over the balcony and saw Peter Legh shoving my son in the chest. Then again. And again, until Elford toppled backwards over some wench seated alongside. The crowd all around him laughed, and the strumpet bared one of her breasts at him, made some little mewing mouth while he tried to regain his feet.

Streynsham's brother-in-law advanced on him again and I was on the point of running to help him when Sir Richard restrained me.

'He would despise you for it, good lady, would he not?'

I knew he was right and, in any case, by then some burly fellow had risen from his own pew, called on Elford's assailant to desist. He had paid to see the players, the fellow shouted, not some feud between a pair of jackanapes, but it was enough to allow my son a dignified retreat.

'My dear,' I said, when he was returned to the box, 'your poor face.'

Such a pair, I thought. Such a brawling brood we are become this day. But he joyfully held up the pamphlet he had secured.

'Do I look such a Whig already?' he said. 'They could take me so easily for an enemy?'

'It would seem so,' said Sir William, taking the handbill from him. It took no more than a moment's study. 'Ah, we should win some prize for divination, I collect. Look at this nonsense. "*A list of crimes against the common people committed by William, who now styles himself King of England, Scotland and Ireland.*" Here, Glencoe. As pretty a piece of treason as ever I've seen. And here, an exhortation for folk to rise up in arms against the tyrant whene'er the time is ripe. God's hooks. Another plot in the making?'

'I doubt even possession of the pamphlets would be enough to convict the scoundrels,' Sir Richard told us. 'They will simply say they found them in the theatre. Blame somebody else. We need a witness who can provide evidence of their direct involvement.'

I leaned over the balcony once more, saw Peter Legh and Ailesbury – though there was no sign of Churchill now – with two other fellows and that gaggle of painted wenches from their company, all leaving the amphitheatre, but not before Legh had stopped to survey the boxes. He noticed Elford first, I think, yet then his eye turned towards me and held my gaze.

'Then it is just possible,' I said, 'I may be able to help.'

It was a month before she messaged me and another before I deigned to reply. By then I had managed to arrange two interviews with William Cavendish, Earl of Devonshire and, of course, Lord Steward of the Royal Household. At the second of these meetings, His Lordship was accompanied by Captain Baker, Master of the King's Intelligence and, it seems, Matthew Parrish's superior. They believed – though Captain Baker seemed less certain of this – that Ailesbury was no longer a threat, nor Churchill neither, though Peter Legh, they agreed, was an unpredictable firebrand and might warrant some watching. The purse for my scheme would be small, however, the war still costing us dear.

It drags on, already in its fifth year, and another defeat, this time for our armies, led by King William himself, and now with the French fielding their Irish Catholic mercenaries. At Landen, in the southern part of the Low Countries.

Katherine Nicks, meanwhile, was living across the river, in Southwark and I arranged to meet her in Pereira's place, at the sign of the Golden Pheasant. It was the very least they owed me and I believed proximity to the diamonds with which she had made and lost her fortune might prompt some enthusiasm in her. She arrived looking even more unkempt than when I had last seen her, her greetings terse though polite enough, and exchanged in Portuguese – her mother's native tongue, of course – through courtesy to *Senhor* Pereira before he left us to our privacy.

'I should have expected something less blunt, more subtle,' she said, 'than this crude attempt at reminding me what you perceive

I may have lost. Yet you are mistaken, Mistress Yale. I expect the Governor's authority to act as his agent here in London very soon.'

'Governor, Katherine? He has not written you? Oh, my dear, how tiresome. You do not know. But, of course, you would have left just too soon to be abreast of the news.'

She shook her head and smirked at me, as though I might be practising upon her, yet her eyes could not mask her inner confusion.

'Some concocted nonsense, I suppose.'

'My own letters arrived on the very day we last met,' I said. 'One of them from Elihu.' I reached into my purse. 'Here, should you wish me to read? No, perhaps not. But he is dismissed, Katherine. Finished. Oh, he will rage and storm and appeal but, in the end, his days at Madras Patnam are over.'

I do not even believe that myself, naturally. Mister Yale would never, I suspect, give up his thirst for trade, deny the gift he believes God has given him, but I must have sounded convincing for I saw her shoulders sag.

'And you, I suppose, will step in to honour the promises he made me.'

'Elihu is still my husband, Katherine. I should be failing in my wifely duties to do otherwise. And how is life in Southwark?'

'I had heard I should be living in a den of thieves. But I always say you must speak as you find – and I have nowhere found anybody to match the deception and fraud practised upon me by you, Mistress. And, I suspect, may now be seeking to surpass.'

'You saw fit to bed my husband, Katherine. My husband. The circumstances of our marriage may not have been entirely normal but I am mother to his children and faithful to him always, in deed, if not in spirit. Oh, you may sneer, but it is true. And hurts you all the more, for being thus. *Você entende-me, Catarina?*' I said, the scornful use of her mother's Portuguese tongue simply by way of emphasis. 'Whether or not you deny delivering his by-blows, you paid a price for your actions and, so far as I am concerned, the matter is closed and my offer to you is a genuine one.'

'I prefer to wait until Elihu's instructions arrive, as they surely shall do.'

'You must face facts, I fear. Great Heavens, you conduct business with more acumen than any woman I have ever known. Yet he has abandoned you. At least for a while. These charges against him will occupy Elihu, body and soul, for a year. Two perhaps. He may then recall his commitments to you, whatever they might have been. There could be some passionate reconciliation between you, and give you joy of it. But meanwhile…'

'Meanwhile I should have the satisfaction of knowing that whatever task with which you desire to entrust me – some nefarious thing, I must assume, in your desperation cannot be otherwise undertaken – remains undone.'

'Meanwhile, *Catarina*, you will be forced to whoring, or worse.'

'You think me thus already, do you not? Elihu held no secrets from me, and such words you chose for my description, he said – drab, harlot, whore. Even when I was nothing but a young and innocent girl. Do you wonder, Mistress, that you were held in such contempt by so many of us in White Town?'

There are times, are there not, when the barbed hazards of our careless tongues snap back to bite us?

'You may wallow in self-pity,' I said, 'or accept the work I have for you.'

'Without surety? Without knowing I might not run straight to whoever may be the target of your latest schemes?'

'In this case it would come as no surprise to the gentlemen in question and, indeed, informing upon me could be the quickest way of securing the desired end.'

Might it not be so? Knowing themselves observed, these Jacobite scoundrels might value their hides too much to risk them further?

'Tell me,' she said, at last.

So I described the intention. If her aim was to eventually act as Elihu's agent in London then let us make it so, sooner rather than later. I was in possession of a modest budget – and no, she did not need to know the details any further – sufficient for the purchase of a certain equally modest property on Devonshire Street, just along from the grandeur of Devonshire House, and across from

Streynsham's place on Red Lion Square. The deeds would show Governor Yale as the owner and there she would establish some business activities on Elihu's behalf. All she must do was to observe Devonshire House itself and, when alerted that Mister Peter Legh was in residence, to put herself in the fellow's way, make his acquaintance. And yes, she could interpret this in any way she chose. If all else failed, a Quaker friend of mine, Mister Northcott, would arrange for her to attend meetings of the Society of Friends, which took place there from time to time.

'You will receive payment,' I said, 'precisely as though you were acting as my husband's agent.'

She had regarded me throughout this outline with something approaching incredulity.

'Why?' she said. 'To embroil yourself in such matters. There were murmurings in White Town of agents acting against the interests of the Company. That Matthew Parrish was somehow more than he seemed. And you…'

'Perhaps you deserve some answer,' I said. 'So let us consider Elihu. Governor of a Crown Presidency. Or was so, when I first began. A loyal servant of the Crown regardless of all else I might say about him. Let us hypothesise, therefore, that Elihu had discovered intelligence of a plot against this same Crown, whomsoever's head it sat upon. What, Katherine? And if the same intelligence fell into the hands of the Governor's wife?'

She seemed to accept that, and I had no need to list my other causes: the way I despised the cavalier faction; the revenge I thought I needed to exact upon them for the injustice suffered by Papa all those years before; Seaton and the death of poor Sathiri; the threat these Tories and Jacobites posed to my Dissenter sensibilities; the level to which I despised the Jacobites' collusion with our mortal enemies, the French; the way in which this helped keep us at these interminable wars; my conviction that confronting their evil, however small my action, might help to build a better world in which my sons and daughters could grow and prosper in peace; and Mama's *mantra* that simply believing the right things about such matters is never enough in itself.

'My appeal to the Privy Council on John's behalf?' she said.

'May proceed exactly as you intended. Why should it not?'

'And this Peter Legh. As soon as he makes the link between myself and Madras Patnam, he will ask about my relationship with you.'

'If he mentions me, you can at least be honest about your feelings. You can vent them all you please, you see? So long as you maintain this story.'

'Is there more?'

'Only this: it is possible – no, almost certain – you will encounter Vincent Seaton.'

I saw her shudder.

'Despicable creature,' she murmured.

'Ah, a point of consensus. At last. Then this, Katherine. That, no matter what the hour, day or night, you will bring me word if Seaton appears.'

Monday 4th September 1693

Such a fool. To believe a spectre like Seaton would be careless enough to reveal himself until he chose to do so. Until this moment.

The dead of night therefore and awoken precisely as I had been on that previous occasion. Or was this simply a recurrence of the nightmare?

Cold silence, the absence of the Maysmore's pulsing heart. Simmering darkness, the light vanished from the first floor night lanthorn. Cloying odour. Not quite decay but sickly sweet as though mortality itself is gone beyond mere corruption. Taste of blood upon the tongue for I must have bitten my lip in some slumbering awareness of the evil, which cometh within. Sitting suddenly upright in my bed, pulling the gown tighter about me for vain protection rather than warmth. Stillness in my bedchamber. The certainty the creature stalked somewhere else within my home.

The candlestick again, the possibility of lighting the tallow but thus depriving myself of its worth as a weapon. So, the heavy brass gripped in my trembling fist and myself creeping towards the door, knowing now the stillness is not precisely as I thought. There is sound, after all. Yet indistinct. Some almost imperceptible rhythm. Almost like – singing.

A voice in my head calling to me, urging me to stay precisely where I am. So what lunacy is it, which drives me on, edging me out upon the landing? The fingers of my left hand brush along the wainscot's rubbing rail.

The stairs ahead of me now visible and the siren's song just a little clearer. I know the tone of it. Of course I do, though I deny it to myself, carry the candlestick just a little higher, readied for my defence, yet suddenly seeming an idiotic gesture. I lower it, take the first wooden tread downwards, wince as it creaks, as it always creaks.

The song. Ursula, of course. It is Ursula.

Two steps more and the words come to me, faint and faltering but discernible.

> *'The hero Prince of Orange came*
> *With forty thousand men.'*

What is that smell? Lily-of-the-valley, I think. Always remind me of funerals. But how would anybody know this?

> *'And with them up the hill he went*
> *Then also down again.'*

I reach the first floor, stop and stare into the darker recesses, the deeper shadows until my eyes ache. *Old Tarlton*. But Ursula does not know this version. And neither do I. It is always *The bad old King of France he came* when we sing it together.

Something there in the blackness? The merest movement – my heart racing in my chest and I almost cry out. Oh, how I wish those thief-takers were still outside. But no, it is nothing. Some trick perhaps played by the sliver of light I can see now under my daughter's door. Yet she shares the room with her nursemaid.

'Susannah,' I whisper at the threshold, my cheek pressed into the old oak. There is some muffled, choking response. And the refrain once more.

> *'The hero Prince of Orange came*
> *With forty thousand men.'*

My hand upon the knob and twisting gently, quietly.

The room is bathed in the feeble light from a single candle burning alongside Susannah's truckle bed and there is the girl herself, trussed like a suckling pig, some filthy piece of rag to silence her, to smother her weeping.

I cannot see little Ursula. Her bed has a slender iron frame, imported from Italy. Iron, I think, so it shall not harbour vermin. No bed bugs. No moths. And thus the extravagance. Nothing too good for the youngest and last of my line. Yet I never envisaged having to secure her from vermin of Vincent Seaton's quality.

> *'The hero Prince of Orange came*
> *With forty thousand men.'*

Oh, how I wish she would just stop.

The corner posts, tall and elegant as willow wands, with the tester they support, and the bars of the head-piece extending half-way around the sides so the child may not fall out accidentally – yet all hidden from me now, Ursula too, by the curtains closed about her. And the stink of those flowers, overpowering now.

> *'And with them up the hill he went*
> *Then also down again.'*

Is he here? Behind the curtain too?

Susannah thrashes about in her bonds and her embarrassment, her distress, the eyes wide, begging me to release her, and her mouth working wildly about the gag. Yet I move forward, ignoring the girl for the present, the candlestick raised once more.

And I grip the curtains, try to still the panic pounding through my veins.

Ursula sings up at me as I thrust back the drape, that rapturous smile on her lips, the tight auburn curls. Her bed is strewn with the flowers. Poisonous lily-of-the-valley and she holds a stem of the things in one clenched first.

'Mammy,' she laughs, and she waves the other thing at me. A small thing, small enough for the fingers of a curious four-year-old. Just small enough. A tiny pocket pistol, the hammer cocked and ready to fire.

'My treasure,' I say, though my head spins with dizziness. 'Put it down, sweet child, and give Mama a big love.'

She looks at the lily-of-the-valley and I set down the candlestick.

'The singing man brought them,' she says. 'Pretty flowers. But Mammy, they stink. He taught me the song.'

'Not the flower, precious. The other thing.'

The flowers, like foxglove, are dangerous enough. But first…

She waves the barrel towards me. Small but deadly.

Then she pulls at the simple unguarded trigger and I try to draw away, to turn aside as the hammer springs forward, as the frizzen leaps, and flint sparks at the pan.

And nothing. Not even primed.

'The singing man,' Ursula laughs, and I run from the room, to retch upon the landing, to heave up my guts as his hand clamps about my mouth, the vomit forced back down my throat.

'Oh, sweet Catherine,' he slavers in my ear while I choke, while tears blind whatever vision I have left. 'How I missed you. But now I am returned, as you knew I must. Indeed, I have been back some time. Oh, if you only knew the times I have been in your bedchamber, watching you sleep, just the smell of you enough to make me – well, you can guess, I am sure. But you have not taken up the offer I made. In the verse I wrote for you. Join me, I said. A simple tryst. Exchange of tokens. Yet still you meet with those traitors to the true king. And I need to know, Catherine. I need to know what you know.'

I think to bite the hand around my mouth but I am still choking, the grip too tight. I had bitten him once before, of course, wondered whether he still carried the scars.

And then Ursula has followed me out onto the landing. I look down into her querulous eyes, her head on one side as she takes in the situation.

'Let Mammy go!' she screams without warning and she smacks the pocket pistol into Seaton's knee with all the tiny force she can muster.

'You whore's bitch,' shouts Seaton and he drags me to one side as he tries to swipe my little girl away.

As the time before, the house begins to stir, the door to Annie and Kate's room beginning to open, light glimmering from up in the servants' quarters.

Ursula swings the pistol at Seaton's leg again and this time he fetches her a backhanded blow, sends her reeling, her head cracking viciously against the balusters. My heart lurches to see it and I kick, struggle even more. Yet his grip has loosened enough for me to clamp my teeth around his fingers, then bite down and down until my jaw aches and I taste his filthy blood, hear him screeching in my ears.

I find myself falling and, as I fall, he cuffs me about the head with his flailing hand, a hand that seems badly deformed. He makes for the stairs, yelling something about God's will, about punishment for sinners, about those who deny the true faith, and about how he will be back – to take from me that which he is owed.

But by then I am sinking into deep and foul waters.

Alas, it had been no nightmare. And after too long confined to my bed I succeeded today in summoning Katherine Nicks to the sign of the Golden Pheasant.

'You must have seen him,' I yelled at her.

'You may rant all you like, Mistress, but Seaton has not been on Devonshire Street. I would swear to it. But you,' she smiles. 'You have seen him, I collect.'

'When I mentioned him. Before. You said he was a despicable creature. What did you mean?'

'You see? If you had spent less time in your hoity-toity world, you might have learned so much more.'

'Just tell me.'

'The embers in your eyes. He has hurt you, I think. Or – your children? Elihu's children? I pray to God it isn't so.'

Sir Richard Levett's personal chirurgeon has been to her twice already. The blow she received and then her poor head slamming against the balusters. At first it seemed she was entirely unharmed, bodily at least. But soon she was taken by fits of tears, such an uncommon trait in Ursula that I was immediately afraid. Then a dullness in those otherwise sharp eyes and the power of speech almost vanished. Apart from that damn'd song. Yet brave little darling, for I have no idea how matters might have transpired had she not run to my rescue.

'Tell me,' I whispered.

'There was much talk.' She began with some hesitation, but then warmed to her topic. 'And I have no idea how much of it may be true. Of things he did to his own body, and to the bodies of others, but always in the name of driving out evil.'

'Specifics?'

'I have none. There are subjects that even the good wives of White Town would not discuss openly over their chatter-broth. Now will you trade? One piece of intelligence for another? Why such interest in Seaton?'

I was almost tempted. There are aspects of the attack I have plainly been unable to share with the Constables, or with Sir Richard – who has now pressed the current Sheriffs to post a thief-taker permanently at the house, or with Captain Baker, Master of the King's Intelligence, who was also alerted, or with Sir William Langhorn. Upon the latter's advice I have written to Streynsham, though providing only an outline. So, no mention of the way Seaton practised upon Susannah – she has now fled from my service, gone back to her family in Dorset. But no, I have no real intention of sharing this with Katherine Nicks of all people.

'I think you forget yourself,' I said, knowing I should become quite mad if I could not drive out the memory of that night, at least for a while. 'This is not Fort St. George and here you merely play the part of the merchant adventuress. Though I suspect it would be entirely out of character if you were not engaged in some peculation of your own. Your sister, was it not, who acted as your agent for the calicoes you sent home?'

'Elihu told you.'

'That you had a sister who receives your trade goods? Yes. But only that. To put a name to her, Dionysia Tombes, and to locate her home, on St. Mary Axe, those I had to discover for myself.'

She seemed genuinely surprised, perhaps even a little impressed.

'I wonder you need my help to garner intelligence at all.'

'And I now wonder that you fetched up in Southwark when your sister is so close. Or that you needed my business when you might have found gainful occupation with her.'

'She was – unhappy to see me.'

'Without the children.'

'In part.'

From the little I had gleaned – with the help of Captain Baker's man and hardly a testing piece of espionage – the sister was a god-fearing woman with a husband and brood of her own, and I found it difficult to believe she had no inkling of Katherine's relationships. Not difficult to picture how I should have reacted if a sister of mine had landed on my doorstep having abandoned all her children, a cuckolded husband and an illicit paramour on the far side of the world.

'And still no word from Elihu?' I sneered.

It would have been less cruel had I slapped her.

'Not yet. But when he writes, Mistress, it will be to my sister's house.'

She spoke the words with such great purpose, such certainty, it caused me to consider her afresh. I tend to view her always as I had first known her twenty years ago, a flirtatious chit, hanging upon Elihu's every word at a time when I, for my part, would never have spared obnoxious Mister Yale even a backward glance. Had I perhaps been wrong all this time, mistaken her for a simple jade when, in fact, there may be something more profound here? And if I am indeed so far from the mark with Katherine Nicks...

'I suppose we must each count our respective losses,' I said.

'And you, I think,' she replied quietly, 'have lost more than you can ever know.'

Oh, I wanted to ask what she meant by that, but I could not. Or would not. Or perhaps I already know.

'There is a saying,' I told her, 'that to lose a husband is tragic, to lose a second simply careless. Yet to lose the same husband twice over must be nothing short of farcical, is it not?'

'Lost him to *Senhora* de Paiva?'

'Was it so formal, there in Elihu's *harem*, at the Garden House?'

She laughed again.

'You think us rivals, Jeronima and me? How could you be married so long and know him so little? Jeronima filled a particular need for a particular time. But then there was the boy. He wants an heir so badly and Carlos makes a better choice than – well, he makes a better choice. Elihu admires *Senhora* de Paiva as he might admire all those other precious items he has collected. Only the boy makes it difficult, imposes a duty upon him he will always honour. He will pledge her his service but never his future.'

I wanted to ask, then, about her own children but could not find the words.

'Then let us back to our business, lest you drown me in melancholy. Have you made acquaintance with Mister Legh yet?'

'What? You hope he will lead you to Seaton?'

'I have business to settle with him now.'

'Well Seaton has not been to Devonshire House, though Peter Legh and myself have certainly met. A chance encounter I could not have engineered had I tried. I went to buy cheese and fresh meat, to celebrate my first weekly purse, and there he was, alongside me at the Holborn Bar shambles. Some clumsy jest about how I must be new to the neighbourhood, for he surely would have remembered me.' She must have seen my expression of incredulity. 'Ah,' she said. 'I forgot. You think me homely. I believe that is the word Elihu said you chose for me. Among others.'

God's hooks, did he share everything with this woman? Had I no privacy to my thoughts?

'And Mister Legh — is there any possibility his interest in you might be sustained?'

'Very easily. He wanted to know my business and when I explained he naturally enquired whether you and I were acquainted. Oh yes, I said. I was chief bridesmaid at your wedding to Mister Yale. In Madras. Though more through his choosing than any desire of your own. Because Elihu and I are such particular friends. Ah, he said, then was I not a friend of the wife? Friends? I said. I have never known such a cold-hearted bitch. And wife? Well, I said, perhaps in name only.'

My turn now to wish she had simply struck me down. And what is it, this thing that rages in me each time she speaks so proprietorially about the husband for whom I have no love? And, God damn them, they used my inheritance from Joseph to create that priceless and unique form of infidelity.

'I have always wondered,' I said, 'about the haste with which you married John. And your eldest, delivered so prematurely.'

She laughed.

'Ten children,' she said, 'in little more than the same number of years. I may be homely, *senhora*, yet I plainly possess qualities that have men unable to survive without them very long.'

'Your husband must then be suffering badly from their absence.'

'Poor John. Always in awe of Elihu. So desperate to accommodate his wishes. Even – well, I have heard from him, at least. He fares badly in prison, curses himself for some of the poor bargains he made, believing they would help your husband's profits. He is a bubble, I fear.'

I found it hard to disagree.

'And these are qualities, I assume, Peter Legh has seen in you also?'

'He may have seen them but it will be a cold day in hell before he samples them. Still, I am invited to a social gathering at Devonshire House next weekend. His mother's birthing day, it seems. So there may be more to tell.'

'It would do no harm if you expressed some discontent about the Crown perhaps.'

'I have already sown the seed. He asked about my accent, the tone of my skin. And when I told him, my mother Portuguese, forced to give up her Catholic faith when she married Papa, how I had hoped, when King James came to the throne, there might be more tolerance. But now, with Protestant William...'

'Best have a care, Mistress Nicks,' I said. 'We need to have you discover the plots of this cabal, not lead them!'

'I was there when they arrested him,' said Streynsham. 'As bold as you like. My mother-in-law's house. Great Heavens, Catherine, you might have warned me.'

He had come to visit, after all this time, to take tea with me. And I was delighted.

'I fear Captain Baker seems to have forgotten to inform me.'

'No need for sarcasm, my dear. Yet you had no inkling?'

'None. It is many months since I passed on the intelligence Katherine gathered, though it seemed precious thin upon which to arrest anybody.'

No more than lists of names for those she had encountered on her infrequent liaisons with Peter Legh. Other Cheshire and Lancashire gentlemen mostly. Names I barely knew. Molyneux. Blundell. Townley. Then, latterly, one that had sparked particular interest in the Master of the King's Intelligence. A certain John Porter. Colonel Porter, Katherine had said.

'Apparently,' said Streynsham, 'Baker was not reliant only on the details you gave him. And this leaf!' He lifted his dish in salute. 'Excellent, by the way. Excellent. Anyway, there is this cove, Lunt.'

'Forgive me,' I said. 'But Lunt…?'

'As you might say, a professional informer. Likely his tales would in other times be dismissed. But so many plots, real or imagined. Such dreadful days. So His Majesty takes Lunt's allegations seriously. Claims to have been a Jacobite himself, part of a scheme to kill the king but now seen the light. Paid to enlist men and buy weapons for fellow rebels he'd met at the papal nuncio's old house in Warwick

Street. It seems that although Monsignor d'Adda himself ran back to Rome after the Boyne, the house itself and the Papist chapel there are still something of a magnet for their fanatics.'

'Seaton?'

He laughed, turned his emptied dish upon the side table.

'There, I thought that might pique your interest. And yes, Seaton. A mass of others too. Some of those same fellows Mistress Nicks says she has seen in my brother-in-law's company.'

'Legh himself?'

'Lunt claims Peter has been sent a commission by James Stuart. A colonel's commission. So there we were, at Lyme Hall. Elizabeth and myself. The little one just stirring with the dawn.' His second-born. A boy, not yet a year old. Legh Master. 'And a score of Dutch troopers turned up with this fellow Lunt at their head. Their house ransacked and, in one of the cellars, a whole case of pistols, but I found out later, of course, about the commission. Still, I don't think they could have found it – even if it exists in the first place.'

'You were arrested too?'

'I was not, though it was the devil's own job to explain myself. Peter they hauled off to Knutsford and thence to Chester gaol where he's been languishing ever since. From what I hear they'll be bringing him to London soon. The Tower. And then – well, we shall see.'

'Those others Lunt has named. To be tried in Manchester?'

'Eight gentlemen of note. All Papists, of course. Yet the wrong place entirely. The jury will be packed with their friends. And even here in London, who is ever going to convict a man like Lord Molyneux? So very old. So many infirmities. Ah, and you mentioned Mister Nicks when you wrote.'

'A letter from Elihu,' I said. 'And such impudence. Finishes by assuming I might, by now, have encountered Madam Nicks and begs that I should relay his service and affection to the woman.'

'In the same breath as mentioning her husband. Extraordinary. Does he have no sense of propriety at all?'

'Somebody told me recently that perhaps I did not know my husband at all, and I fear they may be right. News of John Nicks is almost the first thing he tells me. Following his desire for further word of his girls, naturally. Then the mixed blessing that Sir John Goldsborough's investigation into Elihu's conduct is concluded – though without any findings declared, it seems. And Elihu's own counter-charges, against the Council members in question, all come to naught. He is furious. But at least spares a few lines for Nicks. The garrison chirurgeons sent to examine him in the gaol, found him very ill indeed, ordered he should be confined instead under house arrest at his own home.'

'Poor fellow. Not the worst of men, by any means.'

I thought of Katherine Nicks and her dismissive description of her husband. A bubble, she had said. A dupe.

'He would not be the first to succumb to the perils and pestilences of Fort St. George,' I said, and Streynsham lowered his gaze from mine. 'No, I was not thinking of Joseph or my own, sirrah. But these others Elihu names. Did you know? Three of the four who wrote letters of complaint against him are now dead. And Fraser, the only one of them left alive, now accusing Mister Yale quite openly of poisoning them.'

'Your husband? A poisoner?' Streynsham laughed until I feared he might suffer an apoplexy. 'Why, it is preposterous.'

For Elihu? Yes, it was. But for me – well, that is another thing entirely. My failed attempt at revenge upon Winifred Bridger for betraying me to Seaton in the first place. The Poison Nut seeds. My guilt at the memory comes back to haunt me so often.

'Well,' I said, 'the claims against his brother Thomas now all fallen to the ground anyway, without those three witnesses to corroborate the charges against him. He was due to make his way home, apparently, aboard the *Samuel*. Presumably he will arrive soon, if he has not already landed. Orders to protest to the Privy Council and the king about Elihu's detention – though he seems to have the run of the place. Yet he has already been fined ten thousand pagodas and the final accompt could be many times higher.'

'Your husband cannot be happy about his brother's return. Did you not tell me Thomas had written to the father with news of Elihu's dalliances? And caused his death by doing so?'

'Speculation,' I said, though I remembered Thomas's disgust when I had arranged his discovery of Elihu's concubines at the Garden House, my almost certainty he would indeed then have tried to alert his family. But now? How much was he in debt to Elihu for helping him clear the charges against him? 'Yet I am more concerned,' I went on quickly, 'that Thomas might be the bearer of more brilliants for Mistress Nicks.'

'More?'

'Did I not say? In his letter, Elihu told me he had separately dispatched a packet of diamonds to the woman by the same ship. To the sister's house. He knows Katherine well enough to have that direction, of course. And her receipt of the gems could have ruined my hold over her, given her just too much independence. So I arranged for the thief-taker, Wadham, to visit St. Mary Axe with a warrant. Duty to be paid, something of that order. A mistake, Wadham told Mister Tombes, who had not yet had either the time or the inclination to alert Mistress Nicks. The package, Wadham told him, should not have been released since the ship's inventory plainly showed its nature and now impounded pending settlement of the account. Of course, she will find great confusion at the Customs House when she tries to recover them.'

'Great heavens, Catherine. It will be more than duty to be paid when Mistress Nicks discovers the truth, will it not?'

'How might she discover that? Our Customs Officers are hardly above suspicion.'

'But a whole packet of diamonds?'

'Should you wish to see them – before I take them off to Pereira?'

I thought he must surely choke on his refusal and he was saved the danger of a reply by a knock at the door, Mama and little Ursula.

'Forgive me...' Mama began.

'Please, Mama, you remember Streynsham, of course.' Indeed she did, that most joyous of days, even persuaded my poor daughter to make the necessary obeisance. 'Mama is staying with us a while, since Susannah left us.'

'What better purpose for a grandmother than to act the

nursemaid,' she said. 'Trying to instill some wisdom in the young and their misguided ways.'

'The little one,' said Streynsham, 'still not fully recovered then?'

'You will learn, sirrah,' said Mama, though looking directly at me, 'that the grandchildren are not the problem. Simply our own offspring who cause so much endless grief. Believe me, if I had influence with God Almighty I should admonish him for this fault in his grand design. That He did not grant us the ability to simply skip past the child-bearing and go straight to the next stage.'

'The answer to your question,' I snapped, 'is no, not recovered. She remains listless, her previous high spirits somehow extinguished and the physicians unable to offer a solution.'

A year gone by and no discernible improvement. I have lost count of the consultations we have attended, the last following Sir William Cavendish's investiture, raised from Earl to Duke of Devonshire, back in May. Reward for his services to King William and nobody more surprised than myself when the invitation arrived to see him receive the Garter, the White Staff. And there, having avoided his flirtatious advances, I was introduced to Doctor Harris, the king's physician, as well as to his physician associate, Doctor Briggs, whose specialism is infirmities of the eye and brain. Their prognosis? That Ursula might never fully regain her senses, the possibility her growth might always be stunted.

Seaton, God damn you!

'Well,' said Mama, 'we are off for a stroll while the sun still shines. Presumably it helps the building work, sirrah?'

'At Codnor,' Streynsham smiled. 'Yes, indeed. Though Elizabeth tires of all the distress it brings. Still, give you both joy of your excursion, ma'am.' The exchange of polite farewells. 'I am truly sorry,' he said when they had left us. 'I had no idea. But was there more about Seaton's attack than you have said?'

'Was it not enough? The damage to my daughter?'

'The nursemaid though. To abandon you so quickly. Was she fickle? Or had she other cause?'

'No cause, other than terror.'

'And the other girls?'

'Katie is nine but already as sharp as her grandmama. Constantly pestering me about her Papa and shall she be too big for him to pick her up again when next they meet. Annie – well, Annie is now seven and enjoys her own company far more than mine. My fault, I know, and though I try to repair matters with her, I only ever seem to make things worse.'

'Families!' he laughed.

'Indeed. After Sir William's ceremony I made the journey to Wrexham again, with the girls and with Benjamin. Elihu's mother still blissfully unaware of the trials in Madras and his aunt, Mistress Hopkins, unaware of even what year it might be.' It filled my heart to see him so full of mirth at my impersonation of the old dear. 'But Madam Yale was keen for me to share news of the other boys.'

'I hear Father Ephraim is dead.'

I could see the face of Madras Patnam's Catholic priest as though it were yesterday I had last been in his company.

'Poor fellow, yes,' I said. 'I thought he must surely live forever. Now there was the only man who might ever have converted me to the Church of Rome. Though Madam Yale would only be interested in the ebb and flow of fortunes' tides within this mercantile cosmos we inhabit.'

'She will credit Elihu with the whole expansion of Madras, I would guess.'

'I left her with the pages of Joseph Junior's letter. The city's annexation of Egmore, Puraswalkam and Tondiapet. The ravages of the Roundsmen again, the pirate Tew's attack on the Mughal Emperor's ships.'

The Roundsmen, I thought. Poor Sathiri. And damn Seaton for that too!

'There will be hell to pay for Tew's raid. Aurangzeb sure to blame the English in general. And Porto? Word from Richard?'

'Naturally. Can you imagine a worse disaster in all the history of the world? Fifty vessels sent to the bottom of the ocean, forty taken into captivity, and two thousand souls drowned with them or languishing in French prisons.' Last year's news, of course. The

133

enemy's victory in Portugal's Bay of Lagos, but the full horror of the details had taken a long time to come through. A convoy of two hundred allied merchant vessels and their escort, a dozen English and Dutch warships. Ambushed by the French. 'Richard writes,' I said, 'that families of his friends there are still waiting for word, still hoping fathers, or brothers or sons might be among those that limped back to Ireland. But the ships were packed with writers, or factors, or supercargoes travelling out to factories at Alicante, or Livorno, or Aleppo, or Smyrna itself. There was great loss among Levett's outbound goods and great heavens, Streynsham, Richard could so easily have been among the missing. Or Elford, bound so soon for Smyrna.'

'The hazards of the world we inhabit, as you say. And still questions to be answered.'

'Well, I thank our Lord Jesus the boys are safe.'

'And the girls?' he said.

'We have Wadham on hand,' I replied. 'I think we shall see no more of Seaton.' But I knew this was a lie. I would make sure to see that creature again. And I would need neither Wadham nor anybody else. For there was now, permanently, that comforting weight in the pockets beneath my skirts. And the small pistol was never more without its priming, ball and charge.

'There he is,' I said, and pointed to the shore boat pulling away from the *Samuel*'s side, while the vessel swung at anchor – among that tangled nest of other masts, rigging and yardarms – waiting for a berth at the East India quays. In the stern of the wherry sat Elihu's brother Thomas, surrounded by his personal dunnage.

'I have no idea,' said Katherine Nicks, 'how you persuaded me to this. If there is one person in the world who despises me more than you, lady, it must be Thomas Yale.'

'We have a pretense to uphold,' I reminded her. 'You are supposed to be Elihu's agent here in London, after all. The sooner we introduce Thomas to the idea, the better. Oh, he may express some surprise his brother never troubled to mention this to him but we shall simply shrug our shoulders. Ah, we shall say – that is Elihu for you! In any case, did you not say there is cargo aboard for your sister?'

'Long-cloth and gingham. Though it cannot be collected for some weeks yet.'

'All the same. Perfectly natural you should be here to see your ship come in. And anyway, it is possible Thomas may have brought more brilliants for you.'

It was still a sore point, caused her to bristle. For she had been pursuing a claim against the Customs House. Katherine possessed a witness statement from her brother-in-law, her diamonds impounded pending payment of the necessary duty and I, of course, had been reluctantly persuaded to loan her the coin, with the diamonds as surety, by which the duty could be paid. Except that the Customs House steadfastly refused to acknowledge the problem. The duty had been paid in advance and the package delivered to the proper direction in St. Mary Axe. There was simply no record of any of their officials being instructed to recover the goods. And the very idea the Customs House should have made such an error! The only conclusion? Some clever mark-monger. It had all helped to pull her closer to me, and it never seemed to occur that the mark-monger in question might be myself.

'What shall I tell him,' she said, 'about the diamonds?'

'Best to say nothing at all, my dear.' She regarded me as she often did, uncertain why I should on occasions support her so, yet never quite trusting my intent. 'And we shall see how matters progress.'

The shore boat was almost at the steps, the oarsman pulling strongly against the recently turned ebb tide, and against the head wind with its stench of the myriad middens in London's streets.

'He seems much changed,' said Katherine, and she was correct. He must have been at sea for – what, eight months? But his complexion, never ruddy, was now exceptionally sallow. Taller, considerably thinner than his much older brother, five years younger than myself, the journey and his tribulations seemed to have chewed away even more of his being.

'Changed. But perhaps not so much. See? He has spotted us, already sits more erect, replaces the frown with something that leans almost towards contentment, the ghost of a smile.'

'For you, perhaps,' she said. 'He seems less than delighted at my presence.'

'Thomas!' I shouted, 'give you joy of your return, sirrah.' The wherry bumped against the timber staircase and the boatman rapidly threw a hitch around the mooring rings, fore and aft, before heaving the largest of the sea chests onto his broad back and handing my brother-in-law up onto the steps below us though, despite the care he took, Thomas almost lost his footing on that first pair of sodden treads recently revealed by the receding waters of the mighty Thames.

'What you should 'ave a care, sirrah,' cried the sailor and almost lifted his passenger, the sea chest too, bodily up the rest of the stairs, while Thomas attempted to return my greeting.

'Catherine, great heavens. Truly, there was no need...'

'An' where was you wantin' this dunnage, like?' said the wherryman, once Thomas was safely deposited on *terra firma*.

'Or yes, perhaps some need after all,' said Thomas. 'Would you mind greatly if I took your arm, sister? My legs seem to have developed a mind of their own. You would think I should be accustomed to it, by now.'

'We have a carriage,' I said to the sailor. 'Over there. And you, Thomas, will remember Mistress Nicks, I collect.'

'How could I not?' he said, and offered her a bow slight enough to border on insult. She, on the other hand, returned his greeting with a curtsey so exaggerated it almost caused me to laugh.

'I received your note,' I told him. He had dispatched it when the *Samuel* had come up to the Long Reach, off Gravesend, and before the ship began its lengthy haul upriver. 'Could not resist coming to meet you. Timed it to perfection. And are you cold, my dear? The autumn started fine but there is a chill now, don't you find?'

The boatman finished loading the sea chests upon the carriage, received due payment for his service, while I exchanged more small talk with Thomas and invited him to stay at Broad Street.

'That is kind, Catherine,' he said, 'but I have already taken rooms at the *Pelican*, I fear. King Edward's Stairs. Yet it would please me greatly if you would deliver me there. Dine with me perhaps? Both of you – naturally,' he added, with some reluctance.

I tried to persuade him otherwise, as the carriage threaded its way back to Wapping. Plenty of spare rooms at my house, now Elford has also fled the nest, sailed for Sir Richard's factories at Smyrna.

'So much coming and going,' I said, thinking about the boy and bringing an uncomfortable lump to my throat. 'Always. Comings and goings. Our fate, I suppose. And did Elihu explain we now have a family connection to Mistress Nicks – through her brother?'

'I rather thought,' he said, tersely, 'that the "family connection" was already well established. Very well indeed.'

'Gracious, this is tiresome,' said Katherine. 'Simply my brother in Barbados. A trading contract with your Yale relatives in Connecticut.'

Yet it was like three-day fish cooking on a stove, this question of Elihu's morality – or lack of it – that everybody tries to politely ignore even though the stink is unbearable. And I was unsure how long a tight lid might be kept upon the pot to stop the stench from spreading.

The journey to the *Pelican*, or the *Devil's Own*, took considerably longer than we had expected. Some malefactor meeting his end at Execution Dock and the glutinous crowds so dense that our carriage could move neither forwards nor into the lane just to our rear, which would have allowed us to reach King Edward's Stairs by a more circuitous route through the fields.

'And your voyage, sirrah?' said Nicks, more to break the tedium than from any real interest. 'Difficult?'

'Are they not all?' Thomas replied. 'Four months to reach St. Helena alone. Three of the sailors so badly injured in a storm that the poor fellows lost limbs.'

There was a drum beating in the distance, the condemned rogue being escorted to his end.

'And have you seen my children, by any chance?' she shouted, for there were vendors now, regularly beating upon the sides of our conveyance, hoping for easy sales.

'Elihu persuaded me to accompany him, just once, when he went to visit them. Said it was his duty to keep his eye on them – for your sake.'

'And what treasures have you brought with you, Thomas?' I said, and folded my hands into my lap to stop them shaking.

'Fewer than I should have liked. But a goodly selection of cloths. Nutmeg and pepper. Some rather fine Chinaware. And enough poppy seeds, I hope, to satisfy Apothecary Sydenham's laudanum elixir trade for quite some time.'

'Now there is a habit I never formed,' said Katherine.

'Truly?' Thomas sneered.

'Truly,' she smiled. 'Yet you, Mistress Yale, were somewhat fond of the *soma*, I recall.'

There were ragged rascals attempting to clamber onto our

wheels now, seeking a better vantage point, and our coachman applying the whip to discourage them.

'Some of us form habits that are not for the best, yet are then able to forsake them,' I said. 'Whereas…'

'Diamonds?' she asked, quickly changing the subject.

'I leave that trade to my brother,' said Thomas. 'And I trust you secured a good price for those he sent you?'

I made a great play of almost choking from the noxious odours drifting in through the widows, then spluttered the question I hoped would best divert him from his line of enquiry.

'Elihu wrote,' I coughed, 'to tell us those absurd charges against you are all fallen away.'

The stench was real enough, of course. Carried here by the midden-mired masses packed about us, thick enough that I could taste the slops and filth upon their threadbare shawls, their coarse linsey-woolsey top coats, feel the warts on their cruel faces, sense the frustration of those denied a clear view of the entertainment.

'Mine?' he replied. 'Yes. For want of evidence. Although it was the damnedest thing…'

'I suppose,' said Katherine, 'there can be no help for it, to have fortune smile upon you so broadly.'

Rain now beginning to drum on the carriage roof, screamed complaints from the multitude about the delay.

'Fortune, madam? I should have counted myself more blessed by far had there been proper opportunity to interrogate the fellows, prove my innocence beyond doubt rather than simply have the charges dropped in this way. Neither innocent nor guilty. It is intolerable.'

'All the same,' she laughed, 'remarkable odds. Three witnesses and each of them so quickly dead.'

'I hope, Mistress Nicks…'

'Thomas,' I stopped him, 'I believe Mistress Nicks simply practises upon you with that viper's tongue she possesses. Elihu wrote to explain the circumstances in some detail.'

'To you, Catherine? Or to her?'

There, the three-day fish again.

'Yet you have the opportunity,' I said, 'to challenge this whole case against you both before the Privy Council and the king.'

'I should much have preferred it had Elihu stuck with his plan and sailed home himself.'

'Plan?' said Katherine.

'Did he not say?' Thomas replied, and then an innocent smile spread across his lips. 'Oh, I see he did not. He sought leave to sail with me on the *Samuel*. Permission granted upon surrender of some modest surety. All was arranged, though at the last minute he told me there were still matters to which he must attend there.'

'Matters?' I said.

'Well, sister, I took it he meant...'

We each fell silent a moment, our private thoughts drowned somewhere within the general clamour of our surroundings, the shouting voices, the whores' laughter, the chatter of those closest to the carriage. Yet I thought I could read Katherine well enough. She would assume he would have stayed for the sake of her children – *their* children.

'Surely,' I said, 'he meant he has an obligation to *Senhora* de Paiva and to young Don Carlos.' There, the stinking fish now stinging all our nostrils, Nicks slamming her fist against the carriage door. 'Oh, my dear,' I gasped, 'was that lacking in sensibility?'

'I really do not see,' said Thomas, 'how you can make so light of it. God's hooks, Catherine, how does this all sit with my family? Mama seems to simply ignore the whole mess. And poor Papa, I always feared the news destroyed him. Oh, how I wish I'd never sent that damn'd letter.'

'They never saw it,' I lied.

'Letter?' said Katherine Nicks.

'For pity's sake, the woman is a Jew,' he cried. 'The boy not even baptised.'

'What letter?' she said again.

'Purely a matter for Thomas's family,' I told her. 'And shall you go there, brother?'

'How do you know?' he said, some shred of hope, of possible salvation, beginning to show in his eyes.

Outside there was bawdy singing, a palpable sense of expectation. It was almost impossible for many folk to get near to Execution Dock itself, yet word seemed to ripple outwards through the crowd with news of how things were proceeding.

'Believe me, I know,' I told him, and he nodded his head, smiled gratitude at me.

'My first duty,' he said, 'is to file our papers, trigger the process. But as soon as it's done, yes, then to Plas Grono.'

'You wrote to your family about Jeronima?' Katherine demanded.

'And what shall you tell them?' I said.

There was a roar of satisfaction from the crowd, so that we knew the executioner's work to be complete.

'Now? Nothing, of course. Mama has been through enough.' But he spoke the words without any true feeling and I think I saw the truth – he is now too much in Elihu's debt, too greatly beholden to his brother for deliverance from those charges to risk a family rift. Oh, he might discover that his letter arrived at Plas Grono, but the myth is firmly established that it has remained unread and seemingly lost forever. Elihu's reputation undeservedly intact.

Three-day fish – which Elihu's alchemy seems always capable of turning to the scent of roses.

Monday 1st January, New Year's Day, 1694/5

Oh there is not a loyal home today in England that may exhibit any mirth. There has been none all through Christmas, prayers spoken at every service in every church of the land for our poor Queen Mary. But now...

Smallpox. The king at her bedside these long days past and inconsolable in his grief, they say. With William away at our wars, she has been our rod and our staff, as true to England as good Queen Bess, despite the terrible burden she carried – her own father, James Stuart, exiled in Paris and plotting with our arch-enemies, the French, to destroy our nation, to put our people, my children, back under the yolk of the Church of Rome.

And then, in the agonies of her illness, this saintly woman sent away anyone from her side who had not previously suffered the disease, so they should not be at risk. Even refused a visit from her own sister, knowing they might never see each other again this side of Heaven, because Anne is heavy with child.

As always, conflicting news. One day, the queen much improved. The next, at death's door. Until, three days ago, almost without us needing to be told, the whole city fell silent apart from the half-muffled lament of our parish bells. Mary passed away, and the tragedy slowly revealed to us.

The day before her death, the queen reported some great improvement, a good night's sleep. The pox itself appeared much diminished, her physicians beginning to hope it might, after all, simply have been some measles rash. Yet, by that same evening, her next examination, those fools began to understand the affliction had simply turned within, sunk into her skin. A night racked with pain. Bleeding in her throat, 'tis said. The leeches applied. Hot irons pressed to her skull. Potions and unguents of every sort. And the dear lady told she must surely die.

The most renowned of England's physicians called to her bedside and the queen's condition declared hopeless. The inevitable Communion though Mary herself too weak to pray, begging simply for others to pray on her behalf – as we had all been doing for many days. That evening she weakened still further, tried to converse with her husband but then fell into her final slumber. They say she died peacefully in the end and I hope it might be so. Just thirty-two years of age. England's rose, and taken from us. The king, it seems, collapsed beside her, insensible, needing to be carried bodily from the room. And, since then, rumours he too might die from his grief.

Yet already it is begun. Mama, who has been spending a few days at her own house in George Yard, returned today bearing a pamphlet thrust upon her in the street. A Jacobite pamphlet, needless to say, claiming Mary's death is the judgement of God Almighty upon the poor lady herself for her alleged breach of the Fifth Commandment, and upon the king for his supposed usurpation of the throne. I can barely find words to describe the sickness this brings to the pit of my stomach. And I pray to our Lord Jesu that the work upon which I have set Mistress Nicks might bring at least some of these evil men to the gallows.

Volume Four

London

Ten weeks after her death, our beloved Queen Mary is finally buried.

It has been a vicious winter, the Thames frozen solid for almost two months. But is that the reason for the delay? Of course not, and the gossip on the streets says the king has been so stricken with grief it would have been impossible to agree the arrangements.

We have already been to pay our respects, naturally, risking the ice and snow to reach the Banqueting House at White Hall, where the Queen has been lying in state. Impossible queues, every single day, tens of thousands, desperate to see her embalmed body. Yet today we made the journey once more, joined the throngs crushed behind the black-draped barriers along King Street to watch the funeral procession from White Hall to the Old Palace Yard and thence to her final resting place in St. Peter's at Westminster.

The girls wanted to see the King, of course, but we had to explain to them, Benjamin and me, that such was not the custom, that His Majesty was not allowed to be present, though I could hear mealy-mouthed mutterings behind us that he must obviously prefer to spend the day with his mistress, Beth Villiers.

'Shall we see it, Mama?' said Ursula, mounted firmly on Benjamin's broadening shoulders.

'See what, my dear?'

'The squinting dragon,' she replied. How had she heard that? It seems to be a truism that those with certain afflictions may sometimes make compensation through a heightening of others among their senses. With Ursula, it seems to be her hearing.

Her speech and her features remain somewhat drawn and slow. But those ears. And above the cannons' roar, too. That she had somehow picked up the cruel *sobriquet* by which Madam Villiers is all too commonly known.

'There is no dragon, little one,' I told her and tried to edge Annie and Kate a little nearer the front of the crowd, so they could see, and one of the many musketeers there to hold us back from the procession's path kindly edged to one side, so I might sit them both astride the barrier itself. I had wrapped them in their furs as tightly as I was able, though in that press there was heat to spare even against the blizzard, which threatened to engulf us all.

'Those poor women,' Katie shouted. 'They shall surely freeze to death.'

The spectacle of the *cortège*. At its head, hundreds of women in simple attire, matching black cloaks, representatives of the common folk, I suppose. And behind them, the banners of our not-so-united nations, the apprentice bands, the merchants' guilds, the aldermen, the Lord Mayor, the clergy – so many sections of our society I could not count them nor, I must confess, even remember them all for the purposes of this journal. Yet every person garbed in black, and I especially recall the mass of gentlemen that immediately preceded the Royal Chariot, the bier that bore the Queen's purple velvet coffin – members of both houses of our Parliament, with Sir William, Duke of Devonshire, just one of many I recognised by sight and personal acquaintance. As Katherine Nicks might have said, climbed so high!

Of course, from some among the crowd, the barbs still flew. All the Queen's passion for bathing in asses' milk had not saved her from the pox – that kind of thing. Or, what sort of pox was it, precisely? And...

'How does a husband swing both ways, Mama?'

'Ursula, it doesn't matter,' I shouted. 'See, here comes the poor Queen.'

Eight sable horses, draped in silk of jet and gold.

'Why is Grandmama not here?' Annie demanded to know, abrupt as always.

'You know fine well, girl. She has not been well.'

A flux, which seems to have afflicted her all through these bitter months.

'Will she die too? Like the Queen?'

'Let us pray she will not.' I tried to sound confident, though I know that Mama's health is failing and I am constantly fearful that I cannot have her in my life for much longer.

Immediately behind the Queen's carriage, her Chief Mourner. The Duchess of Somerset, apparently, though I only know that from a neighbouring fellow, one of those who always seem to be present at such occasions, in possession of such profound detail I sometimes wonder at its veracity. A know-it-all, as you might say. And behind the Duchess, all those other lords and ladies, the Maids of Honour, the royal household, the drummers with their doleful rhythm and, finally, the Yeomen of the Guard.

Well, not quite finally for, as the tearful crowds began to break apart, and we fussed the children back, northwards, along King Street, there seemed to be one further mourner, a straggler behind all the others, a large mongrel cur with sad eyes loping along the centre of the thoroughfare in the procession's wake.

And they say already that, when the *cortège* halted in the Old Palace Yard, a robin redbreast settled itself on the funeral bier and rested there until the service began.

They say, too, that those within St. Peter's almost suffered broken hearts when they heard the music Mister Purcell has composed in the Queen's honour.

But my family gathered to pay our own tributes later, at Mama's house. It was good to see her somewhat recovered, though none of us ever seemed quite comfortable with my father's empty chair at the table's head. Yet our guest of honour, brother-in-law Thomas Yale. We were blessed too by the presence of my sister, Roberta, and her husband Richard, he being back for a short while from Porto, where he has struck up a friendship with my Richie. My two younger brothers present also, with my three girls and Benjamin, now sixteen. My three older boys all missing, of course, though it comforts me greatly that brother John in Smyrna is watching over

Elford. Good food, ample flagons of ale, fine wines dispatched from Alicante by my brother Walt, and the elegiac odes to be recited or sung.

This from the Duke of Devonshire himself:

Long our divided state hung in the balance of a doubtful fate,
When one bright nymph the gathering clouds dispelled,
And all the griefs of Albion healed.

Mama had brought a verse by that actor fellow, Cibber, whom Elford and myself had seen at the Theatre Royal, though it was sentimental in the extreme. And one among many, it being almost impossible to cross a street corner lately without having to hand over a penny or more for the latest broadside offering to would-be mourners. Odes by Mister Defoe, by Congreve, Phillips, Glanville or Partridge and a hundred others. Though my most cherished of the collection is most assuredly that penned by Matthew Parrish and sent to me at Broad Street. Composed with much reluctance, he says, for he had written many tributes to Her Majesty upon her considerable achievements while she yet lived. And now?

Saint Peter's arm our Queen enfolds,
While angels watch through endless years;
And every ode her goodness holds,
Or wipes away the marble's tears.

The verse is widely in circulation, adds considerably to Matthew's fame. But his writing to me had an additional purpose, partially encrypted, enquiring after the health of our "good friend, Mistress K" and asking that best wishes might be conveyed to her by associates he has had the good fortune to encounter on a recent visit to Paris – Jack Kent, Robert Priestley, Master Amisty and young Billy Grounds. The names had meant little to me but there was also a whole paragraph devoted to nonsense about how he has discovered a pie-man of great note at The Hague and suggests he will send some recipes to see if anybody locally can reproduce their quality. I had taken this as a suggestion I should meet Captain Baker who, in a clandestine reunion, confirmed that Parrish had sent similar information to himself.

'These are respectively,' he had told me, 'Sir John Fenwick, the Papist priest Robert Charnock, Sir John Friend and Sir William Parkyns.'

Katherine had also reported a sighting of the notorious Jacobite Colonel Porter – then only recently escaped from the Tower – and a hue and cry had ensued to attempt his fresh capture. But he had gone to ground again and now she was set the task of identifying whether any of these new suspects may have been sighted at Devonshire House. And yes, she had reported, these were names known to her, so we are now required to maintain our vigilance, attempt to ascertain what plots are in the making.

'And you, Mister Yale,' Mama was saying as yet another set of serving platters was removed and replaced. 'Here we are, paying tribute to the Queen when you, yourself, have now met the King, I collect. I trust you offered him our respects and condolences.'

'Two weeks ago, ma'am,' he replied. 'The Privy Council and His Majesty. Kensington Palace. And I must be honest, for I was so a-tremble I could barely present our petition.'

'Will they now finally allow him to come home?' said my sister.

'In truth,' I said, 'we had expected no more than that the petition should be dismissed.'

Well, I had provided much of the evidence against him myself, knew it was convincing. All that lack of financial probity.

'Yet just four days later,' said Thomas, 'the Privy Council had me deliver their instructions to the Company's Directors demanding a formal response. And when they received it, their lordships were less than pleased. The Directors simply stating their case again, ignoring the evidence I had given, and repeating that absurd allegation...'

He stopped himself, for we had agreed that the charge against Elihu of poisoning his accusers might not be the best for Mama's health. But personally I was tiring of the saintly status she seems to have bestowed upon this man she has never once met.

'Allegations?' said Benjamin.

'Oh, nothing,' I replied. 'Some foolish fellows have accused my husband of attempting to murther those who bore witness against him'

'Those?' said Mama. 'How many, for Heaven's sake? Preposterous, surely?'

'Of course,' I told her.

'Yet were there deaths?' asked Roberta's Richard.

'Deaths?' I said. 'Of course. It is not Porto, you understand. In Madras Patnam, death is a daily companion. So, three out of the four...'

'One of the witnesses died then?' said Richard.

'No,' I snapped. 'Three out of the four are dead.'

Only the girls continued to eat, the rest all frozen with forks poised before their lips.

'Some pestilence, surely,' said Mama.

'Oh, undoubtedly a pestilence,' I smiled.

'Well,' said Thomas, frowning at me, 'the Privy Council cannot be taking that foolishness too seriously, for the Directors obviously expected the petition to simply be dismissed while, now, the whole matter is referred to the Lords Commissioners, who have made recommendations for the Privy Council's consideration. In two days time, we shall see.'

Indeed we shall, but Sir William Langhorn already knows the outcome. The old East India Company Charter will be "perused"; the bribes they have been paying to the Crown to keep the King's favour will all have been for nothing; and those who have been working towards a "new" East India Company have now built a majority in Parliament, ready to launch. The only spider in the unguent? That Sir William and his associates believe Elihu still to have some purpose for this new John Company and the charges against him may therefore need to collapse. And hence the old Directors shall be required to write to the Council at Fort St. George, instructing them to provide passage, at a time of his own choosing, and in the most commodious of their vessels' great cabins, to facilitate the former Governor's honourable return!

Well, everything has a price. It would have been uncomfortable if I had chosen to spread my first-hand testimony abroad, spoiled this cosy arrangement and thus my silence deserved some recompense, did it not? The obvious thing. That Katherine Nicks's own petition to the Privy Council on her husband's behalf was due to be considered too. And, naturally, it shall now be dismissed.

She was at my door. The insolent bitch. Fletchley had come to inform me though, on this occasion, at least, he had the sense to leave her standing upon the street steps.

'I thought I told you never…' I began, when I had gone to chase her away, to remind her of her place.

'I have seen him,' she said. 'Seaton.'

All my irritation turned to frigid fear mingled with an ice-cold thirst for revenge.

'Where?'

'Devonshire House, of course. Last evening. Madam Legh is in town and hosted a dinner. A celebration of her son's birthing day. He sent me an invitation.'

'Where is the devil now? Seaton, I mean.'

'As coincidence would have it, an inn not too far from that place where we delivered Elihu's brother. Wapping Old Stairs. The *Red Cow*.'

'He recognised you?'

'Well, of course he recognised me. Yet am I to stand out here in the sun all morning?'

'You could have sent a message. Met at our usual place.' I looked up and down Broad Street, certain that somehow she might have betrayed me, either intentionally or otherwise. And if I allowed her inside the house… 'Oh, very well,' I said at last, and ushered her once more into the same lower parlour.

'Ah, the old clock,' she said, as she passed the Maysmore. 'I can still feel the bruises.' She stroked the varnished edges almost with affection.

'It was a long time ago.' Two years.

'Who would have thought,' she said, 'we should become such friends?'

'Would that pass for irony among your Portuguese folk, my dear?'

She smiled, as I opened the door for her, invited her to sit upon the Turkey-weave settle while I took the chair at the desk.

'He asked about you, of course. About whether we had met. I told him only once, to deliver letters from your husband.'

'And he believed you?'

'I think not. There could be no doubting my enmity for you, I think – it is real enough, after all – yet it was almost as though he could taste something else between us, something he could not quite grasp.'

'Who else was invited to this feast?'

'As you might have expected, Sir John Fenwick and his wife, Lady Mary. Such personal hatred for the King as I could barely imagine.'

'He did not trouble to disguise his feelings?'

'He tried, but not his wife. No open talk of treason, simply this endless invective against the King's character, some stories about how he had been slighted when serving in Holland. Trivial stuff, I thought, but they are plainly deeply wounded.'

'Others?'

'The Covent Garden lawyer, Parkyns, and his wife Susannah. He is a fellow so riddled with gout it is scarce credible he can function in whatever scheme they are hatching.'

'They mentioned a scheme.'

'Parkyns only mentioned something about a shipment to Marston. His country house, in Warwickshire, I think. But schemers all.'

'Nobody else?'

'None of those we were asked to observe, but I have a full list of them. Four more gentlemen and their wives. Only I must ask you this, Mistress. Those others we named, the last time. They were all acquitted. Every one of them.'

What would she have told Elihu? I wondered. About our arrangement. She must, I knew, have made some mention of me in her first letters back to Madras. I knew that because he had made mention of *her* in his recent missive to Broad Street. His appreciation that I have been courteous to Mistress Nicks in her unexpected but welcome initiative to undertake some trade on his behalf. *That dear lady,* he writes, *had no need to trouble herself when she has so many other matters of her own upon which to attend and I had only arranged shipment of the brilliants I previously mentioned as a unique transaction.* I suspect he might by now, therefore, have arranged further shipments to her but, if so, they must obviously be insufficient for her to free herself from my patronage. But how long will that last?

'You think these are innocent too?' I said.

'They each seem so – unremarkable,' she said. 'Except...'

'For Seaton. Except for Seaton. And you have seen that other cove, this Colonel Porter at Devonshire House too, my dear. And he, most certainly, is no innocent. So the place is a hotbed of treachery, even though many of its visitors may be entirely without guilt. The Quakers meeting there, for instance. But so often the actions of the evil can be hidden behind a screen of the most Godly. All we can do is relay the intelligence and allow justice to run its course. For now, I am only interested in Seaton.'

'You never told me,' she said. 'Why this passion about Seaton? He is one of the most unpleasant men I ever knew. And you may be right, about him being involved in some sedition. But for you this is a personal matter, is it not? Something – tasty, I think. I can see it in your eyes, Mistress Yale. Fires of hatred, but something else. Shame, perhaps.'

Perceptive, yet I would never admit it, and especially not to that drab.

'Tell me, Mistress Nicks. This talk of the *Red Cow*. Precisely now, what did he say? Ah, Katherine,' I said, giving a fair imitation of the cove's wheedling voice, 'you must come to visit me. The *Red Cow*, at Wapping Steps. But mind, now, for there is an arrest warrant in my name.'

'Arrest warrant?'

'Precisely. He would have gauged from your reaction that you did not know, I think. Then how did you discover his direction?'

'Arrest for what, sirrah?'

'That matters not, for now. Tell me.'

'At the meal's end, some of the gentlemen took themselves off to another room. Excused themselves on account of their tobacco pipes, though it was plain they were anxious to conclude some other business. It was a simple enough matter to ask Madam Legh to show me the room where the Quakers meet. My brother, I said, should be interested when he returns from Barbados. And when we passed the reception room, I paused for a moment to enquire about a piece of Chinaware in the hallway. I heard little enough, but I certainly heard Seaton's voice, angered by something the others had said. And no, he told them, the package must be there by Sunday morning. Nine at the latest. To catch the morning tide. Somebody asked him whether to the same place. Yes, says Seaton, the *Red Cow* at Wapping Steps.'

'And this package?'

'I heard no more,' she said. 'Madam Legh hurried me away. I think she realised I was more interested in the gentlemen's conversation than her Chinaware.'

'I would see his lair,' I told her. 'Will you come with me?'

'Today?'

'Of course today. It sounds like he plans to sail on the morrow. I shall send Fletchley with a note to alert the Constables and the Watch. They should easily be able to apprehend him and this mysterious package before he can slip away again.'

She looked around the room as though she were performing upon a stage.

'You have nobody else?'

If Wadham had been here, I should not have asked her. He has his room in the servants' quarters, part of my permanent household but, at his own insistence, paid simply his keep, as a retainer only. And the old thief-taker has been offered more lucrative business just now, a significant bounty.

'Only my son. Benjamin, you remember?'

'Goodness, yes. He must be – how old now? Almost a man, I collect.'

'Almost a man,' I told her. 'Yet not somebody I should choose for this.'

She laughed then, and I wondered whether it would have been more intelligent to wait for Wadham's return. There was, after all, a warrant still extant for Seaton's arrest and, therefore, a reward available for his capture too. Yet all I was doing, I told myself, was taking a look at the rogue's hiding place. Time enough for Wadham to act later.

'Of course not,' she said. 'For this you need somebody you can really trust. Or somebody dispensable. Is that not so, Mistress?'

The chariot carried us north up Broad Street, then right onto Wormwood Lane to follow the wall as far as the Aldgate, where we passed through the archway before swinging down around the Tower and took the river road all the way east through the pasture grounds to Wapping. And all that way she pressed me to tell her about the arrest warrant, though I refused to reveal any further intelligence.

Wapping is a village I have only visited on that one previous occasion to meet Thomas at King Edward's Stairs yet, that day, I had paid little attention to the place. And this evening, by the time we reached its outlying cottages with their neat vegetable gardens, the day's warm sunshine had turned to cloying humidity, the skies darkening with the threat of rain.

'Monsoon weather,' I said.

'What is it you plan to do?' She barely looked upwards.

There were strident seagulls, swooping and circling frantically ahead of the gathering gloom, as they will do when a storm approaches.

'You threatened to expose Elihu.' I was gazing now towards the river, the ships swinging at anchor and the barge-builders' sheds along the shore. 'Bring disgrace to his girls. You remember? The first demand you sent me.'

'You know I would not have done so.'

'Now? Yes, I do. But then I was less certain of you, Katherine.

Thought you were driven simply by jealousy that it was *senhora* de Paiva who had delivered him an heir. Failed to understand you, at least.'

For I knew now, with absolute certainty, she felt entirely secure in her own relationship with my husband – whatever it might be.

'You think you understand me?' she laughed.

There was a sorry string of cargo hands, almost invisible under the packs they shouldered from the first of the wharfs to one of the many godowns along the High Street, which wheezed and whispered with the rasp of carpenters' saws, chimed with the ring of blacksmiths' hammers upon their anvils, or filled our nostrils with the rare scents of burnt oak from the cooper's yard and coiled cordage from the chandler's shop.

'There,' I called to the driver. 'Turn there.'

A lane running inland along the side of a chapel to St. John the Baptist. Across from the chapel, a charity school and, emerging from its doors, a rat-catcher, weighed down by his wattle cage, filled with squealing and churning captives, on the end of its long pole. At his side, a diminutive apprentice and a twisting tan terrier.

'Did you ever wonder,' she said, 'what they do with all the rats?'

'I understand you well enough,' I told her, as we climbed out of the chariot, making sure to take our cloaks against the certainty of a downpour, 'to know you still need my good will to keep you from the parish. Your sister's trade is barely enough now to feed her own brood.' I had made sure of that, at least. 'Your petition has failed. And there is no sign Elihu is coming back any time soon.'

There was the very slightest chance that Thomas might have told her otherwise before he left for Plas Grono, but I doubted it. Thomas was unlikely to confide in the harlot. And there was nothing in her demeanour now that gave me pause to reconsider. She seemed totally crestfallen. And Thomas would not return for some time, I gathered. The King had proposed a huge grant of land to the Duke of Portland. A reward for services rendered. The lands in question including the ancient Marcher Lordship of Bromfield and Yale. Thomas had been livid, heading north to join the protest

159

by local landowners who wished to remind His Majesty that these lands have, for one hundred and fifty years, known no lord but our Lord in Heaven and the King himself. They would fight, if necessary, Thomas said, to keep those lands simply incorporated in the County of Denbighshire. Bluster, of course, but I wish him well and, if I am able, I shall drop a word or two in the right places.

'We are working on a new petition,' she said, as we neared the lane's end.

'We?'

Back on the High Street once more and heading towards the centre of the village – less promising than the outskirts might have suggested.

'I have hired a lawyer.'

Good. That would be expensive. And futile, though she did not need to know that. Not just yet.

The street was little more than a broad alley, lined with alehouses and victuallers, warehouse, with more narrow passageways leading to small tenements and hovels.

'There,' I said. 'The *Red Cow*.'

A modest frontage, though I guessed it ran back all the way to the river. There was a thoroughfare that disappeared into darkness at the inn's side, so narrow that two people could not pass abreast. It was busy, despite this, a couple of sailors standing aside in the alley's confines while a washerwoman squeezed past, a basket of folded linen balanced upon her head. And such traffic seemed to be constant.

'Indeed,' said Katherine Nicks. 'Well, now you have seen the devil's den. Do we return before we are caught in the rain?' When I failed to answer, she studied me a moment. 'Oh, please, sirrah, you surely do not intend...?'

'Let us walk a little, while I think about this.'

It was at that moment when the darkened clouds were split by a fork of lightning and pellets of water began to cascade down into the restricted gorge of Wapping's High Street, the very fabric of which seemed to tremble with the clap of thunder that followed. We sheltered in a doorway and I called to an urchin running to escape the deluge, offered him a penny if he would run into the

Red Cow and a full sixpence upon his return if he had carried out my instruction.

'He is hardly likely to be there under his own name,' said Mistress Nicks, pulling the hood of her cloak forward as far as she was able. 'This arrest warrant...'

'This is Seaton we are talking about,' I replied. 'We simply need to wait. And, while we do so, what other word from my husband?'

'You know about these foolish rumours?'

'That he murdered the witnesses against him. Of course. If I had not heard it from Elihu, my son was full of it when he wrote. What was the phrase? *Rubbed out his opponents.* But Governor Higginson, at least, appears to be having none of it.'

'It is a torment though, is it not? He so wanted an early report about my petition on John's behalf.'

'Oh, that must be a misery for him,' I replied, pleased she could not see my expression. 'Such a disappointment.'

'And the Privy Council's decision in his favour. The poor man not even receiving that glorious news for another nine or ten months. Ah, here comes the boy.'

And he well deserved the sixpence. Nobody at the inn by the name of Seaton but yes, one gentleman, due to depart on the morrow. A major, it seemed. By the name of Puckle. The back room, overlooking the stairs. But out on business just now.

If I ever had any doubts about whether Seaton might have been complicit in poor Major Puckle's sudden death, they were dispelled at that moment. It would be precisely in tune with the cove's evil sense of humour to murder somebody and then steal his identity. Of course, it left me with the question of whether Elihu might also have been an accomplice but I guessed this was something I would never know.

'Back to the carriage?' said Katherine Nicks for the sixth or seventh time when I had stood contemplating the inn for some while, the rain cascading down the front of my cloak and joining the rivulet into which the High Street had now turned.

161

'The boy said he is not there,' I murmured. 'Seaton is not there.'

The temptation was just too strong.

Along the flooding street, the awning of the chandler's store was so full I wondered it had not ripped asunder and, beneath its sagging belly, another washerwoman sheltered, trying to keep her parcel of smoothings dry while regarding the bulging canopy with open apprehension.

I said nothing to Mistress Nicks but simply ran to the woman, my shoes soaked and the hem of my cloak dragging through the water. It was a simple enough transaction. A full shilling this time if she would allow me to utilise her bundle and bring it back again. Five minutes, I promised her. Oh, and I should need the loan of her hessian shawl.

'What is this madness?' cried Mistress Nicks, hurrying to join me and grabbing at my arm. I pulled it free, angered she should have the temerity.

'Not much of a disguise, I know,' I said. 'And if you want to serve some purpose, you can keep watch – for Seaton, and over my best cloak.'

I wondered at the wisdom of leaving it behind, for it was worth fifty times the shilling I had pledged, though Katherine went on protesting even as I was running back out into the teeth of that awful weather.

Yet, as I had guessed, the disguise was sufficient, for the inn was now crowded by folk sheltering from the storm and I bustled past the busy boards and benches, suffered groping hands upon my person more than once yet seemed to attract no untoward attention when I reached the stairs. I stopped on the first landing, wishing I had pressed the boy to find out more about the precise location of Seaton's room but calculating that the lodgings would be on this level rather than the upper storey. There were creaking floor joints along a dark hallway, lit only by a small rain-lashed latticed window at its farther end, the distortions in each pane so pronounced it was almost impossible to see outside, but I could just about discern the shape of ships out on the water and, nearer, the steps down into the river.

162

A room to my left and another on the right. From the left, the sound of raucous snoring. From the other, silence, and I obviously chose that one. I turned the doorknob cautiously, peered inside. Empty, so far as I could see. I slipped across the threshold, closed the door behind me and set my back to it while my thumping heart settled a little. There was no latch, I noted. Not the sort of establishment where a traveller could expect too much privacy and, so I had heard, it would not be uncommon in such places for gentlemen to find themselves, in the middle of the night, sharing the bed with an additional guest. But I suspected Seaton would have paid the innkeeper sufficient to avoid that iniquity. All the same, space in the room was little more than a malefactor in Newgate might have expected. Another window, as opaque as that in the corridor. A chamber pot, stinking of piss. The bed, with threadbare curtains upon the posts. And a worn travel chest, secured by a padlock, a solid chain passing around the bedpost, the chain's end-rings around the padlock's shank.

But did the chest belong to Seaton?

I set down the damp bundle upon the mattress and reached inside the heavy shawl, pulled from within my petticoats, through the slit in my skirts, that constant companion, the pocket pistol. As a precaution, I cocked the piece and set it upon the bed also, though I feared the priming might be so damp as to render the weapon useless, despite the layers within which it was concealed.

I listened at the door again. Nothing. Then I examined the room's other meager contents. A small table with candlestick and a tallow stump, a brass tinderbox – and this I recognised. Precisely the pattern our local brownsmiths had manufactured for us along the Coromandel Coast, stamped with the Company's chop, the letters H.E.E.I.C. in a small square surmounted by the merchant's traditional sail mark. It could be coincidence, but I set about the task of wrestling with the chest anyway.

It might be worn, but the wood was solid enough, no obvious weakness even if I had possessed some lever to prise at its joints. So I spent some minutes pulling uselessly at the padlock's shank, wondering all the while what I hoped to gain. Only a fool would leave anything valuable in lodgings like this, yet I could not quite bring myself to abandon hope. So I sat upon the floor, holding the lock's old black iron in my hand and recalling a day, perhaps thirty years earlier, when Mama had succeeded in losing the key to my father's small coffer though, being Mama, she quickly found some way to blame her husband for her own carelessness. As usual, he took the setback phlegmatically.

'Never mind,' he had said. 'There is barely a padlock in the whole world that serves much purpose beyond the ornamental.' A device, he said, designed to give comfort to the gullible, one that would deter no determined thief. What had he called it? Some skill he had learned at Smyrna. Rapping, was it not?

And he had taken a hammer, given the thing a few resounding clouts upon its flank so that, sure enough, within moments the shank's claw had been jerked from its station and sprung open.

No hammer.

Yet there was the pocket pistol, small but solid. A fleeting thought that I could damage the lock, or the chest's hasp and staple, with its single shot. The thought dismissed as foolish. The noise, apart from all else – though that, at least, may have been masked by the drumming of rain upon the window. Yet might the weapon be sufficient to replicate Papa's method?

I picked up the pistol, sprung back the frizzen and blew the priming powder from the flashpan. The butt was carved ivory and would be useless for my purpose. Not a hammer, but perhaps…

I clutched the piece in my fist, gripping it around the barrel as though it were a rock, then turned the chest upon its back. It was not particularly heavy, some of the contents rattling inside, but I could only turn it so far as the chain would allow. So I twisted the padlock too until I could aim a blow with the weapon's muzzle at the side of the thing, at the point, I hoped, where the shank's claw might be held by the mechanism, given luck and in view of its apparent age, with less than full efficiency.

A feeble effort.

The second attempt missed entirely and succeeded only in ripping the skin from the side of my hand.

I cursed, dropped the pistol, thrust the bleeding flesh into my mouth, sucked at the wound and tried to stem my tears. And, while I was doing so, even above the noise of the storm, I heard the first of those treacherous floorboards out in the hallway squeal beneath a single cautious footstep.

'Dammit!' I said, half-frozen with fear and fumbling for the gun, even though I knew it had no purpose. Yet Seaton would not know that.

I cocked the piece, scrambled backwards those couple of feet to the farther wall, heard another floorboard creak, this time just outside the room. My hands shook so badly I doubted Seaton would take my threat seriously in any event but, as the door was eased open, I knew I had no choice but to see this through.

'I *shall* shoot you, Seaton,' I cried. But it was Katherine Nicks who appeared in the doorway.

'Well, *senhora!*' She laughed, and glanced back along the corridor before slipping into the room and closing the door behind her. 'Such news I shall have when I write to Madras.'

I could barely breathe and I feared I should soil myself, fought to control my bodily functions.

'God's hooks, madam,' I gasped. 'I suppose it would be too much to hope you brought a hammer.'

'Hammer? We need to leave. And now.'

'Not until I see inside that damn'd chest.'

'You are quite mad,' she said, but she had the chain in her hand, rattled it against the bedpost. 'They say that when the Roundsmen attacked your house, when your *khansama* betrayed you, you scratched out his eyes.'

'Geerthan?' I said. 'An exaggeration. What are you doing?'

She was clambering onto the bed itself, braced her back to the bed post nearest the wall, lifted her feet against its twin, the one around which the chain was looped. And she pushed.

'Well, you might help,' she gasped. 'There is worm.'

I set down the pistol, got to my feet and saw she was correct. The post itself was riddled with tiny pinpoints. I wrapped my hands around it, braced my foot upon the bed's side rail and heaved. It took some small time before the top of the post began to split free from the tester, the curtains wrapping themselves about me. But I could see her purpose and I must admit I admired her initiative. For my own part, I had simply possessed the ambition to secure the return of my lost locket and its chain, yet now it seemed we were bent on stealing the entire chest.

Wednesday 6th November 1695

Two months in which it seemed certain I must surely die. The deadly fever, which almost devoured me.

The soaking of course, and the chill that followed. No more than a simple cough to begin, but then the burning in my head, behind my eyes, followed by the dizzying weakness in my limbs. Inevitable collapse, a swooning from which I could wake only rarely and in whose depths the delirium began.

We escaped from the *Red Cow* with some difficulty, heaving the travel chest and its chain between us, me and Mistress Nicks. Needless to say, the washerwoman had disappeared with my cloak and her hessian shawl was little protection from the downpour. Beyond that, I barely recall our return to the carriage and the fever seems to have shredded my memory entirely, replaced it with rambling visions, twisted nightmares. There is a vague recollection of Ellen the housekeeper attempting to warm and dry me, of Nanny Green's hot broth. Leeches too and regular bleeding, inducements to vomiting so that, at times, I imagined myself as poor Joseph, could see another Catherine staring down at me, assuring me I would be up and about in no time.

'Just drink some of this brew from powdered Jesuit's Bark, my love,' I heard myself saying.

And sometimes Sathiri was there with me.

'Here,' she would say, 'a simple infusion of cinnamon, honey, garlic and ginger.'

Or was it that harlot, Katherine Nicks? Ellen tells me she came to visit every day though, on the first occasion, Fletchley had refused to allow her entrance, as I had previously instructed. But the housekeeper had overridden the order, with the approval of Benjamin and Mama, so that Mistress Nicks was there on the day when Captain Baker came to call, having been notified of my illness. On his instruction, a Constable forced the lock and opened the chest.

Inside, some of Seaton's clothes, though none of any note, for he was never a flamboyant dresser, as Elihu had been. Beneath those, a waxed package of papers the Captain took away with him. Then those instruments that sit on the table beside me as I write – a small scourge, a whip with three sharp stones woven into the lash; and that strange band of chain links, each with a wickedly honed prong, and a fastening strap.

It is strange, because I was not present when the chest was opened and I did not see these items until my fever was almost spent. Yet I am certain that, in the grip of my delirium, Seaton came several times to visit me, gaining access to my room as he had done before, though now kneeling in the corner, tormenting his own flesh with that scourge, first over one shoulder, then the other, until his back was a mess of scarlet weals. And all the time he would be reaching for me, floating just a little off the ground and me gliding backwards, always marginally ahead of him down some endless version of my bedchamber.

'Do you know the essence of Christian faith, Catherine?' he asked me.

'The love of God,' I would say, 'and an invitation for our Lord, Jesus Christ, to reside forever within our lives.'

'Yet the only correct way to love God is to surrender ourselves entirely to Him, every fragment of our body and soul.'

'Your only desire is to surrender yourself and our people to the Church of Rome.'

'It is the one true faith, my dear. All else is heresy. Yet to surrender ourselves fully, we must first possess the substance of both body and soul, practise self-mastery – through denial of the flesh, through asceticism, through penance, through mortification.'

'Was it denial of the flesh that brought you to defile the grave of that poor child?' I said. 'Or to defile my household, damage my daughter?'

He laughed.

'I have atoned for that night in so many ways, Mistress. Yet did you not savour it? Just a little? And I shall come back for you, Catherine. Soon, my dear. I swear it.'

Come back? Yes, I suppose he shall. For, as my actions must have guaranteed, Seaton had escaped.

The travel chest, however, had surrendered one more secret, the object that drove me in the first place to my recklessness since, when the fever finally abated sufficient for me to be lucid, there was a fine gold chain wrapped around my fingers and, gripped in my damp fist, the locket with those precious miniatures of Walt and David.

Two months of my life simply disappeared. Sufficient for me to have missed the wedding of my brother, Richard, though I shall not miss the same celebration for our second brother Benjamin when he marries in February.

More seriously, each of my older brothers taken from us, word arriving from Smyrna about John and, within weeks, about Walter Junior, dead from a boating accident in Alicante harbour. Wicked news I can still barely comprehend and that, for Mama, has been devastating.

Yet, meanwhile, here I am, at my journal once more, on the anniversary of my own marriage to dear Joseph, two days after the anniversary of my marriage to Elihu Yale, and two days after the bonfires and fireworks that now mark a double festivity – Gunpowder Treason Day and the birthing date of our sovereign lord, King William the Third. May God protect and keep him, for it seems that, in my foolishness, it may also have been the Almighty's mysterious ways guiding my steps in that same holy work.

The longest two miles it may be possible to imagine, those between Newgate gaol and the hanging tree at Tyburn. Yet I was determined to walk every inch, to savour every hour of its tortuously slow embrace. To savour it as I have done on each of the previous occasions we have seen those traitors sent to face their fate.

Last month it was that former-priest, Charnock, at whose trial we heard evidence he intended to kill His Majesty with a blunderbuss. And those who took the drop with him, Edward King and Thomas Keyes. Katherine's evidence was not crucial here, though she had certainly seen both Keyes and King in Charnock's company, confirmed them as regular associates. In any case, guilty they were found and, when they arrived at Tyburn, they delivered papers to the Sheriff in which they willingly confessed their crimes – indeed, attempted to justify them.

Thus, the boldness of these Jacobites. The insolence of them, to claim justification in selling us into the hands of French Louis or the Romish Pope for the sake of putting dissolute James Stuart back on the throne. So we shall see plenty more of the rogues tried and sentenced for a while yet. And none shall be jeered to the noose more loudly than he who has principally contrived this latest treason, Sir John Fenwick. For that day we must still wait a while, yet at least he is taken, unlike those others who aided him and have succeeded in slipping the net – this Colonel Porter and Sir George Barclay. Oh, and Seaton, of course.

Seaton who, for me, has come so much to personify the entire Jacobite wickedness.

For his escape, of course, I am severely rebuked. But at least he is gone. France, they believe, like Barclay and Porter. Yet I have my locket once more. And I have the satisfaction of knowing that, while every town and city of this land must surely have its fill of Jacobite conspirators, some of us – many of us – play our part in stopping them, bringing them to justice. So my espionage suddenly has spice again, even though I must sometimes descend to the sewers, wallow in the mire, for the sake of that cause.

Hence today's pilgrimage, with only Wadham the thief-taker for company as we waited with the crowd outside the prison, where I could so easily have ended if that warrant had been successfully served against me.

The Newgate, of course, stands solidly across the street bearing its name. Grand, with its mullioned windows and stone-carved ornamentation. Its portcullis, I suppose, could be lowered if required, to close off the thoroughfare and they say that, at one time, not too long ago, all of its prisoners were constrained within the forbidding rooms of the gateway's twin towers – though it is now extended, of course, southwards down towards the rebuilt courts. But its inmates still enter and leave here, beneath the gate's archway, as did today's traitors, Sir John Friend and Sir William Parkyns.

'Mixed blessing, ma'am,' said Wadham.

'Your pardon, sirrah?'

'Just… bein' traitors, like, and gentlemen too, 'tis less likely they'd die of the pestilence waiting for Hangin' Day.'

That is true, I collect. There are eight appointed execution Mondays – Saint Mondays as we style them – at Tyburn each year, though many die of gaol fever at Newgate while waiting their turn for the drop. But those guilty of high treason have special days just to themselves, for we should not wish to sully the reputation of honest thieves and murderers by having them mix with vermin like these fellows. No, these do not merit even the courtesy of the usual cart to take them on their final journey but, like these two, must suffer the indignity of being hauled forth, lashed to a wicker hurdle, then dragged backwards through the streets, for no traitor deserves dignity in the face of his death. And their executions not confined only to Mondays either.

'I wonder,' I said, 'whether they consider this a blessing.'

The crowd – always in festival mood on a hanging day – seemed especially excited by this particular event. Excited, and smelling none too wholesome. So there were painted nosegay sellers, offering their official wares to those sensible of the stink, and baring their whitened bosoms to fellows who might be interested in more exotic distractions. "Your Honours!" they screeched. "Messieurs!" While the pie-man seared his fingers pushing another dish of mutton pasties into his mobile oven – "kit-cats, lovely kit-cats" – and began to heave the load along the route of our procession behind the condemned villains. Beside us there was a one-legged trader, swinging along on his crutch, a tray of fire strikers slung about his neck and a monkey clinging to his shoulder. "Flints and steels," the fellow yelled. Ahead of us the offal seller, as pink and plump as the tripe and trotters spilling over her barrow. "Neat feet and lights." And thus we progressed, this mass of humanity, several thousand of us, in every shape and stripe, class and creed, the full length of the Tyburn trail.

The crowds even thicker now, so immense we had been on the road almost three hours already. But we could see our destination at least, the corner of the Hyde Park hunting grounds, the open space where Tyburn Road meets Tyburn Lane, and Mother Proctor's Pews in view, the galleries of banked seats erected there by some enterprising souls so that those with the silver to spare could watch executions in comfort. And this was only a small part of the money to be made here today.

'They say there's always one trader to every ten spectators,' Wadham told me.

'I can believe it,' I said, taking a quick tally of the hawkers just in our general vicinity. 'And probably the same number of cutpurses,' I added.

'Safer in the Pews, ma'am. Same seats as before, is it?'

'Not today, Wadham. Today I join the balcony crowd.' I nodded towards old Tyburn House that overlooked the site.

'And me, Mistress?'

'I'm sure there will be room for you too.'

I cajoled Wadham steadily towards the pikemen keeping guard around the house, rooted in my purse for the pass I had received, and we were soon led up through two storeys to the large reception room, its glass-paned doors opening onto a slim terrace with iron railings.

'Gracious, Catherine,' Streynsham jumped up from one of the seats, waving his pipe at me, 'we thought you must surely miss the show.'

'I decided we should walk,' I replied, accepting his affectionate kiss upon my hand, the polite bow and greeting from Sir William Langhorn, and the curt formality of Captain Baker. 'Wadham has been my bodyguard. I trust he might take some refreshment?'

'Naturally, my dear,' said Sir William, and summoned a manservant to take care of it. 'And for you, Mistress, the very best of seats. Has you been here before?'

'I have not, sirrah,' I told him, at the same time acknowledging those others on the balcony Streynsham had named, this year's Sheriffs and some other dignitaries. 'For Charnock I was over there, in the galleries. But a fine view, gentlemen.'

And so it was, looking down almost directly upon the three uprights and cross-pieces forming Tyburn's triangular-shaped gallows. Room for eight felons upon each cross-piece, they say. Twenty-four hangings at one session, if needed, though I have never seen such a thing, for my own interest in attending here is only to see the nation's traitors strung up. A duty to attend, I feel, as it had been my duty in Madras, at times, when wife to the Governor.

'Anyway, just in time,' said Streynsham.

A horse-drawn cart had been positioned under the nearest of the beams, the executioner climbing upon the conveyance to direct a pair of assistants above. They straddled the broad timber and were roughly adjusting the lengths of strong rope with the nooses dangling below. At the base of the upright, a pair of large baskets and two smaller ones, with a long-handled axe resting against the post.

'I fear,' I said, 'that Captain Baker is not entirely comfortable with my presence, gentlemen.'

'Your presence, ma'am,' he replied, 'troubles me not the slightest. But upon my word I find it hard to stomach behaviour that allows any of these rogues to run free.'

'And I have apologised for it, Captain. Almost paid the price with my life.'

'All the same,' said Sir William, 'the papers Mistress Yale helped us recover were invaluable.'

'The papers,' Baker snapped, 'we should possess anyway had Mistress Yale simply reported Seaton's whereabouts, as we would have expected. The difference, sirrah, is that we might have taken Seaton too. Perhaps Porter and Barclay also.'

His reply allowed no room for Sir William to defend me further, and he simply harrumphed.

'Well,' he said, 'it shall be a disappointing day for the anatomists. There'll be little enough of those two coves left for them to study. Have you seen the work of Vesalius, Streynsham?'

'I have, sirrah. Quite a skill, to turn the ugliness of our innards into works of artistic beauty.'

Below, Sir William Parkyns, whose innards might soon be revealed to us, was being released from the hurdle, and hauled up onto the cart.

'What's he saying?' asked Sir William.

'Whether he might present his paper,' Streynsham replied. He has keen ears, for it was difficult to discern many of the words above the crowd's clamour. 'And the hangman has told him all in good time.'

'A paper?' cried Sir William. 'Another confession?'

What do we know, now, about their foul schemes? From the trials and the undisputed evidence against them, from the papers we found and much eye-witness testimony, it is now plain Sir John Fenwick had drawn up a plan by which he and his Kentish Jacobites should rise at an agreed signal, at the same time as a flotilla of French invasion barges would cross the Channel and land at a Kentish port. Then a quick march on London. Meanwhile, some of the plotters –

Charnock and the rest – planned to ambush King William's coach and either kidnap or murder him. Sir George Barclay, under orders from Colonel Porter, and along with others including Sir William Parkyns and Sir John Friend, would also raise a force in London. The content of Seaton's letters had caused our Secretary of State, James Vernon, to launch an extensive espionage network to foil their scheme.

'A pity,' said Streynsham Master, 'that Parrish could not be present to witness the end. He played his part too.'

That was a surprise to me, though I suppose it should not have been. His letters to me are only a little warmer than before and I must heal the coldness between us as soon as possible. But, for now, his missives read more like travel guides, the latest recalling how he has been to visit the elaborate tomb of the Dutch admiral, Michiel de Ruyters, greatly admired by Matthew despite the damage that fellow so frequently inflicted upon us when the Hollanders were our enemies, rather than our allies.

'It could all have ended so differently,' said Sir William. 'So badly.'

'The *Royal Sovereign*,' Captain Baker reminded them.

That venerable old fighting ship had burned to the waterline at Chatham late in January. Negligence, they said, though those of us who knew about the plots had been convinced it was more. And oh, how these Jacobite traitors had revelled in the streets at her loss.

'Ah, the other one,' said Streynsham, as Sir John Friend was now heaved upon the cart, and he definitely appeared the more pitiful of the two.

'But what's this?' Sir William exclaimed. 'Did they not have the Ordinary give them a blessing at Newgate?'

Undoubtedly that must have been so, but now Parkyns was shouting about them both being true Protestants and, as though by some magic, three black-robed ministers appeared from among the spectators and were allowed to approach the cart. By now, the executioner had draped the nooses loosely around the prisoners' necks though he also called up to his assistants to allow them more slack that they might kneel and pray. And the three ministers were hauling themselves onto the cart also, kneeling alongside them.

'Non-jurors, damn them,' said Captain Baker.

Indeed they were. Yet more of those seditious clergymen who had refused to swear the oath of allegiance to King William. And I wondered how many of them were also involved in this intended rising.

'Are they not done yet?' said Sir William. 'This is taking an ungodly amount of time. For pity's sake, what now?'

'One of the priests,' Streynsham told him, 'just asked whether they want absolution.'

'Absolution?' I laughed, as the prisoners and their ministers stood once more, a laying-on of hands and howls of anger from the crowd in response. 'Gracious, have they no shame?'

By February, at least, the plotters had been in disarray, the Jacobites not willing to rise until the French had landed, the French not willing to land until the Jacobites had risen. At the end of that month, the king had gone to Parliament with details of the scheme and, soon afterwards, the arrests had begun. Proclamations read all across the nation declaring that *Habeus Corpus* was suspended for the duration of the crisis.

'And that brother-in-law of yours,' Sir William murmured. 'Is he...?'

'Peter? Arrested again, yes,' said Streynsham. 'Though the good Captain here has agreed to intercede on his behalf. There's no real evidence against him.'

'He'll be discharged next week,' Captain Baker assured him. 'As you say, sirrah, no evidence.'

'Apart,' I said, 'from hosting gatherings of the rebels in Devonshire House.'

'My dear,' Streynsham said, 'these matters look very different in the north. In the West Country as well. So many without work. Without food too, very often, wheat prices gone so high. Trade smashed by the war and then, to add insult to injury, higher taxes so the damn'd thing might be paid for. Other issues that act like a magnet for young men of ideals like Peter Legh. Coiners clipping our silver so often it's barely worth a candle. They are misguided, of course, to lay the blame for such problems at the door of His Majesty. Or to believe the easy lie that somehow James Stuart can help solve them. Take them back to the good old days – as if there ever *was* such a thing.'

'There are always those,' I said, 'who suffer true disaffection, and those who simply exploit the disaffected.'

'That's true,' said Streynsham, 'and if the propaganda is strong enough, constant enough, it's easy to understand why. Always thus, is it not? That the comforting lie is always more acceptable than an inconvenient truth. Peter is more harmless fool than threat to the nation.'

'Unlike those rogues,' Sir William insisted, stabbing his finger down towards the cart, where the words of absolution seemed to have been spoken and both Parkyns and Friend were back on their knees, now in private prayer, the crowd becoming restless, shouting for the executioner to get on with things.

'And Peter Legh's release, I suppose,' I said, 'would have nothing to do with the new John Company?'

Brother Richard had shared the coffee house gossip with me – that a new East India Company would soon replace or absorb the old, Sir William's plans coming to fruition finally. And Streynsham Master, they say, to play a prominent role among the directors.

'You've heard the chatter-broth tales?' said Streynsham. 'Yes, I suppose you would, Mistress Yale.' He exchanged a knowing smile with Sir William. 'A considerable amount of our progress in bringing the old directors down has been due to your own work, Catherine. And we can now risk no threat to the reputation of the new enterprise through – well, through unfortunate associations. My brother-in-law as a guilty Jacobite would be quite an embarrassment. Yet I assure you, my dear, that his acquittal is perfectly genuine. Providential, yet genuine.'

Or a simple favour for your wife, I wondered, while Sir John Friend was holding aloft a paper, asking the ministers to deliver the document later to the Sheriffs up here on the balcony with us. They nodded their agreement to receive the thing, and Friend – seeming to have recovered himself through the absolution – cried out with a voice both loud and clear.

'I have come here to die,' he said, 'not to make speeches. But I desire this paper to be printed after my death. And may the Lord have mercy upon me.'

'And why should the Lord do so?' I shouted down to him. 'Traitor!'

My companions were, I think, a little shocked by my outburst, but the crowd loved it, took up the cry of "Traitor! Traitor!" These two were, after all, along with Sir John Fenwick and the rest, directly responsible for the plan by French Louis to embark sixteen thousand Frenchmen under James Stuart's personal command. Thankfully, with the plot discovered, our fleet had kept them contained in Calais and Dunkirk and then, this very morning, news that Sir Cloudesley Shovel has attacked and destroyed the invasion barges with fire ships.

None of us have any doubt that fighting in the Channel will continue for some months to come, yet the invasion is most certainly dead. And hence, I think, the reason for the exceptional numbers at today's executions. A true celebration.

'Well,' said Streynsham, 'almost over. They've just asked whether they might be allowed to make the sign themselves – for the cart to move off.'

Sir John Friend struggled a little now as his hands were tied behind his back.

'I freely forgive all,' he shouted, 'and I pray God may forgive me too.'

For what? I thought. If you are innocent?

'And Mistress Nicks?' said Sir William. 'What shall you do with her now?'

'I expect I shall allow her to undertake in reality that which has so far simply been a pretense – to act as Elihu's agent.'

'We owe her a great deal,' said Streynsham.

'Oh, so do I,' I replied. 'Our accounts are still far from settled. But I have written to my husband, to sow the seeds, if you understand me. And about other matters too. Poor Richie is unhappy in Porto, wishes to join his brother in Madras.'

'For the Company?' Sir William seemed astonished.

'If so,' I said, 'I should have directed him to yourself, Sir William. No, I think he has ambition towards independent trade. Some scheme to utilise the inheritance Mama invested so wisely for him.'

Poor Mama, still grieving so deeply for the loss of her own boys.

'Did you ever resolve the question of young Benjamin's portion?' said Streynsham.

'Ah,' I said, the other reason I have written to Elihu about Richard's wishes. Cajoling him about Benjamin has done us little good. I thought this might be a more subtle way to prick his conscience.'

Below, the mob had fallen silent as hoods were pulled over the heads of the condemned, though their eyes not yet covered, and the executioner's assistants taking up the slack from their ropes. We could hear Sir William Parkyns plainly now, asking whether it was best to lift his legs when the cart pulled away. Strange, the trivia that will occupy folk in the face of death itself.

'No, sirrah,' said the executioner. 'Best to simply stand. But yes, you may give the signal when you're ready.' Then he pulled down the hoods, covered their eyes, and the crowd began to shout and cheer once more, rising to a crescendo as the executioner jumped nimbly down and moved forward to stand beside the horse. I saw Friend's knee rise and fall twice as he stamped upon the bed of the cart and, without delay, the executioner slapped the horse's rump. The vehicle drew away with a jolt and there was a moment when the traitors' legs dragged a moment on the bed of the cart, scrabbling, as though they tried to impede its forward movement, to act as a brake.

Then their feet fell free, and the two men began to dance and wriggle on the end of their ropes.

'I suppose we must stay until the bitter end?' said Sir William. 'Detestable, though necessary I suppose. Yet you should feel under no such obligation, ma'am.'

How long had it been? In the case of Parkyns it must have been fifteen minutes or more, and still performing the jig, whereas

Sir John Friend had choked almost at once, a great gush of his piss darkening the front of his breeches and finally causing the crowd to fall still. And still they had more or less remained while Parkyns continued his stubborn refusal to succumb. Some clumsiness, perhaps, about the positioning of the rope around his neck.

'No, I shall stay,' I said. 'Besides, I would wish to know whether we have any word of Seaton.'

'None,' said Captain Baker. 'Gone to France like that devil Porter, so far as we know.'

'Not to the pope, sir?' I asked, and noticed the glance he exchanged with Streynsham Master. 'What?' I pressed him.

'It is a complex matter, Catherine,' Streynsham replied, keeping his voice low, little more than a whisper. 'That Seaton was an agent of the papal nuncio is a matter of certainty. But how much he may have been acting with the Monsignor's approval or authority – well, that may be a different matter entirely.'

'Coincidence then? That this same papal nuncio raced back to Rome as soon as the Boyne battle was lost.'

'My dear,' said Streynsham, 'there is little in life more complex than the politics of religion. There are few who know this but without the support of the Pope it is unlikely William would have had the resources to win that victory.'

'The pope?' I laughed. 'Preposterous.'

'Not so preposterous as you might think, Catherine. You know the Papal States have been part of the Grand Alliance. French Louis and his ambitions the common enemy. Pope Innocent – the previous one – wanted to ensure William would bring England into the Alliance also. They scratched each other's backs, as you might say. And then, with Innocent dead and Pope Alexander elected to replace him, there was the Boyne, the battle won. And Alexander hailed William's success as a great victory for the Alliance. Here in England, of course, we chose to not draw public attention to the pope's announcement. It might have been – misunderstood, yes?'

'Misunderstood?' I said. 'That all this time we have been fighting to save our nation from the pope's tyranny and...'

'Catherine, we should never confuse the ambitions of the

Church of Rome as a whole with the priorities and pragmatic exigencies of the Cardinal elected to be its Pontiff.'

'You say so? And now?'

'Our luck still holds. Alexander dead and this next Innocent maintains his support for our League of Augsburg.'

'There, he's gone,' said Sir William Langhorn. 'Gone, at last.'

The executioner, to the crowd's great adulation, gave a final tug on the dead men's legs, then shouted to his assistants to haul up the ropes, while the cart was reversed, allowing the bodies to then be dropped within it, the nooses slipped free. The hurdle was being dragged back too, and Field's corpse hauled down to rest upon it, the clothes ripped off. A gasp and great yell from the spectators as the executioner's axe caught the light, swung down and severed the dead traitor's head. A nimble assistant tossed the thing into one of the smaller baskets – no doubt the heads will by now have been spiked somewhere prominent – while the bloody business began of quartering the remains, a great deal of hacking that, in truth, I could not watch. But the noise of that dreadful butchery – oh, the noise.

'Tell me,' I said, 'those devices of Seaton's. The whip and that thing, the metal garter...'

'I am told,' said Streynsham, 'they call it a cilice – though I have heard that term applied also to penitents' sackcloth, their hair shirts.'

'Its significance?'

The noise abated, the four limbs and their attached segments of the torso collected into one of the larger baskets, and the whole operation begun again with Parkyns.

'Devotees,' Streynsham replied, 'use such things to mortify their own flesh, to impose repentance on themselves.'

'Catholic fanatics?'

'Catholics, Protestants, Lutherans, Presbyterians. There are those who like to sensationalise such things. But even the whip is designed simply to guarantee discomfort rather than draw blood.'

I laughed.

'Great heavens, Streynsham,' I said. 'I could almost believe...'

181

'I thought you wanted to know about Seaton,' he snapped, so harshly it seemed like a rebuke.

'Is he an agent of Rome or not?' I replied, somewhat daunted by his suddenly abrupt manner.

'You hoped, perhaps, for some extravagant yarn about his willingness to sacrifice himself for his faith, yet the truth, we suspect, is likely more mundane. Catholic? Yes. Devout in his beliefs? Most certainly. Immersed in the dogma of the old Cavalier faction? Absolutely. A traitor? Of course. But probably no more so than any other of James Stuart's many agents. Driven, like the rest, as much by his personal ambitions as any misguided nobility.'

'There,' shouted Sir William. 'Finished. And give you joy of your good offices, gentlemen,' he said to the Sheriffs, reaching along the balcony to shake their hands while, below, the crowd began to disperse, the traders pressing for a few final sales and the executioner's assistants heaving their grim baskets onto the cart.

'No more than just another Jacobite agent?' I said. 'And the attack upon my household?'

'As I said,' Streynsham insisted, 'driven by some personal motive perhaps. He certainly had cause to resent your interference at Madras. How shall we ever know, now he is gone?'

'Can we be so certain?' I was wondering how much greater the personal motive might be, now I had left Seaton with that deformity of his hand, stolen back the locket, invaded *his* domain, brought his associates to this blood-soaked punishment.

'With God's good grace,' said Streynsham, 'let us pray it may be so.'

God's grace? I wondered, and I saw in my mind's eye the scales, the good things I may have done on one side, the ill on the other. The balance did not look positive and I wondered whether, to swing the thing once more in my favour, it should not be me wearing the hair shirt and the metal garter.

'I should not be here except I have nowhere else to turn,' said Katherine Nicks, and it seemed to me the tarred skull of Sir William Parkyns grinned down at me, a partner in wickedness, from his spike upon the bridge-gate's battlements. There were boys running about, despite the day's heat, selling copies of ballads and satirical broadsides, all of them making jibes at Sir William's expense, else it might have been difficult to properly identify the blackened lump that had once been his head.

'Truly?' I replied, shifting my goods basket from one arm to the other. 'And there was I, believing it almost time to bring our association to an end.'

We stood in the shade, at the stink-ridden Southwark end of the bridge, not far from the *Bear*, at that place where traitors' heads had once so regularly been spiked, though it has now become a rare spectacle. No, the present fashion is to spike them atop the arch of the Temple Bar, where Sir John Friend's remains are presently and dismally set up.

She had sent a note asking to meet me. Today. And I had dispatched a response setting the hour and place as a suitable point for our rencounter. It somehow seemed appropriate.

'You think the decision rests with you, *senhora*?' she shouted above the crowd's clamour, above the yell of the watermen, above the roar of the Thames as the falling tide thrashed its way between the narrow arches and starlings below. 'I've had no need of your charity these six months past. Not with the treasure dear Elihu sent me.'

It had been a difficult decision, my husband writing me about the further diamond shipment for her, and me faced with the conundrum of whether to waylay the delivery once more. But it would have required a different ruse and suddenly it did not seem worth the trouble. My own trade through the Pereiras' syndicate was flourishing and though I still believed myself entitled to further recompense from her, I could no longer be precise about the actual amount outstanding.

'I understand from Pereira it was a fine batch of gems,' I said. 'Yet it seems you still need my help.'

'What I need is justice. Justice,' she repeated. 'Perhaps through those of your closest acquaintance.'

'The disbursement? Are you thinking about the disbursement?'

I had met her a few weeks earlier at the sign of the Golden Pheasant. Beneath the depths of my skirts that day, within the carefully concealed purse, which I had hefted upon my palm. The satisfying chink of coin, and she caught the purse deftly enough when I tossed it across the table.

'Not guineas, I hope,' she had laughed.

'No,' I said. 'Not guineas.' I wish I had a sixpence for each time I have heard the same comment these past weeks since the recoinage caused the golden guinea's worth to be slashed from its recent meteoric value at thirty shillings to a mere twenty-one. 'Honest silver, my dear. *Pesos de ocho*, unless I am much mistaken – though it would be impolite to enquire about their origin.'

'Disbursement,' she said, skipping to one side as a porter's handcart caught in a rut and spilled two crates of wine onto the cobbles. Portuguese wine, I noted, and thought of Richard as the ruby-coloured liquid splashed about her feet. 'Let me see, Mistress Yale,' she went on, and lifted her skirts to keep them dry, 'is there not something about Greeks...'

'Remittance, not a gift, Mistress Nicks,' I reminded her, and pulled her across the busy street, glancing back to the bridge's shops and dwellings, where a cautious Wadham watched us attentively from a doorway. 'Remember? From others. In gratitude for your efforts.'

184

I steered her away from the *Bear*, between the carts and carriages struggling to pass each other within the narrow confines of Bridge Street, the congestion made worse today by the large flock of sheep being herded across the river from the Southwark side. And then we entered that sombre valley of the bridge itself with its teetering façades on either flank, the buildings held from crumbling entirely only by the wooden beams spanning the chasm to prevent their collapse, either inwards or outwards.

'Blood money then,' she said.

'The blood already spilled. The blood to come. Sir John Fenwick soon, I collect.'

He was taken last month, that vile architect of the plot. In hiding all this time but taken at last though, as yet, no trial – and, according to Streynsham, unlikely to face such a thing. One of the two main witnesses against him, the actor Goodman, disappeared. And the law requires two for the charges of treason to be tried in court.

'His trial date set?' she asked.

'If no trial,' I said, 'then he will surely be sentenced by Act of Parliament. Or so I am assured. And then all those others who will simply be left to rot in Newgate until they too are dead. You did service to the Crown, Katherine, though there were many others whose evidence was perhaps more telling than our own modest contribution.'

'There! Assured, you say. Who is it that assures you so, sirrah? The Duke of Devonshire again, in the same way you came by this payment?'

'At Chatsworth, yes. As you once suggested, even the wife of a humble merchant adventurer may sometimes climb to great heights.'

I stopped a passing nosegay seller, paid her a ha'penny for a lavender wand.

'It was in my mind,' said Katherine, seemingly impervious to the stench, 'that you still have friends in high places.'

I first met Sir William Cavendish at Streynsham Master's wedding, of course. And then attended his investiture. All the same, I had been surprised to receive this particular invitation. And not simply for myself but Mama and my girls too. I hoped it would be good for her, at least. A family affair, if you like. Derbyshire. At the invitation of the Duke himself. To celebrate the completion of his renovations there.

'In any case,' I said, 'the only pertinent thing is that the payment was placed in your hand. Fifty silver dollars.'

'*Dê ao Diabo o que é dele*,' she said. Give the devil his due. 'Judas Iscariotes was worth no more than thirty pieces.'

A file of musketeers – Dutch, I thought – forced their way through the local citizens, and we followed them, towards the centre of the bridge, taking advantage of the space left in their wake.

'You see this as some form of betrayal?' I demanded.

'My mother a Catholic. You know it. Renounced her faith for my father's sake.'

'Your mother...' I began, for it occurred to me I had never enquired after the Barkers.

'My mother is dead. You did not know? No, I suppose you would not. A fever, two years ago.'

'We were often in her company. And your father?'

'The schoolmaster now.'

Yes, I knew that much at least. Appointed when Mister Ord left the position. The school flourishes, Elihu tells me. A fine new room, beneath the White Town Library. Her children all at their studies with him. Including Elihu's children, I suppose.

'You must miss them.' I tried to sound sincere, but I was more concerned, I think, with the fear that I could no longer see Wadham, and I stopped, jostled by those rushing around us until I could locate him again.

'The most foolish thing you have ever said to me, Mistress Yale. My heart aches for them. A terrible pain, which never leaves me, though I doubt you would be much troubled by that. And my worries for their future. I wonder, is that the one thing we might share. The ambition we hold for our children.'

'*One* thing we share?' I said, laboriously moving on again. 'More than just the children, surely.'

186

At that open space where the ramshackle old houses of the bridge – those that survived the fire – gave way to the new, I stopped to buy cordials, sweet and aromatic, sold by a blackamoor literally drumming up business with a small tabor.

'So we must, I suppose,' I said, as we savoured our drinks, 'wait until my husband decides it is more profitable to return than remain, before we see him back in England once again.'

Katherine raised her beaker in mock salute.

'Naturally.'

His latest letter to me says as much. So I imagine he must have told her the same.

'Or perhaps he is simply more comfortable with *Senhora* de Paiva,' I said.

She held the cup to her lip, regarding me for an uncomfortably long while before she spoke.

'Sometimes in the past, Mistress, I have envied you. Your handsome looks, when I am so – homely, is that not how you like to describe me? Your marriage to Mister Hynmers. It always seemed so perfect. I knew you despised me, but even so... And when you were married to Elihu, the way he admired you. The speed with which he took up the chance to wed you. To set me aside. But now? You criticise him for his devotion to trade. But have the things that consume you any more meaning? Make you more satisfied? Weighing the need to protect your boys against the level of Elihu's love for his girls. Measuring Elihu's love for your girls against his affection for my own young ones. Taunting me with whether his devotion to Don Carlos tips the scales against my children. Where does this all take you, *senhora*?'

'You think I fail to understand you all,' I said. 'You. Jeronima. Elihu himself, I suppose.'

But what if you are wrong, harlot? I thought. What if I understand you all too well? I have been in the tropics long enough to know the way that climate can affect morality.

She shrugged her shoulders, passed the drained beaker back to the vendor.

'Why should it trouble me whether you understand us or not? Elihu will be back soon and then we shall see.'

See what? I wondered, though I would not ask her to elaborate.

'Elihu has said so?'

She smiled at me – a taunting smile.

'He made a point of asking me to let you know John Bridger is dead.'

That feeling as though somebody had walked across my grave, the icy chill upon the nape of my neck.

'A shame,' I said, finishing my own cordial. 'I have always liked John.'

And so I have. But surely his death could not be linked to the Poison Nut powder he had somehow taken in error from the glass intended for his perfidious wife. Surely not. I knew he had been ill almost constantly ever since. But great heavens that was seven years ago, almost eight.

'But not Winfriede?' She used Mistress Bridger's Portuguese name. Her Portuguese Jewish name. 'Not at the end,' she went on. 'We all saw it, how you cooled towards her. One day your friend, the next…'

'It is a talent I possess,' I said, and turned my back to her, leaned over the parapet to stare into the swirling waters below. 'The ability to lose from my life those who need to be lost.'

We had ventured back into the ebb and flow of humanity on Bridge Street and bustled past the last of the milliners and mercers, the haberdashers, drapers, iron chandlers and booksellers.

'Yet I trust you will permit me to ask about your boy, at least. Joseph. He has kept clear of the sickness?'

We had all received the news, a mortal pestilence that swept through the Coromandel Coast during last year – might be raging still, for all I know.

'Strange, is it not? That Elihu would trouble to send news of John Bridger, that you might convey the message, yet he sends you no word of my son.'

Joseph Junior, in fact, is no longer at Fort St. George but dispatched to that other factory further south, Tegnapatam – Fort St. David, which Elihu himself had been responsible for establishing. Safe there, I hoped. For there had been other uncomfortable news. The previous year's pirate attack by Henry Avery against the Mughal Emperor's convoy near Surat on its return from annual pilgrimage at Mecca – an attack for which Aurangzeb blames the English and ordered an attack on Bombay, shutting down four of the Company's factories and imprisoning its servants. He had threatened to destroy all English trade in India unless Avery is captured. The result? John Company has paid a huge indemnity and offered one thousand pounds as a bounty for Avery's capture. A manhunt begun but, so far, Avery has eluded every attempt to capture him. No surprise, however, for Avery and his crew will have made enough money to disappear entirely, to be treated like lords for the rest of their new lives.

'Not strange,' she said. 'There was much else to tell me.'

'Since you are so close, I am surprised you feel the need to turn then to his wife for – did you ever tell me, my dear? What it is causes you to seek my assistance? Justice, did you say? Yet do you mind? I did not come, in truth, to see Sir William's blackened head. Simply a convenient place to meet, given my need to visit Hall's.'

'Our petition to the Privy Council,' she said. 'It has entirely failed. No further consideration will be given to John's case.'

'Poor Mister Nicks,' I replied, checking to make sure Wadham was still close behind.

'Yet the Duke, *senhora*. You know him personally. Lord Steward of the Royal Household. With the king away at his wars…'

There were already several customers in the shop, Mister Hall the proprietor and his apprentice busy with the sale of gentlemen's shirts and handkerchiefs.

'If the Privy Council has reached its decision, my dear,' I whispered, 'it is far beyond the remit of the Lord Steward, surely.'

There was a loud fellow required to pay for his purchases.

'But they are shillings,' he was saying.

'Yet,' said the apprentice, 'as you can see, they are clipped so badly…' He weighed them on a small balance. 'Worth only eightpence each, sirrah.'

'Eightpence?' the fellow raged. 'God's hooks, boy, when King James ruled, a shilling was a shilling.'

'The fault plainly rests,' shouted the shop-keeper, 'with those rogues who clip the coins in the first place. What is this country coming to?'

'There is always some cove,' I said, unable to resist, 'intent on exploiting our victory against James Stuart's tyranny.'

'Tyranny?' The customer turned to me, his face red with anger. A familiar face too, though it took me some moments to place it. 'Really, Mistress?' he cried. 'You should perhaps do better to tend your wifely duties than pretend to any knowledge of either trade or tyranny. And you, sirrah,' he said to Mister Hall, 'do you not see how these Whigs and Williamites invent this false news of plots and schemes so they might restrict our freedoms, oppress our lives? Prithee, step out of your door and see the windows bricked up across the way. Window tax, indeed!'

'It is hard upon us all,' I said, 'but such taxation would not be needed except to keep us free from the clutches of the French. Have you no loyalty to our country, sir?'

'The French were not our enemies while good King Charles was on the throne, and then King James after him.'

'No, in those days we were kept at war with honest Protestant Dutchmen, who should always have been our friends. But you, sirrah, would have been too occupied singing *Ho, Cavaliers* with your Jacobite friends to worry excessively about that.'

He took a step back from the serving bench, looked from me to my companion, then back again.

'Do I know you, madam?'

'I rarely forget a face, sir,' I said. 'Though it must be six years ago. At the wedding of my good friend Streynsham Master. You were in company with young Peter Legh, were you not?' I turned to Katherine Nicks. 'Have you met this gentleman, my dear? Mistress Nicks,' I explained to the fellow, 'has often been a guest at Devonshire House. Perhaps you are both acquainted? Oh, and you might also be familiar with Sir William Parkyns. A coincidence, for we just came across him also, at the Southwark bridge-gate.'

It was at that moment Wadham made his entrance. It is his business, of course, to have a nose for trouble and I have retained him precisely for that attribute. Streynsham and others may be convinced Seaton is gone from our lives, but I am personally far from certain, and Wadham now gave this fellow such an appraisal with those hooded, ice-cold eyes that no further words were necessary.

'I am nothing to do with that gentleman,' the man murmured, his attention returned to the apprentice. 'Very well,' he said. 'Damn your eyes. I'll pay your price in silver ounces.'

Within moments he had taken his linsey-wrapped purchases, careful to keep his gaze averted, yet muttering to himself as he skulked from the shop while, for my own part, I also paid somewhat more than I had expected for a pair of Mister Hall's finest cambric shirts, destined for Richie in Porto.

'It seems,' said Katherine Nicks when we were out on Bridge Street again, 'that the conflict between James Stuart on the one hand and your Williamites on the other hurts everybody the same. And do you truly believe it makes the slightest difference to any of these good folk whether one or the other sits on the throne?'

'Let the Church of Rome gain the upper hand,' I replied, 'and you will soon see the difference. When they start burning good Protestants as heretics again, oh, you shall certainly see the difference.'

'The Church burning heretics?' she said. 'You live in the past, *senhora*. And was it wise to let that gentleman identify me with Devonshire House? Well, I suppose you are right. Time to bring our association to an end. A dirty business anyway. Spying. The dead walk in my dreams at night.'

'You were willing enough, I collect. Simply one more piece of trade, no? The excitement of the chase too – is that not the true reward for merchant adventurers, madam?'

'Any reward would be better than fifty *pesos de ocho*.'

'Oh, come!' I said. 'Fifty pieces of silver were just the end of it. You have lived at my expense these three years past. I have financed the stock that gave you the pretense of acting as Elihu's agent – just as I financed his own rise in fortune. And the pretense is now turned to reality. You think you are owed more?'

Of course, I made no mention of the small detail that the financing of this operation has come entirely from the purse provided by Captain Baker. It had been modest, as the Master of the King's Intelligence once promised, but enough for me to make a small profit.

'I think, *senhora*, you owe me at least an approach, or an introduction, to the Duke? When all is said and done, you might despise the wife yet still be gracious towards my husband.'

I sighed and halted.

'All a question of integrity,' I told her. 'My own integrity, I mean. It may be true I am fortunate in my acquaintances, yet you ask me to risk all by vouching for somebody who could well be guilty of the charges levelled against him by the Company. And this is also the man who seems capable of simply turning a blind eye to the wife's infidelities. In my opinion, Mistress Nicks, a husband who accepts his cuckolding as readily as John Nicks is the partner to your crime, not its victim.'

She laughed in my face.

'I should call down a curse upon you,' she said. 'But there is no need. Bitterness such as you bear can bring you nothing but grief. You wear tragedy like a cloak. And in this world of yours there are more hazards than just Vincent Seaton to worry about.' She stretched out her hand just then, placed it gently on the shirts folded within my basket. 'Give you joy of your future, *senhora*,' she said, but I barely heard her, my thoughts suddenly swamped by the memory of that spilled wine, that Porto red wine.

Sunday 13th December 1696

The news, when it arrived, sliced me like a knife and has left this leaden lump in my soul ever since. Tears? Of course tears. But more this awful metallic emptiness. And it took until today, a month gone by, before I finally allowed Reverend Bracegirdle to conduct the memorial service.

'Such kind words,' said Mama, herself still not truly recovered from the loss of her own sons.

'Were they?' I said, shivering despite my warmest cloak. God's hooks, there was a coldness about the place that matched the chill in my soul. 'Perhaps I did not hear them correctly. Many references to the Almighty, to His mysterious ways, to the Kingdom of Heaven, to our Lord Jesus Christ, to everlasting salvation, yet only a rare mention here and there of my son's name.'

Richard, once my darling boy. And I imagined some echo of his infantile laughter as he played with Tanani; or the memory of that rare consolation he gave me when Walter died; or my fear for him when the *sadhu* cursed us – and foolishly I wonder whether Richie's own death is still linked to the holy man's witchcraft.

For an instant I saw young Rich chasing flocks of parakeets up and down along Middle Gate Street. And then the change in him, when his father died, his resentment at Elihu's sudden presence in Joseph's place. His outright animosity when Joseph Junior was sent home and the way he had tried to compensate for this by seeing himself as the man of the house in his older brother's absence. Stubborn Richard, taking this boyish role so seriously he took irreparable offence when it was his own turn to be sent home, screaming that I did not love him, that I was setting him aside. As though I could ever have done so.

And then the silence, when all I heard from him was through Mama, sending me his deepest affection though I knew he had wished me no such thing. The distance between us when I came back to London almost as great as the six-month sea voyage. His obduracy, which had softened only marginally over the years until he finally sailed for Porto. All the things I never shared with him. My Richard. Gone.

'No chance to say goodbye,' murmured Benjamin at my side. Eighteen now and fighting back his own tears. An Oxford scholar, beneficiary of a sizarship. St. John's College, naturally. Where else after Merchant Taylors, and happy to serve as a college servant in return for the privilege. 'I thought this service would help, Ma,' he said. 'But it doesn't.'

I ran my fingers along the polished oak of our pew, breathed in the bitter dampness, the echoing emptiness. There were enough of us there, at St. Peter-le-Poor, to fill the place. Little more than thirty paces, end-to-end, and so ancient the city has literally grown around it, risen so high outside that, without its curtains, passers-by on Broad Street could easily gaze in through the windows. So the drapes were drawn this afternoon, to allow us privacy in our family grief. Our funeral service without even a coffin.

'Will you go there?' said my sister Roberta. 'To Porto?'

She was trying to restrain poor damaged Ursula, who was wriggling like an infant barely half her seven years. Katie, eleven, was busily engaged with brother Richard's baby, little Judith, named for her mother. And awkward Annie, nine, clinging to the skirts of my other brother Benjamin's heavily pregnant wife, Lydia.

'Where do the years go?' I said, to nobody in particular, suddenly feeling my years like a millstone. 'But Porto? No, I think not. Anyway, he is buried in Coimbra. Is that not what your Richard said?'

A letter had arrived from the Reverend Pritchard, chaplain to the English merchants at Porto. A second letter from Clark and Thornton – courteous but no more than the formal and cold condolences to be expected in such circumstances, the chaplain's several pages more comforting. Yet it was the third missive, from my brother-in-law Richard that had been the most illuminating, tragic in so many ways. My own Richie had been dispatched up-country to Coimbra, it seems, his arrival coinciding with a sudden resurgence of activity by the Catholic Inquisition all across Portugal. Little reported here in England, but I remembered dear Joseph telling me tales of his own time in Porto as a boy. The same Inquisition. The burnings he had witnessed. Perhaps the thing that had driven him that night in Madras, the girl Kalai and her *sati* self-immolation. And now in Coimbra alone, ninety converts from the Jewish faith – *Conversos*, Richard calls them, *Marranos* – allegedly lapsed back into their own practices, were burned to death in the town square.

I keep thinking about that scornful barb fired at me by Katherine Nicks. About living in the past. About my foolishness for believing the Church of Rome might still burn heretics. Where is the harlot now? I wonder. Where? Though why does it matter? Except she may be correct, about me carrying my own curse within me. Another of my sons gone before his time.

Brother Richard tells me that when these alleged heretics were led from the palace of the Inquisition, Richie had found himself, by accident, upon the street. There had been a young Jewish woman, no more than a girl, he says, seemingly alone and barely able to sustain herself in her terror. Rich had gone forward to help her. Like Simon of Cyrene, he tries to assure me, helping our Lord Jesus on the way to his own Calvary. Yet a soldier set to control the mob had determined to restrain him. A scuffle, my son struck about the skull with the haft of a halberd. Some companion had carried him away, no obvious damage done, though the following day he had been afflicted with dreadful pains of the head and, two mornings later, he had passed away in terrible agony. I can feel it, every excruciating torment. Yet the local physicians had been unable to help, despite copious bleedings and a botched attempt at trepanning.

My brother-in-law does not say so but there is something between his lines that tells me it might have been this butcher's attempt at penetrating his skull that actually killed my boy –

though I have asked Roberta that this should remain between us. But there is another vision haunting my nights, Richard stretched naked upon the bench, a saw-bones working upon his poor head, blood everywhere. Yet not blood. It is Porto's red wine gushing from the wound, splashes upon the cobbles as it had done that day on London Bridge.

'A tragedy,' said Mama, as we filed out onto the street, 'that he had not been able to secure his post in India as he wished.'

It was freezing enough outside, yet felt positively mild compared to St. Peter's ice-house interior.

'The Lord could not have protected him any more in Madras,' Benjamin replied, 'than in Portugal, I collect.'

'The person who should have protected him is my husband,' I said. And I knew as I said it that there was little logic in my words. None. In fact. For my letter to Elihu, asking him to consider Richie's request, will only recently have arrived there. What difference anyway? Benjamin has it right. But my grief spits in the face of such sensibility. Who else should I blame for failing yet another of my boys but Elihu Yale?

'That is your hurt speaking,' said Mama. 'Such a good man.'

His annual letters and gifts to Mama, the way she reciprocates, it makes me sick.

'I hope,' I said, 'the shirts reached him.'

For some reason it gave me comfort, the idea he might have been warmed by the cambric, felt my love for him through the fabric, even through the pain of his dying.

A boy ran up to Benjamin, demanded a farthing for one of his broadsides.

'Ah,' said Benjamin, 'they have announced the date.' He waved the paper at us. A Bill of Attainder had passed through the Commons, Sir John Fenwick found guilty by Act of Parliament rather than by trial. 'It goes before the Lords,' Benjamin read for us, 'in January and, all being well, the execution a couple of weeks after that.'

And now my dear Mama taken from us too, just a se'nnight past. She has been failing steadily since the death of my father and then my older brothers. I think I have never felt so alone, yet my sadness has been almost eclipsed by the other events of this day.

We buried her as close to Papa as we were able in that crow-cackle churchyard of St. Edmund the King, the family all gathered once more in funereal black beneath an equally morbid sky.

'Together again,' said Benjamin. 'Almost.'

I knew he was referring to Ma and Pa, of course, and I felt proud of him. It helped ease my pain and I linked his arm in mine, gazed up at those sharp and slender features. University life seems to agree with him. He has always been bookish, more spiritual than his brothers, but he seems now to have adopted some of his father's looks and manner. Of course, I never knew Joseph at this age, older when I met him, but I wish I had done so. That dear man. Our Lord Jesus help me, if only he were still at my side.

'I hope they are together, indeed,' I replied, as Reverend Goodgroome made his way among us, offering a final blessing. 'Though I suspect your Grandmama will have found something with which to upbraid him. He was always long-suffering and must, I suppose, now sustain that quality for all eternity.'

I miss them in such different ways. Papa for his simple wisdom, the mere joy of his company. And Mama? Well, perhaps too early to fully understand the loss. For there has been much to distract me, much to arrange, my brothers having left so many of the practical details to me.

'What will happen to the girls now?' Benjamin asked, and I looked across to where they huddled around their Aunt Roberta's skirts, my sister-in-law urging them forward to the grave's edge so they could cast their forget-me-nots upon the coffin lid.

'Katie and Nan are too old for another nursemaid,' I murmured. 'So perhaps boarding school. Or an additional tutor. And Ursi...'

Little Ursula, her growth so stunted, her manner so slow. What shall become of her?

'Ursi, I think,' said Benjamin, 'shall be with us always.'

'Us, Benjamin?'

'I shall not leave you, Mama. Not ever.'

Sweet boy. Yes, proud of him.

'A commitment you might come to regret, my dear. Will it not interfere with your hopes? Your studies?'

'I intend to practise law in London itself if I am able. If nothing else, it shall help me regain my inheritance.'

'Your Grandmama's one regret – that she was unable to secure your future as she had done for your brothers.'

'Everything comes to he who waits, Mama.' He smiled down at me. His father's smile.

My brothers Benjamin and Richard were her executors and early this afternoon we assembled at the cobwebbed office of toad-like Attorney Makepiece to hear Mama's wishes. And how had she described Elihu in the will again? *My worthy and kind son Mister Elihu Yale.* It seems I must have kept the truth from her tolerably well. Joseph Junior too. He has written to her frequently yet, so far as I know, never a mention of Jeronima de Paiva or his by-blows. But thinking of Elihu inevitably dragged me to thoughts of Katherine Nicks. And, as if by premonition, she was still upon my mind when we left the attorney's office and I found Wadham waiting for me on Lombard Street with, it transpires, word of the woman.

I had set the old thief-catcher to observing her activities for reasons that already seem contradictory to me. Still, that imperative about keeping one's enemies bound close to us? Yes, though she was no longer in thrall to me, no longer reliant upon my patronage.

So where was the point? Simple curiosity, perhaps, a professional interest in her business dealings. Something of that, certainly. Concern for her welfare? Stuff! As though I should care. Yet I had to admit that, in a strange way, she provided links. To Madras. Therefore to Joseph Junior. And I suppose to Elihu also.

So, weekly reports: when she moved from the house on Devonshire Street and into rooms above an inn near her sister in St. Mary Axe; when she rented a second godown in Cow Lane; and whenever she had conducted transactions at the sign of the Golden Pheasant. Her business – or rather her agency on Elihu's behalf – seemed to be flourishing, drove me to a compunction for competition.

My own investments are sound enough, for the sale of the Devonshire Street house had turned a small profit, and that small profit multiplied a hundred-fold. Shared fortune with Sir William Langhorn, whose own agent presently operates on our joint behalf at Lloyd's coffee house – Lombard Street, of course, and now the daily haunt of so many bankers, merchants and ship owners for the more informal transactions of their trade.

But our own money, mine and Sir William's? As I write this I am struck by my own hypocrisy – that this gentleman against whom I had helped compile evidence at Fort St. George of the bribes and garnish supplementing his already considerable wealth, has also become my business partner. And I had been correct, of course, for his dismissal as Governor was hardly likely to impoverish him. Yet he does not know any of that and our joint enterprise is more in the nature of assurance, our receipt of premiums against compensation should vessels and their cargoes fail to arrive safety. Lucrative. No rich reward without real risk, of course. But so far, lucrative. And I am now become a regular student of *Lloyd's News*, to follow our fortunes, to calculate the gamble more closely.

Yet I digress, my quill running away with itself, or perhaps fleeing from this evening's ugliness, for I had indeed set Wadham to keeping a watchful eye on Katherine Nicks and now there he was, outside the attorney's office, and in a more animated state than I have ever seen him, wringing his battered hat and scratching impatiently at his cropped and scabrous head.

'You should come, ma'am,' he spluttered. 'Bad business, like. Bad business.'

'Come where, sirrah?' Some emergency, plainly, and at first I feared for the girls, sent home after the funeral in the care of Fletchley. 'My daughters?'

'Daughters? God's hooks, no. 'Tis Mistress Nicks. You should come, ma'am.'

'And what would entice me...?' I began, but Benjamin cut across me.

'What's happened, Wadham?' he said.

'Hurt, sirrah. Hurt bad, she is.'

'Where?' I demanded, annoyed that Benjamin seemed to be dragging me somewhere I did not wish to venture. 'An accident?'

'Barts, sirrah. The chirurgeon sent for.'

'On whose authority?' I said, alarmed at the thought of the price that treatment in the hospital could cost. 'At whose expense? To what end?'

It shames me now to think of my reaction, of course, but at the time – well, even at the time I could have bitten my tongue for my lack of charity.

'The authority of Captain Baker, ma'am,' the rogue replied, and I realised this was no ordinary event.

'I'll find us a hackney, Mama,' said Benjamin and went off along the street towards Woolchurch Market where, often, several carriages stood ready for hire.

'And Captain Baker?' I asked Wadham. 'Because...?'

'The business between you all, Mistress.' The old devil had the temerity to wink at me conspiratorially. 'Know what I means? And this – well...'

The hackney stopped alongside us, Benjamin opening the door, which Wadham held for me while I clambered inside the filthy vehicle, dried vomit on the floor and one of the seats.

'An extra shilling if you get us to Barts without delay,' Benjamin yelled, while Wadham slammed the door shut, muttering the carriage's registration number over and over to himself, against the possibility of some chicanery on the part of the coachman – common enough for those rascals to find some novel way of fleecing the unsuspecting.

'Explain,' I said to Wadham as we rattled and shuddered our way along the thoroughfare, our teeth almost shaken from our skulls. The roads really are a disgrace – uneven barely does it justice, and I have seen carriages toppled twice in the past month. That is without the obstacles, of course. Why, the roads in Madras Patnam are better maintained. So Wadham merely grimaced, cast a doubtful glance in Benjamin's direction and I was unsure whether his reticence was due to the impossibility of carrying on a conversation or his uncertainty about how much my son might have known of my clandestine activities. Both perhaps, and with good reason, at least, so far as Benjamin is concerned.

'Wish – it – were – a – wherry!' Benjamin managed to stammer. If only. But Barts is nowhere near the river and this hack was our only option. So we battered and bumped our way through serpentine, narrow and crooked by-ways, roughly following the line of Cheapside and Newgate Street until it finally dropped us in that rutted lane running along the eastern edge of Smith Field with its stink of cow pats and the grazing ground alive tonight with the lowing of cattle or oxen and the pitiable and distressed bleating of ewes recently deprived of their lambs taken for the slaughter.

The coachman received his extra shilling, though I scolded Benjamin for his profligacy. Twice the approved fare, forsooth. Then we were through the half-timbered gateway, past the side door of St. Bartholomew-the-Less and across the green into the hospital itself, with its overpowering scent of excrement and stale food, the muffled cries and groans of its inmates. They were the same sights, sounds and smells I remembered from our own hospital at Fort St. George, some strange nostalgia from that sad day when I had visited poor wounded Matthew Parrish there, the last time I had entered such an establishment.

'This way,' shouted Wadham, ignoring my demands to know what this was all about and taking the stairs on the north side of the quadrangle. 'Told you, ma'am,' he panted, 'Mistress Nicks. Hurt. At her new godown.'

Well, I supposed that explained Barts, literally on the other side of the Smith Field from Cow Lane, but I followed him anyway until, on the first floor, we came to an open room, one of the small chirurgical amphitheatres for which Barts is renowned. Well, a half-amphitheatre anyway, three tiers of benches rising in a semi-circle around a long wooden table at the room's centre. Upon the table, the reclining form of Katherine Nicks. I could see her quite plainly despite the blood, and I was almost sick. Benjamin too. He was just behind me and I saw him literally turn a strange shade of apple-green.

At Katherine's head was a chirurgeon, dressed in a very fine coat and breeches, his wig powdered, and his only concession to the gore and detritus a butcher's apron as he carefully examined the wounds. Behind him, one of his assistants threaded a long and curved suturing needle.

'What the devil...?' Benjamin gasped.

'Wait outside,' I told him.

'Please!' bellowed the chirurgeon. 'This is not some public spectacle.'

'Doctor Browne,' said Captain Baker from the first tier of benches, 'this lady is with me.'

The chirurgeon muttered some protest but then returned to his examination.

'But...' said Benjamin.

'Do as I say,' I told him, 'for pity's sake. Wait outside.'

Thankfully he required no more persuasion.

'What has happened?' I asked, climbing up the steps, Wadham at my heels, to sit beside the Master of the King's Intelligence.

'What has happened,' said Chirurgeon Browne, 'is that we have cleaned the wound as best we are able, drained it of stinkage and bloody matter, purged this poor creature with suitable enemas, and I am now about to attempt the closure of this excessive laceration.'

'She cannot speak,' Baker explained. 'Or very little. The nature of the injury.'

I looked down upon her, bile rising in my throat again, and I clamped my hand over my mouth. Her face was turned towards me, the eyes closed, her breathing labored. And she was whimpering pitifully. Yet I could see the ruin of her left cheek quite clearly, another assistant constantly swabbing away the blood flowing from a gash running diagonally from the corner of her lips, ripping the flesh apart to expose her teeth, the stark white bone of her upper jaw and the cheek itself all the way to her ear, the top of which seemed to be missing.

And all the animosities I had built up against this woman over the past twenty-five years simply evaporated.

'Accident?' I said, knowing it was an absurd question even as I spoke.

'Will we ever be rid of them?' said Baker. 'I had thought Fenwick might be the last of them.'

Fenwick? I am no fool. They took the wretch's head back in January, on Tower Hill, after the Lords narrowly approved the Act of Attainder against him and, therefore, his execution without an actual trial. And the link?

'Seaton then?' I said.

'So she told Wadham's man. Heard her scream, found her like that. Right, Dick?'

'Did so,' Wadham agreed. 'Old Tom Thumbs says you could've heard it all the bleedin' way to St. Paul's – beggin' pardon, ma'am.'

The surgeon was busy at his stitching, the stink of gore as awful as any charnel house, turning my stomach again, wrenching at my pity for her muted moaning.

'She said nothing else?' I asked.

'By the time I got there,' said Baker, 'she was choking on her own blood. Impossible to understand any of it. Only one thing, and I may even have got that wrong. But I think she was trying to say "hall" – does that make sense?'

It crushed me, but I had already made the connection. That day on the bridge. Mister Hall's finest cambric shirts. The awkward fellow with the clipped silver. What had I said to him? That Mistress Nicks had often been a guest at Devonshire House. Yet now there she was, at Hall's emporium, in company with the same Catherine Yale whom Seaton, at least, knew was a sworn enemy of the Cavalier and Jacobite factions. If this same fellow, whoever he was, had reported the encounter back to his fellow seditionists it would not have taken them long to associate Mistress Nicks with the calamities that had befallen so many of the conspiracies hatched at Devonshire House itself. And Katherine Nicks would have worked that out too. Perhaps even had Seaton confront her with it, depending on how the attack had taken place, the way in which that awful hurt had been inflicted.

I looked back down at her, riddled now with guilt as the needle pushed once more through her flesh, dragged forth yet another burbling howl of pain, and I started as I realised her eyes were wide open, staring back directly into my own. I might have expected nothing there but hatred, yet what I saw was, I am certain, a pleading entreaty. But to what end? I had no idea.

Tuesday 23rd November 1697

'History teaches us,' said Matthew Parrish, 'that in the very depths of our darkest despair, we must always prepare for the possibility of even worse to follow.'

He was taking tea in the comforting warmth of my best parlour, his pipe set aside for the moment, every inch the diplomat in his knee-length dress coat, tawny brown and in the newest style. He seemed travel-weary after his recent return from the Netherlands but still slightly aglow, basking in his notoriety for the part he played at Ryswick, as well as in the flickering firelight.

'I simply never saw it coming,' I replied. 'With the little ones, with Walt and Davy – just babes, Matthew. And with our babes there are always fears. We are taught to expect the perils our little ones must face. The risks. Most of them anyway. To steel ourselves against their fragile mortality. And Joseph? Almost forty. No great age but no longer young either. And Madras. One in five, you remember. A minor miracle that we survived, you and me. So we learn to put our grief away in a box lest it kills us too. Even then, there are the maudlin times. That awful black emptiness.'

In the hallway outside, the Maysmore clock chimed twelve and, from the floor above, squeals of laughter and the clatter of my youngest daughter's playthings.

'The big task, my dear, is to keep alive the memory of them as they had been in health and happiness.'

'Rather than relish the fact they have gone to a better place?'

I know that must be true, for the holy scriptures tell it so, but the thought has rarely given me comfort.

'Perhaps,' he said, 'I spent too much time with Sathiri to put much faith in that concept.'

We were both silent a moment in memory of her and I filled the void by pouring more tea while, upstairs, Ursula's rowdiness simply served to make our own moment of mumchance even more pronounced.

'I have been good at that,' I said at last. 'At rubbing out the worst images of their deaths.'

'Truly, Catherine?'

I had almost choked on the words, for it was a lie, and he could see it. The filthy serpent's fangs buried in Walter's beautiful face. The wet and lifeless bundle that Elihu brought back from the burial ground. My regular nightmares. How could those ever fade or soften, even for an hour?

'Well, perhaps not Walt. But Davy and Joseph? With them I can cloak the final days more readily. Be more rational. Remember them in the best of times.'

'Not Richard though, I collect.'

'There was nothing to prepare me for Rich. I imagined if I could just bring them through their childhoods, see them grow to adults, somehow all would be well in this modern world of ours, the race would be run – that they would all be there to comfort me at my own dying bedside.'

'Life is rarely thus ordered, I fear. The Almighty seems to relish considerable quantities of chaos.'

'But so much death,' I said. 'Walter.' I saw him grimace at my boy's name and I knew the reason, but pressed on, all the same. 'Joseph. Davy. Papa. My older brothers, John and Walter Junior. Richard. Mama. Even when I went to visit Joseph's sister Joanne, it was to find her bereaved only a few weeks before. As though death stalks me.'

'And now Thomas.'

'And now Thomas,' I repeated. Last month. Another journey to Wrexham for his burial at St. Giles.

'I liked the fellow.'

'He was certainly precious to Elihu. Far more than just a brother, he always said.'

I had liked him too, still feel some remorse for having deliberately opened his eyes to Elihu's philandering with his harlots. The knowledge had changed him. His abject horror that Jeronima is Jewish – as though this somehow compounded the thing.

'You've written – to Elihu?' He took up his pipe once more, carried it to the fireplace and tapped out the plug.

'It will go on the first ship to Madras. Though I imagine Mistress Nicks will perhaps have offered him some deeper sense of condolence.'

'You said so without any hint of rancour. I see that I find you changed, madam.'

'In a few things perhaps.'

'Not Seaton though?' He pointed with the pipe's stem at the tobacco pot upon the mantle shelf. 'Would you mind?' he asked.

'The reason I keep it,' I told him. 'That, now and again, some gentleman of my acquaintance might fill the house with that blessed essence. But Seaton? Wadham's thief-takers have torn this city apart. No sign of him.'

And so they had. Every place with any association to the Jacobite traitors or their families. Nothing.

'Baker gave me most of the details. She can talk now?'

He filled the pipe's bowl, took a spill from the hearth, lighting it from the flames.

'A little better. But so disfigured.' I shuddered at the thought. 'We nearly lost her too. Infection in that awful wound. Sweet Jesu, Matthew, I have never seen anything like it.'

'And do we have any clue to reason for his attack?'

I thought once more about my stupidity. That fellow in Mister Hall's emporium – the one Katherine Nicks had seen at Devonshire House and who had now seen she and I together.

'She tried to explain,' I said. 'Finally wrote it down. It was quick and it was vicious. With one slash of his knife he simply said: "This for your treachery." With the second: "And this for Parrish's harlot." Me, of course. Then, as she lay bleeding, a final threat: "Tell her it will be soon." Nothing more.'

'You're in great danger, my dear.'

'I am well protected. Wadham. His fellows. My pocket pistol.'

'You keep it with you?'

'Of course.'

'And Katherine – still with her sister?'

Matthew took his seat again.

'At St. Mary Axe, yes.'

'Does he know?'

'My husband? She forbids me from mentioning it. Says she will write to tell him simply that she has had a minor accident – not serious but sufficient, for now, to keep her from pursuing his business.'

'It's the very devil we've not been able to bring Seaton to justice.'

'It is her obsession. Revenge. When she lay on the table at Barts, that saw-bones working on her poor face, I expected she would despise me, blame me, rightly, for bringing this calamity down upon her. But instead she looked at me with something else in those coal-black eyes. It was only when she could speak again that I understood. She expects me to be the instrument of her vengeance, has sworn me to that endeavour. Besides, I have my own score to settle – the damage he caused to my dearest Ursi.'

Poor Ursula. Yet in truth I was thinking more about Seaton's attack on Susannah, the way I myself had been handled by the creature. Those entirely private matters I would not share with him or any other man.

'Bless her,' he said, oblivious to those images that now crowded my brain. 'When you wrote, I was beside myself that I wasn't here for you. I'm sorry. How is your daughter now?'

'The same. The doctors expect no change. Yet she is always bright and cheerful. A consolation, is it not? That she is at least happy. And you could hardly have been here when he struck.'

'Of course. But still… And the little one a happy child, a blessing, as you say. I must meet her.'

I glanced up at the ceiling, the flaking plaster coming down like gently falling snow, through the pipe smoke's sweet fug, every time the child thumped and banged her way across the floor above.

'It will be difficult to avoid, my dear,' I laughed. 'Can you not hear her? She will appear, bidden or otherwise, by and by. I am amazed Ellen has managed to keep her entertained so long.'

He smiled, but then his face hardened, as I had seen it transformed on occasions in the past.

'But Seaton,' he said. 'You are not the only ones with accompts to balance. If he's not in London, where shall you seek him?'

'First, Matthew, I would wish to settle matters between us. You and me.'

'Are they not settled?'

'You come back from Ryswick where you have helped negotiate not one but six treaties bringing Europe peace for the first time in nine years. Peace with France, my dear. Is that not prime?'

'You know it cannot last. The ink was barely dry before they had begun to argue again, about who should succeed King Carlos. Within a couple of years the Bourbons and the Hapsburgs will be at each other's throats all over again, laying claim to the Spanish throne, England in the thick of it once more.'

'Still, for now, it is peace. You, home again. And we have not seen each other for seven years, exchanged only the most formal of letters, and here you are, turned up on my threshold unannounced to take tea as though nothing had transpired. Yet when you left for The Hague there was a coldness between us I would wish to resolve.'

'Seven years, my dear. Is that not sufficient to thaw whatever you perceive may have been the problem? Though I should tell you that, for my part, I recall nothing that could have given you cause for your perception.'

'Seven years practice at the diplomat's dark arts, Matthew. You are become Machiavelli incarnate, I see. A dissembler, sirrah. For I perceive you remember perfectly well. You were able to forgive me for my betrayal of *Senhor* de Paiva...'

He took a long and thoughtful draw on the pipe, gazed a moment the ceiling, which still trembled from Ursi's raucous pleasures.

'We were all so much younger, were we not?' he said, finally. 'And it is no small matter, to be threatened with implication in regicide – those dwarf Gentue children, the Poison Nut seeds.'

'There was far more. The threat he could arrange to have the finger pointed at my father too.'

'The devil! And threats seeming all the more credible in view of everything transpired since then. I see that. Your impossible predicament. A momentary weakness, and a rare one for you, my dear.'

'Still, a weakness. A wicked sin. But one that, at the time, you thought I tried to hide behind the secrets I kept about Walter.'

'There is no need for this. The truth is that I have felt like a scrub since I left for The Hague. Long before, in truth. Even when I lay in my cot, wounded by that murdering scoundrel's blade. All the way home from Madras. Yet I could not bring myself to discuss it. And especially not to set it down in cold ink. But I knew. The fact you could not even share the thing with Sathiri. The sheer horror you must have gone through.'

There, the chasm opened afresh, and I could not stop the tears from flowing.

'I thought I had done enough,' I sobbed, 'to pay for my wickedness, to settle accounts for de Paiva's death.'

'Catherine, you helped bring to justice some of the very rogues, confederates of Seaton's, who paid to see Jacques killed. For the work he was doing, to help finance our preparations. The debt is paid, my dear, with a considerable dividend. Wherever Jacques de Paiva's soul may now wander, I am sure he knows your part in avenging his murder. And he knows, too, that you're not guilty for his death. That, madam, is on Seaton's slate.'

'Yet he sits upon my conscience, all the same. And now – oh, the irony. Katherine Nicks sits there beside him. Perhaps if Seaton can be brought to the gallows…'

'If not in London, where might he venture? Back to India? And, if so, is that not more reason to warn your husband?'

'Or my son. Joseph Junior is vulnerable out there too. There is evil in Seaton's heart we could never have imagined, Matthew.'

'I can imagine it well enough. Before he pays the ultimate price I shall wring the truth from him about the Roundsmen's raid and the way Sathiri was taken from us.'

'Or whether Elihu deliberately left us so undefended that day?'

The thought still haunted me though, by now, I had rather come to believe my suspicions fanciful.

'I had given up considering that possibility,' he said. 'Happy, I suppose, to close the thing. Easier to focus upon Seaton. For Sathiri, of course. But yes, for Puckle too. Sawcer, of course.'

'Kendal the jeweller?'

'I had forgotten. Kendal, as well. Forgotten, as I say. But then all this about the mysterious deaths of your husband's accusers. It reached me, through Baker.'

'Those charges are dropped,' I said, feeling an unaccountable urge to defend Elihu at least this far. 'And I never set much store by them.'

'I hope you're right, my dear. Yet I shall put Seaton to the question anyway. Though I shall at least await your husband's reaction to Seaton's latest evil.'

'But Mistress Nicks is forthright about this. Elihu not to be told. The strange thing? That I now feel myself in her debt rather than the other way around. She has sworn me to avenge her and she has sworn me to silence. In any case, I think not India. It is almost as though – well, that I can sense Seaton's presence. Still here, hidden in some priest's hole.'

He pondered this for a moment, ran his fingers along the back of the settle as Katherine Nicks had once done, so long ago.

'It is very fine,' he said, 'the boulle-work.'

'Jensen,' I said. 'But I suspect you could do better.'

'A long time since I turned my hand to the chisel. I fear I should make a terrible shambles of it now. It takes all my time to pen the occasional couplet here and there.'

'You see, Matthew? A dissembler.' I reached over to the occasional table tucked away beside my chair, on the opposite side of the hearth, waved the book at him. His latest collection, *Progress and Prospero*, published last year with the help of so many subscriptions – my own included.

He laughed.

'And you have the temerity, Mistress, to accuse me of simply turning up on your threshold for no good reason. Why not with the simple intent to offer my most heart-felt thanks for your generous patronage?'

'Mine and a hundred others, sirrah. Have you so much time on your hands now? That you might take tea with each of your admirers?'

'What have you heard?'

'Nothing more than the rest of London. Matthew Parrish, poet and heroic diplomat of the Ryswick Treaties. The gossip-mongers setting your name alongside – how many is it, Matthew?' I began to count them on my fingers. 'Flanders Jenny. Betty Semple. Annie Duncan. Have I missed any?'

'Gossip-mongering, as you say.'

It was banter, a veneer of the carefree, though each of us knew, I think, it was little more than light relief while we respectively pondered the more profound crossroads at which we had arrived.

'Within every grain of gossip, sirrah,' I said, 'lies a glimpse of the gospel.'

'I always knew I should regret writing that couplet,' he laughed. 'But would you have me repudiate those fine ladies you have named?'

'So it is true,' I said. I attempted levity but I think perhaps I failed and that my voice, at least, may have conveyed some hint of resentment. Jealousy even. And he regarded me seriously for a moment before he answered,

'Perhaps, after all, I need to set the motivation for my visit more plainly upon the table. To make certain there remains no coldness between us.' Oh, how my spirits lifted to hear him say so. 'To offer my condolences in person, as well,' he went on, dampening my excitement again just as quickly. 'To assure myself of your family's well-being. And, finally, this business of Seaton. I have climbed rather in the world, Catherine. No longer junior to Captain Baker. Our fortunes rather reversed, in fact.'

Where was this leading? I wondered. When he had arrived I had thought carefully about the possible impropriety of meeting alone this way. But we had been friends for such a time and never a hint of anything shameful between us, despite whatever Elihu may have imagined. Yet his arrival here today had coincided, strangely, with some wanderlust in my morality. The truth? That I take the sanctity of marriage seriously, as the scriptures require me. Elihu's lack of fidelity does nothing to diminish this, though my decision to marry him, to endow my sons with a man in their life, should have been equally relevant for our girls. A man in their life. A man in mine too.

'Our worlds have changed, have they not?' I said. 'Since Madras.'

'Considerably.' He smiled, a sad smile plunging us both, I believe, into painful memories of Sathiri once more. But then he brightened. 'Why, whoever might have believed I would now find you in partnership with our old friend Sir William?'

Oh, the guilt. More than guilt, the moment between us lost.

'You shall not shame me,' I said, 'with that particular wickedness, Mister Parrish. I was, if you recall, persuaded by you, and you alone, to help gather the evidence against him – to help bring him down as Governor. But he has suffered little as a consequence. And the truth? He seems a different man here in London than we knew in Madras. I certainly owe him for the help he gave Joseph Junior, his post with John Company.'

'And Puckle's death? You're satisfied now he played no part?'

'I am no more satisfied, one way or the other, than I was at the time. Yet it all seems so distant, does it not?'

'I shall get it out of Seaton,' he said, 'before I kill the wretch.'

His matter-of-fact manner, that *sang-froid* I had seen before, shocked me as it always did. The other Matthew Parrish. The man whose attack – many would say ruthless attack – on Condore had made him Parrish *sahib*, Parrish the Devil.

'Perhaps leave it to our thief-takers,' I said, 'and the lawful executioners.'

He shrugged away my concern.

'Perhaps you're right.' He smiled, though it was less than convincing. 'And anyway, first we have to find the devil. But a priest's hole, you say? I wonder...'

213

Matthew Parrish has written that personal loss is like a vortex, a whirlpool, which may suck you down, which spins you slowly around at its outer edge when first you encounter its grip. Yes, slowly. So you remain convinced you can survive this thing, that it may be possible to extricate yourself from its clutches. You struggle against it, though devoid of enthusiasm. Lethargic, the immediacy of staying afloat a cruel diversion. Not quite believing that soon you will be beyond the point of no return, spiralling into the depths of sheer despair. And personal loss need not imply bereavement but, perhaps, those more subtle immersions that have afflicted me today. Loss, all the same.

But first, that terrible winter, which paralysed so much and still seems to have no end in sight. Those awful storms in September and October that buried an entire Hebridean island and drowned so many of its inhabitants under drifting sands, then smashed apart towns and villages all along the east coast and the littoral of our Hollander cousins.

Thus it was that when, early in November, a new prognosticator's almanack joined the plethora of those already published each year, this one compiled by a certain Francis Moore, former astrologer and renowned charlatan at the court of the late King Charles, there were queues at each and every bookshop in the city waiting for the stocks to arrive. The reason? Because Moore claimed to have special insight to the effect of the planets and constellations upon our weather.

And though I normally mock such nonsense, perhaps on this occasion I misjudged. For he correctly predicted the gales, one after the other, the sleet freezing our bones through late December, and the deep snows that trapped us at home for two weeks at Christmas, kept Benjamin in Oxford, kept Kate and Annie in their beds with a sweating sickness. The Thames turned to solid ice and parts of the North Sea too. Whole families frozen to death in the Highlands of Scotland, and added to the misery of the famine that has crippled that country with so many summers of blighted crops. But many folk perishing from the cold here in the south as well. And this month yet more snow, hailstones like musket balls day after day, so that preachers on the streets, whenever they are able to venture forth, and folk are foolish enough to risk stopping to listen, are forecasting imminent Armageddon or Judgement Day.

Yet, in the midst of all that, two weeks before the weather closed in, there was brief respite, a se'nnight of crisp but brilliant December weather coinciding with my visit to Kensington Palace.

'So it is true,' I whispered to Streynsham as he waited his turn nervously among his personal entourage in the King's Drawing Room, the sun beaming in through the high windows, motes of dust dancing in the air where it bounced against the deep red cut-velvet wall hangings. 'About the sun shining upon the righteous.'

Trite, was it not? Yet his discomfiture was infectious.

'Simply my husband's efforts being duly appreciated,' snapped his wife, Elizabeth. She had expressed some surprise – no, surprise hardly does it justice – that myself and Matthew Parrish had been invited. Why had Streynsham not simply told her in advance? I have no idea but it plainly irked the shrew. No sign of her Jacobite brother Peter, I noted, though the children were all present: the little girl, Anne, who must be six now; the boy, about three; and the new babe in its nursemaid's arms. Fine children. And Elizabeth was correct, of course. This about Streynsham's service to the Crown being rewarded. For this is now our modern new world, in which the feudal tenures so recently associated with knighthood are swept away – part of the compromise between Parliament and exiled King Charles within which the Restoration had been foisted upon us – the concept become a personal dignity that can be conferred upon folk of merit for their civic duty rather than their military might.

'And Sir William?' Matthew enquired, as the Yeomen of the Guard patrolled that threshold through which the present king would soon appear.

'Unable to attend, it seems,' Streynsham told him, adjusting his peruke for the umpteenth time. 'A pity. It would have made a very suitable double celebration.'

The invitation to attend Streynsham's investiture had arrived almost on the day when news reached us that the king and Parliament had finally accepted the proposal for the establishment of the New East India Company – both Streynsham and Sir William Langhorn favoured among its Directors.

'He cannot have been best pleased,' said Matthew, 'that the old company is left in place. Heaven only knows how it will play out.'

'Interim arrangement only,' Streynsham told him. 'Three years. And the warhorses among the old Directors know they're under the direct scrutiny of the Crown now. One false step, one hint at obfuscation...'

Well, Streynsham is the gentleman who would know, one of the principal architects of this quiet revolution, along with two other new Directors here to receive their knighthoods as well, Bateman and Harrison. The architects, yes. Along with the absent Sir William Langhorn, of course. And, across the hall, there was that other Sir William – Cavendish, Duke of Devonshire – with whom so much of our story seems entwined. There among the other peers of the realm in their scarlet, their ermine and their full-bodied wigs.

'Did you hear?' Matthew asked, noting the direction of my gaze. 'The good Duke's youngest son, James, and his grand tour?'

'Oh,' I said, 'the Duke writes to me almost daily with word of his sons and their various perambulations.'

'Sarcasm rather becomes you, Catherine,' he scolded me. But I caught the appraising look in Elizabeth Master's eye, as though she imagined something deeper in our banter than was evident upon the surface.

'Your husband still in Madras, my dear?' she said. A simple enough question but, my goodness, how loaded it seemed.

I had expected last summer's letters from Elihu to give some hint at his return. But no, presumably Jeronima de Paiva and young Don Carlos must occupy him too much.

'I fear so, Elizabeth.' I stressed the familiarity, saw her flinch that I should be so fro'ward. 'As your own husband knows only too well, the tribulations for Old John Company's governors facing false accusation can be severe and time-consuming.'

'I find myself blessed,' she smiled, 'that Streynsham was able to deal with his accusers from here in London. Of course, there was so much less to keep him in India.'

The bitch. Does she think she may trifle with me? Had we not been in the presence of so many…

'And James Cavendish?' I said to Matthew, while Streynsham diverted his wife with some frippery about the source of that fine material in which the Yeomen of the Guard were garbed.

'Ah, young Cavendish. Finds himself invited to the Duke of Burgundy's wedding, and imagine his surprise – brushing shoulders with none other than our little-lamented former monarch, Catholic James Stuart himself.'

'Truly?'

'Indeed. The rogue had the temerity to enquire after His Grace's health. Swore he hoped one day to be reconciled with the boy's father.'

How old is James Cavendish now? A similar age to my Benjamin, I had thought, when I first saw him those years ago. And thoughts of Benjamin inevitably reminded me of Richard, so that I was struck that day, as I have been on so many occasions in the past, how impossible it is, even in a crowded room, not to feel utterly alone in the presence or recollection of untimely death.

'If those two were ever reunited,' said Streynsham, dragging me back into the here and now, his wife suddenly busy quelling the impatient wailing of their small son, 'it would only be to allow James Stuart the signing of Devonshire's death warrant. God forbid he should ever regain the crown.'

The crown, I thought, which he lost through the action of Sir William Cavendish perhaps more than any other.

'I may jest about it,' I said, 'but he did indeed remember me.

A brief greeting, at St. Paul's.'

Ten days earlier. The first of those upon which the sun broke through. A great and public celebration of the Ryswick treaties, Matthew one of those mentioned specifically during the service. But that greeting from the Duke of Devonshire – well, I must be honest, he leered at me in the most licentious manner, yet whether he actually recognised me or not is a matter for debate. Leered at me. As though I were some chit of a serving wench. For heaven's sake, I am almost forty-seven!

So, that was the investiture. And then, early in January, news of the fire that all but destroyed the Palace of White Hall. There had been other fires in the past, of course, just one of the many reasons the king had all but abandoned its sprawl – the largest royal residence in Europe, they say – in favour of Kensington Palace after Queen Mary's death. So it is unlikely to have been a target for Jacobite arsonists, though that did not quell the rumours. And our associate, the Duke of Devonshire, could so nearly have perished in the flames. But oh, the loss of such treasures. Michelangelo. Hans Holbein. Bernini. So much more. Not that humble folk like myself would ever have been permitted to see them, but even so...

The thing was still on everybody's lips when, at the end of January, and despite the foul weather, I was surprised by that sudden arrival of Elford, come all the way from Smyrna. A welcome-home dinner, therefore, to coincide with Benjamin's return from St. John's College. I had invited Matthew Parrish as well – and, as was typical of him, he arrived somewhat late, making a great commotion out in the hallway while he shrugged off his topcoat, his shoulder belt and court sword.

'Forgive me,' he said as he took his seat at the table. 'And welcome home, Elford. A long time.'

'Twelve years, sir. Yet I did not expect to find you at our family's table.'

Matthew made an attempt at levity.

'I should have been happier,' he said, 'to find myself here a little earlier. For what have I missed?' Fletchley and the new maid, Martha, were busy removing the first platters. 'Parsnips and oysters? French mutton?'

But it all fell on stony ground, Elford's face hard as mahogany. 'Elford...' I said.

'Mama?'

Where has my boy gone? The tearful little fellow I had rescued from the Fort St. George sea wall the day Akbar was lost. His resentment at being sent away from me so young. The struggle to regain his affection after I came back to England. That night when Seaton left the dead infant in my room and Elford had called out, terrifying me with the thought that he too might be put in danger. The tussle he had got into at the Theatre Royal with Peter Legh and his seditious friends – and when was that? Five years ago. But then he had sailed for Smyrna and a silence had fallen between us.

'Mister Parrish is our guest, sirrah,' I reminded him.

'You must become accustomed to it, Elford,' said Anne. 'Mister Parrish is so frequently Mama's guest these days.'

Eleven, for pity's sake. Eleven, but the tongue of an old hag. A viper's tongue.

'It's true your mama invited me, Elford, but I should have come to see you in any case. Condolences, sirrah. I have fond memories of your brother. But if I'm intruding...'

'La!' Annie laughed. 'You was there all that time ago? Prime. No wonder Papa were always so vexed by your presence when we was little.'

'So far as I recall,' Elford sneered, 'your Papa was vexed at just about everything, Nan.'

Yes, that would be Elford's recollection of Elihu. He never really took to my new husband.

'Hush, Nan,' Katie scolded her sister. 'Mister Parrish was always kind to us.'

Anne slammed her knife down upon the table. Petulant, defiant as ever and I half-stood from the table, knowing I was within an inch of striking her. All that absurd and stale animosity building in me afresh, that Annie had somehow drained the life that should have been Davy's.

219

'You will go to your room, miss,' I spat at her. 'Ellen,' I yelled. 'Ellen.' The housekeeper appeared at once in the dining chamber's doorway and I suspect she had been listening outside in the hallway. 'Please escort Anne to her room and make sure she stays there until I tell you otherwise.'

The girl's face crumpled but she knew better than to defy me further.

'Family bliss,' said Elford, as Annie was escorted from the room, her little shoulders shaking with the sobs she had hidden from me so well – that she always hides from me. But, Sweet Jesu, how I wish things could be different between us.

'And normally,' Benjamin waved his fork at his older brother, 'it is so. You are a disruptive influence, sir.' They both laughed. 'And Joseph? You've heard from him?'

'I have written, of course,' Elford replied. Well, at least he has taken the trouble to do so, even if he has not bothered to be in contact with his mama. 'But it is all so much,' Elford went on. 'Richie. Grandpapa. Uncle John. And then Grandmother.'

Elford had not written to me even though he had sat at the dying bedside of my brother John in Smyrna. No, it was Sir Richard Levett who had broken that news to the family, and this still rankled with me.

'Our family becoming thin, where once it was replete,' said Benjamin with some haste – knowing, I think, I was about to say something I might regret. 'Yet blessed are they that mourn, for they shall be comforted.'

'Matthew Five?' Parrish laughed. 'How apt. And how is Joseph?' he asked Elford. 'Still enjoying the Coromandel Coast?'

'Working, I believe,' said Elford, terse and impolite, 'to restore the wealth he believes – and I believe too – we were denied by Mister Yale.'

'Please,' I told him. 'Not this again.'

'I collect, Mama, you might not be happy with the subject. Your hasty settlement with Mister Yale, after all, that left us with so little of Papa's estate.'

'A settlement,' I said, more abruptly than I had intended, 'designed for no other purpose than to protect you. All of you, Elford. And spare a thought for your sisters, sirrah. Remember the girls.'

'Does he mean Papa?' Kate asked me with child-like curiosity.

'My Papa?' Ursula's simple face beamed. She loved to hear tales of the father for whom she had obviously not the slightest recollection.

'Yes, your Papa. Now, eat your dinner.'

Fletchley and Martha with the fresh dishes, and I spooned out some of the stewed potato, the boiled snipe, onto my daughter's plate.

'And Grandmama,' I heard Elford telling his brother, as I helped arrange the other serving trenchers, 'was hardly generous.'

'A gold Jacobus is no small thing,' said Benjamin, reaching for the roasted pike. 'And our share of twenty pounds? I prefer to make my own way in the world. "*Wealth gotten by vanity shall be diminished: but he that gathereth by labour shall increase.*" And your own investments, brother? Your stock in Levett and Company must be worth a small fortune by now.'

Elford pursed his lips, as though he would make reply, but then thought better of it.

'Well?' I said. 'Your investments?"'

'Perhaps fortune has been less than kind, Elford?' Matthew tried to prompt him, then turned to me. 'After all, madam, of all people you must understand the fragility of trade.'

I needed no such reminder. Sir William Langhorn and myself had established a significant reputation for fairness in the drafting of those maritime assurance policies, the risk under which we wrote our names, pledged sums of our excess income against the loss, capture, fire or other contingencies faced by merchant vessels and their cargoes – in exchange for a handsome percentage of the profits should the voyage be successful. We, and others like us, trading through Mister Lloyd's coffee house, could hardly compete with Amsterdam's Chamber of Insurance and Average but this aspect of London's commerce was growing. And so were the benefits to both myself and Sir William. At least, until the loss of the *Cara* last year.

'Something I am due to discuss with Sir William, it seems,' I said. 'A summons to Charlton House.'

'Is that what you call it these days, brother?' Benjamin laughed. 'A fragile trade?'

'Thick as thieves, then?' Matthew said to me. 'You and Sir William?' And then he muttered under his breath. 'Can this be the same man to whom you bade fair riddance when he left Madras?'

'Trade is trade,' I replied, then turned to Elford. 'What does he mean?' I said. 'Benjamin rarely speaks for the sake of it. What is it he knows about your business that I do not?'

'Elford's secret.' Katie smirked at him, and I recalled the way my brother John had squandered so much of his wealth.

'As Benjamin says,' Elford snapped at me. 'Merely some ill fortune.'

'Gaming? Is it gaming?'

'Another lecture, Mama?' he said. And he too stood from the table, cast down his napkin. 'I shall be in my room. But you should know, Mama, we are decided. Joseph and myself. Benjamin too. We are seeking legal opinion about a claim against your husband.'

'Great heavens.' I buried my head in my hands as he strode from the dining room.

'He is young, Catherine,' said Matthew. 'And Smyrna is full of temptations, they tell me. At least he is home safe for now.'

'But a legal claim. God's hooks, Benjamin, could you not have warned me? You think two years in sizarship at Oxford somehow qualifies you to judge that you have a case?' He shrugged his shoulders, then returned to some child's word game he had been playing with Kate and Ursula. 'And how long,' I said, 'will Elford remain at home, sirrah?'

'How long will any of us, my dear?'

I experienced a sudden frisson of gloom.

'You are going abroad again, Mister Parrish?' said Benjamin. How does he know these things?

'I fear so,' Parrish replied, then turned to me. 'I'm sorry, Mistress. I had wanted to break the news differently. I am bound for France, it seems.'

'We shall miss him,' said Ursi in that slow drawl of hers. 'Shall we not, Mama?'

'I had hoped you might escort me to Charlton House,' I said. 'Not the easiest of journeys.'

'Not in this weather,' said Benjamin. 'But I can accompany you, Mama.'

I saw Matthew flinch but then his face set again into its more customary and affable form.

'A summons from Sir William Langhorn is not to be taken lightly, my dear. If he wishes a private business rencounter, perhaps better to go alone – apart from your servants, of course.'

'I promised to give that some serious consideration, but as I write these lines and recall the conversations, the only thing filling my head is the sense of loss at Matthew's news – that he is leaving me again. As he had said to me himself, personal loss need not imply bereavement but, perhaps, those a more subtle immersion, like this one. Yet his going away leaves me bereft, all the same.

It happened this way – again if I have remembered it all correctly or, rather, if I have not warped the doubtful memories to suit my conscience.

There had been another message from Sir William Langhorn. Imperative I should attend him, he said, at Charlton House. Any time during the following week – this week just gone. And Matthew had been similarly insistent upon my complying with any summons from that quarter as a matter of urgency. It had begun to assume an air of mystery and if Mister Parrish had still been available I should have pressed him to see whether, as I suspected, he knew more about this arrangement than he allowed.

But the weather has improved a little and the arrangements made. Thornton the coachman would convey me to Greenwich by road – the state of the river still too perilous to contemplate the wherry service so far downstream – and I would be accompanied by little Ursi, an excursion I hoped she would enjoy. I sent word to Sir William last Sunday to let him know I would be setting out early the following morning, leaving him no time to gainsay my plans – suggest, perhaps, I should not bring my daughter.

'How long will it take, Mama?' she said as we rattled away from the house.

I tucked the blankets more tightly about her.

'Depends how long to cross the bridge,' I told her. How far? Eight miles, according to Thornton. But that could take at least half a day, perhaps more. 'It will be so worth it though, sweet pea. A very grand house, they say. But first we have to stop somewhere else.'

To St. Mary Axe and Katherine Nicks. I have seen her only once during this harsh winter, just after Christmas-tide, and I still shudder at the memory. Then, a mere eight months after Seaton's attack upon her, the fearsome wound still far from healed, the stitching that held her face together so long it had dragged the left side of her mouth permanently awry, as though it were now a simple continuation of the cut, and adding a slobbering speech impediment to the disfigurement of her features. So we had conversed hardly at all, myself prattling about the foul weather, updating her on the non-existent progress in finding her assailant, mulling over his purpose, and sharing those snippets of gossip relating to Streynsham's investiture. But I had taken her a gift, at least. It was a piece I had among the many of Joseph's sketches brought back with me and which had remained largely untouched ever since. Indeed, I did not know this particular drawing even existed – yet a carefully conceived outline of Elihu. Almost a parody of his features. From when? After little Walter's death, that much was certain. A good likeness though, and I had troubled Dawson the framer to mount it accordingly. But nothing. Not even a comment from her. A strange gift, perhaps, I now tell myself, though my intention was honest enough.

'Who lives here?' Ursula asked, as Thornton drew the horses to a halt outside the house.

'Mistress Nicks,' I said. 'You remember her? Another Katherine. But she had a very bad accident last year and may not be able to receive us.'

'Will she die?'

'I hope not, Ursi.'

It was true, I could no longer wish her ill. In fact, I found her in better health than I had expected. Her sister, Mistress Tombes, was polite – just – and ushered us into a neat parlour where Katherine was working on her accompts, though she quickly hid her face within a long and diaphanous scarlet veil as soon as we were announced.

'Is Mistress Nicks a Gentue, Mama?' Ursi whispered, clinging tight to my skirts.

'Where does she get such things?' I said. 'A mere babe in arms when we sailed. She would not know a Gentue if she over fell one.'

225

'Sisters, I suppose,' replied Katherine, her knuckles wiping at the dribble behind the veil. 'Or your boys.'

'Benjamin, I imagine. All Madras this, Madras that. Though he will never go there. Even if he were inclined, I should not allow it. And trade?' I pointed at her ledgers and she gave a nod of her head, glanced at the wall too, and I saw there the portrait of Elihu.

'Thank you,' she managed to say.

'He will be pleased you have worked so diligently on his behalf.'

'Is that Papa?' said Ursula, finally separating herself from my side. 'He is very fat!'

Katherine ruffled my daughter's hair, earned herself one of Ursi's most scornful scowls in return. And I thought how much she must miss her own children. All this time away from them. They will be strangers when they are finally reunited.

'Dear child,' said Katherine. 'Seaton. The damage he has done her.'

'There are many far worse off. And what she lacks in wits is far outweighed by her nature.'

'Elihu – he knows?'

'He does not. How could I explain it all in a letter? He would never hear a word said against Seaton. So, what would I say? And you? This...?'

I waved my hand towards her face.

'Same. Better he does not know.'

'Then we share another problem. For he cannot remain at Fort St. George forever. And when he returns – well, the evidence of his own eyes. You. Little Ursi.'

'Easier for me,' she said.

A quick resurgence of my old resentments. Was she so sure of him that she believed he would not be affected by her disfigurement? I supposed she might be right.

'Well, I have written to him about Thomas's death.' And having said it, I immediately felt foolish. 'You will have done the same, of course.'

She nodded again.

'I am glad,' she murmured. 'Your visit. And now? Home?'

'We are bound for Greenwich. Charlton House. A summons from Governor Langhorn. More business.'

I saw she had dropped the porcupine quill pen she had been using on the accompts.

'With the little one?' The impediment made it difficult to discern the emotion behind her question, but it seemed to me it was more than casual concern about the journey.

'What is it?' I said.

'Nothing,' she replied, and turned back to her work, as neat a dismissal as I have ever received. 'Nothing at all. Dionysia will see you out.'

Later than I should have liked, Ursi asleep in my arms, we finally arrived at Charlton itself, the village green just visible through the gathering dusk and then the high brick wall, the archway into the grounds, and the gravel beneath hoof and wheel until we finally came to rest before the grand porch jutting stubbornly from a façade stretching away both to left and right.

I had expected the whole place to be ablaze with lights, yet it was mostly in darkness, still and sombre, a single manservant shambling down the steps from the front doors, a curt welcome and Thornton left to unload our travelling chest.

'Wake up, my darling,' I whispered in Ursula's ear as I climbed with her in the fellow's shadow.

'Don't like it here,' she told me, rubbing at her little eyes. 'Can we go home?'

'Tomorrow, Ursi. We go home tomorrow.'

'No, now!' she insisted, and began to cry pitifully. But by then we were inside the entrance hall, dimly lit and the dark oak panelling adding to the profound gloom.

'Sir William is at home, I take it?' I said.

'Busy in the library, ma'am. But if you would follow me to your room he should be pleased if you might dine with him at seven.'

'I need to settle my daughter,' I explained, and caught his look of disapproval. 'And I did explain my daughter would be with me...'

I left the end of the sentence hanging, almost a question, in the hope the old cove would have the manners to at least name himself.

'Archer, Mistress. Though there is no separate room prepared for the child. Oh no, not all.'

I told him it did not matter, that Ursula would be more than happy to share my bed. Especially here. She suffers with nightmares even worse than my own, I fear. Still, I followed him through the sparsely lit hallway into the rectangular enormity housing the grand staircase.

'Are there no other servants, Archer?' I said, struggling up the first of the wide treads, lit only by a single sconce, Ursula still wailing in my arms.

'Sadly no, ma'am. If it had been possible for Sir William to receive more notice, perhaps he might have made different arrangements. But many of us are struck down with an ague and sent away to avoid spread of the illness.'

'Please,' I said. 'A moment.' I leaned against the richly ornamented balusters, catching my breath. 'Just you? For this enormous house?'

'Myself and cook alone, ma'am. Which reminds me.' He pointed back to one of the doors below. 'The dining room, Mistress Yale. Seven o' the clock?'

'Yes, I remember,' I snapped at him, as Thornton finally caught up with us, struggling with the chest, offering to carry Ursula as well. But his presence seemed to reassure her – she was fond of this densely freckled young man – and she willingly agreed to climb the stairs herself so long as she might cling to the skirts of his riding coat. Our bedchamber was on the second floor – in the state apartments, Archer explained, though it was almost impossible to discern wheth-er they warranted such distinction without daylight to illuminate them – and its only candlestick was far from sufficient to dispel Ursi's fears of demons lurking in the deep darkness of the room's corners.

'Will your daughter not join us for supper, Catherine?'

I accepted a small glass of dry sack from Archer, while my host warmed his ample backside before the equally ample hearth. Sir

228

William seemed ill at ease, however, less than his normally affable self and I could not discern whether it was due to Ursi's absence from his table or her unexpected presence in his house.

'She preferred to dine with our coachman, Sir William.'

'Servants' quarters? You permit such a thing?'

'You have no children,' I laughed, 'else you would understand.'

'No children. Nor no wife neither. Not yet.'

Not yet. Did he still have the inclination? He must be approaching seventy.

'Such a waste, sirrah.'

'You say so?' he snapped. 'Truly, you say so? I collect that there were times, my dear, when you had no such high opinion of me.' Cook had arrived with a tureen of pottage, assuring me Ursula had eaten heartily, while Sir William amused himself with some muttered irony about how supper could not properly *be* supper without the soup itself.

'I always had sincere respect,' I told him, 'for the equanimity with which you treated Black Town's disparate communities. I have seen far worse, believe me.'

'Yet there must have been gossip, must there not? Over the ladies' chatter-broth. Rumours of financial impropriety, I imagine.'

'Sir William,' I said, setting down my spoon, 'we have been acquainted again, back here in England, these eight years past. Is it not a little late for questions like these?'

'We have shared adventures, Mistress Yale, yet I wonder precisely how much you truly trust me.'

He thumped repeatedly at his chest, as though his digestion troubled him.

'You doubt my loyalty, sir? To yourself? To the Crown?'

'Ah, the Crown,' he said. 'You know what is afoot, my dear? No, of course you would not. But His Majesty, having happily licensed the New Company, now sees fit to ensure its outposts are properly within his control. Hence, yet another change of governor for Fort St. George. Higginson to be replaced. Tom Pitt already well on his way aboard the *Martha*. Strict instructions, his duty to ensure your husband's return, to demonstrate to him – through my own fine example – what might be achieved with wealth such as we have each accrued.'

Anybody might imagine that news of my husband's possible return should have excited some enthusiasm in each of us, albeit for different reasons, but it was plainly as distressful for Sir William as for myself. Yet my suspicious mind wondered whether he still had things to fear from Elihu's insinuation into London society.

'You believe Elihu will respond?'

Cook had returned to clear the soup tureen, remove our dishes to the side board, replace them with clean plates.

'Next?' said Sir William. 'The mutton pie, I believe. And the kidneys, unless this old nose deceives me. And you was saying?'

'About my husband. You think he will be persuaded? There are certain ties binding him to Madras Patnam, as you are fully aware.'

'*Senhora* de Paiva? The boy?' This was more abrupt than I had ever known him. 'I think you shall find Mister Pitt's argument most persuasive. A man like Elihu Yale does not endure the pursuit of such wealth for so long only to see it snatched away again for the sake of some doxy and his – well, you take my drift.'

'The fortune is his own, however. Or, should I say, *our* own? Mister Pitt would need to prise that wealth from him by force of arms, I fear.'

'If necessary I am certain Pitt would not balk at the challenge. But you need not trouble. Between the sweet bread and the whip we shall bring your husband home.'

Though you do not relish the prospect, I thought.

'The sweet bread?'

'A once in a lifetime offer. He is permitted to fill the *Martha*'s entire hold should he wish to do so. Any goods he may wish to transport in whatever quantity he might choose. An assurance contract guaranteeing the value plus ten per cent against almost any imaginable form of loss.'

'And I assume it shall be your name and mine written under the agreement. The purpose for your kind invitation?'

I tried my best to avoid any trace of sarcasm in this latter part.

After all, business of this sort has always been undertaken through our agents at Mister Lloyd's coffee house. So what *was* this about? I wondered.

'I took the liberty of enlisting others to underwrite this one, ma'am. I considered it more delicate not to have your own name appended. But I have a separate agreement, to be signed privately between ourselves, making it clear that, regardless of those other names, it shall be you, Mistress Yale, who shares my risk and we who shall receive both the premium plus our percentage in the event of the cargo's safe arrival in England. But that can wait until the morrow.'

'Considerate,' I smiled, and took a forkful of cook's very fine pie, even more uncertain now about the reason for his summons and his entirely singular discomfort in my company. 'And the whip?'

'A further liberty, I fear. But this is important to us. His Majesty, and the New Company's Directors, believe your husband has still a part to play. So I must tell you, my dear, that Pitt carries with him a number of denunciations that would see the tide turn once more against Elihu Yale, see him cast into gaol for a very long time indeed. Or worse.'

'Denunciations by whom?' I said, but then I remembered something from long, long ago – Sir William sailing from Fort St. George and the thing I had written in my journals. *Yes, sail into the sunset with your ill-gotten gains.* Matthew Parrish's intelligence, some of it gained through myself, about the bribes and sweeteners from which Sir William had enriched himself. Twenty thousand gold pagodas each year, was it not?'

'Ah,' he cried, 'I collect you may be thinking of another time, another place, another betrayal. And yes, Mistress Yale, the signature on our denunciations is your own.'

'I saw him, Mama! I saw him!'

Ursula was screaming, and I realised I had drifted back into sleep, still in my nightgown and seated at the gloom-cloaked desk beneath the room's heavily curtained window. I had been pondering Sir William's words, as I had done through much of the night, scribbling notes on a piece of parchment for this later transcription to my journal, and my drowsiness had left a spidery scrawl across the page. Worse, the pocket pistol, a permanent accessory to my everyday attire, always hidden within my skirts, had somehow slipped beneath my thigh so that my right leg was now entirely numb, and I almost fell as I stumbled back to the bed and my distressed daughter.

'Who did you see, sweet pea?' I threw a comforting arm around her where she sat up, wrapped in the heavy coverlet. 'Just a bad dream, I think.'

I heard the clock below strike six. How long had I been sitting there?

'It was him, Mama. That bad man again. The singing man.'

'You see?' I hugged her tighter to my breast. 'Always the same dream.'

She seemed to live it afresh each night.

'This time he was here. This time it was different. This time I was awake, Mama.'

'You would have cried out, my dear. And I should have heard, then chased him away like I always do.'

'This time I could not scream. His hand over my mouth. And then...'

'And then?' I found myself suddenly chilled to the bone. For she was right, this was different from her usual telling of the tale. I found myself quickly looking around the room, then shook my head at my own stupidity.

'And then,' she went on, 'it all went black.'

Just after sunrise – a fine though mist-shrouded morning – Thornton knocked at my door, as we had agreed, so he could take Ursula for breakfast with him in the kitchens. But she was reluctant to leave me, the memory of her frightful imaginings still with her.

Yes, unusual.

Still, she obeyed me, as she has always done, and once I had completed my own toilet and adjusted my dress – I had brought only the most amenable of my visiting attire since it was rare indeed that

232

I should have to prepare myself without the assistance of Martha – I retraced the route I thought we had taken the previous evening. From our southwest bedroom through a chamber all hung with Flemish tapestries, a panelled ceiling and a black marble fireplace. Then through the grand saloon, the full width of the house, an enormous hearth flanked by monstrous statues of Greek gods. And so to the staircase once again. But instead of descending immediately I went quietly to the heavily carved door ahead of me, listened for a moment, yet perceived only silence of the other side. I tried the handle, glanced inside and gasped. The long gallery, perhaps forty paces from one extremity to the other, six huge windows along its outer wall and, at each end, wide stained glass so that, to my right, a rainbow of blue, yellow, green and red flooded the polished floor and reflected upwards onto the strap-work ceiling. Magnificent!

One day, Mistress Yale, I said to myself, you shall have such a wonder for your own.

I ran my fingers along the oak wainscote, breathed deeply of the beeswax, listened to the echo of my own footsteps, then crossed to the farther side where, at its centre, the mid-point of all that fenestration, there was an alcove, part of the tower I had just been able to discern on our approach. Almost a miniature of those flanking the Tower of London's old keep, I had thought. A narrow spiral staircase climbed up to another and final level. The view, I decided, must be exquisite up there and, after a moment's hesitation, I determined to take a quick look.

Correct. The view superb. Just to the north, Charlton village, a deal of common land beyond and, further still, the Thames, Greenwich and neighbouring Deptford hidden by the higher ground to the north and west. On the road from that direction, in the distance, an early coach and two outriders, coming fast. Closer to the house itself, enticing glimpses of the gardens, some outbuildings and, to my surprise, a figure scurrying for the gate. Old Archer. Strange! The only manservant in the place and, from his attire, not planning to be back any time soon to wait upon his master.

There was little room up there, however, for the space was large-ly occupied by a great lamp, a huge lanthorn, of the sort, I imagine, they must employ in the lighthouses I have occasionally seen on my voyages, or those that more frequently shine from church steeples along the coast for similar purpose. Yes, I thought, this must be what it is like, perched upon a cliff's edge, a beacon for mariners lost in the darkness. I touched it – then quickly withdrew my fingers again, burned at their tips. Hot. Still hot. But why? And how? I was certain it had not been lit when I arrived.

I climbed down again, crossed the long gallery, back to the staircase, licking at my stinging fingers and hoping they would not blister. My adventure had briefly dispelled memories of Ursula's nightmare and, indeed, of Sir William's behaviour the previous evening. Yet both now returned to vex me.

'You have forged my signature?' I had said, and he gave some glib response that he had not done so personally, any more than his actions had been driven by personal motivation. In a similar way, he imagined, that my own reports to the Company in conjunction with Matthew Parrish, about his own activities, would not have been personally motivated either. But my signature on the denunciations had been so very necessary, he claimed. To make the documents more authentic, ensure that Elihu has no choice but to return.

'Duty, dear lady,' he had insisted. 'Simply duty, is it not? The greater good.'

I had questioned him further about his true purpose in bringing me here but he would not be pressed, insisting all should be revealed at the breaking of our fast. Eight o' the clock, he insisted. And, now, there was the clock itself, below, chiming that precise hour.

I chose the wrong door. Two of them, side by side at the foot of the stairs, each of the doors twelve-panelled, each panel carved by a master craftsman, and above each door a coat-of-arms. All of this I had barely noticed the night before, so ill-lit had been this charming inner section of the house. I was also mistaken into thinking the door on the right was the one I had previously taken to enter the dining room. But it was not. This was the chapel, pews along its flanks and a baptismal font at its centre. I retreated quickly, took the other door and myself to the correct place for breakfast. Again, I was shaken by how different the room appeared in daylight, the curtains thrown open, light flooding the windows and illuminating the splendour of its décor.

Sir William was already seated but his plate was empty even though the side board seemed amply supplied with platters.

'Give you joy of this fine morning, Sir William,' I beamed, in the absence of any greeting from my host. He was gripping the edges of the table and seemed deep in thought. 'I took the liberty of visiting the long gallery, noticed Archer heading for the village.'

He harrumphed loudly, then again.

'You did?' he snapped, then seemed to think better of it. 'Yes, I suppose – Catherine, there is something I should explain…'

A man's voice, behind me.

'And spoil my surprise, sirrah?'

I spun around, knowing that supercilious tone of old. Ursula's singing man. Seaton, ethereal as ever, slithering from a place of concealment, the recess at the far side of the dining room's great fire hearth. He was armed, I saw, a baldrick over his right shoulder and, from its hanger, a sheathed rapier.

'How could you?' I spat at Langhorn. 'You lured me here for this?'

'Little choice, I fear.'

'Oh, don't believe him,' Seaton laughed. 'Sir William had plenty of choice. Now, my sweet, shall you not partake of this fine repast? See, we have cold meats a-plenty. Fresh bread and butter. And a pot of new-brewed chocolate, I collect.'

He gestured towards the breakfast platters with a gloved right hand. I was quaking inside, hoping beyond hope he might not know of Ursula's presence, but at the same moment certain she had imagined nothing – that he had truly been in our bedchamber. Still, I forced myself to laugh as gaily as I might.

'God's hooks,' I said. 'Did I truly damage the hand so badly when I bit into your devil's hide, Seaton?'

'How ungracious,' he replied, looking down at the glove. 'Did I not allow you to take back the locket?'

I touched the jewel at my neck without intending to do so.

'Allow?'

'Of course. You think I would have left that flea-pit without a watch being kept? And you found my playthings. Stole those, too. They amused you, Catherine? Excited you, perhaps?'

Oh, I remembered them. The scourge. The cilice garter. And I remembered the broadsides he had shown me, that day in Madras when he had persuaded a younger, more gullible Catherine to betray Jacques de Paiva – anti-Papist broadsides displaying the vile practices of Romish nuns, broadsides he claimed to have discovered in my home, broadsides he promised would incriminate my father in seditious activity. And I began to sense the start of a red rage rising within me.

'You set your depraved hands upon my daughter,' I cried. 'You creature!'

'I merely lulled her back to sleep, my dear. Yet she is a sweet and simple child. A temptation, that much I must allow.'

I was across the intervening space in a trice, howling like a harpy, determined to rip that insolent face with my claws, though he caught my hands, twisted me about and forced me down onto the nearest dining chair. Then I felt the knife he had taken from within his coat, holding it to my throat.

'Enough, Seaton!' Sir William shouted, half-standing from the table. 'You have business with this lady, so proceed. Yet you shall not torment her.'

'Please do not trouble to act the gentleman now, sir,' I sobbed in my frustration, and clutched at my skirts. An act, of course, a pretext for me to prepare my next move. The pocket pistol. Yet where was it? A sudden awareness that its familiar weight was absent.

Sweet Jesu, I thought. I had left it upon the bedside table when I was comforting Ursi – to ease the numbness of my leg. Foolish, foolish woman!

'Sir William, a gentleman?' Seaton was saying. 'Had you not best explain to her, sirrah?' Sir William, however, simply stared down at that redundant plate. 'No? Then you should know Sir William is no willing accomplice in our reunion, sweet Catherine. Yet he was biddable. My mention of all those unspeakable acts in which he is implicated. That fool Sawcer. Troublesome Major Puckle.'

And my husband, I wanted to ask him – was he involved in Puckle's death too? Or in leaving us so unguarded for the pirate raid upon Fort St. George? But no time for that now. I could not chase from my head the vision of Seaton's hand upon my daughter. We were in terrible danger and I knew it. I saw again the damage he had inflicted upon Katherine Nicks, the way he had terrorised young Susannah, and I saw the way his fingers played around the rapier's guard as he leaned close beside me, stroked my sleeve with the gloved hand. It was repellent, though I knew our only salvation might lie in remaining rational.

'Another crime to add to your account,' I said to him. 'That you go abroad armed in contravention of our laws.'

'This?' he sneered. 'My trusty blade? How foolish of me. It had entirely slipped my mind. Fine for a gentleman to carry a sword in his own defence – yet only if he is a Protestant gentleman. Oh, how equitable are Dutch William's laws. Well, might as well be hanged for a sheep as a lamb, eh?'

'God's hooks, Seaton,' Sir William shouted. 'Tell her what it is you want.'

'Oh, there is so much.' Seaton gazed down at me. 'You remember that night? After the serving wench? When I held you, Catherine. The agonies of desire that brief moment left within me. The penance and purification I had to endure for the wickedness you sowed. But I have purged my flesh so many times, cleansed my soul entirely of that longing.'

Yet his eyes told a different tale and I could feel my gorge rising, swallowed back the vomit in my throat.

'For pity's sake...'

Sir William had collapsed back into his chair.

'But that leaves me, sweet Catherine, with only my master's business to complete.'

'The pope's business,' I said.

'Great heavens, I wish it were so. But His Holiness seems to have as much empathy with this heretic King Willie as his predecessor.'

237

'God's voice on earth,' I said, hoping that time – or Sweet Lord Jesus – would bring some miracle. 'Is that not what you Papists believe? The pope, infallible? How can you gainsay his support for our anointed king?'

'Even His Holiness can be tempted by Satan, my sweet. We must always be able to discern the devil's work, act accordingly. God bless King Louis that he has seen the light in this, ruled that the true power of our Faith rests with the ecumenical council – and not with the Holy Father alone. The Edict of Fontainebleau.'

'By which your godly King Louis initiated such persecution of his country's Huguenots. The same fate that would eventually have befallen Protestants here had James Stuart remained on the throne. So who do you serve, Seaton – Catholic James or French Louis?'

'Does it matter? The enemies of one are the enemies of both. As your snake-tongue harlot Katherine Nicks had to be taught. Clever to use her, though. Such a ruse. It must have amused you, to employ your husband's whore for your own ends. Indeed, it was her tongue I intended to take – until I was so sorely interrupted. Do you feel no guilt at all, my dear, for bringing such a fate down upon her? Well, I suppose at least Elihu will not find her so attractive now – though I have no idea why he should have chosen her above you in the first place. The fellow is indeed a bubble.'

'And do you have in mind the same punishment for me?'

'Gracious!' he laughed, in that madcap way I recalled from when we had first met. 'You have an imagination, ma'am. But no. For you there is a different task entirely. You see, there are enemies and then – well, there are enemies. Are there not, Sir William?'

'He means Cavendish,' said Langhorn.

'The Duke of Devonshire, sirrah? But he is your friend, Sir William.'

'Friendship on the one hand,' said Seaton, 'disgrace and loss of fortune on the other. Those were Sir William's only options. And Cavendish? Without that traitor as their ringleader, the initiator of the seditionists' merry dance, there could almost certainly have been no invitation to Dutch William, no way to allow him to usurp the crown of England. Of the Three Kingdoms indeed.

There were the others, of course – Talbot, Lumley and the rest. King James will deal with those in his own good time after his restoration. But justice for Cavendish cannot wait. I had intended the White Hall fire might have disposed of him, but the wretch escaped unharmed. So then it was all a matter of how to get close to him without arousing suspicion.'

'Through me?' I said.

'In this case I could think of none better. Personally close to His Grace. A heretic Dissenter yourself. Well-connected through your family to this so-called Society of Friends. How did you describe your father once – a fellow-traveller, was it not? So when I heard Cavendish was coming to Deptford, in his official capacity – Lord Steward indeed – to the Meeting House of that town's Quakers this very day, with Czar Peter indeed – well, I thought, an opportunity.'

Something in the back of my mind, a few snippets I had seen in several of the broadsides, though not a mention of his visit to England in the *Gazette*. The Czar of Muscovy's fascination not only with our shipbuilding and the dark arts of seamanship but also with the doctrines of the Society. These dual interests have kept him in London since January and I had quite forgotten he has been resident in Deptford this past month, to be close beside the King's Yard where he is alleged to have worked with his own hands. I could be forgiven for my forgetfulness, however, for this has been no pomp and ceremony state tour. Quite the reverse. They say the Czar has been travelling under a *sobriquet*. Peter Mikhailov, or something of that ilk. Strange, and I am not entirely certain I believe the yarn, yet when I read those brief reports I thought I should like the fellow for his common touch.

'I might not have come,' I said.

'Then you should have been fetched, my dear. Though there were other similar opportunities we might have explored on later dates.'

'And why…?'

He held up the gloved hand, sneered at me.

'Please, please do not ask me that absurdly foolish question, Catherine. It would be quite beneath your intelligence. You already know the answer, do you not?'

Of course I did. It had frozen my blood these past several minutes. Ursula was the lever he would use this time to bend me to his will. Ursula the reason I would do his bidding.

'If I had not brought her…'

'The same response, I fear. We should have taken her in any case.'

'If you hurt her,' I spat, 'I *shall* kill you, Seaton.'

'Forgive me, my dear, but death holds no fears for me. To die in the cause of the True Faith? Eternal grace?'

'Then somehow I shall see your soul in hell. Where is she?'

And where, I wondered, was Thornton? Was my daughter not supposed to be in his charge? Why, if he had allowed harm to befall her – but then I heard her, those gut-wrenching screams from the passageways of the house, from the echoing expanse of the stairwell beyond the dining room walls. The agony and anger flooding my brain, gave me the strength to leap up, despite Seaton's restraining grip, despite the blade at my neck.

The door slammed open.

'Mama!'

She was hauled into the room by some pox-faced poltroon, a polished pate and many days' growth upon his jowls.

'Bitch,' he was shouting, his accent plainly Irish. 'Feather-brained little bitch. Bottom though, sirrah. The bitch has bottom.'

I struggled towards her, beside myself with fury, blind to everything but poor Ursi's impossible distress.

'Have you not done her enough harm?' I yelled. 'Look at her. In Jesu's name, have pity.'

'Mama, please…' Ursula sobbed.

There was rage in me, yes, but there was horror too, and that dreadful quaking impotence.

'You blame me for her lack of wits?' Seaton snarled, gripping me tighter about the neck.

'She was a healthy, growing child until that night,' I said. 'Until you slammed her head against the balusters. God damn you to hell for that alone, Seaton.'

Ursula was screaming incoherently now, then fell into a swoon.

I felt his hold upon me slacken a little and he muttered something I did not quite catch in my confusion. Something in Latin, perhaps.

'You do not need the child,' said Sir William.

No, just set her free, I wanted to shout, and I shall do anything you wish. Yet some small voice inside me knew it would never happen and I bit down upon my lower lip.

'Of course we need her,' Seaton replied, but some of his self-assurance seemed to have ebbed. 'Though we certainly need her in prime condition. Be careful with her, Colonel. She is a valuable commodity. Without her I suspect Mistress Yale might be appreciably less amenable to our scheme.'

'My coachman?' I said. 'What of my coachman?'

The ruffian shook his head and grimaced. A colonel? Truly? Of what, pray? I wondered. And Ursula was beginning to stir once more in his arms, eyes rolling in her head.

'It seems,' said Seaton, 'he is another who has paid the price of loyalty to you, Catherine. How heavy your conscience must be. Unfortunate, but...'

No, not Thornton too. I choked back my tears and, as I write this, I hope they may have been shed for that faithful young man, though I suspect they may have been driven more by the ferment of my trepidation for my daughter, or even by fear for my own life.

'You murderous rogue,' I shouted. 'You shall dance at Tyburn for this. All of you.'

'And my cook?' snapped Sir William. 'Another of Colonel Porter's victims?'

Porter? The same who had been involved in so many of the Jacobite plots, who had escaped the Tower and fled to France? It made sense, of course. Though I had somehow imagined him very different to this cove. Still, his cold-blooded reputation, my worst imaginings confirmed now with Thornton's murther. Oh, the ferocity of my convulsions as I fought to break myself from Seaton's hold.

'Safe and sound in her kitchen,' said the Irish colonel. 'Safe and sound – more or less.'

'Mama...'

I tried to close out Ursi's piteous stirring, to conceive some means by which we might escape.

'There,' Seaton was saying to Sir William. 'And give you joy of cook's talents. She has made my sojourn here in your inestimable company quite delightful. A pity that, today, it must all come to an end. But you see, Catherine?' He pulled me to him once more and I could smell the rancid sweat of his body. That, and the frenzy that gripped my innards, caused me to retch, so that he pushed my head away. 'Hell's teeth, woman,' he swore, 'not upon me.' And I emptied the contents of my stomach instead upon Sir William Langhorn's fine floor. 'Yet we are determined upon our goal,' Seaton said. 'One more death means nothing to me. And later, if you have played your part, you may be lucky enough to be reunited with your daughter. Though, for now, you must bid her a fond *adieu* since, sadly, Colonel Porter insists on taking her to another place. A safer place, he says, where you shall never reach her unless we permit it.' Then he smiled to himself, amused by some inner thought. 'By bell, book and candle, I swear you shall not.'

Hard to recall much of the following minutes. All confusion in my mind. Yet there was this: Seaton half-dragging me through the house, back to our bedchamber to collect our travelling cloaks and, all the time, my crazed pleas and ill-formed threats that he should release my daughter; Ursula's heart-rending wails from below; my desperate hope I should be able to find the pocket pistol where I had left it; and my desires so badly dashed. Something worse too. I had folded our cloaks neatly into the travel chest and was kneeling at its side, careful to keep my gaze away from the bedside table yet trying, at the same time, to calculate how I might reach it. It was obvious to me now how I had failed to see the weapon earlier because I had thrown Ursi's nightgown across it in my haste to see her dressed when Thornton – poor Thornton – had come to collect her. But Seaton was otherwise distracted. At the desk beneath the window.

'God's hooks,' he said, 'what's this? A journal. You keep a journal, Catherine? Let me see...'

I jumped to my feet, Ursula's cloak falling to the floor.

'There is nothing of interest – ' I began.

'Truly? But this scrawl. Last night. What have we? Your cosy chat with Sir William. Elihu coming home? Gracious, though hardly any longing in your words, my dear. And here. Sir William truly had no idea how much you had betrayed him until I broke the news? But gracious, do I get a mention in these pages, sweet lady?' He laughed. 'Oh, I see by the blush in your cheeks that I do!'

I bent down to pick up the cloak again, and to retrieve my own from the chest, then slowly backed around the bed, trying to control my trembling, my chaotic breathing.

'Frequently,' I gasped. 'But my journal is my own, sirrah. My most private thing. For the eyes of none but myself.'

'Now you make it irresistible, of course. How could anybody miss the opportunity of delving into the inner thoughts of my otherwise coy Mistress Catherine Yale?'

'My daughter's nightgown,' I said. 'Perhaps...'

'Yes, yes, take anything you think she may need.' He was busily poring through the pages, and I had turned from him, gathered up the cotton gown, the pocket gun too within its folds. Then his hand upon my arm. 'What have you there, madam? And why, prithee, might you think your daughter's night dress so necessary?'

He had thrown the journal carelessly upon the bed, was trying to pull the gown from my hands.

'I simply believed...' I stammered. But then the pistol fell to the floor. He stared at it briefly, thrust me at arm's length away from it. And I thought of that night, when I had pulled it so cautiously from Ursula's fingers. The smell too. 'The Lily-of-the-valley,' I said. 'Why?'

'The scent of death. I guessed it might signify the same for you also. And their poison, another hazard to set beside your daughter. A test. For you. For her. To see whether the Almighty would spare her. And He did. For this greater purpose.'

'You are mad, Seaton. And you have tormented my family enough,' I said, as he stooped to pick up the small gun.

'You kept it all this time,' he laughed. 'This other plaything

I left for your daughter. I had almost forgotten. How sweet. You kept it on the offchance. And when you had the chance to use it – oh, this is so elegant!' He pushed aside the baldrick, opened the front of his plain rust-coloured coat to show me a brace of similar weapons hidden beneath its folds. 'You see? Now a third chance to kill Cavendish. Such a gift you have brought me. Loaded and primed too, I see. Magnificent. So, lady, the cloaks and we shall be away.' Then he halted, reached down onto the bed. 'But I shall take the journal too, if you please. To entertain me afterwards.'

I hung out of my carriage window until she was almost out of sight, smothered in Colonel Porter's riding coat to deaden her screams yet, to my ears, they still carried clear upon the wind. The Irishman was heading north, towards the river, and I could scarce believe he might avoid detention in Charlton village by some law-abiding citizen alerted to such a rogue absconding alone with a distressed child upon his saddle. Yet no, he seemed to have made his escape unimpeded while my own conveyance, Seaton at the reins and shouting instructions at me as we trundled and bounced relentlessly towards Greenwich and Deptford, his sword and baldrick hidden from view beneath the driver's seat.

I had been forced to endure the horrors of seeing Thornton's body, his skull a mass of blood and matted hair, dragged from the kitchens and dumped unceremoniously in the stables. Of the old cook I saw no sign at all, nor Archer for that matter. But Porter had hitched and harnessed my horses, and he seemed to know his business in that regard. Seaton's saddled mount was tethered behind, while Sir William made various vain attempts to quench my ire though, finally, he simply stood mute and wretched, watching our departure from the stable-yard gateway.

Could I have escaped, jumped from the carriage? I thought about it constantly, yet once upon Black Heath I knew my chances of successfully following Colonel Porter were non-existent and that, whatever might befall in Deptford, I was, at least, marginally more assured of finding allies, assistance, means of escape there than upon this barren waste.

Thirty minutes later we had descended the hill to by-pass Greenwich, and clattered over the Ravensbourne bridge, below Deptford Creek, to make our way up the byway I now know to be Butt Lane, which serves the three disparate settlements of Deptford itself as a kind of high street. And towards the upper end of Butt Lane, where the enclosures and sparse cottages give way to more condensed brick-built housing, stands the austere bulk of the Friends' Meeting House – unmistakable, of course, for the crowd it had attracted on this early spring morning. A little further still, alongside the site where a new church was being built, the yards of Trinity House affording us watering and safe-keeping for the beasts and carriage – though we attracted many questioning glances from the ostlers set there for that purpose, Seaton little troubling to disguise his rough handling of my person. Yes, he told them brusquely. The Quaker gathering.

What was I feeling? Terror, naturally, for my daughter – even more than I might have felt for any of the others, if such were possible. Ursi is so vulnerable at the best of times. Frustration too, at my feeble helplessness, once again fit for nothing except to comply with Seaton's murderous intent. And a simmering anger that all the infamies for which I and others were owed justice against this devil now seemed so far from punishment.

'Simply walk naturally, my dear,' he murmured in my ear, close behind me in his coachman's cloak. He was sporting a straw-coloured periwig surmounted by a tall and stiff-crowned beaver, very much in the Puritan style. 'You must remember, the first of these pistols will be for you, Catherine – sad as I should be to see you dead – unless you do precisely as I have instructed.'

As we approached, several elders attempted to still those who were plainly present through curiosity rather than any sense of reverence.

'Prithee,' one of the elders cried, 'this is a place of worship not a race meeting. Be gone, unless thou hath business here.'

'My name, Friend Elder,' I said, delivering the lines Seaton had given me, 'is Mistress Catherine Yale and I am here at the behest of His Grace, the Duke of Devonshire.'

245

The elder examined Seaton closely.

'And thee?' he said.

'Friend Catherine's coachman,' Seaton replied. 'Vincent by name and a Convinced Friend, meeting for worship most frequently at Gracechurch Street.'

The serpent sounded convincing, had adopted a gentle West Country accent to complete his mummery.

'Then pass, Friends,' said the elder, and he began to clear a path for us to the front doors.

'Now, Friend Catherine,' Seaton hissed, and I felt the barrel of a pistol, concealed within his pocket, pressed into my kidneys.

The gloomy packed interior of the Meeting House was even more austere than the exterior had promised, though I had expected no less, having occasionally accompanied Papa to such meeting rooms as a child – crucial to my education, he had frequently said, to understand the philosophies of the Religious Society of Friends. And how I wished, now, as Seaton squeezed us onto the end of one of the crowded benches near the doors, rudely pushing an old fellow with a walking cane further along the pew, that I had my father's wisdom to guide my steps.

There were other women here, I saw, though for any normal purpose we should have been confined to our own room. Yet this was a special gathering and there, at the farther end of the high-windowed hall, facing us from the tiered benches of the gallery set aside for visiting ministers – no other liturgical symbolism here, naturally – among the most senior of the elders, sat a weathered fellow in his mid-fifties, rubicund, simply dressed and sporting his own hair, shoulder-length. I knew him, of course, for the same reason – the occasional public gatherings with Papa at which I had heard this gentleman speak alongside George Fox. William Penn, no less. Something of an enigma, but I was shaking too much to permit me any great consideration of his past – though Seaton was not so troubled.

'Does it not confuse you, my dear – that this leader of the Quakers should have been so close to our Catholic King James? How can you revere the one, yet so revile the other?'

James Stuart's closest personal friend, was this not what they claimed about Penn? But where the devil was His Grace the Duke? And what would I do when he finally appeared? For the pistol was still at my back.

'What was it you said, Seaton?' I hissed. 'That even the pope can be tempted by Satan? The same, I suspect, must therefore also be true of an honourable man like William Penn. Lured by the weasel words of Catholic James – a coarse and vulgar creature who employs wretches like you to conduct his cowardly assassinations for him.'

'Yet it is your own precious usurper who has had Penn arrested so often on account of his friendship.'

'Well, they are reconciled now, it seems.'

Penn had risen to address those crowded upon the hall's benches and in the galleries above. A long speech, about how he had been beguiled by the previous king's Declaration of Indulgence, how he had feared a return to persecution and intolerance following the king's exile. And how wrong he had been.

'It is the Devil has him beguiled now,' Seaton sneered.

Yet Penn's words were lost in the clamour from beyond the doors, both of them thrown open and held wide by a pair of emerald-coated equerries. Upon the steps, some jostling, another uniformed lackey, his back to us, clearing the way for those who came behind. I caught a glimpse of William Cavendish himself and, for a moment, I imagined the fellow at his side must be intending to ride a pony or ass into the Meeting House, for he towered above the Duke by – what? A foot or more?

'No,' I said. 'The Devil is occupied elsewhere this day. With my daughter, sir.'

I knew, of course, with absolute certainty, that whatever Seaton's true plans, they would never include some blissful moment in which I was lovingly reunited with my darling girl and then both of us released unharmed. It was not in the nature of the beast. But nor could I see any obvious escape from my predicament. Porter was away with my daughter and without Seaton to inform me, I doubted I should ever be able to rescue her. On the other hand I could scarcely stand by and see such a loyal peer of the English realm assassinated in cold blood and, even then, have no assurance – far from it – that doing so would restore my daughter to me anyhow. Between the cliff-face and the whirlpool indeed. Yet my father and Mama had taught me well that the greatest sin in all the world is for good folk to idly observe the actions of the bad and take no steps to impede them.

'I see your thoughts, Catherine,' murmured Seaton, as Mister Penn noticed the arrival of the royal party, called down God's blessing upon the Czar of Muscovy. 'But prithee remember,' Seaton hissed, 'if I do not escape this place, Ursula will suffer the most evil death you can imagine.'

There was, of course, no pony, no ass, simply Czar Peter, astonishingly tall. I think I can never have seen anyone taller. But strangely narrow. Narrow especially in the shoulders, narrow in his head. A moustachioed head, which otherwise had not seen a razor in a week or more. A dark and unkempt peruke too, to match the dark and unkempt coat. In contrast, before him, came a resplendent dwarf, a fellow almost as broad as he was short, all gilded lace and silver-powdered periwig. No pomp and ceremony perhaps but nor was it the modest incognito I had expected. Indeed there was quite an entourage, royal bodyguards in great number and, among these, two faces I knew only too well. Yet how did they come to be here? Wadham the thief-taker close beside the Duke and, at the Czar's side, Captain Baker, Master of the King's Intelligence, this whole array pressed so closely about His Grace that I doubted Seaton could possibly ever have a clear shot.

'I think, sirrah,' I said, 'you are ditched.'

For the first time, he seemed troubled.

'If I am ditched,' he sneered, 'then so are you, sweet Catherine. But perhaps not just yet.'

Something had changed. Out there, beyond the doors, beyond the press, something had changed. A scream. Another. Somebody roaring in a language I did not know, Russian, perhaps? The Czar was turning. The sound of a shot? And one of the men at Czar Peter's side fell, so that all now faced about: the dwarf, desperately trying to push through the forest of legs; Wadham, struggling to free a pistol from his belt; Captain Baker, his hand upon the hilt of his sword; and the Duke of Devonshire, shouting at the top of his voice.

'Assassin!' yelled His Grace. 'Protect the Czar!'

He was exposed, of course, his back to us, and Czar Peter the same, while Seaton was pushing past me, one hand emerging from the pocket of his cloak, cocking the small pistol as it came up, the other drawing a second weapon from beneath his arm-pit, the left aimed precisely at the open target of the Duke's spine, the right at Czar Peter's head. Whatever might be happening outside, the true assassin – a double assassin – was in here. One step, two. Gasps from the Quakers all about us – and I was moving even before I could give it any thought, shouting warnings drowned by the cries of the crowd.

Yet I had the presence of mind to snatch the walking cane from that old fellow on our bench and I swung it with all my might at the back of Seaton's skull.

Crack. His head jerked forward. The pistol in his left hand flashed and roared, impossibly loud in that confined space for such a small piece. The sulphur stink of its smoke billowed about us – though my vision was still clear enough to see the Duke of Devonshire drop. At the same moment Seaton, fast as the cobra strike, which had killed poor Walter, spun around, smashed down upon my arms with the still primed second weapon, knocked the stick from my hands and threw his arm about my neck, the muzzle of that pistol in his right hand now pressed to my temple.

'Stupid whore!' he shouted, his composure all gone.

Wadham, I saw, was at the Duke's side where he had fallen, the old thief-taker staring wildly around, his weapon pointed into the interior, which from out there on the threshold must have seemed dark indeed. Across the steps, Czar Peter had either crouched low or been pushed to the ground by his guards, the dwarf's back pressed against him, arms spread as though to protect his master. And Captain Baker, sword in one hand, horse pistol in the other. It was Baker, I think, who perceived my presence first.

'Mistress Yale?' he shouted, without any true surprise at seeing me there. 'Are you hurt?' But I could not reply, such was the grip of Seaton's forearm upon my throat. Indeed, I thought I must swoon.

'Unhurt for now, Spymaster,' Seaton cried. 'But I will blow out her brains before I am taken.'

'At least release the girl,' said Baker, 'and perhaps we may parley.'

'Master of the King's Intelligence? God's hooks, you are exceptionally ill-informed. You have the thing quite awry, sirrah. The girl is sequestered in another place and unless I have safe passage neither mother *nor* daughter shall survive.' Then Seaton whispered in my ear. 'It seems I must be content with simply Cavendish dead, my dear. Yet I shall have to punish you for your foolish interference – you understand, do you not?'

Captain Baker was shouting instructions, speaking with the Czar – in Dutch, I think – but careful to keep that horse pistol trained always upon my captor. As Seaton had demanded, a passage soon began to open up through which he dragged me, looking all about him but never once taking the muzzle from my head. Yet at least the grip on my throat had slackened. I coughed, gasped for air.

'Never fear, Mistress,' said Wadham, as we passed the stricken Duke. 'Never fear.'

'Shoot the devil,' I implored him. 'Shoot, for pity's sake. For myself and my daughter are both lost.' Lost indeed. I had played Seaton's game, then tried in the end to foil his plot, and I had failed. But I suppose I knew Wadham would not do as I proposed. And Seaton knew it too.

'How careless,' he sneered, 'with your daughter's life!'

He was right. It was eating away at me, my brain filled with every possible mischance that might already have befallen poor Ursi. But then the moment was gone. The Czar was on his feet once more, a bemused look upon his irregular face and my only grain of solace was that, as I glanced back for the last time towards the doorway, I thought I saw Sir William Cavendish stir – though I knew Seaton did not see it. He was too occupied taking account of the escape route before him, through the confusion and pandemonium of the royal entourage, at the outer limit of which was another scene of conflict. A great bear of a man was struggling furiously under restraint by a dozen fellows or more. A decoy, of course. And oh, how nearly the assassinations had come to terrible fruition.

He hauled me backwards up Butt Lane, past the elaborate carriages waiting at the roadside, past the shoemaker's, past a candle shop and past other premises towards the half-built church.

'And now?' I said.

'How did you do it?' he snapped. 'Alert them – that useless old thief-taker and his friends.'

I had no more idea than Seaton but I was never about to admit this. And I was more enraged than curious, the thought dawning upon me that I and my daughter had been used by more than just Seaton alone.

'Your scheme was always doomed, Seaton. And what do you gain now by harming me? Or my daughter. You may have no fear of death, but living to fight another day – what of that?'

'Oh, you can hardly imagine the satisfaction it would give me to harm sweet Catherine. Though I shall perhaps simply leave you with a token to remember me. For when I send the girl back to you she will be so broken you will wish both she and yourself dead, my dear.'

I always disliked Seaton, that much was true. Despised him, in fact, for most of the time I knew him in Madras Patnam. But this venal hatred for me? Simply due to my espionage? Enemies, yes. Yet this confusion in which, at one moment, he seemed to desire me, the next to see me tortured to the depths of my soul.

We were not entirely alone, of course, for a score of armed fellows from Czar Peter's entourage had followed us cautiously, spread thinly across the road, or the vegetable patches to either side, and Captain Baker leading them, urging them to keep a safe distance, to do nothing that might endanger me further. Those citizens closer to us, there at the junction, needed no such warning and, as soon as they perceived the situation, scurried away or crept back within doors.

251

'Then you have a dilemma, do you not?' I said. 'To leave me this token with which you threaten me, yet not give Captain Baker the chance to take you down?'

I should have known better, for he quickly transferred the pistol to his left hand, pushing the barrel up, under my chin. And from within his coat he pulled a knife, brandished it before my face. I thought of ravaged Katherine Nicks again and the terror surged within me afresh.

'Oh, this shall do nicely, I think,' he said, and dragged me into the Trinity House yard once more, across to the stables where my carriage stood unhitched among several others. The horses – Seaton's saddle horse too – were being walked about the cobbles, enjoying their nosebags of fodder, the ostlers confused by our return, unexpected in both its timing and its manner. 'My horse,' he yelled at them. 'And quick about it!' The smell of horse dung, the jingle of harness, and while his mount was readied, Seaton reaching up beneath the driver's seat of the carriage. 'Where is the damn'd thing?' he muttered.

'This?'

A voice from behind the coach. Parrish. Dear Matthew Parrish, holding aloft Seaton's baldrick and sword in one hand, my journal in the other. But how the devil did he come here? There was only one answer and I saw it now as I should have seen it earlier. A trap. Not the one set by Seaton but, here, by my closest friends, as I had supposed them. Myself and poor Ursula as bait, tethered to the post as I had seen goats employed in India to attract the man-eaters.

I think I saw a smile twitch across my captor's lips as perhaps he reached the same conclusion. But then Matthew had thrown the sheathed blade towards Seaton and, without thinking, the wretch had to release me in order to catch it, so that I fell upon my rump. It was a fumbled catch, naturally, for the cove was encumbered with pistol in one hand, knife in the other, but it gave me the chance to skitter backwards, away from him. And now Captain Baker was in the yard. Seaton was at bay, his desperate gaze falling first upon Parrish, then to me, then to Baker. Uncertainty, but he chose swiftly, pointed the pocket pistol at me.

'She dies first,' he said.

'Mister Seaton,' said Matthew, tossing my precious journal back inside the carriage, 'that was a risk we took into consideration when we set this performance for you. Sir William Langhorn – indeed, His Majesty himself – would never have played your game, never have allowed Mistress Yale to be summoned here for your purpose, without understanding the risk she might become the sacrificial goat.'

'Liar!'

'Am I? Had it not been for Mistress Yale I should have settled with you that day at the tomb of Joseph Hynmers. I owe her nothing. But you, Seaton? Oh, I owe you so much, sirrah.'

'Your Gentue whore?'

'She would hate me for it,' said Matthew, 'but there is revenge to be had.'

Behind me, I heard Captain Baker cock his pistol.

'Do not toy with him, Matthew,' he said. 'I have the warrant here for his arrest. We should see him hanged.'

'There,' said Matthew. 'You may shoot Mistress Yale if you wish, Seaton. But then you shall be taken and you shall be hanged – well, hanged, drawn and quartered to be precise. And you may be certain I shall pay the executioner very well indeed to ensure you do not enjoy his mercy, that you shall be alive for every precious moment. Or you may face me like a man.'

He drew his own blade, though Seaton simply smiled.

'Ah,' he said. 'You do not know about the child?'

'Ursula?' Matthew asked me. 'Is she not still at Charlton House?'

'She is not,' I snapped. 'Porter has taken her. He rode off this morning towards the river. Fatal flaws, sir. And Ursula's life now more in danger than even your foolish plan could have placed her.'

The yard was beginning to fill. A travelling carriage with Czar Peter's dwarf driving, a file of soldiers, onlookers by the dozen, even Mister Penn, begging that there should be no further bloodshed, no more violence. But it was unlikely any there would heed him.

'I knew we should have watched the house more closely,'

Matthew insisted. 'But Sir William was certain this rogue would scent any spies we set about the place. My fault. I should not have listened. But you, Seaton, perhaps there is a bargain to be struck after all. You tell us where the girl's been taken and I shall make sure you are not, after all, conscious when the headsman pulls out your tripes and burns them upon the scaffold.'

'Oh, I think not, Parrish. If you were happy to see sweet Catherine as the sacrificial goat, you must have calculated the same for little Ursula. A poor gamble, sirrah. But I shall take your test.' He lowered the pistol, dropped it into a pocket, tossed the knife across the cobbles, under the wheels of a waiting carriage, threw aside his hat and that absurd straw-coloured wig beneath. Then he drew his sword and cast away the scabbard, crouching into an *en garde* position.

'What are you doing?' I cried. 'For pity's sake, just shoot the wretch. Wound him so we may put him to the hot iron, force the truth from him.'

'Here, Mistress,' shouted Captain Baker. 'To me.'

I obeyed, scrambling to my feet, taking shelter just behind him as Seaton's rapier and Parrish's much shorter court sword began to exchange lunge and parry, riposte and quinte, Seaton with the advantage of reach, Matthew's the lighter, faster blade. Yet Seaton seemed to possess all the elegance, Matthew more brutish, his long-repressed thirst for revenge causing his steps to sometimes falter. There was nothing of the poet and philosopher in him now, gone the diplomat. And I feared for him then, suddenly knowing that here was a fight he could not win. No escape for Seaton either, of course, though that thought was secondary to me, mattered little against the certainty Matthew would perish. Yes, secondary, I realised. Even despite the harm in whose way he had placed us.

'Shoot!' I screamed at Baker. 'Shoot or Parrish will die.'

The chink and chime, the slither of steel on steel. The laboured breathing as each man struggled for balance, encumbered by their heavy coats. The stamp of their feet on the cobbles.

'He would never forgive either of us, Catherine,' Baker replied. 'It is all in God's hands now.'

Karma, I thought, and there was something in the ringing chatter of the blades that reminded me of Sathiri's laughter. Was she watching this? I hoped not, for Seaton had advanced rapidly, made a feint towards Matthew's hip and then, as Parrish tried to deflect the blow, the rapier's wicked point whipped around and up, struck home, deep into Matthew's arm, his sword arm. Seaton gave a grunt of satisfaction, of triumph, as he pulled the steel free, began to circle for the kill. Matthew gripped the arm with his left hand, the sword hanging useless at his side.

'Now,' I cried into Baker's grim face. 'You must finish him now.'

But he simply shook his head.

'Not such a bad day after all,' Seaton was panting. 'Cavendish and Matthew Parrish both.'

'You are mistaken, sirrah,' shouted Captain Baker. 'His Grace received no more than a flesh wound, a graze to his scalp. You have failed, Seaton. Failed.'

'Not in this, though,' Seaton replied, readying his rapier once more. 'Well, Parrish...'

I saw Matthew transfer the blade clumsily to his left hand now and, at the same time, I saw a dark shape materialise from one of the other waiting coaches. A shadow, no more than a shadow. And for a moment I truly believed it to be Sathiri's spirit come to take Parrish once more to her bosom. The shadow crouched, picked something from the ground beneath the carriage while, just in front, his back to the apparition, Seaton took up his fighting stance again. Matthew seemed to look past Seaton's shoulder, retreated a pace of two, and Seaton paused in his attack to follow the direction of his opponent's glance. And so it was that, in this one instant of foolish distraction, Matthew's steel pierced Seaton's black heart while the discarded knife picked up by Katherine Nicks plunged into his spine.

Czar Peter's capacious carriage shook and swayed all the way back along the Greenwich road, the elaborate dwarf flogging the six-horse team without mercy, his master alongside him on the box, yelling encouragement and occasionally bending that strange head down towards the uncurtained window to check the condition of we who were thrown about inside.

'*Alles goed?*' he would ask.

And yes, I would shout back to him, also in Dutch, that all was indeed good. It was easier than attempting to tell him the truth. Two hours or more now since I had seen Ursula taken away by Porter. But to where? Captain Baker had questioned me carefully about it. What had been said? Precisely what? And I had been forced to clear my mind, shovel aside the worry and confusion. To a safer place, I had told him. That was what Seaton had said. Porter was taking her to a safer place, where I should never reach her unless they permitted it.

'Reach her?' the captain had said. 'Strange choice of words. Yet perhaps a boat. Would that make sense of it? They must have a boat, after all.' He reasoned they could not have expected to remain safe in England if, God forbid, they had succeeded in their plans. And was I certain there was nothing more?

'No, nothing,' I had replied. 'Except – well, something amused him. He swore by bell, book and candle I should not find her.'

Whatever I had said seemed to stir him, and he was out there now, somewhere ahead of us. Captain Baker, riding Seaton's horse like a madman, dressed in that coachman's cloak – poor Thornton's cloak – and sporting the straw-coloured periwig, the tall stiff-crowned beaver hat.

'A needle in a haystack,' he had said. 'So many wharves along the river. But if Porter went north, then perhaps Woolwich. And in Woolwich…' He would not be pressed further, except to apologise yet again that this plan to catch Seaton had not gone as he and others intended.

But the Czar, it seemed, had several vessels at his disposal, both there at Deptford and also at Greenwich. Thus, messengers were dispatched, his boats to make all possible haste downstream, to watch out for any unusual activity. But where to look, and where to rendez-vous?

'It's a slim possibility,' the captain had told the Czar, still in Dutch, 'but Seaton may have given us a clue, despite himself. If you would be so good, Your Majesty, to instruct your sailing masters, no further than Gallions Reach. That they should patrol Gallions Reach.'

And he had galloped away in his makeshift disguise, as though the devil himself was at his tail.

Yes, he had apologised. Yet did he truly think that myself and Ursula could be placed in harm's way like this, and a mere apology would somehow put things right?

'All of you?' I said to Katherine Nicks. She was doing her best to help the Czar's physician who, in turn, tried to staunch the bleeding of Parrish's wound. Matthew slouched in the corner, pale, slipping in and out of consciousness. The injury was a serious one, Seaton's blade having passed right through the arm, but Matthew had refused to be left behind. 'You all knew about this scheme?'

'All of us,' Katherine replied, one hand gripping the back of the seat to steady herself, the other employed in mopping Matthew's brow.

'I told you,' Parrish murmured. 'Seaton approached Sir William... weeks ago... threatened to expose him. Swore he would find witnesses... testify about Langhorn's involvement... Puckle's death... other things.' Katherine gave him a sip of water from a leather bottle, but most of the liquid simply dribbled from his lips. 'Seaton had details... Czar's itinerary... and Devonshire's responsibilities as his escort. Too much of a temptation. And all he needed... was a means... to get close.'

'Me,' I snapped. 'Me and my daughter.'

Matthew's head lolled against his shoulder.

'You should not press him so,' said Katherine Nicks. 'Repeating the story will not make it better.'

She was right, I suppose. Most of the puzzle's pieces I now possessed. It had seemed like a good plan, Parrish had said. Sir William's summons for me to attend Charlton House. The arrangement for him to light that signal lamp in the north tower once I had arrived. The complication of my note that I would be arriving with Ursula, too late to change the arrangements. The house cleared of servants. And Archer sent out early to Charlton village to find a post boy, warn Parrish and Captain Baker that the game was afoot. The certainty that, if they had tried to apprehend him at Charlton House itself, Seaton would certainly have sensed the trap.

No, Parrish had insisted. The plan had seemed a good one. They had simply not allowed for Porter to take my daughter. That was unforeseen and, when it happened, Sir William had no way of launching a further alert. And they had certainly not allowed for a second assassination attempt. The bear-like fellow restrained outside the Friends' Meeting House. Sedition in the making in Muscovy itself, the would-be killer one of the *streltsy*, those elite soldiers of the Czar's army yet now in revolt against him for many years past. The network of agents for French Louis was, it seemed, wide indeed.

'I still do not understand,' I said to her. 'Why you?'

'Mister Parrish believed I was entitled to see Seaton captured,' she replied, wiped her hand across the black veil. 'That the Crown owed it to me.'

'And Our Lord Jesu be praised you were there,' I said. 'Otherwise Parrish, I think, would be dead.'

'Blood on my hands, all the same,' she murmured. 'So much blood. Yet the Crown owed it to me, Catherine – and I owe nothing to you. Not any more.'

'I cannot argue with you. We were all owed revenge upon Seaton, though you more than any. But the Czar – did Matthew explain why…?'

The final occupant of the carriage was Wadham, of course. He had so far spent the journey, as best he could, checking the priming on his pistols, for we had no idea what we should find at the end of our ride. I had even recovered my own pocket pistol from Seaton's corpse – the corpse now destined for the gibbet.

'Maybe I can fill that corner, Mistress,' he said. 'Seaton were an agent of French Louis, like you knows. But the Captain, 'e says them Frenchies are all in bed – beggin' your pardon, ma'am – with the Turks. An' the Czar, 'e's been tryin' to put together this Alliance against the Turks. Well, French Louis don't like that.' Wadham rubbed together the thumb and first finger of his right hand. 'Bad for the Frenchies' trade, like. For French Louis 'imself. So…'

'Yes,' I said. 'I see the picture.'

Matthew had come to his senses again, struggled to sit upright while the physician finally seemed satisfied the wound was cleaned, applied a dressing.

'We knew the Czar was threatened,' he said, weakened from loss of blood, 'but he would not cancel any of his appointments.'

'Baker told me,' I replied, 'that when he set out on this Great Embassy of his, he had hoped to fight under England's banner against France.'

'I fear he holds me personally responsible for frustrating that plan.'

'You, Matthew? How?'

'Ryswick. The treaty. End of the war.'

In other circumstances I might have smiled, but I was still very far from forgiveness.

'And now?' I said.

'Now? I believe the Czar's friendship towards England... may be stronger than ever. The king's ministers have been keen... to strengthen our trading opportunities... with Muscovy. And all this, I think... will serve that purpose very well.'

Trade. Always trade.

We were descending the hill at devastating speed, woodland still bare of leaves flashing past to the right, then a church to our left – perhaps a brace of churches, now I come to think of it. A first glimpse of the shipyards before we swung down into, I supposed, the high street, running in parallel to the river.

'Such a bustling place,' I said. 'I should have expected those rogues to have concealed themselves in a more secluded hideaway.'

The sounds of industry from the yards, the heady aroma of hemp and cordage from the rope walks that must be somewhere near, and a mantle of metallurgical smoke hanging over the farther side of town where, Wadham told me, the royal ordnance and munitions arsenals might be found.

'And there, Mistress,' he pointed to the hills up beyond the out-skirts, a cluster of buildings among the trees, 'beggin' your pardon once more, but Mount Whoredom – an infamous place of soldiers' resort, ma'am. Take my meanin'? Woolwich Militia. Two more blackguards among this parcel of rogues – who might notice, eh? Seaton an' Porter. Perfect place for them to hide. That was Captain Baker's guess. 'E 'as a fine nose for these things, does the Captain.'

He leaned out of the window, thumped on the side of the door. 'Your Worship,' he yelled. 'About 'ere, if you please.'

'*Natuurlijk*,' cried the Czar, and the carriage began to slow, the horses skittering to a halt.

I found myself in a narrow alley, Bell Watergate Lane according to a faded sign at its southern end. There was a deserted inn, all boarded up now. On the other side, a couple of chandlery shops. The alley turned down towards the river's noxious odours and we followed our noses to the very end, where a flight of watermen's stairs dipped down into the ebbing tide between wharves of weed-slimed upright timbers.

And there we discovered gallant Captain Baker, quite dead. He was surrounded by scavengers, his mount already disappeared and a couple of rogues attempting to steal his boots, another grappling with the heavy coachman's cloak. That absurd periwig lay a yard or so away and it was stained almost black from the awful wound in the captain's head. A pistol shot at very short range, this much was clear as we chased away those vultures, the Czar lifting one of them bodily, hurling him into the swirling current below. But, to my shame, I cared almost nothing for all that.

Captain Baker killed meant his instinct must have been right. Captain Baker killed must mean he had encountered Porter – and Ursula. But where? I scanned the waters, screaming her name like a mad woman. Nothing. Vessels up and down the Thames, naturally. A constant procession of them. Yet mostly sailing barges, or larger ships being towed or warped upstream against both wind and tide. But then –

'There!' I yelled. She had been hidden in the lee of a coal barge anchored just at the margent of the main channel, readying her sails perhaps. Yet now she broke from her cover, a small two-masted yacht, a three-man crew, so far as I could tell, and all working a-fury to get every inch of her canvas aloft. Something, just something…

'*Uw dochter, mevrouw,*' said the Czar. Your daughter, madam. '*Kunt u haar zien?*'

No, I told him, I could not see her. But I was certain. As certain as a mother can be. And that was good enough for the Czar, even before Porter himself appeared on the yacht's deck, though no sign of Ursula. I prayed then as I have never prayed before that she was somewhere safe, below, and not already harmed. By then, the Czar was scanning the river himself, this way and that – until he finally saw the thing he sought. The dwarf had seen it too, produced a thin golden pipe from within his coat, a ball at one end, some sort of boatswain's whistle, which he placed to his lips and pierced all of that Woolwich clamour to bring another boat, a boat with red sails, healing over towards us across the turbulent stream.

We chased them in the *Dove* for more than four hours, with the Czar at the helm, Matthew left behind – against his debilitated protests – in the care of Katherine Nicks and the physician. Myself and Wadham on board, though I fear more of a burden than a blessing. There had already been three men sailing the boat and, with four more of us added to her load, we seemed unable to make any headway towards catching our prey.

We had passed, early in the chase, close to another of those vessels the Czar had instructed to patrol along Gallions Reach, a larger yacht with cannon on her deck, but the *Henrietta* had got herself entangled with a moored bomb ketch while coming about and was still nowhere in sight.

Worse, His Majesty did not seem the most competent of seamen. It is hard to spend as much time as I have done aboard our East Indiamen without learning at least a little of the navigator's or sailing master's dark arts, and I could see from the glances exchanged between the three seamen, the way they tried to trim and play the sheets, that the crew was less than happy with the royal helmsman's performance.

'Shall we never catch them?' I asked Wadham, my arm wrapped about one of the shrouds.

'She's a game bird this one, ma'am. An' you never knows. If the wind turns a bit, all this fore-and-aft spread might just give us the edge. But, for now...'

For now we seemed to be capable of nothing more than keeping pace, always a quarter-mile apart, it seemed. And every now and again, that cove Colonel Porter would make his way to the stern of the two-master, hang on to the daviots from which her shore-boat was suspended, and put a spy-glass to his eye, study us for minute after minute.

'I wish I could see inside her hull,' I said. 'Just for a moment.'

'Mustn't fear, Mistress,' Wadham tried to reassure me.

'No? You think not? Oh, I fear, Wadham. I fear all about me are betrayers. That any one of you could have alerted me to the danger. Confided in me. At least made some effort to intercept us on my journey to Charlton House, ensure my daughter be taken out of whatever equation you had all devised.'

He made no answer, of course, except to keep up an occasional commentary about our progress – or lack of it.

And Nicks, I thought. There I was, in her sister's house, and she said nothing. She, a mother too. It all went round and around in my head as we coursed through the starboard turn at Tripcock Point, the long straight haul along Barking Reach to Cross Ness, then tack and tack about all the way through the twists and turns to Crayford Ness, Dartford Creek, past the dismal expanse of the Rainham Marshes and through the Long Reach, the tide slackening as we swung north to Broadness Point, and a tedious wallowing final hour with the wind almost abated but the myriad masts of Gravesend in sight. The *Henrietta* in sight also, astern, and labouring at the task despite her greater press of sail. It was hopeless, I concluded, yet the Czar, despite his lack of total competence, was plainly unwilling to give up the chase, frequently attempting to reassure me that, while we could not catch them, neither could our enemies escape.

'*Het is allemaal een kwestie van tijd,*' he said, over and over again. All a matter of time? Yes, I supposed so.

Then, just after we had passed Gravesend itself, dusk gathering about us, the Tilbury Marshes off to our left, the wind still negligible, we saw activity aboard the two-master, the daviots being readied to lower the shore-boat. And there, on the deck, just barely discernible, a small figure wrapped in her riding cloak. Ursula. Surely my daughter. Colonel Porter again, the spy-glass pressed to his eye, watching us. Watching. He gestured to one of his crew and the fellow pushed Ursi forward, lifted her and threw her into the tender. What were they doing?

'Not stupid, that one,' said Wadham, and I hoped we had both made the assumption about Porter's plan correctly. If they dropped the shore-boat with my daughter aboard, left her adrift, we would plainly have to manoeuvre in order to rescue her, to luff up and lose our wind entirely. We would save Ursula but, as darkness fell, we would lose Jacobite Colonel John Porter.

She was safe, at least. Shaken badly but safe. And now tucked up securely in bed at Charlton House, the physician having given her a draught to make her sleep. It seemed the best option for, by the time the wind and tide turned in our favour, delivered us back to Woolwich, it was almost midnight. Mistress Nicks had left us a message – with a local urchin we found huddled upon the wharf, waiting for the second half of a generous reward – that Sir William Langhorn, having finally been appraised of all that had transpired, had sent a carriage to collect Parrish, the physician and herself.

The household, it seemed, was now fully restored to its more usual complement, and toddies of hot cordial, bowls of steaming broth, were being served to all of us gathered in the Great Hall. And it was quite a gathering, despite the hour. Yet I searched in vain for Katherine Nicks, uncertain whether I should embrace her for saving Matthew's life, or curse her to hell for failing to forewarn me, since our brief discussion in the carriage had resolved neither of those impulses.

'She would not stay,' Sir William Langhorn told me, seeing me search among his guests. 'The scars, I suppose. That awful wound. It must be an embarrassment to the lady.'

'Still,' I said, 'she was revenged at least. Whereas I...'

'Should have preferred to see him on the gallows, I suppose. As should we all. But Catherine, if I might explain?'

I looked about that huge and beautifully proportioned chamber, the full width of his house, two storeys in height, oak panelled to first-floor level, the ceiling strap-worked in the most elaborate of patterns.

'Explain, Sir William? Why, you have all this. Exquisite. And Seaton threatened it. There must have been a dozen ways to deal with him. Yet you chose to fall in with his plans, allow him to use me and, at the same time, to use me yourself. You may have considered it a clever double game, but I almost lost my daughter, sirrah. Captain Baker dead. Poor Thornton too.'

'You must allow me to make arrangements for the fellow. Your coachman, I mean. Funeral arrangements.'

'Harder, I think, to explain all this to his family. His mother. His sisters.'

'I am sure I can find some way to recompense them?'

'That was not quite my meaning, Sir William.'

'Yet can you forgive me, Catherine? Great heavens, I have been a virtual prisoner in my own home these weeks past. Seaton coming and going at his leisure, knowing myself constantly under observation. Only Archer able to escape from time to time, acting the witless fool, to carry messages to Parrish and our friends. For when Seaton arrived here, making his threats, it seemed an opportunity too good to miss.'

'And you sent your servants away to keep them from harm.'

'Of course. Though it suited Seaton's purpose too.'

'Then it is good to know, Sir William, you thought more of your servants' safety than my own.' He looked even more distraught, began to mumble some apology, perhaps explained himself badly. 'No,' I said, 'I intended no irony. It does not assuage my anger though I think it is the best way I may answer you. It speaks well that you considered them so. For most would not.'

'It was a calculation I made. Though not entirely philanthropic, I fear. We needed to light the great lanthorn, yet the rest of the house darkened, and hence the absence of servants. The signal to

Seaton, wherever he was hiding, perhaps across the river, that you were come. A signal to others that the trap was sprung. Another calculation – through Parrish, I collect, by these others of our notable circle too – that Seaton might be lulled into a false sense of security only if you, yourself, played the most natural of parts in our deception.'

'And if he had not this plan in which to work, his alternative schemes would have been hidden from us.'

There had been plenty of time aboard the *Dove* – all that fearful voyage down the Thames, not knowing what I should find at its end, and then the journey back with Ursula wrapped in my arms, shivering and terrified by her ordeal – for me to make those calculations. And yes, I was still angry I had been deceived. Yet I was almost as resentful that Sir William had felt himself capable of playing the deceivers' part with Seaton so well all those weeks, while having thought me incapable of doing likewise. How little he knows me. And Parrish too, it seems.

'Precisely my own opinion,' he was saying. 'Better the devil we knew, so to speak. Though I have to tell you, Mistress, that as providence would have it, whatever our errors, whatever our losses, our risks, I console myself with the thought that your intercession in Seaton's plan almost certainly saved the life of both His Grace, the Duke of Devonshire, as well as that of His Royal Highness, Czar Peter.'

'That,' said Wadham, who had come to join us, 'is undeniable, ma'am. The Crown owes you a great deal this day. I seen Seaton knock the cane from your 'ands. You'd struck 'im, I collect?'

I smiled despite myself.

'I wish I had struck that blow, which in the end fell to the privilege of Mistress Nicks. Yet it was revenge of a sort. But you, sirrah. Between yourself and Captain Baker, you smoked the devil.'

'For my sins,' said Wadham, 'I were born and raised in Woolwich. But Captain Baker, it seems, knew it better even than me, ma'am. I know all the streets reachin' down to the river stairs very well. Five o' them. Hog Lane an' that fine establishment, the Green Dragon. Warren Lane. Ship Lane. Talertree Watergate

Lane, an' the Blue Anchor. But it were only when we got there I remembered. The last but not the least, Bell Watergate Lane – where my father were a frequent patron of that old waterin' hole we saw closed down. Boarded up, you collect? Seaton must 'ave known it too. The old Book an' Candle. It could simply 'ave been coincidence – yet it was all 'e possessed, an' the Captain played 'is inklin' well.'

'Well, God bless his soul,' I said. 'The idea those devils should have carried out their threats against my daughter.'

The shiver down my spine at the very thought. What was it Porter had called my precious girl? A feather-brained little bitch. Yet more value in that one damaged child than a thousand Jacobite traitors. How I wished I could have paid him for those words. And now he had escaped. Well, one day...

'Friend Catherine!' None other than William Penn, our circle enlarged this time by his presence in company with the Duke of Devonshire, Czar Peter and his whole entourage – the dwarf too, of course – and I found myself flustered by their collective attentions. 'Give you joy of your safe deliverance and that of your daughter, madam. But gracious, what a day.'

'I thank the Lord Jesu as much for deliverance from my own ire, Friend William. I had not realised I was capable of such fury, nor such thirst for revenge. I believe that terrified me more than the ordeal itself.'

'Take succour, perhaps,' he said, 'from the knowledge of the complexities with which the Lord has endowed us all. The wider and more profound the well of a person's humanity, the mightier the monster that, pray God, shall remain leashed in its depths.'

'Amen to that!' said the Duke. His head was swathed in a dressing, his full-bodied wig balancing precariously above. 'Yet Mistress Yale and myself are old acquaintances. Why, we was together at that special service to celebrate the peace. Though no chance to chat, eh, my dear?'

So he had recognised me that day after all. The day he had leered at me as though I were one of his whores.

266

'No chance, Your Grace,' I replied. 'And then I gave thanks for your deliverance from the White Hall fire. Did you explain, Sir William?' I said to Langhorn. 'It seems Seaton may have been responsible for that too.'

'The devil!' said the Duke. 'And I had only a temporary lodging in the Cockpit there too.' I could only imagine why this Duke of Devonshire might have been residing in the annexe to the White Hall palace that had, before the days of King William and Queen Mary, always housed one or more of the royal concubines. 'Spies everywhere, I fear,' said the Duke. 'Yet you are so in looks, my dear, as always, despite your travails. So in looks. You must visit me.' He had not changed, I saw. Still the old lecher he had always been. 'Must find some reward, eh? God blind me, so we must. Wadham here tells me Seaton would have had a clear shot at these old bones had you not given him a lick with a stick. Eh? Eh?'

Mister Penn was translating the conversation for Czar Peter's benefit. And yes, Friend William was a strange man indeed. Friend to Catholic James Stuart. Now friend also, it seemed, to both King William and this Czar of Muscovy. The concept, I thought, for this Society of Friends, taken to its extreme.

'*Ik ben je mijn leven, mevrouw Yale.*' The Czar reached down, took my hand in his own rough and grime-stained fingers, kissed the knuckles gently enough, even so. But was it true, that he owed me his life? It seemed absurd, and I had to concentrate hard for a few moments before I could piece together the Dutch words I needed for reply.

'Your Imperial Majesty,' I said at last, as carefully as I was able, 'I think in truth it may be I who owe you – for the life of my daughter. Without good Wadham here, without poor Captain Baker, we should not have known where to begin. But without you, sir, without your boats, there should have been no happy end.'

The dwarf jumped up and down in delight, clapping his hands and shouting something in their own Slavic tongue.

'You are a brave lady,' said the Czar. He smiled at me, as he had done several times during our adventure aboard the *Dove*. A kind gesture, though one, I thought, that must show simply one facet

267

of this man, this giant of a man. Tales of the cruelties inflicted by so many of the Muscovite rulers in their own lands, against their enemies, real or imagined, are the stuff of legend. And can it be that here was the exception to the rule? I believe not. Yet it is enough he played such a part in restoring Ursula to me. Certainly not as uncivilised as I might have imagined had I not met him. He shall always have a place in my heart.

'Brave indeed!' said William Penn. 'And you know what they say, Friend Catherine? Satan quakes when the innocent take up arms.'

Innocent? I thought. Me?

'Thank you, Friend William,' I said. 'But if you gentlemen would excuse me, I should rather like a few words with Mister Parrish before I retire.'

There was a great deal of bowing, more kissing of hands, before Sir William Langhorn finally succeeded in extricating me from that web, leading me to the far end of the Great Hall where a settle had been arranged to accommodate Matthew, now surrounded by a veritable company of female admirers. Yet Sir William stopped me before we quite reached our destination.

'My dear,' he said. 'There is one thing more.'

'You fear, sirrah, somehow I might have changed my mind about the financial arrangement that brought me here.'

'I fear,' he said, 'you might have believed the whole business to be a fabrication.'

'No, Sir William. Never that. It is true I seem to be left with more questions than answers. Not least about whether you have truly used my name on those denunciations against Elihu. But our private underwriting of my husband's cargo? On that, at least, I am happy to shake your hand and sign the contract.'

'What did he mean?' Matthew asked me when he had finally dismissed his cohort of admirers – dismissed, I think, more brusquely than he intended.

He was somewhat revived since I had last seen him all those hours earlier, yet something in his eyes that spoke of an influence akin to the *soma* I had once been wont to enjoy. A sleeping draught for my daughter, a stimulative for my friend, it seemed – though I saw it did little to dull the pain in his arm. 'Sir William,' he went on. 'I heard him press you. More questions than answers?'

'And so I have, Mister Parrish. Though the hour is late and they are perhaps best left until the morrow.'

'Nonsense, my dear. Look, you see me bright as a button.'

Hardly, I thought, but I understood he was intent on keeping me in his company a while longer.

'Then questions it is, Mister Parrish. Of them all, you have most certainly never troubled about my ability to act a part. Why now? There, that is my first.'

'True,' he said, shifted his wounded arm to a more comfortable position, as far as its swaddling would allow. 'But it might not have been politick to share the full extent of your talents with any but Baker. And, God blind me, how I shall miss the honourable fellow. He would have agreed with me, I think, that the whole value of women intelligencers, my dear, is that gentlemen think you incapable of this purpose. Long may it remain so.'

'The deception you were abroad? Entirely necessary?'

The Czar's physician came to make a final inspection of his patient before himself retiring. Was he German? I had no idea, though he smiled a great deal, nodding his head and snorting sounds of satisfaction, then made some effort to bid us goodnight in badly broken English.

'Necessary?' said Matthew, when the fellow had gone, the rest of the Great Hall clearing quickly also now. 'Not entirely false, I should say. I had received word of my posting – indeed, my passage to France was arranged, my dunnage all stowed aboard – when Sir William sent me his first warning. The most difficult decision of my life, Catherine, whether or not to keep the truth from you. But Seaton is gone now. And he was indeed a devil. I am certain he could have smelled a trap, or the presence of any set to capture him, had we played it any other way. At least, I hope that is the way you shall record it in your journal.'

I felt the anger rise in me again.

'The journal is my own, sir. Entirely my own. You had no right to open it!' Last night I had felt more defiled by Seaton having touched it, read some of its content, even than when he laid hands upon my person. Even than that long distant night of my wedding to Elihu when he had seen my legs bared to ridicule – that absurd ritual of the garters. Even more than the day he desecrated the tomb of little Davy and my dear Joseph. And now it was almost as though Matthew too had supplemented those indignities. 'How much did you read?' I snapped.

'Catherine,' he protested, 'I would not offend you further for the world. Your title page only. Yet, Volume Four? There are three more of those jewels? Great heavens, I merely glimpsed the first words, your mention of Queen Mary's funeral and – well, my ode to her. I was simply touched that you should have given my verses such prominence, the feeling perhaps... No, let me say nothing more for I read nothing more either. Though truly, no others have shared this wonder.'

'Seaton, as I told you, last night, and to my shame.'

'The shame is that you do not discuss your work with others of like mind.'

'Of like mind, sirrah? I fear Marcus Aurelius and Plutarch are both long dead.'

'What? You think the art of the biographer, the commentator, the social historian, the letterist died with the ancients?'

'In truth,' I lied, 'I have rarely given it consideration.' The truth? I have wondered many times whether my solitary writing is an aberration peculiar only to myself. Surely not.

'If so, Catherine, I have to correct you. It may be true there are few, if any, in these times interested in the publication of such things. But does it not occur to you that those of us who consider ourselves poets must also keep regular notes of our daily thoughts and inspirations? Or those who study the natural sciences. Music, all the rest.'

'That is, Matthew, entirely different. I have no claim to such academic purpose. I simply scribble what I see each day.'

'Why, madam, London itself is full of such observers of the city's daily life and they, in turn are all in touch with each other.

There was a fellow, Pepys – you will not recall him but once Secretary to the Admiralty, though long retired from that position.'

'Oh, I recall him, sirrah. We discussed him once, you and I. He was among the parcel of fools who saw no threat to their own faiths from popish James Stuart and thought themselves his friends.'

Like William Penn, I thought.

'Indeed. A member of the Cavalier Parliament for a while. And when I took up my duties after King William came to the throne, Pepys was one of the first I had the pleasure of arresting for his Jacobite sympathies. A pleasure because I disliked the wretch so much. We never brought charges against him as it happens. Insufficient evidence. And he was vouchsafed by Mister Evelyn. You know Evelyn, of course.' I smiled. How could I possibly not know Evelyn? One of our most prolific writers on almost every subject under the sun. 'Apologies, my dear. Of course you know him. But perhaps you did not know that he and Pepys have long shared the same passion as yourself. Daily journals. Private journals. I doubt they shall ever see the light of day but I had the honour of becoming familiar with their work during my investigation. And through them I discovered this entire web of others. If you would wish...'

'How monstrous,' I said. 'I can think of nothing I should like less than to endure the ramblings of others if they are as chaotic as my own scribbling.'

The Hall was almost empty now, Archer moving slowly around the wall, snuffing out each of the sconces in turn.

'Time for bed in any case,' said Matthew. 'I shall ask the old fellow for a manservant to light my way and help me up the stairs, I think. And you, Catherine, the rest of your unanswered questions must wait until the morning, I fear.'

'Oh,' I said, 'I think I may now have exhausted them.'

For most of those that remained must, I know, now rest unsettled forever, their solutions died with Vincent Seaton. I was still no wiser about whether the rogue's allegations against Sir William were true or not. Had Governor Langhorn been actively involved in Major Puckle's death? In that of Sawcer, the calico sorter? And apart from these possible crimes of Sir William's, what of Elihu's involvement with Seaton? My husband's defence of Seaton had always been unquestioning, less than natural. Why? More secrets? Had Elihu truly paved the way for the Roundsmen's attack on Fort St. George – an attack in which, I had no doubt at all, Seaton was embroiled.

And there was this. Something else that regularly troubles me. That when Seaton had forced me to the affidavit betraying the diamond trade, Jacques de Paiva, all I had actually done was confirm Seaton's suspicions. But who had it been that had planted those suspicions in his mind, that had divulged de Paiva's work on behalf of our faction in the first place? It occurred to me I might know the answer, after all.

Why, in heaven's name, had I not embarked upon that line of enquiry earlier? I had thought to find some answer from Katherine Nicks herself but since Seaton's death she seems to have become even more reclusive than usual.

Besides, I had Ursula to attend. She fell ill with an ague that lasted all through April and soon also struck down my other girls, as well as the tutor, Mister Smedley, engaged for the furtherance of their education. I have toyed frequently with the idea of boarding school, certainly for Kate and Annie, yet cannot quite bring myself to part with them, despite the obduracy which seems to afflict the younger of the two, worse with each month that passes. The girls were at their studies this morning – even poor Ursi, though her ability to digest education remains sadly limited.

'Perhaps she will be better once your husband is home,' said Benjamin, now returned to us from Oxford and commenced at the Inns of Court where, with the end of Trinity term yesterday, he is released from his studies at the Central Law Courts, though still without a placement in any of the barristers' chambers.

We were taking breakfast together at George Yard, a private booth in my brother Richard's coffee house, so we should not breach the prohibition against women customers. Not that anybody could have observed me anyway, through the fug of pipe smoke, the clamour of Richard's clients.

'I wonder whether the timepiece would be better here than at Broad Street,' I replied, determined to ignore his reminder of Elihu, and still excited by the precious gift's arrival. At present, as

I write, it sits upon the cabinet next to my writing slope. Dispatched by Czar Peter of Muscovy himself. A geographical clock, he had written – and written in person, too. It incorporates a thirty-year almanack, capable of telling me what o' clock it might be in any part of the world, day or night, the times of the sun's rising and setting, the arc made by the sun and each of the zodiacal signs above or below the horizon, and many other curious natural motions. And the Czar had been thoughtful enough to have one of its smaller, jewelled faces labelled in gold. *Madras.* And another, *Smyrna.*

'Why ever should you think so, Mama? It was a mark of personal gratitude from the Czar, after all. An insult, perhaps, to install it other than in your own home. And it gives me joy that my brothers are thus so frequently in our thoughts.'

'At every chime of the quarter-hour,' I smiled. 'Though it simply seems too grand for our humble abode.'

'Yet not too grand for this place?' said Benjamin. 'And the time settings – I suppose Smyrna's appropriate, given the number of our Turkey merchants.' There was a group of them, standing about one of the tables, waving their papers at each other and haggling ferociously over the price of Ottoman tobacco. 'Madras too might serve. Though the third dial, if I remember correctly, is set somewhat closer to the hour here in London. A fifteen-minute difference. Hardly worth the trouble, one might think. Ah, Paris, perhaps?'

'You are impertinent, sirrah.'

'Is he giving you trouble, sister?' Richard arriving at our table with a steaming pot of fresh chocolate.

'We all imagine,' I told him, as he re-filled our saucers, 'that our children are at their most troublesome when they are small. A mistake, Richard. You will learn, to your peril, the reverse is true, that they become a greater source of concern with every year that passes.'

'Mama,' said Benjamin, as soon as brother Richard had moved on, 'if I had a florin for each time you have bidden me mail your letters to Mister Parrish I should now be a rich fellow indeed.'

'Business,' I snapped. I have often wondered how many among my family, friends and acquaintances might assume a liaison between myself and Matthew that does not exist beyond their imaginations. At least...

'What? Progress reports on the state of decomposition of Seaton's remains?'

They still hang within an iron gibbet at the Southwark bridge-gate.

'Among other things,' I told him, realised I must have sounded petulant, 'you do not know Matthew as well as the others, but he insists on regular news of your fortunes. And there has been much to tell.'

So there had! Joseph Junior writing from Fort St. David to tell me his intention of seeking retirement from John Company, his covenanted time now being served, and making application to enjoy the privilege of being a free and independent trader. Oh, India, I thought. In my blood and my sons' blood, Walter's blood and Davy's blood, left in those distant lands. It made me think again of the voyage I had made aboard the *Rochester*, how close we had come to disaster. I still have nightmares about it.

Then, from Elford, the alarming announcement that he had been struck down by smallpox – usually a virtual death sentence – but introduced, through the new chaplain for the Smyrna factories, Mister Chishull, to a Turkish physician skilled in the strange practice of engrafting and, therefore, able to provide the treatment known as inoculation, which I do not fully comprehend. It smacks a little, to me, of Turkey witchcraft, and I am certain I should have forbidden it, given the opportunity. Yet I recall the apparent efficacy of so many Black Town rituals and medicaments and, as it happens, Elford only wrote to me when he was already cured.

'You have kept Mister Yale similarly informed, I suppose?'

He was goading me. I knew that.

'His last letter only just arrived here. You know that full well. And if our intelligence is correct, by the time I can dispatch a reply aboard one of our outbound vessels, he will already have left India.'

Two of those same tobacco traders had now almost come to blows.

'He's confirmed his plans to return?' Benjamin shouted to make himself heard over their rowdiness.

'Barely a mention. But the same. The new governor, Mister Pitt, will only now be arriving there with all the instructions and arrangements.' The offer for him to return with his fortune intact, of course. That priceless cargo whose value is so secretly assured by myself and Sir William Langhorn. If it arrives safely, and the premium is paid, the stipulated dividend forthcoming as we hope, that should at least provide some compensation for any requirement upon me to take up wifely duties once more. The truth? Ten years as my own mistress is a treasure I shall resent losing.

Of course, there is an alternative scenario – one in which this sweet bread, the concession he might bring home his wealth entire, may not be enough to persuade him, and that Pitt will be forced to apply the whip, those denunciations against Elihu and bearing my falsified signature.

'He asked about the girls though?' said Benjamin. 'Their father, after all.'

Difficult for him, I know. I shook away all thought of the reunion I might expect if Elihu knew about the denunciations. Benjamin never knew his own father and always hoped, I think, Elihu might treat him as his heir – though, in reality, he now simply resents my husband for his retention of that portion I had secured for him.

'Of course. Yet even if I could reply, what should I tell him? Ursula's life threatened by his friend Seaton? I doubt he should believe me.'

'And Mistress Nicks?'

'Well, naturally. How could my husband bear to write an entire letter without at least three paragraphs dedicated to her praise and welfare? God damn the woman, Benjamin. I thought I was past all this.'

'Perhaps damnation would be better directed towards Mister Yale himself. What of his son?'

Jeronima's boy. Charles. Carlos. How old now? Eight, of course.

'No. Simply word that Madam Paiva, as he styles her, sends her kind regards. How generous.'

Benjamin smiled at this.

'As generous as Mister Yale himself,' he said. 'You know, Mama, we now have sufficient advice to open proceedings against him. I shall have my share.'

'It is your right, Benjamin. Though might it not be better to wait and see what happens when he gets back? I am assured he will be returning with his fortune intact.'

Well, I hoped this would be the case.

'His fortune?' he said. 'This new law will give him free rein to pick up his old trade again.'

The Trade to Africa Bill. For those of us cloistered within the confines of the merchant adventurer's world, its progress has been followed with monastic dedication. The decision to shatter the monopoly of the Royal African Company and open up the most lucrative of trades with that dark continent to all comers. Merchants from Bristol and elsewhere have finally managed to garnish sufficient numbers in Parliament to push through the decision, and thus earn the ability to break into the priceless triangular trade: gewgaws and antique weapons from England to buy cargo from slavers in West Africa; slaves from West Africa dispatched to the Caribbean and Americas and sold to plantation owners as chattel; the goods from the plantations, sugar, tobacco and the rest, sent back to England and converted to gold. Is that not the way of it, this trade in human misery? And too few voices raised against it, I fear. But gracious, our noble Parliament. So long debating freedoms and rights – the freedom and rights for any who might so choose to be able to trade in human misery. Oh, England, how fair and just thou art!

'Elihu and the slave trade again?' I said. 'Somehow I doubt it. But we shall see. As it happens, that is almost the least of my concerns about my husband's return. Yet, for now, I think you may be correct. The geographical clock remains where it is!'

I climbed from the coach at Aldgate, entirely exhausted, rousing the girls and giving my thanks to those other passengers who had made the journey moderately more tolerable, endless hours helping to entertain my daughters and keep them as warm and comfortable as possible. But now? We would need a hackney to get us home. Already dark. And that was when I saw her, stepping from the doorway of the *Bull*, wraith-like as usual in her cloak and long black veil.

'Great heavens. Katherine!'

'How was it?'

'Wrexham? How did you know?'

From the inn, the smell of chops a-cooking and I put a hand to my stomach to still its grumbling. We had not eaten since the *Goat* at St. Albans.

'I needed to speak with you and went to Broad Street. Benjamin told me.'

Her speech has lost most of its slur, though she talks now only through the right side of her mouth, for the scarring has left the other entirely inoperative.

'A letter from Elihu's mother,' I said. 'It arrived two days before Christmas.'

'The aunt, was it not? Mistress Hopkins. The lady who lost her wits in the colonies. Tawny savages, I collect. A dreadful attack.'

God blind me, was there anything at all my husband had not shared with her?

'Already buried in the family crypt at St. Giles by the time the letter was sent. But Madam Yale, herself ailing, asking me to bring her granddaughters as soon as I might be able.' So we had made that execrable journey again. I had only been there last year for Thomas's funeral, and an annual visit was too much to bear. 'Five days there,' I said, 'a week at Plas Grono, and six days back. But the girls enjoyed it, did you not, my lovelies?'

Six days back because we had stopped an extra day at Birmingham to visit Joseph's sister Joanne, still grieving the loss of her own husband.

'They have winter,' said Ursula, rubbing at her sleepy eyes. 'Real, real winter.'

The coachmen were slinging down the travelling chests, and I summoned a waiting urchin to help us move our own cases and my large valise.

'Snow,' I said. 'And the local river thick with ice.'

In London it had been one of the mildest winters anybody could remember. No Frost Fair this year.

'Elihu's mother,' said Mistress Nicks, 'ailing, you say?'

'I doubt she will survive to see the bluebells in flower.'

She lifted her hand to the veil, a gasp of genuine concern, I think.

'We went skating every day,' said Kate.

Children can be such sweet distraction from the unpleasant realities of life.

'And you, Nan,' said Mistress Nicks, 'you enjoyed it too?'

That grated upon me as well. I had only ever heard Elihu call her Nan.

'I should rather have been here,' Annie told her.

'Well, we need a hackney,' I said, thinking to send the same urchin to find one.

'I have already taken the liberty,' she replied. 'It should be here at any moment. Benjamin says you never replaced Thornton.'

'I have not quite been able to bring myself to do so. The carriage sits idle at Mister Benson's livery stables. The horses must be enjoying the respite and he cares for them very well, but it shall not answer in the longer term. Ah, the hackney. Come, girls, home at last.'

'Might I travel with you?' Katherine asked. 'There are things I must discuss.'

The hackney driver loaded our baggage, once more with the urchin's assistance, and I tipped the lad a sixpence for his troubles.

'You have heard from my husband?'

'He must have told you the same. How much he looks forward to being reunited with his mama, sharing family comfort with her after Thomas's death.'

'They were very close,' I said. 'The news must have been devastating for him.'

'My Papa is coming home,' Ursula told her.

Coming home. It seems such an alien concept. And his own letter to me, still insisting he should have been allowed to erect a monument to little Walter. His main regret, he says. The thought he might leave Madras Patnam without that deed fulfilled. I hope he means it, that it is no mere deception, that he has not defied my wishes, regardless. For I had made my views on the matter very clear indeed. No vainglorious obelisk for my son to match the monstrosity beneath which I was so foolishly persuaded to lay his father. No, Walter shall remain sleeping beneath that simple cracked headstone with his Papa close by to comfort him.

'Yes, coming home,' Katherine Nicks replied, as we all bundled inside the hackney, despite the protests of the coachman that we were too many and some of us should take a separate conveyance. Yet I told the rogue we had his registration number and would report him to the proper authorities should he not deliver us, post haste, to the direction I had given him. 'Yet I believe,' she told me, over the top of this altercation, 'that his brother's demise makes his return more certain. Though Sir William seems to think the thing is without question.'

'Langhorn?'

'Of course. I pressed him for the details.'

Aldgate was behind us now, the city wall to our right as we made the corner turn into Beavis Marks where, despite the hour, torches were all ablaze and there was a great to-and-fro of hauliers, workmen busy about the synagogue being constructed there. Strange to think of it, really, this great warren of London's Jewry, the same Sefardis who had been expelled from Spain and Portugal all that time ago, as the Jews had for so long been expelled from England, and only welcomed to settle here again by Lord Protector Cromwell. The same Sefardis who had also been welcomed to India, who had styled themselves the Paradesi, and who had made their homes at Madras Patnam and elsewhere. Strange that my life should seem so bound with them.

'I needed to speak with you about Sir William,' I said. 'Perhaps later.' But I suspected I might not do so. And would she know? Was she the guilty party? Might she tell me the truth in any case? Anyway, with Seaton dead it somehow seems less important to me, now, to know the source of his information about Jacques de Paiva's clandestine activities. And Elihu's possible involvement with Seaton? If he is coming home, I suppose it should be more important. But sleeping dogs? Perhaps, for the girls, that might be best. Yes, sleeping dogs. On this, and on those denunciations also.

'As you wish,' she said. 'Yet I've received word from John too. He says if Elihu sails for England, he will journey with him. The children also. The girls anyway.'

'You have children, Mistress Nicks?' Kate asked her.

'Yes,' she said. 'A great many children. Some of them now fully grown. Did you know? Rowley, Pelle, Jenny and Nance. Oh, and Dionysia – though we tend to call her Donchy. The younger ones almost the same ages as yourselves. Betty and Ursula…'

'That's my name too,' Ursi clapped her hands with delight.

'And young Elihu, I collect,' I said, as sweetly as I was able.

'Oh,' said Nan, 'did you name him for our Papa?'

'Well…' said Mistress Nicks.

'Ah, look,' I said, as a night watch brazier illuminated a familiar junction. 'St. Mary Axe. Should we drop you here, my dear?'

Tonight I thought I would be glad to see the back of her.

'I should prefer to travel a little further with you,' she said. 'Still much to discuss.'

Ursula begged for her to stay and, by then, we had passed the junction anyhow, making our way along Camomile Street, that den of thieves and debtors.

'Quiet, Ursi,' I whispered. 'You'll wake your sisters.' They were both dozing again. 'Arrangements,' I said to Mistress Nicks, 'for your children perhaps, when they arrive?'

'Catherine, I will not be here.'

There was a finality about her terse statement that confused me.

'Something takes you out of London? How can you be so certain when we do not have the date?'

'To Fort St. George. I sail next Saturday with Captain Lesly. The *Neptune*.'

I remember being entirely stunned. Still feel that way as I write the lines. Worse, I recall the absurd sense of bereavement, the realisation I should not wish her gone from my life. Is that not bizarre? Though I was damn'd if I should reveal this foolishness.

'I think I do not understand.'

'John is penniless. He would, I know, become a burden upon me. And the children, I would not have them see me like this.'

'If I am honest,' I said, as quietly as I was able, despite the shake and clatter of our wheels over the cobbles, 'I never truly understood why you married him. And in such haste after my own wedding to Mister Yale.'

She turned away then, began to play that finger game, Odds and Evens, which Ursula enjoys so much – and at which she is uncannily adept, as Mistress Nicks was just discovering.

'So, sweet one,' she said and held out her clenched fist towards my daughter. 'What do we think? Did I marry for love?'

Ursula thrust out her own fist too.

'One… Two… *Three*,' she yelled, and their respective fingers stretched out.

'Let me see,' said Katherine. 'Three of my fingers, two of yours. Five. Odds. So not for love then. For money, perhaps? And my turn to count.' The same result. This time only three fingers, so not for money either – though that much I already knew. For protection? Not that. Three fingers once more. Because she admired her husband-to-be? No again, seven fingers this time. 'Yet what,' she said, 'if I was obliged to marry?' Three fingers each. 'She is a perceptive child, Catherine. She knows me far better than you, I see.'

'Obliged?' I said. 'How could you be…?' Perhaps I have always suspected, somewhere deep within me. 'A babe?'

'I was sure Elihu would marry me, was about to tell him when the Governor made the announcement to Council you were both to be wed. I had not seen him for a few weeks, as it happens. I think he had been avoiding me. But then, the announcement made – well, I needed a new plan. And John was always willing, as you'll remember.'

'The…?'

'I lost it just a week later. John never knew.'

'Wait. My own letter from Elihu. A reference that did not signify when first I read it. About not knowing how he would cope with London. You expect him to follow you to Fort St. George, do you not? You have planned it so?'

'You make the whole thing seem so sordid. What did you expect?'

The bustle of Bishopsgate, where we were delayed some while before we could cross into Wormwood.

'All that time,' I said. 'I feel such a bubble. Your liaison began even before we were wed.' It almost made me laugh, that extent of my cupidity. 'And then, with your husband away at Porto Novo…'

'Catherine, this is in part what I needed to tell you. I have my secrets, but this you should know. That none of my surviving children are his. Not Elihu's.'

'I should believe you?'

'It matters little to me whether you should or should not. But it is the truth. And when, as I believe he will, he returns to Madras, it will be to his own son and heir, not for my sake.'

'Don Carlos,' I said, recalling the time when I had read Elihu's letter to her, about Joseph Junior visiting the Garden House and claiming Jeronima had practised upon him, about the boy.

'Don Carlos,' she said.

'Who is Don Carlos?' Ursula asked, turning first to one of us, then to the other.

'Just a little boy we both know,' said Katherine Nicks. 'Perhaps you shall meet him one day.'

'Is he nice?'

'Yes. Nice.'

I somehow felt as though my world had turned upon its beam end. A little like the time aboard the *Rochester* when I had been certain we must surely broach, only to have that brave vessel right herself again. But confusion still reigned and I found myself fumbling at my skirts, the pocket pistol returned now to its usual hiding place. For Seaton might be gone but out there somewhere Colonel John Porter still lurked, and other enemies too, I imagined. Enemies. Like Katherine Nicks? I wrapped my hand around that small but deadly weapon. Oh, it would be so easy!

'Your own Ursula,' I said. 'Young Elihu…'

'I named them in honour of your husband, Catherine. He is their godfather. Nothing more. I told you so once before. Don Carlos, though, is his heir.'

Godfather only. Yes, I remembered. And the letter I had received from Joseph Junior, all that time ago. He had not believed it, I think, and neither had I. And did I not count the months when her youngest was born? Had I not been certain John Nicks was in Conimere at the time of the child's conception? Have I been wrong, all this time?

'I always thought myself a perceptive person, one who understands the world in which I swim. One who understands those others around me. One who understands my inner self. That is what I learned from Matthew Parrish's Sathiri.'

'The person we think we are,' she said, 'is not the person seen by others. The person we think we are does not exist. We hide from ourselves the characteristics others might see plainly. And no other person truly knows us either for the same reasons. We are in part a conglomeration of everybody else's image of us.'

Was she right? I remembered those lines from Julius Caesar, of which Elihu was so fond. Her Cassius to my Brutus, telling me that, acting as my mirror, she could discern my innermost thoughts about Elihu and about our narrow little world even before I was aware of them myself.

'Shall we not meet again?' I said, as we clattered along Wormwood and swung into Broad Street, the two girls stirring as Ursula shook them awake.

'There will be much to keep me in Madras, I think. After all, I am part owner of a worthless diamond mine – the purchase of which put me in considerable debt, remember?'

'And when Elihu called in that debt, it stopped you bringing your children home. How can you bear to lose the opportunity of being reunited with them now?'

'I can bear it because I must. And I have always considered the debt called in by Elihu was at least an honest transaction. Whereas, Mistress Yale, the debt under which you placed me...'

I recalled the diamonds destined for her, which Wadham had waylaid – the diamonds of my own that Ferñao Pereira had sequestered for so long against Elihu's repayment of the silver the syndicate dispatched to Jacques de Paiva, not knowing he had died. It had been a tangled web and I was only pleased she did not comprehend the full story.

'The mine?' I said. 'Well, who knows, perhaps it shall yield some benefit to you after all.'

'That would be a fool's errand indeed. But Sir Stephen Evance has provided a contract for me to investigate the diamond trade once more. That, at least should be more lucrative.'

Evance had been useful to Thomas in Parliament, his appeal to the Privy Council on Elihu's behalf. Elihu, in turn, had made certain investments for Sir Stephen. And now, as Jeweller to the King...

'Another contact through Sir William?'

'Naturally. And a small enough reward from the Crown for the services we rendered.'

'I remember that time at my dinner table, at Fort St. George, you said how much you should love to see London? Now you have seen enough?'

We had come to a halt outside the house, light appearing from the doorway, Fletchley, Ellen the housekeeper and Nanny Green coming down the steps to greet us.

'Enough. I have served your husband's business interests sufficiently here, I think. And I shall continue to do so back in Madras. Until he is ready to take them up again himself. He trusts me, Catherine.'

Yes, I see that now. She must, I think, be the closest friend Elihu ever had, perhaps the one person in the world he trusts entirely. For some reason, it makes me think of my own return to England, safely landed from the *Rochester* despite everything. And then the poor ship sent to the breakers' yard because she was finished. She had given her soul to bring us home, me and my three tiny girls. And now Katherine Nicks would make her own last voyage, a similarly selfless voyage on Elihu's behalf.

'We two,' I said, as Fletchley took our cases from the still grumbling hackney driver, and the girls were hurried indoors, 'have been through a great deal together.'

'But never truly trusted each other, I think.'

She began to climb out of the hackney herself.

'Fate? *Karma*?' I said.

'I believe in neither. We are the masters of our own fate, Mistress Yale.'

'At least keep the hackney,' I said, paying the coachman and including the additional fare for her return to St. Mary Axe. I could almost hear Elihu. *Julius Caesar* again. *The fault, dear Brutus, is not in our stars, but in ourselves.* 'And a pity,' I told her. 'It should still have fallen to me to kill Seaton.'

'Oh, you did, Catherine. For it was you who brought him there to his execution ground. So I would give you this final piece of advice. John's letter. He mentions one more thing. That the ship which brings them back will not carry our two husbands alone, but also Winifred Bridger.' I felt as though somebody had walked over my grave, trembled, and remembered the *Revanche*. Those premonitions of retribution. 'John wrote something strange,' she went on. 'Something about how Winifred seeks revenge. Seaton she named, apparently, having finally seen the evidence that it was he who concocted the evidence against her own husband, the evidence that ruined him. Well, too late for her to seek justice in yonder quarter. But it seems she also made some comment about her husband's cold-blooded murderer. Does that make sense to you?'

Of course it does. Had I not wondered, so many times aboard the *Rochester*, how my schemes at Fort St. George might play out? Well, here I am, ten years on, and the chase still not fully run.

'To make sense of the irrational,' I said, 'requires the logic of Elisha.'

'Then God go with you, Mistress Yale, for I doubt we shall meet again. Not in this world.'

'Is that him, Mama?' said Kate, as we stood at the Billingsgate Stairs, a warm breeze blowing up the river towards us, twisting around the edges of the busy dock to whip dishevelled hair into our eyes despite our bonnets.

'I am sure it must be,' I told her, though to be honest I could not be certain. Instead I remembered that night in Madras Patnam when we had first gone on the *masula* boats to visit the Company's new Garden House, which Governor Langhorn had conceived, and Streynsham had seen completed.

'"*The barge she sat in,*"' Elihu had quoted, in some strange and embarrassing premature attempt to flatter me, '"*like a burnish'd throne, burned on the water.*"'

And here was his own gilded barge or, rather, the Long Ferry from Gravesend, its upper hull above the black rubbing strake indeed painted sunshine yellow. He stood in the bow, one foot upon the gunwale and his back resting against the forrard of her two short masts, arms folded across his chest to embrace his walking cane. Every inch the hero returning from his conquests. He had changed though. Ten years changed. Fifty now, heavier in every way, and it was more the elegance of his attire that marked him for the Elihu Yale I remembered. Difficult at this distance to determine the precise colours of his justaucorps and breeches, but some dark shade, maroon perhaps, his silk stockings adorned with ribbons to match. Yet his long waistcoat blazing like a beacon, scarlet with silver thread to match the silver-grey of his peruke. Peacock!

'Mama, it stinks here.' Ursula glared up at me, little fingers pinching the sides of her nostrils. She was right, of course. Seaweed, but the stench of fish everywhere too, and the normal noxious odours wafting down to us from the chaos of the bridge itself, away to our right.

They were still some little way from the quay, the ferrymen playing the twin spritsails to bring her across the flood tide, towards the steps. But he saw us just then, began to wave both arms like a loon, then shouted back towards the canvas awning, the tilt that gives these vessels their name, which provides shelter from the elements along the aftward portion of the deck for both passengers and cargo.

'My family,' he was shouting. 'My family.'

But apart from the occasional disinterested glance, the tilt boat's crew seemed entirely unimpressed. They had begun to shift his dunnage out from beneath the striped canvas, ready for offloading.

'Mama,' Ursi clutched at my skirts, 'he is very big. Very loud.'

'He has a bark, my dear. Like Cabal, I suppose.' The deerhound, which resided in the house just two doors from our own on Broad Street. 'But how gentle is that old dog when you come to know him.'

Great heavens, it almost sounded tender to my own ears. What did I expect from this homecoming, after all? I had no idea. Still have no idea. Yet I could almost sense my independence slipping away from me at every boat-length with which he drew nearer.

'Why so long,' Annie demanded to know, 'to get here?'

'You have asked me this every day since we had word of him, Annie. The answer, I fear, is still the same.'

The *Martha* anchored in The Downs ten days ago and Elihu had troubled to send messages ashore, letting me know his plans. They were due to arrive at the Long Reach, Gravesend, two days later, where the bulk of his cargo would be unloaded and shipped by lighter to the East India Company's warehouses at Blackwall. But he himself would not disembark until he could do so with the private chests he had brought with him in the *Martha*'s great cabin. And that would not take place until today, once they had been fully inspected by the Customs Officers. He apologised for the delay in our reunion – a delay, I must confess, which I did not entirely regret – wished me to express his affection to the girls, and sent me the tidal calculations made by the Long Ferrymen with an estimate of his arrival time. That should have been an hour earlier but – well, here he was, the sails let go, hauled down, along with the sprit itself, and the helmsman giving her tiller a pretty enough touch, slewing the boat round to bring her alongside the wharf, while one of the hands launched her rope fenders over the side and another threw a stern line turn around a mooring post.

'Oh, my beautiful girls,' Elihu cried, bounding up the stairs, his eyes brimming with tears. 'Darling Kate.' He passed me his walking cane almost without a second glance, lifted her in his arms – or tried to do so. 'God blind me, you are grown tall as a bean-pole.'

'You expected her still to be four, Elihu?' I said. A colder greeting than I had rehearsed. 'That is ten years' healthy eating you are attempting to hoist.'

Then he looked at Annie, thought better of raising her up as well and settled instead for a clumsy embrace.

'And sweet Nan. Yet my goodness, wife, you have indeed fed them well, I see.'

It was all so formal. But when he turned to Ursula, his brow furrowed, as though he were trying to calculate something. Ursi, for her own part, refused to be separated from my skirts so received merely a paternal stroke of her hair.

'Yes,' I said, in an effort to help him. 'Ursula is small for her age, is she not?' He nodded, stooped down to examine her, tweaked her plump cheek and gave her his widest, warmest smile, though she simply buried her face deeper in the folds of my peach-striped silks. 'And your travelling companions? I had not expected you to arrive alone.'

'Ah, dear lady.' He took my hand without affection and kissed it. A stranger's kiss, though his eyes, I saw, were always upon the dunnage now finally being hauled up onto the sand-blown quayside – three large chests, seven smaller cases and two separate writing slopes, one of them fabulously inlaid in the Indian style with ivory, tortoiseshell and mother-of-pearl.

'Has Papa brought us gifts?' Ursula asked me in a loud stage whisper, while her sisters scolded her for such impertinence.

'Careful, you rogues,' Elihu laughed. 'Did you not hear? Those chests contain precious gifts for my girls.' Then he turned to me. 'All of my girls,' he said, quietly.

It was the thing that had been troubling me since I first heard he was coming home. Is it possible? To simply turn back the clocks? Not just the ten years we have been apart but long, long before that, when there was at least some modicum of substance in our marriage.

And while I was mulling this over, searching for a clever riposte, Elihu was fishing in the pockets of that silver-threaded waistcoat for small coins, crossed each of their palms with a shilling while he finally answered my own question.

'Poor John Nicks,' said my husband, 'suffered badly during the voyage. His girls too. So they took coach direct from Gravesend, the sooner to be reunited with his wife.'

'Ah, Elihu...' I began, but he was in full flow.

'And Winifred Bridger, her two girls, have gone first to Rochester. Some relations there. Though I wonder you should trouble to ask after her. You hardly parted as friends, I collect.'

The time for news of Katherine Nicks seemed to have passed, at least for the moment. And I did not regret it for I still expected him at any moment to reproach me yet again for having cheated her in the sale of the mine. Or to raise those damnable denunciations with my forged signature.

'Tanani?' I said. 'Have you news of Tanani?'

'Still working at the Garden House. *Ayah* to...'

He stopped himself, needed to say no more. *Ayah* to his whore, Jeronima.

'Well,' I said, 'we have my carriage at the *Lion and Key*.' I pointed towards Thames Street where we had left the conveyance and the driver I had hired from Mister Benson. 'What should you wish, husband? Some victuals at the *Lion* or straight home to Broad Street?'

I had made this assumption, of course, and half-expected him to counter with some apology that he had arranged lodgings elsewhere. Or perhaps simply hoped he might do so. One of his many associates, maybe. But he did not.

'I could eat one the Gentues' sacred cows,' he said, snatching back his cane. 'What say you, girls? Some good English food at last. God's hooks, I am so tired of pickled goat.' Katie and Anne dutifully wrinkled their noses at the very thought, while Elihu turned to see the tilt boat's crew now making the vessel all safe and snug, pending the turn of wind and tide. 'You rascals,' he yelled. 'A silver croker a-piece if you will carry my boxes to the *Lion and Key*.'

It was plain they intended visiting one of the local establishments anyway, so we gave them instruction, then went ahead while they set about the task, though with Elihu frequently looking behind to make sure his valuables were not left unattended or abandoned, particularly as we pushed our way past the stalls and arcades lining that side of the dock.

'Benjamin regrets he could not be here to greet you, by the way,' I told him, seeking a gentle way to break my other news to him, and trying to herd the three girls before me, to keep them focused on our path and away from the vendors' attractions surrounding them on every hand – the currant and meat puddings, the water flagons. The boating capes, ironware and pottery, and the wines. Wines from France. Wines from Porto. Ah, Porto! I think Elihu noticed the markings on the casks at the same time.

'Benjamin, yes. But Catherine... Richard – my dear, how inadequate my words must have seemed.'

The first sign of any warmth from him. Did he know, after all, about the denunciations?

'Not at all. And there is much else I must needs tell you.'

But the noise. How might I compete with the fishwives, screaming from their places on the further side of the dock, the Tower outlined against the sky behind them. It was all "Handsome cod!" and "Yarmouth bloaters!" or "Fine fat mussels!" and "Alive, alive oh!"

'Of course,' said Elihu. 'And so much to do. The probating of Papa's will. Wrexham, to see Mama.'

'There, husband. I was hoping for a better moment, but you must hear this now, I fear. I was at Plas Grono myself, at the turn of the year. Your Aunt Hopkins had passed away.'

'Oh, that is bad news indeed, but at least the poor dear is now at peace. I have been thinking about her a great deal. My uncle Edward Hopkins made a great bequest, did you know? Established the Hopkins School in New Haven. Connecticut. Is that not prime? Mama will miss her though.'

'Are you talking about Grandmama Yale?' said Anne. 'Oh, Papa...' And she took his hand, looked at him most pitifully.

'My dear?' He looked down at her.

'Elihu,' I said, 'I fear I had not long arrived home when word reached us that your Ma too...'

'Oh, say it is not so.'

'She was plainly ailing badly when I saw her. I suggested staying to care for her but she insisted she would soon be well again.'

My offer had hardly been effusive, truth be told. But my wifely duty, I had supposed. And both Annie and Kate now moved to his side.

'Are you crying, Papa?' Kate asked him.

'Dead and buried, both?' he sobbed.

'I fear so, husband. The funeral in February, though I could not be there.'

We had reached that jumble of stones, all that yet remain of the old watergate, and Elihu stopped at the corner, looking all about him as though lost, or seeking something undefined, trying desperately to hide his tears from the girls. And a brace of ruffians, mistaking his purpose, rushed up to him, shouting the service they thought he was seeking.

'You blackguards!' he yelled, swung at them with his walking cane. 'How dare you, sirrah!'

They dodged the blow neatly enough, cursed him for a madman with profanities that, I hope, my daughters did not comprehend, and ran off to ply their trade elsewhere.

'My dear,' I said, touching him for the first time since his landing. 'They are simply touts for the wherrymen.'

'But they were offering...'

'No,' I told him. 'It has become the thing now. Part of the wherrymen's canting tongue. They were offering you "oars" – not...'

He produced a kerchief from his pocket, blew his nose, made some excuse to the girls about his foolishness and no, he had not truly meant to strike those fellows.

'But come,' he said, 'we shall eat and try to be merry. This should be a day for rejoicing, when all is said and done.' Yet I could see that news of Madam Yale's death had shaken him badly.

We turned along Thames Street and crossed Dark House Lane – all fish and fruit, oysters and ice houses – to reach the *Lion* while I kept up a steady stream of chatter, which I hoped might break the ice.

'Elford though, did I tell you? Smallpox in Smyrna, though thank our Lord Jesu he is recovered. And do you have word of Joseph? He wrote to tell me he intended application to become an independent trader.'

'Great heavens, no. The new governor – Pitt, do you know him? I suppose you might. Fine fellow, we shall do some business together.' Then he looked me straight in the eye. 'No secrets between Pitt and myself,' he said, and there was a chill to his words. 'But in any case he told your boy he is far too valuable for such nonsense. Promoted him to Provisional Mintmaster.'

'Nonsense?' I said. 'You seem to have done passably well from independent trade.'

'Well, we shall see,' he said, as we were shown to a table in the inn's haze-filled dining parlour, at a grimy window overlooking the yard.

'Yet you mentioned Benjamin. He has a place now?'

'The Chambers of Sir William Williams.'

'Speaker of the House? Great heavens, my father knew him well. Prime!'

How was I to tell him that much of Benjamin's time seems taken in preparation of the court case he intends to pursue for recovery of the full inheritance from which he feels Elihu has cheated him?

He ordered a shoulder of lamb, dishes of buttered potato and braised summer vegetables, claret, and anything the girls might desire, while I pressed him for more news of Winifred Bridger, trying to assuage this concern that would not leave me.

'You are correct, of course,' I said. 'We could have parted on better terms.'

'Not the most forthcoming of women,' he said. 'A Jew, you know?'

'Well, yes...' I wanted to make some comment about his concubine, his by-blow's mother. But in front of the girls, I must confess to having been left quite speechless.

'And changed still more since she took the widow's weeds. A little deranged, I think. Spent much of that interminable voyage telling me she has debts to settle. And I do not think she intended financial debts. Though she seemed to imply I should know her meaning.' Did he? I think not, but I could not help the feeling that, through Elihu, Winifred Bridger was sending me a message – and it made me fearful. Could she have fathomed that I was perhaps the cause of her husband's death? 'Are you listening, wife?' Elihu was saying. 'You look pale.'

'I am perfectly well.'

The tilt boat's crewmen provided safe distraction from further interrogation, seeking us out and d'offing caps to tell us they had found the coachman as directed and the chests were now all loaded. Elihu checked through the window, poured from his purse the promised groats.

'Then – where was I?' he said, as the sailors shouted coarsely for a table of their own. 'Ah, Mistress Bridger. Still holds me accountable, I think, for her husband's fall from grace. The Garden House and so on. Yet it was Vincent, of course, who discovered all his wrongdoing. Whatever became of him, I wonder?'

'Seaton?'

Here was something else I had never been able to consign to the written page – nowhere but in these journals, of course.

'Yes, Seaton. You do not still harbour all those foolish suspicions about him, I hope.' He laughed to himself. 'And where *is* our dinner?'

'Mama,' whispered Ursula, 'have you told Papa about the singing man?'

Elihu glanced at her, pulled forth his kerchief again and made some pretense of mopping sweat from his face, but murmured to me from behind the linen.

'Why *is* the child so small? And so...'

'So simple-minded?' I muttered, with my face turned towards the parlour's other diners, allowing my words to float away from my daughters. Then I turned back to face him. 'Yet she is the most joyous of infants. A godly child, always at her prayers and never happier than when we are at church together. Her injury may have stunted her growth in many ways, yet it seems to have awoken something in her spirit that was absent before.'

'Injury?'

Dinner arrived, the innkeeper flicking the remains of the previous customers' debris from our table.

'Elihu, it is an incredibly long story. And not fit for...'

I glanced towards the girls, and he studied them too for a moment.

'Ursula,' he said, cutting into the lamb and sharing slices between their plates. 'This singing man. Who is he, my dear? Some friend of your Mama?'

His tone had adopted a sharp edge, a suspicious edge. God blind me, what was he thinking? And Ursi looked up at me, waiting for my permission to speak. I nodded to her.

'He hit me, Papa,' she said. 'The singing man. I banged my head. And he hurt Susannah.'

'Susannah?'

'Our nursemaid,' I said. 'But I have told you, husband, a long story. Do you not think...?'

'It seems you have allowed some wretch into your home – some fellow. And that this fellow...'

'Elihu, it was Seaton.'

He dropped the knife, splashed some of the meat fats across the girls.

'You – and Seaton?'

'Your suspicions could not be further from the truth,' I snapped, and bade them clean their faces with a napkin. 'And you cannot imagine, Elihu,' I hissed, 'how much I despise both the suspicion and the hypocrisy. But you should know one thing. One thing only. That Vincent Seaton is now dead, sirrah. Executed by Matthew Parrish.' He threw up his hands in exasperation.

'Oh, I might have known Parrish would feature somewhere in this fantasy.'

I could see Katie's face begin to crumple. Not precisely how she had envisaged her father's homecoming either.

'Executed by Matthew Parrish,' I hissed. 'And by Mistress Nicks also.'

'Katherine Nicks? What in heaven's name…?'

'I told you, a very long story indeed. Now, girls,' I said to them, 'there is no need to be upset. Papa and I simply need a word together. Katie, you are the oldest. Take care of your sisters a moment.'

'But Mama…'

I stood from the table, went to stand near the door, from where I could still observe our table, the sad and troubled expressions on the faces of Kate and Annie, the usual innocent curiosity in Ursi's eyes.

'Katherine Nicks?' said Elihu again as he came to stand at my side. 'My dear, I do not understand any of this.'

'John Nicks,' I said. 'He comes home with his fortune made?'

'What has this to do with…? Never mind. No, penniless. Entirely penniless.'

'I see. Perhaps that explains one thing, at least.'

'But Mistress Nicks has been compensating for her husband's lack of business acumen, I think. Would you not agree? Why, she even managed to make good the loss she suffered from that damn'd mine you sold her. And then again when those diamonds were stolen.'

'Stolen? I thought the diamonds were impounded by the Customs House.'

'Great heavens, Catherine. Did you not know she smoked that one? She wrote to me to say she had discovered the truth. Some strange claim the brilliants were stolen by a thief-taker. I have no idea what she intended but she was punctilious enough about replacing their value.'

She knew? My heart sank as fast as the *Johane* had done. Thief-taker? Surely she could have intended none but Wadham. But how? Through Wadham himself? And not confronted me? Sweet Jesu, that woman has depths I never fathomed.

'We worked together,' I said. 'To bring Seaton to justice. For the Crown, Elihu. For the Crown. Vincent Seaton was a Jacobite traitor. Oh, I see you do not believe me. Yet you shall do so, I am certain, when you know the full story. "*Let me have about me men that are fat.*" Is this not what you might have told me? But Seaton was lean, hungry, indeed. Yet still a story for another time.'

'And you put my daughters in danger in the process. Catherine, this must stop. I am home now. Your husband. We must try to pick up the pieces of our lives. Begin again, perhaps. But this about Seaton...'

Is it possible, a new beginning? I know not. But I recall the pledge I made to myself when I left Madras. That I should play my part. Have I done so? A small part, I suppose. Ten years. The uncertainty then of James Stuart's exile. Would he return to place us under the thumb of the Romish Church? Or would good William of Orange free us from that threat? I thank God it has been the latter. And yes, a small part, I suppose.

As I write, I look at the geographical clock, that gift from Czar Peter of Muscovy who claims he owes me his life. And Sir William Cavendish, Duke of Devonshire, the same. Yet, as always, these scribblings in my journal give me pause for doubt, a lack of certainty about whether I have set the record correctly. I am in two minds, doubtful in that way also.

About the future I am doubtful indeed. Is it possible for me to set aside all those questions remaining unanswered at Seaton's death? And possible to set aside Elihu's infidelity – at least so far as Jeronima de Paiva is concerned? Possible to believe Katherine

Nicks that Elihu is indeed no more than her children's godfather? Possible to become a family again, with Elihu at its head? Possible to avoid Winifred Bridger and whatever vengeful intentions she may harbour? Possible to discern the reality of whatever may be passing through the devious mind of Katherine Nicks? Possible that I may one day be reunited with Matthew Parrish and perhaps reconcile whatever it is that exists between us? Possible I might now be free of the politicks and intrigue that – as Elihu correctly says – have so endangered our lives, damaged my daughter?

Ah, but I see I have paused in my narrative, left the telling of our reunion in the *Lion and Key* incomplete. It is strange since, to some extent, this feels like my wedding night afresh. I am married again, that much is beyond dispute. My freedom gone once more. But my husband in a room of his own, as he was then, the decision that it should be so simply tacit, needing no debate. And in the *Lion*…?

'Stop?' I said. 'Yes, I can promise you, husband. Seaton was the end of it. I am done with politicks and intrigue.'

'Then let us say no more.' He touched my arm. Hardly a tender touch, but enough to reassure me – or perhaps simply to delude me – that, if indeed he knew about the denunciations in my name, those too might now be set aside. 'And I shall look forward to hearing the tale,' he said. 'Both from yourself and, I hope, from Mistress Nicks too. I suspect she may already have shared the thing with her husband.'

There was some longing in his voice, a distance in his eye, which filled me with irritation, with spite. And there I stood, with the one piece of knowledge that I knew would wound him.

'Oh,' I said, feigning surprise as best I could. 'With her husband? I hardly think so. But did she not write to tell you…?'

The End

Historical Notes and Acknowledgements

As readers of *The Doubtful Diaries of Wicked Mistress Yale* will recall, I stumbled into this particular story through a chance discussion with our excellent Member of Parliament, Ian Lucas, early in 2018. He had developed a fascination with one of our Wrexham (North Wales) constituency historical celebrities, Elihu Yale, whose elaborate tomb stands in the old burial ground of St. Giles Church in the town's centre. Ian's fascination was infectious, though I soon became even more intrigued by Yale's wife.

Original research allowed me to follow Catherine's real-life story – and yes, to embroider all manner of fictional inventions with which to fill the many gaps – from 1672 until her return from Madras in 1689. My intention, of course, has been to tell the story of nabob collector (and slave trader) Elihu Yale through the eyes of his much-maligned and largely overlooked wife – and thus to tell a very different tale from that which we normally hear of the god-fearing philanthropist who gave generously of his fortune and his name for the benefit of one of the USA's most famous educational establishments.

But, in this second part of the trilogy, I was faced with a different dilemma if I was going to tell the next chapter of their stories but without Elihu appearing directly even once through the entire novel, except at the very end. That was a bit of a stretch but hopefully it works well enough and allows readers to continue enjoying Catherine's saga, from the time of her own voyage back to London through to Elihu's return ten years later.

Ten troubled years too, all the way through the Glorious Revolution and the turmoil of an England in the grip of one Jacobite plot after the other. And it seemed natural that Catherine should be embroiled in those troubles as she had previously been involved in the politics of Fort St. George. For these sections I relied heavily on Nadine Akkerman's *Invisible Agents: Women and Espionage in the Seventeenth Century*.

Once again, the story is told entirely through Catherine's secret journals, so maybe a word here about diarists of this period. I was particularly interested in the paper written for the *Eras* journal by Elaine McKay: *The Diary Network in Sixteenth and Seventeenth Century England*. This paper makes the point that those years saw a great flowering of diarists but whose work never came to public attention until a long time after their deaths. So Samuel Pepys's diary not published until 1825, John Evelyn's not until 1818, Lady Margaret Hoby's only in 1930, and the journal of Reverend Roger Morrice (who appears in the third part of the trilogy) only in 2007. Diaries and journals were known, of course, but only those of the "ancients" – Marcus Aurelius, Suetonius, Plutarch and others. Yet Elaine McKay cites the work of William Matthews, who has listed no less than 328 known diaries from England, Scotland and Wales between 1440 and 1700. And while those might not have seen the light of day while their authors were alive, their works show the diarists themselves were often "connected" through shared interests – so that, for example, Pepys was familiar with the journal-writing of John Evelyn, and both of them were associated with diarist Sir William Rider and, through Sir William, to Arthur Annesley and others. The diarists were frequently also essayists or correspondents on their shared interests – science, politics, religious belief – though the diaries and journals themselves remained personal and private in the extreme. So this was a theme I want to explore a bit further in *Wicked Mistress Yale, The Parting Glass*.

Otherwise, and apart from the resources listed in *The Doubtful Diaries of Wicked Mistress Yale*, I had to get through additional research on Wrexham in the 17th Century; on politics and religion in the 1690s; on life in London during that same decade – for example, to get a real sense of St. Paul's Cathedral still without its iconic dome but also as a symbol of the city's re-birth after the Great Fire; on the upheavals within the English East India Company; on the diamond trade; on Czar Peter (and his dwarf) during their Great Embassy to Holland and England; and on the relationship between Elihu Yale and Katherine Nicks – principally from the Yale University Library Manuscript and Archive Collection of letters (more than fifty of them) between them both, beginning in early 1699 and ending with her death, in Madras, during 1709. And much more from those letters, of course, in part three of the trilogy, *Mistress Yale's Diaries, The Parting Glass*. Full details of the various resources in question are listed in full on my website, www.davidebsworth.com.

But then there are all those historical points with which I took certain liberties. For example, the precise circumstances of the deaths of Elihu's father and elder brother, David, are lost to us, though the dates of their deaths are a matter of record. In fact, David Yale Senior and Junior both died in January 1691, rather than 1690 as I have them here.

Second, there is considerable confusion about Katherine Nicks and her children. Yale's biographers usually detail her as having ten children, with varying degrees of suspicion about whether the youngest four might have been sired by Elihu himself. She certainly seems to have shared his garden house at Fort St. George along with Jeronima de Paiva (or Hieronima as she is more commonly known) and Jeronima's son, Carlos – and there is little or no doubt about whether Yale was Carlos's father. It is then usually claimed that Katherine Nicks sailed back to England, alone, to present her husband's petition to the Privy Council, and remained in England virtually until Yale's own return in 1699. However, that cannot be the case. The archives at Yale University hold that remarkable collection of letters between Elihu Yale and Katherine Nicks, and these plainly show that her four youngest were all born in Madras during the 1690s. Perhaps, therefore, she was in England only a short while, long enough to present the petition. Or perhaps she never left Madras at all. Whatever the truth, I have chosen a version that suited the story, with those children of a more similar age to Catherine Yale's own girls.

Sir Streynsham Master is an interesting character but I have brought his knighthood forward a year to 14th December 1697 instead of 1698. As fate would have it, in my first novel, *The Jacobites' Apprentice*, I killed off a character called Sir Peter Leighton of Lymewood Hall – based on the real Jacobite plotter, Sir Peter Legh of Lyme Hall, and brother to Streynsham Master's wife.

Then there is Sir William Langhorn and I hope nobody will take offence at my depiction. Likewise those other real-life and extraordinary characters who stroll through these pages: Captain Baker, Master of King William III's Intelligence (and factually survived longer than my fictional portrayal, I think); Sir William Cavendish, First Duke of Devonshire; Sir Richard Levett; and several others.

And, last but not least, I have also taken a liberty with the date for one of Czar Peter's visits to the Deptford Friends' Meeting House and, of course, the boat chase – though students of the Great Embassy will know there is a factual vein running through this fiction. Czar Peter was indeed residing in Deptford during February and March of 1698, he met with Penn, conferred heavily with the Quakers, visited the Deptford Friends' Meeting House on more than one occasion, crashed his sailing boat at least twice – once in an unfortunate collision with a bomb ketch – and succeeded in causing untold damage to his accommodation at Sayes Court, Deptford (owned by the diarist, John Evelyn), during several of his many drunken sprees. But, in truth, Czar Peter was actually in Portsmouth and the Isle of Wight between 20-26 March 1698, so that his eccentric appearance in this story is plainly another invention. A warning here too, not to become beguiled by *this* Peter the Great. Peter the well-travelled visionary thinker? Certainly. But Peter the sadistic tyrant? Yes, that also, though if any ruler's story deserves the title "stranger than fiction" it must surely be that of Czar Peter.

I very nearly blundered, as well, by locating old Devonshire House in Boswell Street when, in fact, the thoroughfare only acquired that name in the 1930s before which it was more relevantly known as Devonshire Street, and I am sure there must be many more confessions to be made, so perhaps allow me to finish with the catch-all disclaimer that, naturally, any other accidental errors in the history are entirely my own.

Finally, my personal thanks to my excellent editor, Nicky Galliers; to my hugely supportive beta-reader, Ann McCall; to Dennis Verheul from Maltop Media for his advice on the Dutch language phrases; to my regular publishing team; and, once again, to Joe C. Dwek CBE and his Family Trust for their considerable support in the publishing process for this novel. Last, but by no means least, there are those who – in the best traditions of publishing in the 17th and 18th centuries – "subscribed" to *Mistress Yale's Diaries, The Glorious Return*, by pre-ordering copies, therefore helped this yarn to ever see the light of day and thus deserve their place on this list:

Joan Roberts; Paul Jeorrett; Dylan Hughes; Bernice Daly; Jude Lennon; John Isherwood and Mary Land; Ian McCartney; Judy and Bob Jones; Sheila Browne; Gary and Charo Titley; Peter Booth; Bill Fairhall; Beverly O'Sullivan; Steph Wyeth; John Haywood; Chris Remington; as well as Deborah Swift and Waheed Rabbani for their hugely appreciated back cover endorsements.

Catherine's trials and tribulations continue in the third part of her journals, *Wicked Mistress Yale, The Parting Glass*.

Lightning Source UK Ltd.
Milton Keynes UK
UKHW011804151119
353603UK00002B/150/P